"Vibrant, bold, and bursting with original concepts … a writer willing to bypass all the familiar territories and stake out a new narrative landscape all his own."

– Thomas F. Monteleone

"Michael Bailey has that rare ability to terrify readers and break their hearts—often in the same paragraph."

– Norman Prentiss

"Ambitious, inventive, in love with language … Bailey turns plots, characters, expectations, and even words inside out with courageous abandon. His desire to tell different kinds of stories (and to evoke complex emotions—sorrow, loss, melancholy, awe—as well as dark fiction's more familiar shock and dread) is relentless."

– Douglas E. Winter

"Michael Bailey continues to amaze. He is on track to becoming his generation's Ray Bradbury."

– F. Paul Wilson

"Like the drug he's invented, Michael Bailey's *Psychotropic Dragon* is addictive, scary, and at times, mind-blowing. But it's the human element that keeps you turning the pages, the wounds to the psyche which we recognize immediately. The human element ... and a fierce narrative style."

– Jack Ketchum

"After the publication of *Palindrome Hannah*, I did not think it possible that Michael Bailey could ever top that mind-bender of a novel. I was wrong. *Psychotropic Dragon*, from its perception-altering structure to its gut-wrenching and deeply moving and frightening narrative, makes recent cross-genres look like they were written by a three-year-old. Did I say 'cross genre'? My bad. This phantasmagorical show-stopper of a book defies categorization. It is, in the truest sense of the word, *unique*, something all too rare in publishing today. Beautifully written, stunningly illustrated, and guaranteed to blow your mind (not to mention scare the bejeezus out of you). *A* staggering achievement."

– Gary A. Braunbeck

"If you try to hold on too tightly to the narrative, you might get hurt. My advice is to let it sweep you up. And to read it twice, or more. *Psychotropic Dragon* is a modern classic you will want to return to again and again."

– Christian A. Larsen

NOVELS

Palindrome Hannah

Phoenix Rose

NOVELLAS

Agatha's Barn
(a Carpenter's Farm story)

NOVELETTES

Our Children, Our Teachers

COLLECTIONS

Scales and Petals

Inkblots and Blood Spots

Oversight

The Impossible Weight of Life

PSYCHOTROPIC DRAGON

BY MICHAEL BAILEY

for Josh Malerman & John Skipp

PSYCHOTROPIC DRAGON

THE BEGINNING OF THE END

The artist outlined wings on Julie's abdomen, pressing her skin flat as the needle pulsated. Between attacks, he wiped away the surfacing red, sometimes with a wet washcloth, sometimes with surgical-gloved fingers. Her skin: a canvas for complication.

The tattoo took shape, lines sharp, black, and tribal. Unbuttoned jeans rolled over her hips as she lay on her back.

"I'd expect you to have more piercings," she said.

"I'm not a fan of needles." The buzzing stopped as he peered over the rims of his glasses. On his wrist was a single tattoo of a semicolon, small enough to fit under a dime. Underneath his clothes could tell a different story, but what he shared was minimal. "Try not to laugh. Your stomach jumps around too much."

She had visited a number of tattoo shops before deciding upon this one. Every artist she'd met had been covered in ink and scattered with piercings, yet something attracted her to this particular tattooist. He didn't look the part, yet his artwork was incredible, his lines sharp.

"Have you been doing this a while?" she asked.

"It's my first day and you're my first customer," he said. "No, fifteen years."

"And you don't have a single piercing, and the one tattoo. I'm guessing you're not all tatted up under there," she said, motioning to his shirt.

"I guess it's not my thing. I'm in it for the art. Other people are my backdrop. You doing okay? We can take a break if you want. This is going to take about three hours, maybe longer, and that's just for the black. We'll have to schedule color fill and detail another day."

"No color."

"Still have to come back to finish. Lots of black. Lots of pain."

He wiped Julie's stomach and handed her a small mirror so she could see the progress. He had traced the lighter image stamped onto her body, bringing it to life. The mythical creature appeared tribal, with thick black lines forming into pointy wings of swirling black. They attached to an arching body, a mix of reptilian and serpentine. Sharp claws reached for her bellybutton.

"It's okay to cry," he said.

Julie welcomed the pain.

"I'll be fine."

The two-coil tattoo machine droned to life as he detailed the spine, neck, and head of the creature. He stopped an hour later when he made it to the middle of the tattoo, at her waistline. The rest of the design consisted of a long tail that required her to undress.

"So, you dodged my question earlier." He pointed to her stomach with the needle. "I see a lot of skin with this job—not that the stretch marks are noticeable—so I assumed ..."

"She's three now. I don't know what I'd do without her."

"What's her name?"

DRAKEIN

Julie ignored the question, tilted her head back and dropped two beads of *Drakein-5*. Warm tears welled beneath her eyelids as she blinked in the drug, an instant rush.

The young man straddling the barstool next to her had cropped-messy hair, a semi-scruffy face, a hint of a smile and a dangerous stare. Lovable. The *D-5* made him transparent. A muddy blue aura wavered around him.

"You're not supposed to ask a woman her age, not so directly. I'm old enough to catch your attention. That's all that matters."

"True, you did catch my attention," he said, his face turning a shade darker as he swiveled in his seat. "Don't get me wrong. You are absolutely stunning. Mesmerizing, even. You just look young, and young could get me in a lot of trouble. And, you're at a bar."

"So you want to sleep with me or something?"

The bar clattered with noise, glasses clinking, forks and knives scraping over cheap dishware, laughter and crossing conversations.

"I'd like to buy you a drink first, but right now it's a tossup between alcohol and soda."

"How old do you think I am?"

He took a long breath.

"The little devil on my left shoulder wants to say twenty-one and share some shots and get wild, but the little angel on my right says younger, and wants me to walk away. Nineteen?"

Julie smiled and signaled the bartender by holding up a ten-dollar bill she fished from her pocket. She worked the move flawlessly and caught her new friend stealing a glance at the black thong rising above her low-cut Capri pants. His eyes moved upward to the matching tank top. One of her boob shirts, as she liked to call them.

"That which sees," she said under her breath. "That which flashes or gleams."

"What'll it be?" the bartender said.

"Couple shots," Julie said, and motioned one for each of them.

"ID?"

The bartender looked past Julie to the young man, who chuckled and dug for his wallet, and slid his license across the counter. Julie wondered how much cash he carried.

The bartender held the card to the light and took a long time inspecting it. Sometimes he'd ruse the guys trying to get in her pants.

"Your license expired last month," he said and slid it back, "and you're twenty."

"What?"

"Relax. I'm just messing with you."

He poured two shots.

Julie slammed hers down, her glass thudding hard against the counter. It didn't take long for the alcohol to mesh with the *Drakein-5*. Jack burned down her throat. Tingling warmth rode her spine. She wanted to reach down and feel herself.

"Julie Stipes," she said, holding out a hand.

"Elliot Cartwright."

She held his bony hand for an abnormally long time, watching intently until the drug made the metacarpal bones ripple beneath his skin. Julie flinched and pulled back.

"You okay, there?"

"Yeah, sorry."

"Are you on Ecstasy?" Elliot sipped his drink, grimacing in a cute way. People sipped whiskey. He probably wondered why they were shooting it.

"Your eyes are kind of undressing me a little," he said, "and I think you just made love to my hand. Not that I mind. I like your nails. Not too many people wear black."

"Do my eyes look strange to you?"

"Distant, maybe, but not strange."

Julie held out her hand, half-expecting bones to crawl through her skin, or her fingernails to peel back.

"*E?*" she said. "No. I'm afraid of pills. I won't even take Aspirin. You know *E* is actually *3,4-methylenedioxymethamphetamine*. MDMA for short. I know, it's a mouthful, but I can spell it. I wrote an essay about it sophomore year. Got a B- because my chemistry teacher thought I was a junkie. I read somewhere they're trying it on cancer patients now. To help with anxiety."

Elliot flinched when she grabbed his knee, but let it stay there.

"Sophomore year of college?"

"Does it matter?"

"Not really. I'm just curious about you." He looked to the empty shot glasses, nervous. "You look young for twenty-one."

"I never said I was twenty-one."

Julie's hand turned skeletal, fingers spider-crawling up his leg in a blurred slow motion. They stopped short at his belt and the black legs transformed back to fingers.

The psychotropic effects of the drops were both amazing and terrifying. She wanted the spider to keep crawling, to see how far the dragon would let it go. The street coined it 'dragon.' Chasing the dragon, some said, like with heroin. Some called it *D*, or *D-5*, or its original name, *Drakein-5*. Every syringe housed freaky-crazy liquid sex and ran five hundred per milliliter. Injecting it into an eight-milliliter bottle of Visine would dilute it to last about twenty-five doses, if taking two drops at a time, one in each eye. "Always dilute it," her supplier told her. Chase, her first dealer—an appropriate name, overall—told her, "Don't drink it, don't inject the shit directly, just dilute it. One drop in each eye."

She remembered holding the syringe that first time, hands trembling. Such a small thing—a third the size of your typical medicinal syringe, the needle a quarter-inch long. Smaller than a cigarette. "Looks like water," she had said to Chase. The clear liquid inside appeared iridescent under direct sunlight, as if having an oily consistency. She heard it turned bluish-green under black lights. "What happens if I take more than two drops?" Chase had looked away, then, smiling out of the corner of his mouth. "It's like any drug. Affects each differently. Two drops, no more. It'll last a couple hours max, and then it's back to earth. After you level, you can take more. Take it with sex and you'll orgasm with electricity shooting up your spine. How old are you, anyway?"

Elliot signaled the bartender for another round as Julie rejoined the world.

"I'm sorry, did you say something?"

"I asked your age again and you told me I didn't have to worry."

She wanted to lean forward and kiss him, wanted to taste his tongue. She leaned forward to see how he would react.

The aura around him fluctuated and reddened as he shifted in his seat.

"You're a quiet one," Julie said. "No more small-talk. Tell me about yourself. Tell me why you deserve to have me. What makes you intriguing? What makes you lickable?"

"Lickable?"

Julie leaned close, moved one hand behind his neck, and passed her tongue over his right cheek. He tasted a bit like apples, his stubble soft sandpaper.

"You have this strange—" he started.

She pushed him back. "No. This isn't about me; this is about you. This is where you tell me something about you that sets you apart from all the other losers. Look around us. The two guys at the end of the bar are staring at me." She waved and they turned away. "They want to get me drunk and feel me up. The guy behind you—don't turn around—he's not even paying attention to his wife. I think it's his wife; he's wearing a wedding band. He's looking right through her, to me, undressing me with his eyes like I undressed you when you first got here. I know what he wants, just like I know what I want, but he's not going to get it. The balding perv in the corner with the burns on his face, he hasn't stopped staring at me since I got here. So, no small talk. Tell me something about you."

"Like what?"

"Tell me something you've never told anyone before. Something embarrassing. Something you would never tell your mom."

"I have a thing for girls in flip-flops."

"Yeah, who doesn't? Give me something real. Something dark."

The new drinks arrived and Elliot held his shot with both hands. "You won't laugh?"

"How about this? If I laugh, we go back to my place, and if I don't laugh, we go back to yours. Either way, you win."

Julie shot the whiskey, let it burn. She couldn't laugh, no matter what. She'd bite her lip if she had to. Earl and Helen Heimlich gave her a home, or the closest thing to one. She often thought of them as unrelated grandparents with love to share and a spare bedroom to use if things got out of control. "We're not using the room," Earl told her the first time they'd met, "and I'd rather you stay with us than on the streets. Everyone needs a bed."

Everyone needs a bed.

She blinked and Elliot's skull jolted outward from its skin. A second later it returned and she focused on his concentrating face. She had about an hour before the drug would fade, about an hour before she could take it again. Hormones kicked in, as expected. Miniature sparks of electricity erupted within, her nipples sensitive and showing under the tank top. She had to focus to keep from reaching underneath and squeezing them herself.

"Well," he said after a breath. "I once killed a cat."

"You what?"

Julie bit her lip to keep from laughing until she tasted copper.

"I killed a cat. This was back in New York, long before I moved here. After 9/11, my mom wanted to move us as far away as possible, hence Washington."

"Why would you do that? I love cats."

"Before I got my license to drive, I used to ride my bike everywhere. Sometimes my mom would have me run errands, like picking up a gallon of milk at the gas station down the street, or returning something at the store."

He sipped his whiskey and continued. "One evening I rode my bike somewhere, I don't even remember where, and the sun was setting. I'd get in trouble if I wasn't home before dark, so I booked it back home, taking up part of the road. A car passed on my left and had to swerve to drive around me and hit one of my neighbor's cats crossing the road, a little black cat with white spots on its backend and paws. He didn't run over it, but hit it. I remember it tumbling across the pavement and the sound it made."

"You didn't kill it. The car did."

A similar thing had happened to her cat when she still lived with her parents.

Sox.

"You caused the chain reaction resulting in its death. Sort of like the butterfly effect, only more localized. You flapped your wings."

"No, I killed it. The guy in the car slowed, knowing he'd hit something, but he didn't stop. He sped and continued on his way like nothing happened. The cat still breathed when I rode up to it, on its side, panting, with its front legs facing the right way and its back legs facing the wrong way. Blood dabbed the white spot under its nose. It looked scared, confused. I knew it wouldn't survive and a vet wouldn't be able to do anything, but it was in a lot of pain and would probably take all night to die."

"What did you do?" Julie said, holding one of his hands.

"I helped it die. I held its mouth closed and pinched the bridge of its nose. It didn't struggle much, just sort of spasmed under me as it tried for one last breath."

"I wonder if it knew it would die."

"It wanted to survive at the end."

"You did the right thing."

"Sometimes I wonder if I did the right thing. I never told anyone before."

His eyes changed from blue to gray to black, an effect of the drug. She blinked and they glowed soft blue again. He forced a smile and his teeth prolonged and retracted, his aura all but gone.

"I don't think I've ever had someone look at me so intently."

"I do that."

"You're addictive, aren't you? Now it's your turn. I confessed murdering a cat. Tell me something dark about you."

"There is lot of dark about me."

Julie thought of her father. He came home drunk one night from work and sat next to her on the bed while she slept. She remembered waking up with a hand on her thigh and her mother turning on the light, cussing, and taking him away.

Seven years old.

A year later, she found a bent spoon between the seat cushions of the couch and asked her mom about it and she told her it was none of her goddamn business. Burnt—the way glass looks after holding it against a flame.

In sixth grade, she had to see the school counselor to explain bruises. She said she fell trying to skateboard, too afraid to admit she couldn't remember which of her parents had hit her last.

"I used to cut myself."

Elliot didn't react as she expected. He didn't react at all.

"Sometimes I used to feel so dead inside, as if it didn't matter what I did in life because we all die anyway. We live. We fuck. We die. The magical triad of existence. If you pick any other animal, those are the three important things it will do in life. I used to think life was some kind of wheel rotating around and around on some endless cycle. It is, but I'd like to believe it's something more than that now. Life is what we make of it. Cliché, I know, but true. Someday I want to write children's fables. I've always wanted to do that. I want to run a marathon, learn another language, travel around the world, maybe go to Iceland, have kids someday. Two, I think. I don't know, maybe only one. I want to do everything I can before I die. You know what I mean. When I die, I want part of me to stay behind. I used to cut myself because I didn't want any of that before. I cut myself because I felt dead inside and sometimes the pain would let me know there were still things I could feel. Cutting wrought pain, but it let me know I was still alive. Sometimes what hides inside wants out, and skin is confinement."

"I'm sorry about your parents."

"They can fucking rot in hell for all I care. They're the reason I was a cutter."

Julie pulled her tank top aside to expose three parallel scars below her collarbone.

"See? Nothing too bad, but they will always be there."

"Scars from the past design your future," Elliot said. "Hurt creates uniqueness. You're probably the only person in the world with three little marks like that. Some people have birthmarks, or little moles on their faces they like to call beauty marks. Some people get tattoos." He pulled his shirtsleeve over his bicep to uncover a skinny clown with a scary face, like something on an old tarot card.

"What the hell is that?"

"This," he said, "is one of my own little scars. We all have them."

"Tattoos?"

"Scars."

Julie traced the black edges with one of her nails. A menacing face wearing a purple and white motley-patterned jester hat held a malevolent grin.

"What does the clown say about you?"

She expected his skin to melt.

Elliot finished his second shot of Jack.

"The clown reminds me every day to watch my drinking. We used to pay one of our friend's older brothers to buy us alcohol. Sometimes we'd inject oranges with vodka to make portable Screwdrivers and we'd slowly get drunk between classes. This was in high school. After graduation, we all got shitfaced. I woke up at two in the afternoon with a massive hangover and *this* guy on my arm, smiling at me. I don't remember any of it, but I haven't gotten drunk since."

"I've always wanted a tattoo."

"If you want one, you should get one."

Julie yawned and blinked and when her eyes opened again, gray ribs arched outward from Elliot's chest in a flash display of morbidity, as if his skin withdrew and his insides protruded. Within the ribcage, she could see a liver and some other organs, and a red beating heart pounding rhythmically before the mess returned to his body where it belonged. The hallucination lasted a moment, but long enough for Elliot to notice her change in expression.

"Are you okay? You did that jumpy, freaky thing again, like you saw a ghost or something."

Julie rubbed her eyes. "So, you don't think I'm a bad person because I used to cut myself? Most people get freaked."

"It's in your past, and I'm not most people."

"Good. You want to get out of here? Burn Victim in the corner's creeping me out. He's still staring at us."

Elliot swiveled.

"The guy in the trench coat?"

The guy in the trench coat threw a wad of bills onto the table and headed to the door with a limp in his step. The man defined gaunt. He stared at Julie as he walked out and past the large window with reverse-letters of "Pete's Pub" etched onto the glass.

Streetlights revealed a shaved head, as if he had buzzed it in the dark while heavily medicated. A red rose tattoo with black-trimmed edges ran up the side of his red-leather neck. The drug created an aura of dark green and black wavering off his body like smoke.

"What a creep," Julie said.

They waited in silence for a while before Elliot added, "He should be gone by now. So, where to?"

"I didn't laugh."

"What?"

"I didn't laugh."

The blur of city lights captivated Julie as the drug thinned. Some of the lights streaked bold and heavy white and meteoresque as they passed her blurred vision; others changed colors or melded with stars. The constellations and their invisible connecting lines shifted about like drunk maps.

"Are you sure your car's going to be fine left at the bar?" Elliot said. "It's not the best location. A friend of mine had his stereo stolen from there a week ago."

"I don't have a car."

Elliot stared at her for a beat, and then she told him.

"I walked. The place where I'm staying is less than a mile away."

"How do you get around town, or to and from your job?"

"Friends. Cabs. Tell me about your dad."

"Stepdad. You really don't have a car?"

"Why is he a prick?"

Elliot sighed. "It's one thing to live with your parents when you're twenty-one, and I have my reasons, but it's another to be twenty-one and having a forty-something year-old man rubbing your head and calling you 'sport' or 'champ.' The next time he touches my hair like I'm some kind of troll doll, I swear I'll knock him flat on his ass. Not really. I'm not a violent person; it's just annoying, you know? You ever have someone do that to you?"

Julie remembered the way her father used to look at her when he'd come home from work. Every so often he'd rub her hair and say, "How's my little girl?" He'd expect a hug or a kiss, some 'sugar' as he liked to call it. "Come sit on my lap and tell me about your day at school," he'd say, but he never cared about her school. He wanted to feel her weight against his lap. The brush of his mustache against her face, the warm beer on his breath, his eyes and the sheen they'd get when her mother left the room. "Give your dad some sugar," he'd say with a hand on her thigh. Even if she didn't want to give him sugar he'd find a way to take it. Sometimes his breath smelled like chocolate. She remembered the M&M's on the side table next to the sofa. Julie could have one of each color for being a good girl. She could have sugar if she gave sugar. "Don't spoil her appetite," her mother used to call from the kitchen because she knew about the candy. Sometimes Julie would hear her name as a question, which meant Mom needed help with dinner and she could leave, but before she slid off her father's lap, he'd rub her hair, say things like, "That's my girl ..." and kiss her again.

"I know what you mean," Julie said, her eyes beginning to tear; she tried to wipe them unnoticed, but Elliot noticed.

"Are you okay?"

"It's just these lights."

"Because if you're not, it's not a problem. We can do this some other time. I could give you my cell and we could talk all night. I like talking to you."

"We are talking, and I'm okay. Honest. My eyes are just a little sensitive. Plus, I don't own a cellphone."

"How can you not own a cellphone?"

Julie dug in her purse for the small bottle of eye drops. She leaned back in the seat, dropped a single bead of *Drakein-5* into each

eye, blinked, and felt the rush. It burned for a bit but then warmed the rest of her.

Elliot eyed her but then returned his focus to the road.

"Everyone I know has a cellphone," she said. The side of Elliot's face, and part of his arm, melted away as her body tingled. "Why would I need one?"

A skull with a gaped jaw turned to her and asked, "How can you not have one? What if there's an emergency?"

The last few words came out low-pitched and slow.

She wanted to taste him.

The dragon working its magic.

She unbuckled her seatbelt, knees straddling the emergency brake as she leaned over with her mouth to his ear. She reached one hand around his neck and her other deep into the right front pocket of his pants. He hesitated and flinched, but adjusted to let in her fingers. Part of him stirred as she pulled out his cell phone. She returned to her seat, buckling in, smiling. Through parted lips, he let out a shaky breath.

"See? I'm never more than a few feet away from communication at any given time. Mind if I put in my number?"

"I thought you didn't have a phone."

"Technically, I don't. It's not my number; it's my … it's the number where I'm staying. If some old guy answers, that's Earl. He's like a grandfather to me. If some old gal answers, then Earl's out taking a walk and you've reached the answering machine. Helen hardly ever answers the phone. Is that your house?"

The car slowed and pulled up to a humble, single story home, gray like the thunderclaps overhead, and with blue trim as dark as the sky trying to peek through. A light rain specked the windshield as sprinklers hissed on and sprayed the front lawn. A single bulb illuminated the front door with a yellow triangle of light. A black cat waited on the doorstep.

"Where I grew up," Elliot said.

"Red doors mean passion, which also means suffering. I read that in some *feng shui* book a while back."

"I've always thought the door looked creepy, especially at night. Used to give me nightmares."

"The *cat* is creepy." The feline stared straight at them with pompous, proud eyes. As the cat yawned, its face peeled, revealing a set of elongated fangs. Julie knew if she returned the stare long enough, the cat would crawl out of its skin completely in another of her hallucinations.

"Her name is Spooks. She comes around whenever it rains because our neighbors don't have a covered porch."

"She brought you a present."

Half of a dead mouse lay at its feet in a red lump. Julie had to look away. Her eyes landed on Elliot. He seemed uncertain, or concerned. It made Julie want him more. She bit her bottom lip as a tingle of current crawled along her spine. She unbuckled her seatbelt and slid closer.

Unbuckling his belt for him, Julie crossed the center console and straddled him on the seat, un-tucked his shirt and put her hands around his waist. Not much room in the cabin, but she made it work. He trembled, his skin as soft as silk and ticklish. She took the air out of his lungs in a single hard kiss and had to pull back to catch her breath. She moved one of her hands to his neck and let her sandals fall to his feet as she sank further onto him and tasted his earlobe. Kneeling on the seat, Julie spread her legs wider and wrapped around his body. Rough hands reached underneath her tank top to crawl up her back. They grabbed her shoulders and pulled before sliding down to her hips and then greedily up again, thumbs pressing under her ribs as she arched her back and gasped in ecstasy. She nearly came when he slid his fingers around her waist. He kissed her clavicle and then her neck. She fell against him, her breasts tender and sensitive, pressing against his chest. She wanted him to pull the tank top off and toss it to the seat next to them, to unfasten her bra so he could taste the skin hidden beneath, to reach his hand down and feel the wet warmth inside her. As soon as his tongue danced around her lips, she let him in, and for a while she couldn't breathe. Her mouth finally let go and she leaned back, shivered. Julie grinded against him and when her back found the steering wheel, the car horn screamed.

Julie laughed.

A single car occupied the street behind them.

"You get a dimple on your cheek when you laugh," Elliot said. "Just the one." He pointed to her mouth before pecking that spot with his lips. "Don't roll your eyes … it's true. You smile more on that side. I bet you don't hear that a lot. You ever notice Kiera Knightley? You have the same smile. You could be her little sister."

She smiled for him, bit her bottom lip and gave Elliot her best, 'I want you to fuck me' face. It wasn't difficult; she wanted him to, just not in the car.

"Do you have coffee?" Julie said, moving from his lap to the passenger door. She let herself out and circled the car before he could react. She stood on the sidewalk, her feet bare, and beckoned for him to follow as she walked toward the house.

Elliot got out of the car. "You're amazing, you know? I'm sure there's coffee in the house. I'll brew a pot. Aren't your feet cold?"

She hadn't noticed before, but Elliot wore a belt, like something you'd wear with a pair of black chinos. She had forgotten the coffee. She had forgotten the rain- and sprinkler-water under her feet. When he caught up to her, she grabbed the buckle and pulled him close so their hips connected, and kissed him. He pushed away, about to say something, but she stopped his words by sliding a hand down the front of his pants to feel what had pressed against her in the car. As she wrapped her fingers around him, she felt a gasp in her mouth as he melted into her and reconnected fervently to her lips. He grabbed the wrist buried into his waistline and guided her hand out.

Julie backpedaled, smashed against the front door, avoiding the remnants of the sacrificial mouse. Elliot fished for the right key to open the lock, their mouths and hands attacking one another. Finally, the door opened. Still backpedaling. Elliot dropped his keys to the floor and flipped on the lights, his eyes closed; she knew this because she watched their tremors with hungry eyes of her own. He tried to kick the door shut behind him but it bounced back and rattled on its hinges. Julie worked the buttons of his shirt free and let it drape over his shoulders a moment before falling to the floor. She pulled at the band of her ponytail and freed her hair. Their mouths inseparable. Fingers danced at the base of her tank top, so she lifted her arms to the ceiling and let him pry off the damn thing. It landed over a tableside lamp and dimmed the room. She worked his belt loose but gave up. She concentrated on her Capris, sliding them down with her feet—her sandals lost in the car—until they crumpled on the carpet. The back of her knees buckled against the sofa behind her. They nearly toppled, but Elliot saved them from falling with a firm hand on the cusp of her back, the other warm against her ass.

Never once did Julie feel vulnerable as she melted into his arms, wearing nothing but a matching black bra, thong, and her painted fingernails and toes. Like something off the cover of a romance novel. "Not too many people wear black," he had said to her in the bar. It meant he noticed the little things about her that most ignored, like the color of her nail polish, or the single dimple when smiling. She could trust him with the things that made her dark.

He feather-kissed her sternum and the exposed flesh around her breasts and placed a hand flat against her stomach, his thumb circling her belly button. The tickling sensation sent pleasant shivers down the rest of her body. His fingers slid beneath the elastic above the small patch of silk at the front of her thong.

"I don't want you to think I go around to bars—"

Julie stopped his hand from descending. She brought it up to her mouth and kissed his fingertips, looking deeply into his eyes.

An awkward silence filled the room for seven heartbeats. Julie counted them as they pounded within her chest.

Her focus pivoted between Elliot's eyes and his puzzled emotions. Was he scared, frightened, smiling? She could only look to his eyes for answers because she stood so close, his whiskey breath nothing like stale beer or chocolate. She wanted to taste his tongue again, to let the electricity flow through her like a Jacob's ladder when they connected.

This was something more than the *Drakein-5*. This was emotion.

And she wanted to share it with him.

He kissed and pulled back so she could see his smile.

"If you want to wait, I'm okay with that. We've only known each other for a couple of hours. We have plenty of time."

Julie brought his fingers to her stomach, then guided them under her thong. She used her hand to help him discover her center, one of his fingers passing inside and pressing a place that caused her other hand to rake across the skin of his lower back. Pulling her own hand out, she wrapped it around his neck and lost her breath.

She loved the slickness of sweat on his lower back.

His hand malformed to a tarantula crawling outside her, body rising and falling beneath the black silk, legs curling, stretching, curling, as they tangled in her hair.

Elliot pulled the spider free when the front door slammed against the wall.

The gaunt man from the bar stood in front of the door, his trench coat dripping on the hardwood floor. He held a twelve-gauge shotgun singlehandedly like a witching stick, the barrel teetering in his hand and traversing the living room.

The aftereffects of fire climbed his neck and covered his face, along with a rose tattoo.

Julie covered herself as best as manageable and attempted to hide in the small space between Elliot and the sofa. She sat on the armrest and brought her knees together, crossed her arms to cover her chest, brought a hand down to cover the rest of her, brought it back up, unsure what to do. She thought of reaching for her tank top on the lampshade, but modesty doesn't matter much with a hole in your chest. With the shotgun pointed at her, she could only think about hiding the parts of her she had so readily surrendered moments before.

"Whoa," Elliot said. He had lost his chattiness, left with only a single word. He looked scared out of his fucking mind.

The man in the trench coat took three hasty steps forward. A vibrant aura wafted off him like fire, red and as frightening as blood.

Elliot backed into the couch, with his hands held high. The barrel of the shotgun met his mouth and pushed hard until he let it in between his teeth. He gagged when it hit the back of his throat, and she could almost taste the oily metal in her mouth and steel against her teeth.

Julie bit her bottom lip hard to keep from crying. She crossed her arms to cover her breasts, put her knees together. Her fingers traced the cut lines below her collarbone. For the first time in her life, she felt ashamed of her body.

"Take your clothes off, Julie."

Heart pounding within her chest, Julie met his eyes, to see if he was serious.

Elliot tested the man's reaction and lowered his hands, which resulted in more deep-throating of the barrel.

"Take the rest of your clothes off or I'll do it for you."

Julie shook her head no.

She was practically naked already, but she didn't want to be naked in front of this man—in front of either of them—for fear of what she imagined would happen next.

"Your scanty underwear or this guy's fuckin' head; one or the other comes off in the next three seconds."

No, I can't do it.

"Three."

No-no-no.

"Two."

Fuck!

Julie turned slightly away, enough so to make her feel a little more comfortable, and reached around to the bra strap to unlatch it.

"One—*that's* my girl."

She slid the straps off her shoulders diffidently, still clutching the bra to her chest to cover her breasts. When she turned back to him, Elliot was looking away. He, too, was ashamed.

"Are you happy?" she said.

"All of your clothes, Julie. Don't be modest. You have nothing to be shy about, remember? We think you're beautiful."

Julie turned away from him.

"All of it."

The man with the rose tattoo pushed the barrel into Elliot's throat enough to force him back a step, the sofa lurching.

"Look at her!"

Elliot obeyed.

The man with the shotgun didn't show any interest in her nudity.

Julie let the bra fall to the floor and folded her arms, all without exposing any more of her body than necessary. She had watched herself undress in front of the mirror: the scars, the self-inflicted wounds, and the puzzle-shaped birthmark on her left inner thigh. Julie imagined her reflection now, a cold shivering body trying to hide its beauty, the tears and mascara running down the sad woman's face—a scary clown like the tattoo on Elliot's arm.

Moments ago she was willing and eager to shed her clothes. Now it felt dirty and wrong and made her think of her father.

"Now the rest."

With her right hand holding her left breast, she felt the rigid nipple beneath and the fast pulsation of her heart pounding against her fingers. She let her other hand fall to the side and hesitated before sliding a thumb underneath the thin strap holding her thong in place.

She turned to the side again, her body folding as she pushed the dainty garment around her knees. The hand returned to cover where she had previously allowed the tarantula to wander. It sickened her now to think she once let it crawl there, fingerlike legs trying to sneak inside. Julie stood upright and brought her foot up like a derrick to let her toes pull the rest of it to the floor.

"That wasn't so bad now, was it? What a modest little girl you are. And to think … how could just a few triangles of cloth and some string make so much of a difference?"

Completely naked, she covered herself.

"Apparently it does; you've only replaced the cloth with your hands." He stood there a moment, admiring her. "Isn't she to die for," he said to Elliot, "so slender and sleek, so innocent?"

The man with the gun smiled.

Elliot shook his head *no* and the smile vanished.

"Don't you want to see the rest of her? Don't you want to see what she's hiding from you? Fine. Stay silent. I know what you want and don't want; the bulge in your pants says it all. Julie, show him what he wants to see or I'll show him for you."

As if frozen in curtsy, Julie held her hands outward, palms up, letting them see her complete naked self.

"See, Julie? He likes that. See how you're turning him on?"

"Fuck you!" she said.

The barrel of the shotgun retracted from Elliot's mouth and the stock swung hard, slamming into the side of his head. He fell to the floor and Julie ran to him, embracing him.

"Please don't hurt us," she said. "Whatever you want, just leave us alone."

"While you're down there, Julie, reach into the pockets of your pants—furrowed on the floor—and pull out what's there."

"Anything you want: money, drugs … I have some dragon!" she exclaimed, remembering the eye drops. She pulled out her wallet, the small bottle, and a Chapstick sized container with a hidden syringe of clear liquid stashed inside of it. She removed the syringe from its container and showed it to him, took all of her cash from the wallet, about forty bucks, and held it out as an offering. "This is everything I have. Please, take it. If you need money, the *D-5* in the syringe is worth five hundred. Use it, for all I care. Please, just let us go."

When he didn't take any of it, she tossed it to the floor in front of him.

He only seemed curious about the drugs.

Julie concentrated on a particular knot of wood on the floor.

"What are you doing here with a girl this young?" he said to Elliot. "So innocent, yet so beautiful … you were going to break this flower, weren't you?"

Be a good girl and give me some sugar, she could hear her father saying. *Give daddy some sugar and you can have some sugar, too.* She envisioned the bowl of M&M's on the side table next to the sofa back home, imagined their sweet taste as they melted on her tongue, her father's bitter-rotten breath wafting in the air. She could even feel his hand on her leg, sliding like a serpent under the hem of her dress and across her thigh, skin as rough as kitten kisses.

She looked up to see the shotgun pressing at the nape of Elliot's neck, pushing him forward a few inches, the fingers on the trigger starting to squeeze.

"What do you want from us?" Julie said.

"What do *I* want?"

Neither answered.

The shotgun turned her way, to her chest. She sat up, arching her back and looking away, her hands crossing her chest like the deaf sign for 'love.' Sharp, oily steel pushed against her belly and moved up her chest until one of the twin barrels swallowed a nipple. The barrel pushed against her flesh and soon the cool metal pressed hard against her ribs until it hurt to breathe.

"Your turn, Elliot. Lie on your back and take off your clothes. All of them."

Elliot's eyes remained closed as he said, "No." His bottom lip quaked as he considered his options: strip naked or die.

The shotgun pulled away long enough to fire at the ceiling, rattling the room, and then returned, hot against her chest. Pieces of ceiling rained around them.

"Want to say 'no' again?"

Elliot kicked off his shoes, slipped off his socks, and then lay flat on his back as he reached down to unzip his pants.

Julie looked away, but a firm hand seized her chin and forced her to watch.

"Wait, I've got a better idea," he said. "Julie, this is familiar territory for you, isn't it? Looks like you already got his belt loose when your hands were down there playing earlier. Take off his belt for him and I'll point this thing elsewhere."

Julie did as she was told and grabbed the buckle and pulled the belt free, held it up for him to see. The man pointed the barrel at Elliot's face instead.

"Elliot, sit up so she can tie your hands behind your back."

He sat upright and placed his hands behind his back. The gun followed his movements, the end of the barrel slipping in his tears.

"Tie it tight, Julie. If he gets loose, you both die."

Julie scooted closer and wrapped the belt around his wrists.

"I'm sorry I got us into this, Elliot. I just wanted to feel—"

"Shut up," the man said.

"I wanted you. I like you, honest. I wanted to be with you and—"

"Shut up and do it!" the man screamed.

Julie fed the belt through the loop and pulled until it was taut, fed the pin or whatever it was called into the closest hole she could manage without hurting him.

"Help him out of his clothes, Julie."

The gun trained on her again as the two of them orbited Elliot's horizontal body, and then he forced the end of the barrel into Elliot's mouth.

Julie no longer felt embarrassed about her own appearance. It was beyond that now. She had to do what this man wanted or they were both going to die. She only hoped Elliot felt the same as she kneeled next to him and unzipped his pants, worked them free around his hips and pulled them down around and over his ankles. She threw them toward the living room and thought about what they might have to do. She wondered what was going through Elliot's mind as she undressed him. Seeing him exposed like this was mind-mesh of confused emotions. She had wanted him, but not like this. She wanted nothing to do with his body now, and a part of her hoped Elliot felt the same as she removed the last of his clothes.

Maybe this guy was just trying to make some kind of sick point. Maybe he'd leave after seeing them both naked and humiliated.

Elliot mumbled around the barrel in his mouth to the man standing over him. Water ran down his cheeks from a constant gagging.

"You want me to pull the trigger and let her go?"

That silenced him.

"We've done what you've asked," Julie said.

"I haven't *asked you* to do anything! Now help your friend Elliot realize what he's been missing. The eye drops next to you on the floor … be a good little girl and share."

That's my girl, she thought and reached for the laced bottle.

The dragon wouldn't hurt Elliot. It might freak him out with the hallucinations at first, but wouldn't hurt him. "Two drops, no more," Chase had told her, "… after you level, you can take more. Take it with sex and you'll orgasm like electricity's shooting up your spine."

Oh god.

"We have to do what he says."

Either Elliot nodded, or the man used the tip of the barrel to make him puppet nod.

Julie hesitated.

"Don't be afraid," the man said. "You were going to do more than this before I showed up and ruined your evening. Sit on his lap like you're going to ride him. Don't worry, you won't be having sex. Push it down and out of your way. It won't bite."

He shifted around to give her room. The barrel never moved from Elliot's mouth.

Julie unscrewed the cap and straddled Elliot with shaky legs. She slowly lowered herself onto him and had to push down with more force than she initially anticipated because he was still hard. She sat on top of him and slid her hand out from between them, his erection pressing firm and hot between the folds of her labia, pulsating rapid heartbeats between them. What she felt wasn't pleasure, but confusion as thoughts of her childhood rushed through her mind. She sobbed over him as she leaned forward, her tears dripping against his chest.

"That wasn't so bad now, was it? One drop in each eye ..."

Elliot's pupils dilated after applying the *Drakein-5*. There was not much he could do but look back at her with those horrified eyes, the shotgun wedged in his mouth. In a matter of seconds, his body pressed harder against her as the drug shot ecstasy through him. As he bit down harder on the barrel, she imagined how she must look from his position, and couldn't for the life of her remember the aura color for fear.

She imagined it looked like fucking.

"Now you," the man said.

She leaned back and brought the bottle to her eyes, but he stopped her.

"Set it on the floor."

"What?"

"You're going to shoot the syringe," he said, pushing the end of the shotgun deep into Elliot's mouth, which caused a loud gag and some bile to rise out of his throat.

The small medicinal syringe held a single milliliter of pure *Drakein-5*. Julie had only used it in a diluted state. Chase never told her the side effects of shooting it directly—only to never do it.

"It won't kill you, if that's what you're thinking," the man said. "Either you shoot, or I shoot. You have five seconds."

Was it possible to OD on the stuff?

"Four."

How bad would the hallucin—

"Three."

Would it—

"Two."

No!

"Okay okay okay!"

Julie brought the needle below her left bicep, pumped her hand open and closed—she had seen Chase shoot heroin before in his apartment—then shot a few drops out of the tip to clear any bubbles, and plunged the quarter-inch needle into her skin.

The *D-5* burned hot up her arm before blacking her out.

"Julie, how did you get the bruise on your arm?" her mother asked while making her a peanut butter and jelly sandwich for lunch, crusts cut off and set to the side. She pushed the plate across the table before pouring a glass of milk.

"I dunno," she said, her eyes on the sandwich.

"Roll up your sleeve and let me see."

Julie was five and wore her favorite white and yellow sundress, the one with the lace around the hems. It had short sleeves and she rolled the left one up over her shoulder. A yellow-purple bruise wrapped around her skin like fingers.

"Did your father do this to you?"

She sat quiet and swung her dangling bare feet from the chair as her mother inspected the wound. Julie grabbed the sandwich with both hands and took a bite. With a full mouth, she said, "No," swallowed, and took another bite.

"Julie, stop eating and tell me who did this to you."

Whenever she heard the loud adult voices, it meant she was in trouble for doing something. She listened to them arguing all night sometimes before falling asleep. The adult voices scary. Her mother realized this, because she then lowered her voice and asked her again who had squeezed her arm hard enough to cause the bruise.

"Your father's at work right now. He won't know we ever had this conversation; this is just between you and me. You aren't in any trouble, Julie. I just want to know what happened. Did your father do this to you?"

Julie nodded and took a sip of her milk, wiped away the milk mustache.

Her mother squeezed her hand around the jelly knife until her knuckles turned white. She set it on the table and looked away to the floor, closed her eyes and mumbled something with the word *fucker* in it—a *bad* word.

"Is this the first time he's hurt you like this?"

Julie nodded.

"Has he … has he ever put his hands on you anywhere else?" She could barely get the question out. Words caught in her throat.

Julie took another bite of her sandwich. She didn't want to get in trouble.

"Does he touch you?" She took the sandwich away from her and set it back down on the plate. "Julie, I want you to get down from the table and take off that dress."

Shaking her head no didn't seem to matter. Her mother grasped her by the wrist and made her get down from the chair. "Arms up," she said and lifted the dress. It stuck for a bit around the neck and then was free, and she was suddenly standing in the kitchen in only her panties. Her mother checked every inch of her body, turning her around and around and lifting her arms, her legs; she even had her remove the underwear to check the places Daddy sometimes touched.

¤ ¤ ¤

Elliot fellated the shotgun. One of his teeth had chipped. The man stood over them with a disconcerting look on his face as he watched them having sex. They were both glistening sweat.

How long?

Julie uncontrollably gyrated against the naked man between her spread legs. She slid wet around him, numb from the waist down, minute electric flurries blossoming deep inside. She leaned over Elliot, her hands on his chest to keep her body upright. Her mind spun from the drug as something powerful controlled her body. A raw and primitive part of her wanted the sex while another part of her wanted it all to end and begged to die.

She couldn't help but wonder how he had gotten inside of her. Had she done it on her own accord? Had she slid him in? She must have, or the drug must have caused her to do it, because Elliot's hands were still bound what looked painfully behind his back, and the man standing over them had his hands busy with the shotgun, one of his fingers tapping the trigger.

The last thing she remembered: shooting the needle up her arm, a memory of undressing in the kitchen back home when she was five, and then waking up to this ride.

The sex was by no means consensual. Less than an hour ago she wanted to have sex with Elliot and she was certain Elliot wanted the same in return, but it all changed the moment the psychopath with the rose tattoo barged in on them. He had made them strip, belittled them into miming sex, forced Julie to straddle him on the floor. And somehow during Julie's drugged and unconsciousness state she had opened herself up and let the man trapped underneath her inside.

The *D-5* rushed through her like never-ending shivers. It felt so wrong yet felt so right. Secretly she didn't want the sensations to end, so natural, so innocent. But it was wrong. The shotgun in Elliot's mouth reminded her of this.

Consensual rape, is there such a thing?

"I'm sorry, Elliot," she said. "I can't …"

She arched her back and moved her hands from his chest to his thighs, rocking gently against him. The ceiling blurred. She tried to focus but her eyes watered and stung. She thought of the rocking horse she'd gotten for her sixth birthday: wood-carved and painted white with a brown mane and big beady eyes, handlebar ears and peg stirrups. She had asked for one for Christmas but had gotten it instead a few months later as a birthday present. Rusty springs meant it wasn't the one she had picked from the catalogue, but she had fallen in love with it at first sight and called it Daisy. A palomino, she told her mother. She remembered leaning back sometimes after she'd gotten the horse going, hands behind her on the saddle.

Small flowers of eruption filled her body with warmth. *Had they put on a condom?* Only skin separated them. Julie wanted to stop, to jump off the ride, quarters spent, but grinded away without her blessing. Julie opened her eyes to pleasure and pain.

Through hallucination, the skin peeled from Elliot's face as he strained to keep his eyes open. His lids not cooperating. The skin melted around his mouth leaving a dry skull with jaws clamping on the shotgun barrel. Despite his expressionless face, she knew the rest of his body couldn't help but enjoy the sex. She felt a tremor underneath her as Elliot's ribcage violently extracted from his body, the skin gone, the white bones revealing the organs underneath, the lungs expanding and collapsing, the heart beating spastically, and then everything contracted and hid behind the skin.

The man standing over them: a laughing corpse, his jaw stretched as if the bottom half of his face were thawing and melting away. His canines elongated like dripping wax. Julie imagined his laugh played out on a record player with someone's finger pressed against the vinyl to lower the pitch and slow the pace.

"You're both enjoying this quite well," the voice said.

Elliot's stomach erupted once more and out of instinct Julie pushed the gore back down, her fingers sticking in the mess seeping through his ribcage. She pulled clean fingers away, and so she pushed back down, the heart pushing hard and wet and warm against her palm. Some sort of perverted CPR. And then the gore disappeared.

Julie leaned back, raked fingers through her hair. Her body continued to grind. A mesmerizing aura held them in a figure eight of luminous colors, their bodies like two opposite poles in a magnetic field displayed by prismatic light. Soon it would end. Soon the electricity between them would break.

Too much pleasure for one not to climax, her eyelids clenched. If she were able to open them, she'd die, remembering her father once telling her something similar about sneezing. The only funny thing he ever said to her.

She had wanted this, something magical. Her friend Frankie once said sex was ethereal, that an orgasm was the closest you could come to death without dying, that your heart would stop beating and your soul would let go of your body long enough to peek through the veil without having to cross over. And wet.

Electricity shot up her spine as he came inside her.

The man with the rose tattoo on his neck pulled the trigger, turning Elliot's head into a crimson flower on the floor.

"Let me see, Julie," her mother said.

Julie ran to her and held up her thumb. A small bead of red bled from where the rose thorn had pricked her. She had tried picking a yellow flower, but she managed only to bend it before gouging herself. Her mother had spent the morning lining the fence in the backyard with heritage rosebushes, the kind you bought from the store. There was a dozen of varying color.

"You have to *cut* roses. You can't pick them or they *bite* you."

Julie imagined one of the buds opening up and smiled. And then she noticed the yellow and green-striped caterpillar, thicker than her thumb and twice as long, inching along the top of the roots. It would fill her palm if she held it. She wondered if it too would bite.

"Do you want to help? I have one more to plant."

The remaining rosebush waited at the corner of the yard where the back and side fences joined together at an angle, roots and topsoil still trapped inside a green plastic bag. Her eyes must have said yes because her mother held out the spade and gardening gloves.

"It rained a little last night, so the ground should be nice and soft. You need to dig the hole deep enough to hold the roots, just enough so everything in the bag can go in. I'll be inside for a bit, so call out if you need help."

Julie admired a black-spotted ladybug crawling along the spade. It flew off as soon as she grabbed the handle. She put on gloves too big for her petite hands as the sliding glass door opened behind her. Inside, her father yelled at the baseball game on television before the door closed, hushing his words.

A yellow rosebush full of blooming flowers had bit her. The rosebush in wait contained only one red, black-trimmed rose, which looked burnt and withered, the color almost fake. She imagined someone with a paintbrush had given it life, but then it dried. The rest of the plant looked dead as well, the thick trunk above the roots dry and cracked and covered in bulky thorns.

She looked for the caterpillar, but it was gone, probably hiding camouflage in the leaves.

Rotted wood stuck out from the ground where she was supposed to dig. Painted letters had faded. Most of the wood crumbled under her gloves. Slugs crawled along the pointed end where the wood was nearly as soft and dark as the ground. Julie threw it aside and dug with the spade. Her mother was right—the rain the night before made the ground soft—and within seconds she was a foot deep, so she placed the plastic-covered rosebush temporarily into the ground. A few more inches and she'd be there.

The rest she dug with her fingers, tossing handfuls to the side. She counted five worms before she felt something hard, like roots. Pulling firm, they ripped free. With a crunch she pulled out a handful more. Within her hands she held not the remnants of roots, but several curved bones—a miniature broken ribcage. In the hole she found the skull of the small creature once buried there. She knew at once it was Sox and screamed. The sliding glass door opened.

"Julie, is everything alright?"

They got her as a kitten from the SPCA. Julie named her after the Boston Red Sox, a team her father hated. He was a hardcore Mariners fan, yet every time the Red Sox played the Yankees, he'd suddenly turn into a Yankees fan, even wore a pinstriped NY hat sometimes. After some arguments, they decided on 'Sox' because of the white boot-like feet. She had a white-tipped tail as well, but the rest of her was striped tabby orange. She was indoors/outdoors, and one day when she was outdoors, she ran into the road. Julie found her body on the side of the road while getting off the school bus. Julie carried Sox to the house and later that night she and her mother buried her in the backyard.

She had forgotten about the grave marker.

The sliding glass door closed.

Julie returned the bones into the grave, tried to hide her tears by wiping smudges of dirt across her cheeks with the gloves. She quickly untied the green plastic bag around the roots of the rosebush, ripped part of it free, and set it into the hole. She gave one final sob before piling the rest of the dirt around the roots and packing it down. She imagined the plant forever soaking up her dead pet. The single red rose seemed to stare back at her, petals more alive.

She tasted gluey copper, teeth grinding against a pebble of bone—part of Elliot's skull or face or maybe a tooth. She let it dribble from her lips. The flower on the floor was nothing more than a conical display of red and white and gray matter splashed in her direction. Julie peeled a petal from her left breast and examined it before casting it aside. Petals covered her body. She and Elliot connected, both naked bodies covered in the hot gore that had once been Elliot's head, neck and chest. He had died rooted inside of her. She clenched around his hardness, the spasms slowing. Even after death, he came.

The man with the shotgun stood in silence. His lips moved, but the deafening blast covered his words with a constant drone. Emotionless, he raised the shotgun and dented her left breast with the barrel.

He squeezed the trigger.

Julie welcomed death.

Click.

The man in the blood-covered trench coat, the man without a name, with the self-buzzed haircut and the week old stubble on his cheeks and the rose tattoo running up his neck, he smiled. He lowered the weapon and limped out the door, never turning back.

"What's wrong, Julie?"

Her mother didn't see the rotted piece of wood next to the rose-bush, only the dirt smeared around Julie's eyes from her crying.

"Did you get bit again?"

Julie shook her head and sniffled, and winced at the hand on her shoulder.

The shotgun blast … was it only her body erupting from within, some sort of hallucinatory effect of the drug taken at such a high dose? Two diluted drops brought the anatomy-popping visuals and the heightened sex drive Julie was used to experiencing after dropping, but she had taken an entire syringe of concentrated *Drakein-5* directly into her bloodstream, an amount normally diluted. How many drops filled a standard Visine bottle, a hundred? She had taken so much *Drakein-5*, she could no longer interpret fantasy from reality as the room changed around her.

Her surroundings turned to watercolors, the air visible and salty, everything blending with everything. The lamp on the end table flickered purple then yellow then red and finally white. The magnetic aura connecting her body to Elliot had broken and lifted away like sun-soaked dew as the room spun around her.

A cacophony of train cars shook the entire house, the picture frames on the walls tilting askew, the refrigerator door and the cabinets in the kitchen opening and slamming shut, repeatedly, monstrously loud, silverware and dishes shuddering in the sink, the furniture, everything vibrating. The ceiling fan turned counterclockwise on its own accord, the pull chains in continuous pendulum. The cool hardwood planks glided beneath her like sheets of ice.

Elliot's headless body shifted under her, and she realized the worst part of it had been real. The man with the shotgun had blown Elliot's head off. The blast still echoed in her ears.

The entire house darkened, as if the power went out. Light from a full moon filled the house with silhouettes and shadows of what Julie remembered from the living room.

Such as the dead body she straddled.

Elliot was dead and inside her and still she rode him. A car drove by, illuminating the room, and Julie looked down in time to see a headless corpse with melting flesh. Julie fell to her side and felt a banana slug slide out of her, a sensation that made her uncontrollably giggle. Light from a second passing car revealed a body arching and rising from the ground. Snapping and crackling broke through the drone as the rest of Elliot dissolved. Waxy skin and tendons and organs liquesced and flowed onto the floor in a viscous black pool, leaving nothing but bones.

Julie crab-walked backward and met the couch. She somehow found her black panties and bra in the dark and absentmindedly dressed as she concentrated on the morphing skeleton.

The body arched further, like a gymnast, ribs grinding together and fracturing, the eyelets in the pelvic area staring straight at her.

The bones in both hands and in both feet—holding the skeleton suspended over the floor—extricated into four separate halves.

Hugging her knees, she thought back to her human anatomy class. She recognized the humerus bones of the arms, which connected to the ulna and radius in the forearms. She recognized the large femurs of the thighs, which connected to the tibia and fibula below the knees. The smaller bones in Elliot's forearms separated, as well as those in his legs, until the four appendages holding his torso aboveground had become eight. Two clavicles dangled like pedipalps at the head of this dead creature, like miniature hands to feed the mouth.

Elliot's corpse had transformed into a man-sized arachnid skeleton. It crawled toward her, but ceased when Julie cowered against the couch. One of its legs rose and reached outward to touch her— once a left leg; now a tibia, part of an ankle and two small bones hanging loosely to broken metatarsals.

Julie closed her eyes.

Something dry passed over her cheek, and she wondered if a part of Elliot lived in this morbid creature trying to wipe her tears. When it pulled away, she opened her eyes to a face of pelvis and sacrum, blood still dripping from its body. The creature almost looked sad and Julie could no longer be frightened. Its legs tapped against the hardwood floor, sliding in its own blood, nearly falling as it smeared black lines in its wake. A dotted line of gore trailed behind.

The spider crawled into a darker section of the house where Julie remembered a counter-height oak table with matching chairs and a large metal centerpiece filled with hand-woven balls of wire. She had glimpsed the kitchen beyond that room before the chaos, now a flat wall of black, a room of shadows in which the spider could hide. Halfway there, the spider turned its pelvic head to find Julie peeking around the corner of the couch.

Was it prompting her to follow?

The body disappeared into the mysterious.

Part of her trusted the giant arachnid and wanted to follow into the darkness. She rose to her knees, with a mixture of fluids flowing warm down her leg, and another part of her wanted to die.

A saucepan lid fell to the floor and spiraled to a stop, which returned her attention to the kitchen. Tiny footsteps clattered on tile. Two choices: run for the door, or follow the spider into the abyss. The decision reminded Julie of the poem by Robert Frost about two paths diverging in a wood. She had to memorize every line in seventh grade:

> *And be the one traveler, long I stood*
> *And looked down one as far as I could.*

Julie peered into a dining room filled with fuzzy black. Metal clanged onto the floor. She imagined the legs of the spider stumbling in the dark to the counter or the stove and knocking over utensils. It would be much easier to run out the door and into the rain. Slipping in the blood beneath her toes, Julie chose the more difficult path.

> *In leaves no step had trodden black*
> *Oh, I kept the first for another day!*

She reiterated the poem and imagined leaving bloody footprints.

> *Yet knowing how way leads on to way*
> *I doubted if I should ever come back.*

She stopped at the dining room table, mostly to catch her breath. *You're one messed up girl, Julie Stipes.*

A knife waited for her on the kitchen tile—one of the items that had clanged to the floor. It took effort to bend down and pick it up.

Headlights from a vehicle illuminated the small kitchen. Ambient shadows moved across the walls, the odd triangle of light revealing a giant spider silhouette climbing over the sink, its back legs holding it upright and front legs skittering on the countertop.

Standing behind the creature was a young girl, no more than three. Her eyes met Julie's as the light passed through her semitransparent body. Julie took her in: wet black hair, ash skin and sunken eyes, a rain-soaked white dress that disappeared when the light passed over it, and brown sandals caked in mud.

One moment she was there; another she was gone.

The room filled with darkness.

Julie slid the blade across her wrist, deep enough to remind her she was awake and capable of pain. She imagined the little girl walking toward her—a girl resembling herself at three—and materializing from the fuzzy black, holding out her hand and wanting Julie to take it. And it would feel cold and dead if she could feel it at all. Julie cut again, deeper this time. A trickle of blood found her palm and ran cool along her fingers, drops ticking against the floor.

"Julie, what are you doing in there?" she remembered her mother calling after knocking hard against the bathroom door.

"Nothing," Julie had said. "I'm using the bathroom."

"You've been in there awfully long."

"I'm fine, Mom."

She was far from fine. She had cut a little too deeply and held wads of red toilet paper against her shoulder. It was the first of three self-inflicted scars obtained as a teenager.

"Julie?" her mother had said, the doorknob jangling.

"Help her," a child's voice said, bringing Julie out of the memory.

Julie dropped the knife and backpedaled into one of the chairs, sending it screeching across the floor. Rain pattered against the kitchen window. A soft rumble of thunder rolled over the mountains far to the east. Strobes of silent lightning exposed the girl shifting closer. She held out a curled hand, as if holding something.

The spider stayed at the sink, entranced by the window.

"Help her," the girl said, her tone pleading.

Another flicker and she was a step closer. Sad eyes looked to Julie. The dead girl rounded the corner of the dining room, shifted down the hall and stopped, motioning Julie to follow, wanting to show her something.

"Who are you?"

Prune-stained lips smiled and said, "Hannah. That's one of my names."

"Are you—?"

"Dead?" she said and nodded.

A few gray freckles pocked her cheeks around a puzzle piece birthmark below her left eye. She floated down the hallway, looked to the floor, and passed through one of the doors.

Julie followed her through the dark, using the walls as guides. She pushed open the door as electricity returned to the house. Everything behind her lit up. The soft buzz of some kitchen appliance returned to life.

The door led her to a large bedroom. Julie flipped the switch on the wall. A king-sized bed centered the room with a nightstand on one side and an alarm clock blinking midnight in red. A few paperback books lined the headboard but Julie couldn't read the titles because her eyes watered from strain.

The nearly invisible girl stood at the far end of the room. Another door. She motioned Julie to follow as she stepped inside.

The doorknob rattled. "Julie, what's going on in there?" her father had said. "When your mother asks you to do something you do it, you hear? Unlock this door right now."

"I'm fine."

"You have to the count of five before I break down this door."

"I said I'm fine. Leave me alone."

"Don't you *talk* to your father that way," her mother said, and then in a softer voice, "Maybe she's in there writing one of her stories. You know how secretive she is about those."

"Are you writing another damn story?"

"Cal."

"I don't care what she's doing in there. She's not minding, either you or me. And those stories aren't right. Kids don't write like that."

The cut on her shoulder had mostly stopped bleeding. Julie left a few strips of toilet paper stuck to the wound and fixed the straps of her bra to cover herself, but her System of a Down T-shirt hung over the side of the bathtub. Before her father could say three, the door flew open.

Their reflections in the mirror looked to her own reflected image: a scared, half-naked teenager with blood on her shoulder and a red wad of toilet paper in her hand. Their eyes moved to the knife on the toilet seat.

The little apparition girl climbed on top of the toilet and to the counter. She scooted on her knees to the left side of the sink and pointed to the oak-trimmed mirror in front of her.

"Her," she said, pressing her finger through the mirror.

Julie realized the girl didn't have a reflection.

"Why do you need my help?"

The ghost shook her head.

"No, *her.*"

Mascara ran from the reddened eyes of the young woman in the mirror. Arms folded across her chest to hide the underwear barely clinging to her skinny body. One of the thong straps had fallen from a bony hip, the small triangle of black askew. A malnourished ribcage surfaced with every breath.

"I don't understand."

Hannah reached through the mirror and the once flat surface rippled around her arm. Rivulets of liquid glass found the edges of the frame as she leaned forward and stuck her head through, and then her shoulders. She disappeared through the glass.

The vanity light burned out and the bathroom door slammed shut as loud as a gunshot, hard enough for the oak framed mirror to shatter and come crashing down at the sink.

Open this goddamn door right now!

[fists pounding, doorknob rattling]

Julie shriveled to the floor over shards of glass.

You give your father some sugar, or he'll take it from you.

Julie remembered the bowl of M&M's on the side table next to the sofa. One of each color if she was a good girl. A red one and an orange one and a yellow and a brown and a light brown and a green. Six. Mom wouldn't have to know. Mom wouldn't have to know anything happened. It was a secret.

[the hand on her leg]

You wouldn't tell on Daddy, would you, Julie?

Stale beer and sometimes chocolate tainted his breath.

[her bedroom door creaking open]

Sometimes at night, her bedroom was black with a white rectangle of light around the door, dark unless the moon striped her window through the mini-blinds. Sometimes the mattress groaned when he sat on the edge of the bed. Her dolls and teddy bears watching from across the room.

[her father's shoulder slamming against the door, over and over, a soft line of white peeking underneath, the shadows of angry feet]

She sank to her knees.

Open the door so Daddy can fuck you, her mother said, but it wasn't her mother.

The voices, they couldn't be real.

She knows now, Julie, her father said. *She knows and she's mad because you've been a bad girl. We both saw what you were doing with that boy. It's warm when it runs down your leg, isn't it Julie?*

Julie rocked on the floor and found a large shard of mirror to help it all go away. She used the edge to cut another line next to the others on her shoulder. Blood seeped from the wound and ran along her bra strap—the pain deep and comforting—and down the side of her breast, past her navel, welling at the elastic band around her waist before spilling over and traversing warm over the triangle of fabric between her thighs.

And then they faded: the bathroom, the fabric, the darkness, the shard of glass.

Julie held a sharp piece of jawbone, bloody at the tip. She had used it to cut herself. She still straddled Elliot's dead body in the living room, his arachnid skeleton beneath her. Spilled rose petals splashed over the hardwood where his head used to be—bloody fragments of skull and brain matter, splinters of wood and buckshot.

The room gyrated, flashed red and white. Within the strobe lighting, two plump caterpillars crawled across a leaf that had blown inside. A green caterpillar with yellow stripes. A yellow caterpillar with green stripes. Characters from a fable she had written as a child. But that wasn't right. Why were they here now? One of them reared. She blinked and they were gone.

Hallucinations, Julie told herself, although something more than the drug caused the strobes of light. *Most of this is real.*

She forced herself from rocking against the skeletal frame, which continued to flicker beneath her in horrid phantasms of flesh versus fleshless. Something dead and wilted slid out of her body as she lifted off him.

Julie retched and vomited two shots of Jack Daniels. She rose to her knees with the last of her strength and fell to the side, her head hitting hard. The syringe crushed beneath her shoulder.

Elliot's arm enveloped her, cold fingers around her wrist.

◻ ◻ ◻

"Julie?" her father said. "Your little negro friend is here."

"*Calvin!*" her mother said from the kitchen.

"What's wrong in calling her that?"

Julie joined them, but her father's hand held her back.

"She doesn't mind," he said over his shoulder. "What you got there?"

"Reese," Frankie Jones said, holding up a clear container.

She lived two doors down. Sometimes they'd go to the park to turn over loose wood or rocks to search for skinks or bugs. What they found usually went into mason jars or coffee cans with wax paper held over the openings by rubber bands—holes punched through so the creatures wouldn't die. Frankie held up an aquarium she'd gotten for her birthday for Julie's father to see. Inside, a small tarantula hid behind a chunk of bark: Reese.

"Can Julie play?"

"Where?" her father said.

"Huh?"

"Where do you want to play? I'm not taking the two of you to the park to look for no goddamn bugs. We've got plenty enough around here."

Frankie looked to the ground.

"Here?" he said.

Frankie nodded.

"Can we?" Julie said from behind him.

"Let her in, Cal," her mother said from the kitchen.

He let out a disgusted sigh.

"We're not feeding her. She can go home for lunch. Julie, go around back and let her through the gate. I don't want that thing in my house."

Whether he meant Frankie or the tarantula, Julie didn't care. Only playing mattered.

Julie ran through the house and slammed the sliding glass door of the kitchen behind her. She found Frankie Jones already at the gate—she must have run, too—and pulled the string connected to the latch to let her in. Gravel crunched under their feet as they walked down the narrow path leading to the backyard. Rusted lead pipes rested against the house, as well as an old wooden dresser weathered and warped by the rain and sun. A few of the drawers next to it sprouted weeds. The girls traded turns kicking a beer can as they walked side-by-side.

At the edge of the yard, Frankie held up the aquarium for Julie. Reese withdrew into the corner. Stretched out, the spider's longest legs would have each measured an inch; the two in front caressed the plastic, but the rest of the grayish-brown creature scrunched together, its body like a hairy Tootsie Roll pinched in the center.

"I found him under a brick next to our garage."

"How'd he get under a brick?"

Frankie shrugged.

"Does he bite?"

"No. I don't think so. My dad says they don't like winter 'cause they're coldblooded. That's why he's just sitting there. Do you want to touch him?"

She slid part of the pink lid to reveal an opening.

Julie reached through to brush the spider's body with the back of her index finger. The spider felt cool, clammy, and not hairy at all. She slowly pulled her hand out and smelled her finger, but it didn't smell like anything.

For the next hour, they lifted rocks and moved oak logs stacked in the woodpile by the fence, but found nothing worth keeping. They almost caught an alligator lizard, but it darted into the neighbor's yard. They fed a few beetles to Reese, but he let them crawl around in the aquarium, sometimes over his legs.

"Wanna swing?" Frankie said.

"Okay."

Only one of the swings worked. The other blue seat broke a long time ago and hung from the chain. Julie didn't have many friends, so she figured it got tired of not swinging and died one day. Now that Frankie Jones was here, she wished it hadn't. They took turns, each trying to out-swing the other. Frankie said she almost got one of the swings in Canford Park to go all the way around once, one of the big swings, but Julie knew it was impossible. Once you got high enough, you'd just fall hard onto the seat as you came back down.

Frankie was moderately high when she launched. She landed ten feet in front of the swing set and kept on running to the house.

"I'll be right back," she said. "I've gotta go to the bathroom."

Julie's mother let Frankie into the house and peered out from the sliding glass door.

"I'm running an errand," she said. "You two play safe while I'm gone. I won't be back until five, so make sure Frankie gets home before noon. If you're hungry, there's leftover chicken in the fridge."

"Okay," Julie said, and then she was alone.

She took over on the swing, but only sat on the plastic seat, waiting, rocking with her feet dangling over the sawdust.

Julie watched the spider for a while, counted his legs. He had wrapped one of the beetles in a cocoon while the other waited for death. The tarantula didn't look hungry, but had killed anyway, for later, she knew. And the other beetle wasn't going anywhere. Sometimes her father took two cans of beer from the refrigerator and it was kind of the same thing.

The combination clock/thermometer on the back of the house said it was seventy-eight degrees and that Frankie had been gone for five minutes, and then ten.

Julie checked the half bathroom, but Frankie wasn't there. She wasn't in the full bathroom either because Julie heard her father's cough behind the door. She wasn't in Julie's room playing with her toys, or the kitchen or living room area. Julie found Frankie naked on the edge of her parent's bed, tears running down her face to the pile of clothes beneath her feet. She had been sobbing.

The two of them looked alike without any clothes, only Frankie had brown skin instead of almond white, her hair was darker, and she didn't have a birthmark.

Neither said a word as they stared at one another.

Frankie's eyes moved away from Julie's, to a place behind Julie and then to the floor. She wiped her face with the back of her hand and then tried to cover herself.

A heavy hand pressed hard on Julie's shoulder as her father leaned down and whispered in her ear, "Frankie's had an accident and needs to wash up."

His breath hot and foul, like beer and roasted peanuts.

"Go to the kitchen and heat up some chicken. Your mother said there's leftovers in the fridge. I need a few minutes more with your negro friend."

Julie couldn't pull her eyes away from Frankie. She didn't look embarrassed from wetting herself; she looked like a naked doll sitting lifeless on the edge of the bed, eyes sad and dark, cheeks bruise-red and tear-smeared, and her mouth a flat line.

"You said she had to go home for lunch. You said—"

"She'll stay for lunch and then go home." He turned Julie around and pushed at her back. "Frankie, why don't you start getting dressed?"

Julie looked over her shoulder to Frankie pulling on white underwear with blue butterflies. Julie had a similar pair, but hers had green and blue butterflies instead of only blue ones. She was about to ask if they were hers, if Frankie could borrow some of her clothes while they washed her dirty ones, but the door between them closed.

The cold fingers around her wrist belonged to a hazy young woman dressed in a dark blue uniform. She suppressed the blood spilling from Julie's wrist.

"Her pulse is weak," the woman said to another in the room.

"What the hell happened in here?" he said, his voice warbled and far away. "This is why I'm a vegetarian. Inside, we're all just meat."

Julie squeezed Elliot's jawbone.

"Shut up and wrap this for me. I'll get the stretcher."

Red welled from her wrist when the woman let go as another set of gloved hands dressed the wound with gauze and tape. She couldn't feel any of it. She couldn't feel anything at all.

"You think it was a failed murder-suicide?"

This new voice came from nowhere in particular.

"What do we know about her?"

"Nothing."

"What about the other?"

"Elliot Cartwright. He lives *here*, according to his driver's license. We found his wallet in his back pocket. No money and no credit cards."

The female paramedic moved into Julie's blurry vision. Their eyes made contact, and then she pried open Julie's mouth and looked inside. The room spun.

"Eyes are solid black, skin clammy and she's barely breathing. She's OD'd on something. We need to move her ASAP."

"We need more photos."

"If we don't move her now, she'll die. We're moving her."

"Give me ten seconds. Vargus, get over here! Put that thing on automatic and start firing. I want pictures of anything and everything. Murder-suicide, my ass. That's a shotgun blast on the floor and I don't see a shotgun anywhere. Do you?"

"We're still looking."

"Get some pictures of her face before the paramedics clean her up. Nelson, get some swabs for blood comparison. Some of this blood might not be theirs."

Feet danced around Julie on the floor. All at once the room became crowded and overbearing. Someone in the room retched.

Elliot's corpse lay next to her, sticky against her leg. Still naked, she imagined all the strange eyes in the room staring at her. It was either the gore or her naked body to look at, and she guessed no one wanted the gore.

A dozen flashes turned everything white.

When Julie's vision returned, the paramedic still holding her head looked to her sadly and said, "Can we at least cover her up?"

[flash]

"Not yet."

[flash]

"Get a shot of her arm. What *is* that?"

[flash]

"A puncture bruise from an injection. There's a small syringe smashed on the floor next her. Looks like *Drakein-5*."

[flash]

"She injected it?"

"More reason to move her now. If we don't get her into detox, there's no telling what could happen. I've seen people OD on *D-5*, but never at this high of a dose. This girl is in la-la land. I can see it in her eyes. It looks like she's trying to say something."

[flash]

"You better be done with the pictures, because we're going."

Julie tried to tell her about Hannah in the other room, and the mirror through which she passed. *He took her*, she failed to say.

[flash]

The paramedic wiped her face with a white towel that striped red. Her skin peeled back to reveal a perfect white skull and then she was beautiful again. A pale and out-of-focus yellow aura surrounded her head like a halo.

"We're moving her," the woman said. "Lift on three."

On three, someone lifted her legs while the woman over her lifted her by the shoulders. They moved her onto a stretcher, strapped her down, and rolled her into the back of an ambulance. Julie convulsed.

The woman paramedic disappeared, but her voice read numbers to another in the back of the van who held her down despite the constraints.

"Temperature one-oh-three. Heart rate one-forty and rising. Blood pressure … one-sixty-eight over one-forty. She's hypertensive and burning up. How long until we reach—"

Warmth ran up Julie's arm as they injected something into her. The shakings calmed and then stilled as the voices and everything around her faded.

Julie sat upright on a metal gurney. No longer constrained. The windowless white room resembled the patient quarters of a psychiatric ward she'd seen in a movie once, minus the padded walls. White ceiling tiles and florescent lighting meshed and turned the scars on her skin purplish. A sickly bruise surrounded the injection. The floor consisted of polished ceramic tile. Everything but the gurney was white, even her paper gown and the gauze around her wrist.

A mirror with an oak frame faced her, the kind you'd expect to see in a home improvement store, barely noticeable against the white because that's all it reflected. Someone had etched a word into the top of the frame in a strange script, but she couldn't read it. Curious, Julie slid off the gurney.

The reflected woman was all but unrecognizable: hair in tangles, makeup running, and reddened eyes sunken and exhausted. Julie touched her face to make sure the woman in the reflection would do the same.

And then she saw the little girl approaching from behind. Somehow she knew Hannah wouldn't be there if she turned around, but she looked anyway.

Semitransparent and difficult to see in the overly bright room, the little apparition girl stopped at the gurney and put her hand up to it. The reflection of the gurney rolled a bit.

Julie touched the glass and her finger passed through. The surface rippled like water. She pulled back and let it turn placid.

"Where am I?"

"This is the trial room."

"The trial room?"

Hannah nodded.

"Bad things happen here."

"What kind of things?"

Hannah looked to her feet and shrugged, as if she were too afraid to say anything.

"What kind of things, Hannah?"

The girl simply pointed at Julie in the mirror.

Blood welled beneath the paper gown in her reflection, a dark crimson stain against the white around her. The red flowered through the fabric and ran down her leg.

A sharp cramp bent her in half and Julie grabbed at the pain. She pried her fingers away, expecting menstrual blood, but her fingers came away clean. Looking down, the blood was gone, despite the intense but otherwise familiar pains of a period. Pain troubled her again as Julie faced the mirror. The lower half of her hospital gown welled with blood in the reflection, flowing down her inner thighs. Sticky red covered her fingers.

Hannah rocked on the balls of her bare feet and rolled the fabric of her dress between her fingers. She wanted to say something, but couldn't.

What other name or names did she go by?

As quickly as the blood in the mirror appeared, it disappeared, yet the pain intensified, like a hot coal migrating past her stomach and beneath her intestines. A firm hand against her abdomen felt something moving inside, something hard, something pushing back.

"Can you feel it kicking?" said Hannah.

Pain dropped Julie to the floor. The pressure inside moved lower and severe cramping made her cry out in the empty room. Her

scream reverberated off the walls and when she looked underneath the hospital gown and lifted her fingers from her crotch, they came back tacky and red, like her reflection only moments before.

Julie's body contracted as blood spilled freely from between her legs. The tips of two black, skeletal appendages tore out of her. She felt the urge to push, and when she pushed, more of the creature came out. Slimy, jointed black legs clawed at the air, each nearly eight inches long, stretching her body wider, multiple elongated legs grazing her skin, cutting into her like knives as they struggled in the wet for leverage to escape the warm prison of Julie's womb.

"Get it out of me!" Julie screamed, no longer crumpled on the floor.

She sat at the edge of a hospital bed in a room flooded with light. A young woman's head rose from between Julie's spread legs. She wore a blue facemask and looked scared out of her mind from the outburst. The nurse next to her tried to calm Julie down.

"This will only take a moment longer."

The legs of the spider pressed hard and cold from within.

"I'm nearly finished," the examiner said, "but I need you to hold her down so she doesn't hurt herself. We still need fingernail scrapings and hair samples."

"Please," Julie pleaded, "get it out of me ..." Sobs interrupted the rest.

"Everything will be fine," the nurse said. "You're reacting from the drugs, but please try to stay calm."

The examiner's head was not much more than a skull, her raw jaw elongated beneath the mask, the remaining skin melting like wax from her sleek face. Then the horrible image was gone. She held up a metal instrument and a long cotton swab dabbed with blood, which she slid into a small envelope and set aside next to a dozen others on the stainless steel tray. Next to it was a clipboard and a plastic box with S.A.F.E. KIT stenciled on the side.

"What are you doing to me?"

"This is standard procedure for sexual assault."

The plastic box was a rape kit. She remembered seeing one on a crime scene show the Heimlichs watched regularly. S.A.F.E. stood for Sexual Assault Forensic Evidence. The victims on television often appeared more violated after an exam than the actual rape.

"I wasn't raped."

"Everything will be fine," the doctor said. "This shouldn't take much longer. Another fifteen minutes at the most. I know you're scared and confused, but I need you to remain calm. I need you to—"

"I don't have to be fucking anything!"

Julie kicked out and knocked something metal onto the floor.

"Get it out of me."

She tried to slide off the examination table, but the nurse grabbed her by the arm until it hurt. Julie envisioned the spidery legs inside of her, trying to crawl out.

The woman between her legs struggled to hold Julie's knees apart despite their dire need to connect. Something cold stuck inside of her and it hurt to move. Something hard and metal—not the legs of a spider, but something foreign.

"Julie," the nurse said, releasing the pressure a bit. "I know this is uncomfortable, but it needs to be done. You agreed to let us perform the exam when you first got here; you offered consent. You've been through a lot tonight, but we need you to go through just a little more."

Clammy fingers touched her hand; she could barely feel them at all.

Hannah stood at her side. She wasn't smiling, but seemed tranquil. The puzzle-shaped birthmark on her cheek appeared like a shadow, or an absence of ghostly skin. She looked up at Julie with a bashful air and thin purple lips, with deep-set eyes. She resembled Julie at three, only dead, and held a red rose with black-trimmed petals. Everything about her was semi-transparent, everything but the rose. A few of the petals surrounded her feet, as bright as blood.

"That's better," one of the women in the room said, but Julie was leaving them. She turned her head to the side, to Hannah.

Hannah held the rose as if she wanted Julie to smell it. Julie leaned closer and inhaled a pleasant aroma. She tried to squeeze the little hand within her own, but her fingers simply passed through and the apparition girl smiled.

"What's she doing?"

"I'm not sure, but I want to finish this before she starts kicking again. I recommend getting fingernail scrapings before she acts up."

"What is she looking at?"

Innocent eyes. Translucent skin.

"She's holding something."

Julie's hand opened to take the rose—her fingers pried apart by an unseen force. Hannah slid the flower across Julie's palm, the thorns cutting into her to create new blossoms spilling through her fingers to the floor.

"And it's cutting her."

Keep it safe, the little girl said.

Julie's hand opened like a flower, the petals scarlet.

"My god …"

Hannah smiled and turned away, taking the pain with her. Barely visible, she held the rose behind her back and walked to the other side of the room where a full-length mirror floated against utter whiteness. She knelt in front of it and placed the flower on the ground before stepping through. The glass rippled around her like water rivulets.

Don't go.

Julie wasn't sure if she said it aloud.

"What?" a voice said.

"It's a piece of bone. Three teeth still attached. She's been holding onto a part of someone's jawbone this whole time."

"And you didn't notice?"

The little girl at the door was all but gone, fading as the rest of the examination room restored around her: the white walls, ceiling and tile, the stainless steel instruments and furniture, the Formica tables, the examiner with the mask, the nurse next to her with the horrorstricken expression as she held up something red and white to her counterpart with a shaky, rubber-gloved hand—part of Elliot's lower jawbone. She moved out of sight and returned with gauze. She pressed hard against the lacerations on Julie's palm.

Then the girl was gone, passing through the rest of the thin frame as if it were an open window. The rose remained at the base, reflecting bright red against the otherwise white. She expected the flower to vanish, like the girl, but wished for it to stay—the same way she wished for Hannah to return and stand by her side, to hold her hand, to get her through the pain, to show her everything she wanted to see.

Julie needed to protect the flower.

Hannah's aura floated through the mirror in her wake, as visible as the petals.

The women at her side scraped something rough beneath her fingernails and combed through her hair.

"We're almost done," one of them said.

The dragon would call for her soon if she didn't drop.

The rose ... was it there at all?

If she had another syringe, she'd shoot the whole thing into her arm to tell the craving to shut the fuck up, to stop the sounds of scraping around her, to stop the clattering of metal and the ringing in her ears and the buzz of florescent lighting.

They scraped Elliot's blood from underneath her fingernails.

Julie pulled her hand from the nurse, but a stronger hand pulled back. Tape and gauze wrapped the wrist where she had cut herself with the glass or bone or whatever she had used at Elliot's. The pockmark where she injected the needle was a purple hole.

A few drops, one in each eye; that's all she really needed.

She could hang with Chase and they could drop together. Maybe he'd let her have a sample if she promised to buy more. Half a grand for another syringe. She'd call Chase as soon as she got out of the hospital. She didn't have money, but could convince him she was good for it, or she could even—

Julie blinked and the room disappeared. Surrounded in white, the rose stood out like a splotch of paint thrown against an empty canvas.

She blinked again and found herself in a cold chair, still in her hospital gown, bandaged hands on her lap. Two men in uniform stood in front of her, one with folded arms, and the other with a pen and notepad. Their faces melted as the room materialized around them. The room was cheap hotel ugly and smelled like cleaning solvents. Sweat poured off her, although Julie shivered.

"We need to ask you some questions," the man with the folded arms said.

Julie covered herself, feeling exposed.

She shook her head 'no' because his voice sounded familiar, too much like the man with the shotgun.

You want him to fuck you. Is that it … you want to fuck 'er?

"What happened to Elliot?"

"Tell us your name."

Julie turned away from them, but couldn't make them go away.

The man with the notepad was the detective from before.

"We realize you've been through a lot tonight, but anything you can tell us—"

"We know there was someone else at the scene," the other said. "Footprints in the blood suggest a male. What did he look like?"

"He … I can't—"

"Yes, you can. What did the man look like?"

"He had a tattoo," Julie said. "A—a red rose on his neck, climbing up from his collar. It looked burnt, or his skin was burnt."

"What's your name?"

"I don't remember."

Julie lied.

The man in front of her started to change, his skin no longer dripping. His body reconstructed, unsettling in its normalcy.

"Was he tall, short? What kind of build?"

"He looked sort of like you, only his eyes darker, sunken in. Strange hair, like he cut it himself with clippers." Julie imagined the man in the trench coat staring at them from across the bar, not the man with the shotgun in Elliot's house. "He limped."

"Why did he do this to you?"

"I don't know?"

"Did you catch a name?"

"No."

"What's your name."

"I told you I don't remember."

"Did this guy with a limp know the deceased?"

"No."

"Are you certain?"

"Yes. No. I don't know. Yes. I don't think Elliot knew who he was. Elliot—"

"So you remember your boyfriend's name. What's your name?"

"He's not my boyfriend."

"Why do you think he came after the two of you?"

"He must have followed us from the bar."

"What were you doing at the bar?"

"Drinking, looking for someone to hook up with."

Julie didn't want to tell him she was there for cash, to find a gullible guy concerned more with hooking up than the contents of his pockets. It had become natural for her to steal. It was the only way to pay for the drug. The goddamn dragon. She was riding it hard.

"Are you underage? Were you drinking?"

"Yes, but—"

"And this Elliot …"

"Elliot Cartwright," the other said.

"This Elliot Cartwright, he hooked up with you after some drinks at the bar and brought you back to his place, is that correct?"

"Yes, but—"

Had she told them this?

"And the two of you were sexually involved?"

"Sir," the other said.

"I'm just trying to get the facts straight."

"Don't you think some of this can wait until—?"

"Were you and the deceased sexually involved?"

"No. Yes."

"Which is it, yes or no?"

"Both."

She didn't want to talk about any of this. Not now, perhaps not ever. Not to anyone. Julie stared at the wall next to her and rocked on the chair. She thought of Elliot. Julie had only wanted his money at first. She wanted to draw him in and then dupe him like the others. And then something changed during their conversation at the bar. He had dark secrets and didn't care about her past.

The room slowly spun around her as thoughts turned to the giant arachnid spider rising from his fallen, headless body—the charred, blackened bones, arching from the floor—and the guilt of their bodies grinding together just before. *Don't worry, you won't be having sex*, he had promised. *Just push it down and out of your way, Julie. It won't bite.* But it did bite. Sometime after shooting the drug she had blacked out and upon waking his promise had—

"Julie, I want you to look at me and tell me the truth." Her mother's words always seemed more powerful with a hand in the air.

The floor wanted Julie's eyes. Her cheeks wanted the water dripping out of them and then the floor wanted her sadness as well and so she told the floor her secret.

"I can't remember."

"Don't you lie to me."

Julie tried to find a reflection of herself in the black of her mother's eyes, but there wasn't enough light in the room and everything was blurry.

"I can't remember," she said again, and it was the truth.

"Why did you break the vase?"

She had cut her palm, but it wasn't deep and didn't hurt. The blood a watercolor rose with liquid petals. She couldn't remember breaking the vase, only wanting to grow a flower in her hand.

"I watched you do it, Julie."

The hand that had slapped her mouth remained in the air; instead of slapping her a second time, the hand came down and squeezed her wrist, making her drop the shard. Bones in her wrist mashed together.

The secret flower stretched along the lines of her hand, down her wrist, and cried onto the carpet. Julie could see herself now in her mother's eyes and tried disappearing into them.

Julie pulled her hand from the nurse and slid off the examination table. She wasn't expecting the ground to be so far away and she landed hard on the balls of her feet. She was barefoot, the floor cold. Her feet slid in something wet.

Someone said to hold her down. Another said to take it easy and everything would be all right. Another grabbed her shoulder and she shrugged it away. She told them all to leave her alone and backhanded one across the face. Three or four of them in the room. Trying to touch her, smothering her … hands reaching out, hands trying to hold her down. Fingers as cold and rough as her father's.

[what aren't you telling us?]

Don't you lie to me.

"Get away from me."

[we need to sedate her]

"Get the fuck away from me!"

The words cracked, reminding her of a song called "Raven" by the female growler band, Kittie: *Get away from me! Stay the fuck away from me!* There was such hatred behind the chorus repeated over and over again. Frankie called those types of bands microphone-eaters because they screamed into the mike.

A needle slid into her shoulder and broke.

Her elbow connected with someone's mouth and a few of the hands let her go. Intravenous tubes pulled taut against her body like rubbery strings before stretching and tearing away, and at first she suspected her father was behind those strings somewhere, making her dance. She felt something slide out from the back of her hand. Metal trays clanged to the floor. She couldn't understand any of the frantic voices around her because the beeping and her father's words drowned them.

Just close your eyes, Julie.

"Don't touch me!"

The ground beneath her slipped away as she ran for the mirror through which Hannah passed. A part of her knew only she could see it. The others would see a blank wall, or perhaps the door leading out of the room, but Julie knew it was there. Along with the rose left for her beneath it. Hannah wanted her to follow, wanted to show her the magic on the other side, perhaps a better world.

A firm hand grabbed her shoulder and dug underneath her clavicle. She slipped and fell hard, smacking the back of her head on the tile. Either a tile or her head cracked, making an awful sound that turned the world around her black.

"I used to cut myself," she had told Elliot at the bar. "Sometimes I used to feel so dead inside, as if it didn't matter what I did in life because I was just going to die anyway."

The thought came to her out of nowhere.

How easy it would be to die.

How alive it felt to see the blood, to feel the sting of the blade.

Daddy won't hurt you, honey.

Sometimes she'd pry open the wound and it would make her forget all the bad things: Frankie crying naked on the edge of the bed, Julie on his lap, her father holding Reese in his palm and squeezing, sticky fingers touching her shoulder—the same place she used to cut herself.

Julie sliced the air, raking fingernails over flesh that easily peeled away. Someone like her mother screamed through the black.

The rose pulsed red through the darkness like a heartbeat, guiding her. She crawled to its warm light. She reached blindly for the rose and it was there, the thorns cutting into her, making her feel alive, making her forget. As soon as she latched onto the stem, the face of the mirror turned white to offer a reverse silhouette—a rectangle of white against the black. Her hand passed through the invisible glass, the surface cool and rippling around her touch.

A clammy hand on the other side grabbed her wrist and pulled her through.

"Julie," her father said.

"Yes, Daddy?"

"Julie!"

"Yes."

"You listen to me when I talk to you. Hear me? Now, come on."

"Yes, Daddy."

Her wrist crumpled within his leathery hands and her skin burned underneath, the way it did sometimes during recess when Paul Williams gave her Indian burns by wringing her wrist like a washcloth. Some of the other kids said he must like her, teasing her and whatnot, that he *loved* her and wanted to have secks with her, but Julie never understood why someone would want to hurt someone they loved, and whatever secks was, she didn't want to have it with Paul Williams, especially if it hurt.

Julie's mind often wandered, but she was listening to her father. He eased a bit on her arm.

Nothing but empty white surrounded them; all but the wooden frame to Julie's back from which she entered this nothingness.

"I'm not going to run, Daddy."

"What?"

There was only one way out of this place: through the mirror.

"I'm not going to run. You're hurting me. I won't, I promise."

"I'll show you hurt."

"I won't run this time."

He raised a hand in the air and it stayed there long enough for Julie to know it wouldn't strike her this time. It was only a warning. She saw something bad in his eyes whenever it was more than a warning. His eyes would become glossier, always trying to focus.

"I didn't mean to do it."

"Do what?"

"Whatever I did. I didn't mean to, Daddy."

The hand returned to his side while the other tugged her along.

"Come on, Julie," he said.

"Okay."

They walked for an insurmountable time before Julie looked over her shoulder. The mirror was quite a distance back. A small dot against the white and nothing more. If they traveled any farther, it would disappear. They would be alone. Something Julie didn't want.

"Can we go back, Daddy?"

The mirror was gone.

They were alone.

He pulled her wrist and they walked onward.

She was going to ask her father if they could go back soon, but he was gone too, a different hand wrapped around her wrist.

"Come on, Julie," Frankie said.

Frankie Jones led her now. Perspiration glistened from her dark skin. She had been playing hard and smelled of dirt and sweat, a pleasant alternative to her father's aftershave. Faster they ran and they laughed and soon Julie's lungs burned. Where they were going, she didn't care. But they had been running from something, Julie knew, but it must have been something imaginary chasing them because Frankie smiled as she dragged Julie along.

"Come *on*."

"What's back there?"

"Wolves."

"Wolves?"

"Yeah, can't you see 'em? There's two."

Julie looked over her shoulder to blank white.

"Yeah, I see 'em," Julie told her friend, but she didn't know why. "We're never going to make it, though. They're going to catch us."

"No," Frankie said. "We'll make it. Hurry!"

"They're gaining on us."

"*Hurry up!*" her mother said, who had taken Frankie's place. "We're never going to make it. I told you we'd be late."

"But the wolves—"

"I want you to stop with the nonsense."

It was hard to follow her mother without tripping over her own two feet. Her mother's arm stayed rigid at her side and she held Julie's hand as if attached to her hip. One arm swayed as she speed-walked; the other was a wooden board with Julie's hand nailed to it.

"I told you to get dressed over an hour ago and now we're going to be late because of you. You never listen. Do you know how much trouble we'll be in if we don't make it on time?"

"Where are we going?"

They weren't going anywhere.

"You're not listening, Julie."

"Where are we going?" she said to the white.

Her mother was gone.

"Away from the trial room," Hannah said.

The little apparition girl had taken her mother's place, no longer ghostly, but a normal little girl leading her along an invisible path. Her hair was not dirty and black as before, but light brown, her skin soft and light instead of transparent, and the puzzle-shaped birthmark on her cheek profound. Freckles peppered her skin. Julie had to bend her knees as they moved along.

And then she saw it: a red splotch against the white.

The rose.

"Who are you?"

"Hannah, and …" she said, trailing off.

Her hand was cold and small.

"I know, but *who* are you?"

Hannah shrugged and said, "I'm me."

"Where did you come from?"

"From my mommy."

"Who's your mommy?"

Hannah shrugged and some of the hair on her shoulder moved. At first Julie thought walking had jostled the hair, but then she noticed a small, hairy appendage hiding beneath. And then another. Reese freed himself, his front two legs feeling at the air as she had remembered him in Frankie's plastic aquarium all those years back.

"There's a spider on your shoulder."

"I know." Hannah brushed her hair back, which fully uncovered the tarantula. "He tickles sometimes. You can pet him if you want. He won't bite."

Julie brushed the back of her finger against its body and he stretched to her touch, cold and clammy, exactly as she remembered.

"Is this Reese?"

"I don't know, but you can call him that if you want."

"What's he doing here? What's he doing on your shoulder?"

Another shrug.

"He likes it here, I guess."

Within all the whiteness, and without any sense of direction or linearity, the rose seemed to float before them, full of vibrancy.

"He dropped it," Hannah said.

"What?"

"The man dropped it."

"What man?"

"The man who took it from you."

She had retrieved it from the floor at the base of the mirror, the thorns digging into her, cutting her, but somewhere between the hand grabbing her wrist and pulling her through, she had lost the flower and had forgotten all about it.

"Was it my dad?" He was the first Julie remembered dragging her along. "Did my dad take it?"

"Who's your dad?"

Julie shrugged and it made her think of the little girl and how she had shrugged when Julie had asked her a similar question. How could she describe her father to a girl like Hannah?

"My dad is a very bad man."

She imagined twirling the rose with her fingertips and it brought her warmth. The flower was flawless, almost cartoonish. As red as blood.

"Oh, then it was probably him."

"Why do you say that?"

"Because the man who took it is a very bad man."

Thoughts returned of the red gore flower left from the shotgun blast …

"It can't be my dad," Julie said, pushing away the image. "I don't know why I asked you if it was him. It can't be him."

"Why?"

"My father's dead."

"Oh."

A soft prickle at the back of her neck, and then a cold shiver.

Hannah's expression turned grim. "Then it was probably him."

"Why would you say that?"

"I don't know. 'Cause *I'm* dead."

Am I?

It was highly possible. Maybe all this was part of some sick after-life. Maybe after the very bad man had pulled the trigger and ended Elliot's life he had ended hers as well. The drugs in her body … perhaps they were stuck in her system postmortem, causing after-life hallucinations, such as the arachnid skeleton crawling out from beneath her—rising from Elliot's fallen body like a phoenix rising from its ashes—and leading Julie to the kitchen window where it seemingly wanted out [or through] and tapping its boney legs against the glass. And the ghost girl, Hannah, admitting she was dead.

Memories flooding in and flashing before her eyes—didn't this transpire with death, a light at the end of the tunnel? Was she walking through that tunnel? Was she in the light? The whiteness was overbearing in its brightness.

"No."

"No what?"

"You're not dead."

"How do you know?"

"I brought you here. If you were dead, you could have brought yourself."

"Oh."

Julie picked up the rose and smelled the fragrance—like the heritage roses she and her mother had planted in the backyard the year she'd accidentally unburied Sox. She grabbed the stem tight and welcomed the thorns. "Can't pick them or they *bite* you," her mother had said about the roses. The pain: a reminder that she was still alive.

"You have to cut *them*," Julie said, thinking both of her mother and of the scars below her collarbone.

"Huh?"

"Nothing. It's beautiful, isn't it?"

Hannah smiled with Reese camouflaged in her hair.

The rose was mesmerizing.

"Where do we go from here?"

"To find the bad man."

"Why?"

"Because he needs to make things right. Took what wasn't his."

"I don't understand."

"That's why we need to find him. He understands now."

"Now?"

Hannah nodded, as if all this made sense.

"I don't want to see him, I want to go back. How do I go back? I want to go home."

"You have to see him."

"He killed my … my friend. Elliot. Shot him and killed him while I was … with him. He made us do bad things. He's a very bad man, Hannah. If he sees me again, he'll kill me."

What she wanted, what she really *craved*, was more *Drakein-5*, some dragon to make the chaos seem normal. A drop would be fine, one in each eye. She could feel her fingers pinching the bottle, the slight burn as she blinked in the drug, the sudden rush.

Julie squeezed Hannah's hand and it squeezed back, clammy like the spider. Holding the rose was comforting. Whenever she held the flower, what Julie could only describe as power flowed from one hand, through her body, and to the other, but it wasn't enough. She knelt next to the girl and asked sincerely if they could go back to the mirror from which they entered this strange place.

"That's where we're going," she said, and pointed ahead.

Directly in front of them was a black spot deep into the white. Julie glanced over her shoulder; behind them was nothing but white.

"But—"

"This way," Hannah said.

Before Julie could completely stand, Hannah had taken a few steps forward and tugged on her arm for her to follow.

"Come on."

They walked for quite some time in silence, the ground beneath them barely there. Neither body cast a shadow. Julie checked over her shoulder every so often. It was unsettling not having a perception of space, but she experienced neither imbalance nor vertigo. With the same white at their back and front, above and below and side-to-side, they could have been walking in place for all Julie knew, or floating on an invisible plane. They were moving forward though, toward the black dot slowly growing in size, her only insight as to whether or not they were moving at all.

A part of Julie expected the man from the bar to sneak up from behind, his black trench coat dripping rainwater forever onto/into the white, the double barrel shotgun swaying at his side, his burned, crooked jack o' lantern smile ever so menacing. Breath like her father's.

"He can't hurt you here," Hannah said, as if reading her thoughts.

"Why not?"

"I don't know, but he can't."

"Can I hurt *him?*"

"No."

Julie thought this over as she and Hannah walked in the white emptiness toward the unknown object. *Because he's dead, too? Is that why he can't hurt me here? Is everything in this place dead but me?* Her mother told Julie that Calvin Stipes had died in prison, where he belonged. *Was that true?* Reese hid behind Hannah's hair somewhere, validating her suspicions. As a child, she had watched Reese die.

Frankie's had an accident and needs to wash up, her father had said after Julie found them together. *I need a few minutes more with your little negro friend.*

Those words had stuck with her, as well as the burned image of Frankie's shame. She remembered not being able to look away from her friend and thinking maybe her father liked her and wanted to have secks with her like some of the kids at school had teased. The door between them had closed then, but afterward, after lunch, Julie asked her father if he liked Frankie Jones that way. The secks way.

What the hell do you know of that? Are they teaching you that in school?

Julie told him 'nothing' and 'no' while Frankie stared at her shoelaces. She didn't understand the word, couldn't even spell it.

I don't want to hear nothing more of it. Frankie, it's time for you to go.

She left, forgetting the plastic aquarium with Reese inside. She didn't look up from the floor as she made her way to the door. She didn't even say goodbye.

What are you going to say to your mother when she gets home?

Julie remembered reaching down to the aquarium at her side and keeping her eyes on Reese so she wouldn't have to look at her father while answering.

Just that—she started to say, but he had interrupted her.

Just nothing. Look at me, Julie. I said look at me!

He stood in front of her in a matter of moments, forced her by the chin to look at him. Hurt enough to later leave bruises. Brought her to the ground, whether he had meant to or not.

You will say nothing. You hear me?

He moved her head up and down to make her nod as she lay on her back. With one hand on her jaw, he used his other to open the aquarium lid and reached inside for Reese. He grabbed the tarantula as he'd sometimes grab a handful of M&M's—always avoiding the brown and light-brown ones—and brought it above Julie's face. A few of Reese's legs tried to escape. He held the spider inches from Julie, out of focus.

Your little negro friend ... she's just as fragile as this guy. You would never wish for anything bad to happen to your friend, would you?

Blurry spider seeped from between his clenched fingers and dripped over her.

A menacing smile.

"I never meant to hurt anyone," the voice of her father said.

Julie pulled free. She no longer held Hannah's hand, but her father's. Smashed spider coated his palm.

Lost in memories, they were at their destination, the black dot no longer a dot, but a giant floating window, through which this man had apparently stepped. He wore a black trench coat dripping rainwater. Stubble peppered his cheeks in patches around thick burn dells covering his face, chin and neck, his shoddy hair cut unevenly.

The man from the bar: her father.

"Hannah!" she said, stepping back and wiping off the mess.

"I'm here," she said from behind.

She found Hannah standing there as if nothing were out of the ordinary. "He's not real," she said. "He can't hurt you."

"I'm not real," the man said.

"Stay away from me."

"Julie," he said, taking a familiar limping step.

"You're not him. They took you away when I was a kid for all the bad things you did. The police took you away and Mom hated me for it. She hated me for ratting you out. You can't be him because he's dead. You're not—"

The man in front of her resembled both her father and the man from the bar. The burnt rose tattoo previously climbing his neck was gone; no, not gone … somehow Julie held it, and he wanted it back.

The bad man stepped forward as Julie stepped back.

Hannah took her free hand again and gently squeezed.

Julie squeezed the rose, letting the thorns dig deeper.

Blood dripped into the white, creating red rivulets at her feet.

"You acted like you didn't recognize me at the bar," he said. "I'm your father and you didn't even recognize me."

"No," Julie said, shaking. "Mom told me you killed yourself in prison. You set your cell on fire and hung yourself with bed sheets. That's why she took all those pills. The man at the bar looked nothing like you."

But he did. Despite the skin deformities, the limp in his walk and the lack of hair, it was her father, only older and more weathered. His face was overcooked and as age-damaged as a meth addict's, his eyes sunken and his cheeks as well. She could see it now. He had been gone for years, dead in her mind, but she could see it now and it was even more unsettling to learn this after the horror he had put her through. His face was nearly melting with every step and changing into something sinister—Calvin Stipes emerging.

"You only see what your mind wants to see," Hannah said.

"How do you think that made me feel," he said, "to have my own daughter not even recognize me? After all the love I gave you."

"Get away from me."

"I wanted to see you, Julie. I wanted to see if you still loved me. I saw you sitting there with that boy, and you looked back at me like I was some kind of pervert. You rolled your eyes. I was a complete stranger to you. I tried to love you and you pushed me away."

He was looking at the rose, reaching for it. He staggered forward as if hypnotized. "My little angel, all grown up. So beautiful and full. A flower bursting with splendor. My broken flower."

"You broke this flower," Julie said. Hannah remained at her side as they backpedaled. "You ruined me. I am so *fucked* in the head because of you."

"You made me so *furious*," her father said, touching himself.

Rain continued pouring somewhere behind the glass of the floating window. A flash of silent lightning and Julie could tell it was the living room of Elliot's home on the other side; she counted the seconds *one thousand one, one thousand two, one thousand three* and the thunder discharged.

"You are not Calvin Stipes," Julie said.

The man resembling her father pulled a pocketknife from the trench coat pocket. Both hands reached out as skin dripped from his face, aging him further. A black burnt face surfaced with eyes glowing as red as the rose.

"Give your daddy some sugar. Give your daddy the pretty flower. I just want to smell it. I just want to smell your sweet flower. Don't tell your momma or I'll cut your throat."

"You can't hurt me."

"Then give me the flower or I'll cut your daughter's throat."

"She's not my daughter, and you're not going to hurt her. You can't do anything."

"Is that what she told you, I'm dead and worthless? Well, so is she, and there are things far worse than death to worry about here."

He slid the blade against his wrist and a red arc spurted into the white; blood pumped from the wound and collected at his feet.

"Do the dead bleed, Julie? I may not be able to hurt you, but I can do worse to your fuckin' daughter."

Julie stepped in front of Hannah.

His expression changed from sinister to sweet.

"It's not me saying these things, Julie. I don't mean to scare you."

"You don't scare me anymore."

"I don't mean to scare you. The bad things in my head just make it that way, make me do things I don't want to do. Things I *have* to do. I expect you to understand more than anyone, Julie." He wiped his arms and held them out to her, wrists up, the blood no longer pumping, but streaked in finger-thick lines like war paint. A puffy scar remained where he had cut himself. He dropped the knife and walked forward, leaving bloody footprints. "We're the same, you and I. We've both got scars. See? I just want to set things right. You're just a reflection of me. I want to bleed the bad out of me to make things right, like you. I am a part of you and you are a part of me. Please believe me."

"How can I trust anything you say after the things you've done?"

"I can only hope you'll try."

Hannah tugged her sleeve and said, "He's only as bad as you make him here. He's not real." She pointed to the rose.

"Why do you want this?" Julie said to her father, a man who no longer looked menacing. She tried remembering the good things about him; there were few.

"It's a part of my past. A scar. It reminds me of everything that made me bad. In that world—out there—I wear it as a reminder. I can't take back the things I did. I can never take them back, but I can be penitent. The rose is my scarlet letter. A burnt flower. Something beautiful destroyed by my hands."

Julie realized she made him say these things and that was the sole reason he said them. She had power over her father here, wherever here may be, and she could make him say whatever she pleased.

"I'm sorry, Julie."

And for Frankie.

"And for Frankie Jones. For everything I've done. Beth—your mother—told you I died in prison, and I wish I had. I wish I had died in my cell. If only it were that easy."

You deserve worse.

Bruises covered the area on his neck where the rose tattoo with burnt petals should have climbed, as if sheets had strangled his neck after jumping from his bed to end his life.

"I deserve a fate worse than death."

Julie handed him the flower, his eyes never leaving it.

If he could have it, maybe he'd go away.

"No," Hannah said, more as a whimper.

He grabbed the flower in both hands and brought it to his nose and drew in the scent. A dark red aura of smoke traveled from the petals and into his nostrils; some of it surrounded his neck like a noose, strangling him. He smiled and backpedaled until he met the frame of the floating window … the man from the bar, her father, the man who wasn't real.

"I'm sorry there is darkness in the world, Julie. I know it probably doesn't mean much to you now, or if it means anything to you at all, but I love you."

Julie put those words into his mouth.

"I need you to do something for me," he said. "I need you to talk to your mother. Really talk to her. She needs to know the truth, about everything. Tell her what I did to you. Tell her about Frankie.

You've kept things from her and the two of you have grown distant because of it, because of me. When's the last time you two talked?"

"I won't do that."

"You need to sit down with her. She deserves to know why you are the way you are. She won't like what you have to say, she may not even believe you, but you need to talk to her."

"Why would I do anything for you?"

"Take care of yourself, Julie, and help her."

He peered through Julie, to the child at her back.

This wasn't her father, Calvin the monster, but the caring father Julie had always wanted as a child.

Saying what Julie wanted him to say.

And now it was Julie looking through Calvin Stipes, her father—past the façade to the monster within. The one that smiled. The one that lied. The bad man with the bad touch and foul breath. His hideous face housed a devilish grin. If Julie had some of the drug remaining in her system, the rest of his skin would melt and drip to the floor, leaving behind his true ugly form.

Her eyes craved the drop.

Calvin dropped what remained of the flower, which burst to flame. Ash petals fell like black snowflakes from his fingertips. His neck singed at this same moment and burned with it, the rose tattoo regaining shape: blackened skin and blistering.

Hannah rushed to his feet for the flower.

"No," Julie said, but it was too late. Her feet were cement blocks.

"Save her," the man said, but Julie's mind put words into his mouth; Julie's words flowing from her father; what she had willed him to say, as she stood petrified.

He snatched the girl by the waist before stepping through the placid glass and disappeared into the blackness.

A child's scream.

Cut short.

Hannah.

With the exception of the floating window/mirror and its fluxing surface, her father's blood, and the pocketknife, Julie was alone.

She willed herself to follow, to save the child, but she couldn't move. Something stuck in her throat, possibly her own trapped scream. The liquid surface returned to its once placid state and it was only then Julie found the courage to move. She reached out, fingers splayed, expecting to pass through the glass, yet the window was cold and impenetrable. On the other side, through Elliot's empty home, her father ran with Hannah under his arm.

"No!"

Julie pounded against the glass.

"Hannah!" she cried, fists pounding.

Calvin Stipes deliberately paused at the front door and turned around so she could see his smile. She couldn't get through, not yet. He looked across the room, forcing Julie to do the same, to a cheap clock with oversized hands above the fireplace mantel. There was something peculiar about the time, but her thoughts were set on saving Hannah. The time: some kind of message to her. Hannah, too. With a malevolent grin, he walked out the door.

Hard as slate, the glass wouldn't break.

She crumpled to her knees.

"NO!" she said, her voice hoarse.

The backs of her fists slid against the glass on her way down, unable to break through, though it seemed so easy. Trapped, Julie could only watch him take her.

She found the knife at her side, along with Reese crawling over the blade. He must have fallen off her shoulder during the struggle. The knife was hers from high school, the one she had used to cut herself so many times before. Calvin had left it for her.

Julie pulled at her tank top to reveal the three parallel lines. She tried the blade against her skin to make a fourth, but it wouldn't cut, sliding over instead, as dull as a butter knife.

It will only cut if I want it to.

◻ ◻ ◻

"What are you doing?"

"Nothing, Frankie."

Julie hid the pocketknife in a closed fist. She pulled the strap of her tank top to cover the cut, the black material concealing the scars.

"What is that?" Frankie said.

"Mascara."

"Do you always apply it to your shoulder?"

"I was testing the color."

"Black?"

"Yep. Like you."

"Funny. Just because I'm the only black girl at this school and you happen to be my friend, doesn't mean you can just go around wearing my color. You don't see me wearing white mascara in *your* honor. Anyway, I thought your mom said you couldn't wear makeup until you turned thirteen. Let me see." Frankie held out a hand. "Come on, fork it over."

In the Brenden Middle School restroom, Julie watched her best friend in the mirror, the hand wanting the knife. This wasn't the first time Frankie had caught her cutting.

Julie wore mascara and some of it ran down her cheeks. By twelve, she had perfected the art of wearing makeup by making it unnoticeable, for the most part, and by taking it off before returning home. Mom always said makeup was for sluts. Makeup made boys want to fuck you and that she wasn't old enough. The mascara always ran before she cut. She couldn't hide anything from Frankie, who reached over and pulled the left side of Julie's tank top off the shoulder.

Three lines, healed over.

Julie turned away.

"Well," Frankie said, "don't let me stop you."

"Frankie …"

"No, here, if you don't want to do it in front of me, let me have the knife. I'll do it. I'll cut you. Come on, hand it over. What, you don't want to do it now? You *scared?*"

Julie planned to reopen the first wound—the oldest of the three.

"Let me cut you. I'll do it. I wanna do it."

This was typical Frankie sarcasm. It usually worked.

She held out her hand to Julie.

"Didn't you come in here to pee or something?"

"I can hold it. This is more important. Let me cut you."

She wouldn't do it. Frankie would take the knife from her and hide it or throw it away and she'd have to buy another one. She had done it before.

Their eyes connected in the mirror.

"Okay," Julie said. She slid the other side of her tank top down, exposed the blade of the knife, and held it out to her, fingertips pinching steel. "This side, though." She shrugged her left shoulder back into the tank top. "This side is mine."

Frankie took the knife.

"You serious?"

"Not too deep. Slide it across," she said, pointing to the spot on her opposite shoulder. She scratched a line with her fingernail.

One of Frankie's eyebrows raised, but she took the knife.

"Here?" she said, poking Julie with the tip.

"Ouch! Yeah, but don't stab me with it; slide it across, slowly."

"Ouch?"

Julie smiled as Frankie ran the cold metal over Julie's shoulder, as dull as a butter knife—the backside of the blade.

"Like that?"

Julie nodded.

Frankie flipped the blade over and just as gently slid it over her skin. A soft tickle, then the sting, and then the prolonged continuation of the sting as she drew a line of red.

"Doesn't it hurt?"

The slow burn as the body tried to recover from the wound.

"That's the point. I like the way it feels. Reminds me that I can still feel, you know? Even though it's pain, at least it's something."

Sometimes Julie wouldn't even let a wound heal properly. Sometimes when things got really bad she'd cut herself, but sometimes she wouldn't need to and would instead dig into one of the newer wounds with a fingernail and pry it open again, and then hold her finger against the cut to make it sting. When the sting abated, she'd do it again, and again, and again.

"You need help."

Frankie pulled the knife away and the two of them stared into the mirror, watching the thin line bleed red down her chest. It was comforting, the cut, and also having Frankie with her. "What now?"

"Go back to class," Julie said. She already had a wet paper towel at the ready and used it to wipe away the blood. She pressed her finger against the cut and enjoyed it for a bit.

Frankie rinsed the knife in the sink and wiped the blade. She rolled up her sleeve and sliced into the meat of her bicep and jolted.

The pocketknife clattered into the sink.

"What are you doing?"

"I wanted to know what it felt like."

"I want to know what it feels like," Johnny Rutherford said.

He and Julie had been "going out" for two weeks. Going out meant they held hands between classes, and sometimes on the way home if his friends weren't around to give him trouble. Sometimes they'd kiss, but it never meant anything. The longest was over two seconds. Most relationships in fifth grade rarely lasted so long.

"Stop," she said.

Julie pulled his hand out from under her shirt, what Johnny and his friends called second base. Not yet. Not Johnny. Julie knew a little about baseball because her dad had played on a company softball team one summer. All she could remember from it was a snack stand and a bunch of drunken guys with ugly caps cursing at each other and drinking beer and her dad driving them home drunk afterward.

He found his way under her shirt again, fingers tickling like a bug. His hand was harder to push down the second time. Their hands struggled for power, but then she let it happen. At least it would be done and over with.

One of his hands felt her for a while, uncomfortably, mostly skirting around the edges, sometimes over the top, and that was okay, but then he slid a few fingers under the material across her breasts, brushing her nipple. Julie grabbed him hard around the wrist and forced his hand out from under her shirt. She twisted his fingers until he cringed.

"What'd you do that for?" he said.

"I don't know. Maybe pushing your hand down the first time was a sign I wanted you to stop. You think?"

"You could have said so."

"I did, the first time you tried to touch me."

It was the first time a boy had ever felt her up.

Johnny stopped holding her hand. He stopped talking to her, stopped looking at her. He no longer thought of them as 'going out,' even though he never officially broke it off, which was supposed to happen in relationships, Frankie told her.

"I break up with *all* my boyfriends," Frankie had said.

And then she told Frankie the real reason why Johnny Rutherford pretended she didn't exist. She felt like a boy under there. Under the bra, it was all flat—a boy's chest. Yeah, she wore a bra, but there's nuthin' under there but little bumps. Those were his words. Mosquito bites, some teased, even the girls. In school, hurtful words spread cancerously, whether or not they were true, and then they became more hateful, more hurtful.

The words stopped two years later when Julie took off her shirt for Simon Lekowski. It was right before P.E. when all the boys left the boys' locker room and all the girls left the girls' locker room and they waited as a group for the gym teacher, who was always five to ten minutes late. Julie grabbed Simon's hand and dragged him away from the others.

She took him to a hidden place where a few of her friends sometimes smoked pot. A gap between building E and building F completely hid them from the rest of the school campus. Julie thought he was cute at the time. Simon didn't seem to mind.

"Where are we going?"

"A secret place," she had said, pulling him between buildings. She peeked once to see if any faculty had seen them, or if any of the other P.E. students had followed, but they were alone.

"Do you like me?"

"Huh?"

"Do you like me?"

"*Like*, like?"

"Yeah."

"Then yeah, I guess."

They held hands for a moment, about waist level, and then she let go and pulled off her shirt—laying it over a pipe—and unstrapped her bra, crumpling it into his pocket. Only in gym shorts, socks and sneakers, she put her hands on his hips, leaned in, and kissed him. A long one. Julie could tell he was nervous by the way air escaped his lips. He tasted like bubble gum. He hugged her and seemed scared of touching her, so she moved his hands for him over her chest, where they stayed, immobile, for the next few minutes. He didn't try anything more than what she let him do, but he trembled.

Julie pulled back so he could look at her before she put her shirt back on. She walked away, leaving him alone with what she could only hope were positive, confused emotions.

Simon Lekowski didn't come back until well after the gym teacher had arrived, which got him marked as tardy for class.

"Why were you late, Lekowski?"

"I—uh, well—"

"Twenty pushups. All of you. Twenty pushups."

Julie watched Simon during the pushups. After the tenth or so rep, he pushed the bra further into his pocket because it had started to slip out.

Classmates looked at her differently that year, especially boys. They took interest in her, whispered to their friends after she passed them in the hall, some would do the head nod thing, which was supposed to make them look suave. Simon never said anything to the other boys. He didn't have many friends.

He and Julie never 'went out,' yet sometimes he'd see her in the hall and smile. A part of Julie was mad he never tried to win her heart. But he never told anyone.

Brandon told. Brandon Wilson, the jock; he had rounded second and had tried for third in this adolescent sex game called baseball.

Tried.

This started the rumor mill. If she wasn't on her period, she may have let him.

Julie's first period.

Eleven years old.

Khakis capris.

Her desk at the back of the class.

The bleeding …

On the floor, Julie doubled over while holding her stomach. The floating window ahead revealed a different image: the hospital room, from which she first entered this strange world. The surface was clear glass, like most windows, but there was enough reflection to see the dark, familiar stain forming beneath her hospital gown.

Her father had disappeared through the frame, replaced by the nurse she had struck. She doubled over as well, but to retrieve fallen medical supplies from the floor. Metal objects, bandages, and tubing littered the room.

Julie pulled her fingers from between her legs to find blood

She imagined the black spider climbing out of her, the sharp, slick appendages reaching outward and bending to pull the body free. Something inside wanted out.

"Hannah?"

She looked around for Reese, but he was gone as well.

Alone, Julie fell through the glass.

"Get it out of me!" Julie screamed.

Shards surrounded her on the floor, not clear glass, but mirror.

A man dressed in white held her feet. A nurse and some orderlies held the rest of her to the floor. Someone stuck a needle in her leg and shot her up with a warm fluid. Her legs kicked, and then they kicked a little less. Her back arched like the arachnid skeleton, and then relaxed.

Pieces of glass everywhere.

"Please, get it out," she said to the man holding her feet.

The blood between her legs gone, the florescent lighting began to fade.

"Please," she said as they lifted her.

Blood streaked the glass. The frame of the mirror remained on the wall, as well as some of the glass. In a broken spider web reflection, Julie watched her body float away. And then everything turned black. The dragon opened its wings …

Julie opened her eyes to white. Then she saw the tape on her hand. The tube. The plastic bag on a metal arm. They were flushing the dragon out of her.

Bands strapped her ankles and wrists to the hospital bed, but not tightly; enough to protect her from hurting herself, or perhaps from dislodging the safe drugs they were pumping into her system.

"Glad to see you awake," a female in blurry blue scrubs said. "We can take those off of you now. We have you on a drip system to help you rehydrate while your body works against the bad stuff. I would recommend eating something. There's food under the alien-space-ship-looking thing next to you, and some orange juice."

The woman in scrubs set a patient chart next to the food, untied the straps and checked the catheter and IV.

"Running a little low," she said, and left the room.

Julie sat up dizzy. She lifted the lid off the food tray to find some kind of sandwich, a fruit cup, and baby carrots. No utensils, which made sense. Teary eyes blinked out of control, everything blurry.

Someone had cleaned up the glass and had removed the rest of the broken mirror and frame from the wall, leaving behind a dirty oval outline. Someone else had patched up her arms. Her wrist throbbed, synchronous to her pulse. Her body shivered, naked beneath the hospital gown. The air conditioner vent on the ceiling buzzed. Her clothes were probably under analysis by the police or thrown out as hazardous material. She had read once that blood fell under hazmat laws.

Police were waiting for her. She had to get out of there.

How much did they know?

The room, so cold.

Julie reached past the food to grab the clipboard the woman in scrubs left behind. She would be gone for only a minute.

The top of the page had Julie's name: UNKNOWN, which meant the detective on her case figured out her license was a fake. Someone Frankie knew made them so they could sneak into nightclubs. She had expected to see a cliché DOE, JANE on the chart. Her age listed as APPROX 17/18 with a bunch of other UNKNOWNs marked on the page, as well as her weight, but she couldn't remember them

weighing her. She flipped through the rest: medications and what-not, scribbled notes about the *Drakein-5* overdose and lacerations.

SELF-INFLICTION.

She opened her hand, expecting the pocketknife, although she had only held it in her mind. Someone had taken the jawbone.

"Hello?" Julie set down the chart. "Cop at the door?"

Silence told her she was alone.

Cloudy white surrounded her.

Tape holding the catheter to her hand took hairs when she peeled, the skin underneath swollen and red. The tube, longer than she'd expected, caused her forearm to spasm as she pulled. She threw it to the side and let it dangle like some kind of bloody-mouthed worm.

Scrubs would be back any moment.

Julie stole her patient chart from the clipboard and folded the pages into quarters. Her ass hung halfway out of her gown while she scrambled around. She drank the orange juice and took the sandwich and fruit cup and tried her best to keep the gown closed in back with her free hand. Poking her head out the door, she found the hallway empty, except for an orderly checking with the patient next door.

"Everything okay, Mrs. Kenseth?" the orderly said.

Mrs. Kenseth either slept or nodded because the orderly left.

When she turned down the hall, Julie poked her head into Mrs. Kenseth's room. The sleeping woman looked thirtyish. An overnight bag lay open on the chair next to the bed, like something a pregnant woman would bring to a hospital.

Barefoot, Julie entered the room and kneeled next to the bag. Mrs. Kenseth was out cold. A framed family picture sat on the bedside table next to her: a portrait of the woman, her husband, a boy, and a girl that looked somewhat like Julie when she was a child, only without the strawberry-blonde. Julie's age when her father first touched her. In the photo, Mrs. Kenseth had a third-trimester tummy bump, which meant the husband was most likely at the hospital and returning soon. Julie rifled through the bag and snagged a pair of gray sweatpants and a long-sleeved shirt a few sizes too large, as well as a pair of flip-flops.

Everyone loves a girl in flip-flops.

She dressed in front of the sleeping woman, devoured the food. Before leaving the room, she removed the band around her ponytail and ran fingers through her hair to alter her appearance. She stole the woman's money and stuffed it between her hip and the elastic waistband. She drank the woman's orange juice.

Scrubs passed through the double-doors at the end of the long hallway. She held an IV bag and another patient chart.

Giving her maybe thirty seconds.

Julie turned the opposite direction and headed down the hall toward the green EXIT sign, which pointed her to another hall with another green EXIT sign. She upped her pace after rounding the corner and followed the semi-blurry signs. They led her past the cafeteria and lobby and eventually to the double-doors leading out of the building. Her borrowed sleeves barely covered the bandages. Julie hoped no one would notice her appearance.

Frankie would have called her a hot mess.

No cop cars. No waiting police.

Julie walked free from Brenden Memorial, no one stopping her.

She never looked over her shoulder.

"Where to?"

Julie sat in the back of a taxi, not remembering even flagging one down. How far had she walked? Where? What time? Nothing looked familiar. Car horns and city static and narrow streets told her somewhere downtown. Brick buildings tagged with graffiti surrounded her on either side. Streetlights, crosswalk lights, and neon signs lit the early morning. How far had she walked?

"Ma'am?"

Eyes, nose and mustache filled the review mirror.

She flipped through the cash: twenties, a five and some ones.

Violated in so many ways, she craved a shower.

"How much to Foer Street? 4,884."

The driver tapped the address into a GPS.

"Shortest route … eighteen and change. Twenty at most."

She had taken seventy-eight from the woman.

"You got change?"

"I make change."

A short ride took her to the Heimlichs. They lived in a modest post-Victorian on the outskirts of East Brenden. A driveway void of cars. The clock on the dashboard displayed 8:03. Twitchy, Julie searched for answers.

"Is it Sunday?"

"Sunday, yes."

This meant Earl and Barbara were at Ed's Diner for breakfast. They'd go nearly every Sunday morning. They always invited her, always kept her fed, and always gave her a place to sleep for the night. Grandparents by proxy.

"Ma'am?"

The eyes, nose and mustache.

For a moment, she saw her father in the reflection, and then pity.

"What's the damage?"

His reflection turned from Julie to the meter.

Julie counted the money a second time, flipping through the bills. Seventy-eight. Twenty would get her a few doses of D from Chase. But he wouldn't sell her any. She stole the syringe, now gone, wasted after the man with the rose on his neck forced her to shoot the entire fucking thing up her arm. But Chase didn't know the story. Chase didn't know it was gone. She had a buyer in mind, she could say, although he wouldn't believe her. She was already late with the money and had used a similar story once before. Seventy-eight minus the taxi ride plus her stash in her room at the Heimlichs in the music box with the ballerina dancing on ice made of mirror with the Swan Lake song, and whatever money was crumpled in the bottom of her other purses or hiding in her dirty clothes pockets … she maybe had a hundred; not enough to bring her straight with Chase. Maybe he'd understand, let her have a few drops because she was good for it, or he'd let her pay some other—

"Uh … machine is broken. Numbers jumble sometimes. Let's just say five."

"Five?"

Five would get her a shot of Jack.

"For you, ride is on the house. No pay."

"You said twenty at most. I'll pay you twenty."

"Eh … no, this trip on me. Good day."

The piteous eyes, nose and mustache added a smile.

"You sure?"

Julie held a twenty.

He pondered a moment and said, "I am sure. You be safe and have good day. Pass on kindness to another. That is payment."

"You have no idea how much this means to me, so thank you."

"Yes."

When she closed the door, he drove away.

It wasn't until she let herself in and saw her reflection in the bathroom mirror that she realized why the driver had been so generous. A purple bruise stained her left cheek. Lacerations held together by butterfly bandages on her chin, above her right eye and on her opposite cheek. As if someone had hit her. A bruise swelled on the back of her hand where she had pulled out the catheter. White bandages wrapped tightly where she had sliced open her wrist with the shotgun-blasted section of Elliot's jawbone.

Three teeth still attached, the nurse had said. *She's been holding onto a part of someone's jawbone this whole time.*

It was gone now. Someone at the hospital had taken it.

The Heimlichs were gone as well.

She had the house for at least an hour, Julie guessed, based on the time. The Heimlichs were methodical when it came to Sunday breakfast. She'd love to see them, but not like this. She looked and felt like shit, run down, dragged through the garden, raped, but not really. But kind of. They didn't need to see her like this.

Julie's feet were red and raw. She peeled away clothes on her way to the shower, stepped inside, turned the knob and let cold water flow along her neck and back. She stood there until the water heated and steamed, hands pushing against the wall to hold her body upright. She sank to her knees and leaned toward the drain until the water scalded, let it beat down until it was overbearing, eventually adjusting it back to cold. Water drained counter-clockwise and held her attention, reminding Julie of her downward-spiraling life.

Diluted-red from her wounds circled beneath her. She wanted to throw up, but couldn't. Her meal from the hospital stayed inside, and instead she produced bile and spit, which she fed to the hole staring up at her. The drugs in her system, she imagined them washing away. The filth and sadness and everything else disgusted her; she let the water take those things, and with them, the memories: the bar and everything leading up to that moment, Elliot and her mixed feelings about him, the staggering footsteps and struggling breath as they embraced, backpedalling to the door with each other's hands crawling hungrily, and the man with the shotgun, forcing them into a situation they both originally wanted anyway ... the drugs shot into her arm had taken over, controlling her uncontrollably, her naked back arching, her body rocking against the man under her, the wonderful explosion and horrid gunshot, simultaneous ... Elliot, his face gone, the red blooming flower ... the spider leading her to the little girl.

"Hannah," Julie said.

But she wasn't there.

Was she ever?

The images flashed through her mind.

A dozen flashes turning everything white, like the police photo-shoot.

This is the trial room, Hannah had said.

[flash]

The little apparition girl.

"What do you want from me?"

Bad things happen here, the girl had said.

[flash]

Julie opened her eyes and pulled open the shower curtain, alone, hands shaking. She had imagined the words of the girl.

She was still coming down from the drug. Such a high amount of the *Drakein-5* had entered her system, undiluted. The IV at the hospital had helped, but the drug was still there.

The dragon was part of her now, she knew, a tattoo on her skin she couldn't simply get rid of; she had to wean her system off the dependency, one drop at a time. She had to feed the dragon, lest it would kill her. And then she had to feed it less, and then less, and then less until her body no longer craved the fix.

The cold, the sweats, the shakes: those three ghosts would soon come for her.

She imagined a tattoo artist working a needle next to her navel, outlining a tribalesque dragon in black, pointy wings outstretched over her ribs, claws grasping her belly, the scaled body slightly arch-ing and a tail sinking well below her waistline.

[flash]

Julie sat naked on the edge of the bed, wet, but drying.

A memory of her father's hand creeping.

[flash]

Elliot's hand spider-crawling.

[flash]

Her room at the Heimlichs housed few of her personal belong-ings. Most of what she owned remained at her mother's.

Get the fuck out of my house!

Those were her mother's final words to her.

Her mother didn't want to hear about the bad things.

There was a picture of her and Julie in a small frame on one of the dressers, and another of Julie and Frankie from a few summers past. They had stayed friends, even after Julie dropped out of high school. Frankie would graduate in the spring.

[flash]

"Julie, you okay?"

Frankie's voice from far away, from the phone at her ear.

"You're scaring me, Julie. I told you to stay off that shit."

The phone cord coiled from the wall to the bed.

"Caller ID says it's you. Julie?"

"Frankie."

She couldn't remember dialing and cried.

"Stay there, Julie. I'll be right over."

"No—"

[flash]

The doorbell rang. The phone in her lap yapped at her to hang up, so she returned it to the wall. How long had she sat there? The bell rang again, followed by knocking.

[flash]

"Damn, Julie!"

Frankie rushed inside, trying her best to shield Julie from the outside world because Julie stood naked at the open door, coated in a cold sweat. The door slammed shut, like a gunshot. Julie tried to cover herself, like she had tried in front of Elliot with the shotgun to his head—the tip of the barrel gagging the back of his throat. A throw blanket wrapped around Julie as Frankie escorted her to the couch.

"What happened?"

Julie tried to tell her, but nothing came out. Her body shook instead.

Frankie held her for a while.

"What can I do?" Frankie said.

"I need a ride."

"Where you going?"

"I don't know."

She needed a ride to Chase.

"I'll see if you can stay at my place for a few days."

Julie shook her head and said, "I just need a ride."

"Looks like you need to get *off* the ride for a while. You using?"

Julie shook her head no and then nodded yes.

"Look, it's all right. We'll get you through this. What happened? You look like a wreck, but you didn't do this to yourself, did you?" It wasn't really a question. "Who did this to you?"

Julie shook her head no.

"Your wrist, my god! Tell me who did this to you so I can beat their fucking ass."

When she stopped crying, Julie released her tight hug around Frankie and said, "Look, right now I need to see someone. I need a ride to see someone."

"Julie, what you need—"

"Trust me, Frankie. Please. Can you do this for me? Can you give me a ride?"

"Julie—"

[flash]

Frankie covered the bruise with makeup and helped Julie dress: a black tank top and long-sleeved shirt to go over it, some low-cut capris and pair of flip-flops. She didn't have many clothes from which to choose. Julie wrapped a long necklace around her wrist multiple times as a bracelet to hide the bandage, in case she took off the shirt. The small lacerations on Julie's face stopped bleeding and didn't warrant the butterfly bandages, so she took those off as well.

"There," Frankie said after applying some cover-up.

For the most part, Julie looked ready for a night out.

"I look okay?"

"You're beautiful."

"Thanks, Frankie."

"But you *look* terrible."

They both smiled.

"I need a ride there. You don't have to stay. I'll find a ride back."

"You're crazy if you think I'm taking you to that douchebag. I'm not taking you, Julie. You don't need to be doing that kind of shit, not now, not ever. And you don't need to be calling me for rides for this kind of shit. It's not fair. You need to clean up. Stay here. Get some rest. I'm sure Earl and Barbara will let you—"

"I need to talk to him. He's a close friend."

"Bull*shit* he's your friend."

"No, really. I don't even want anything."

"Why you need to see him so bad then?"

"To pay him back. See?" Julie dug in her pockets and pulled out the crumple of cash she had stolen. She must have found more money in the house before calling Frankie because she held out close to two hundred dollars. She couldn't imagine stealing from the Heimlichs, but maybe she had. "I owe him for the last time. *The* last time, I promise. I just have to pay him back so we can be square."

"You're crazy if you think I believe that. Why you got to lie to me, Julie?"

Frankie had taken Julie once to see Chase, before she knew he was a dealer, before he had gotten her hooked on the drug.

"What's going on with you lately?"

"I'm crazy."

"No," Frankie said. "What's the drug? What's this fucker got you on? Julie …"

"Look, it's only *Drakein-5*."

"What the hell's that? *D?* Damn it, Julie! You're taking *D?*"

"It's not like *3,4-methylenedioxymethamphetamine*," she said.

"You roll it off your tongue like you say it every day. I wrote my chemistry paper on the properties of soap, and you almost got expelled for writing yours on an illegal street drug."

"*Drakein's* not bad. It's like *E*, but, you know, more sexual."

"Not bad?"

Drakein differed from *Ecstasy* in that it was nearly instantaneous. One drop into the eye was an immediate turn-on; one in each eye was even better. With *E* you had to take a pill and wait. *D* often bore strange, visually horrific side effects, but the pros outweighed the cons. The high lasted thirty minutes or less and she could take another dose the moment the previous trip ended. One time Julie had tried a second dose soon after the first, but nothing had changed. A waste of drops and nothing more. And until this point in Julie's life, not once did the stuff exhibit addictive behaviors. It called for her now, though, feeding the lies to the one person to whom Julie never lied.

"All street drugs are bad, Julie. That's why they're called street drugs."

"Not this one."

"Can you buy it at Wal-Mart?"

"What?"

"I *said*, 'Can you buy it at Wal-Mart?'"

"No, I can't buy it at fucking Wal-Mart."

"Can you buy it in a grocery store?"

"No."

"Can you buy *D* at a gas station?"

"No."

"Can you buy it in a *drug*store?"

"I get it, Frankie."

"No, I don't think you do!"

"Stop it. Please. I'm not taking anything, not now, I promise. It's what I took from him. *Took*, as in past tense. Tense is all that matters sometimes. I only had a few drops of *D*. Chase trusted me with an entire syringe to sell and promised me a cut, but it dropped, broke."

"I know when you're lying to me."

"Five hundred bucks and I'd get to keep a hundred if it sold. That was our deal. I need to talk to Chase to figure out what to do. I don't know what to do!"

"What are you even talking about, you're a dealer now?"

"I just thought I could—"

"Tell him you lost it. Lie, like you're lying to me. Tell him you were mugged and had it stolen from you. We can take off some of your makeup and he'd be sure to believe it."

"It's not that easy."

"Try me, Julie. Better yet, why don't you tell me the fucking truth? You're lying to me, still. I see it in you. You've always told me the truth, about everything, and now you can't even look me in the face, after all we've been through. I haven't heard from you in months and you call me from out of the blue, simply breathing into the phone, not saying a word, and I come rushing over to help and you finally talk to me, but I can't make heads or tails of your lies."

Julie wanted to tell Frankie everything about the previous night, the drugs, Elliot, the spider, the girl, everything meshed together like some kind of nightmare, but she couldn't. Not yet. Someday, maybe. Why she and Frankie had grown distant these last few months was a mystery as well. They were always so close before. They told each other everything.

"I stole it."

"Stole what?"

"I stole some *Drakein-5* from Chase the last time I saw him. He paid me for two syringes I helped sell. Two hundred bucks. But I needed more. I needed the money, Frankie, but I don't expect you to understand because you don't know the rest of the story. He went out of the room to get the money, and the small leather case was just sitting there. I opened the lid. Ten slots for ten syringes, four of them empty. I thought maybe he wouldn't notice if I took one. Maybe he'd lose count because of the meth he smoked. Five hundred bucks, sitting there for the taking."

"Julie …"

Finally some truth. She knew Frankie could see it.

"If I sold it myself, without him knowing, I'd make enough to not need him anymore. Five hundred would get me by long enough to find a job, start making some real money. I honestly didn't think he'd remember the count because he was so high. How could he?"

"I wish I could help you, Julie—"

"I can't get a break. I've submitted resumes, but no one's hiring. School dropout. No one wants to hire that shit. Somehow they know I'm not in school. No one is hiring. No one. And this was five hundred, waiting for me. The syringe, it busted open and I lost it all."

She didn't tell Frankie she shot the entire syringe into her bloodstream, at gunpoint.

"I need to see Chase so I can snag another."

"You need help."

"I need your help."

"I won't take you. That's my way of helping you. I love you, Julie, but I won't do this for you. You don't need to do this to get out. I'll help you find a way. You've got options."

"There *are* no other ways!"

"You're not going, Julie."

"You sound like my mother. You're not my fucking mother! Who the hell do you think you are? Fuck you, then. Fuck you, Frankie!"

Julie slapped her across the face.

Frankie took it, her eyes not angry, but saddened. She had barely moved, as if expecting the slap.

In silence, she turned and walked away.

"Frankie, wait … Frankie, I'm sorry."

[flash]

Frankie was gone.

ECLOSE

[a fable by Julie Stipes]

Two caterpillars once grew up together, one green with yellow stripes, and the other yellow with green stripes, both the size of a finger. The color of their skin didn't matter much to their friendship. They were inseparable.

"What do you want to be when you hatch from your cocoon?" said the yellow.

"I don't know," said the green, "but I hope I'm beautiful."

Beauty can be an ugly word sometimes.

"Not me. I don't care if I'm beautiful," said the yellow. "As long as I have wings and can fly away, that's all that matters to me. My wings can be black and ugly."

"Don't you want to attract a handsome boy moth? Handsome boy moths look for beautiful girl moths, and if you're black and ugly, no one will want you."

"Not true," said the yellow. "Some like black and ugly."

"I hope so," said the green. "My parents were like that. I don't want to grow up to be like them. I want to transform into a beautiful moth with vibrant colors. Orange, I hope, or maybe shades of yellow, like you. Maybe I'll be a monarch …"

The two caterpillars shared the maple leaf. Both knew they had to fill their stomachs to prepare for the long sleep.

"Do you think it hurts?" asked the green.

"You should never be afraid of pain. Pain's temporary and lets you know you're alive. The more pain you go through when you're younger, the more complex your wingspan will be when you're older. I hope it hurts a lot."

"Me too."

The yellow caterpillar inched along next to the green. Neither led. Both took turns, not necessarily following one another, but simply remaining companions on their journey through the impending change. They were stronger together.

"Over here," said the green, venturing wayward beneath the shade of a fallen branch.

"There's not a lot of food over there," said the yellow. "There's still some left—"

"Trust me."

"Okay."

The yellow caterpillar with the green stripes followed her friend this time. The fallen branch held two small maple leaves: one a lively green, the other a dried yellow.

"Hey, just like us," said the yellow.

"Quiet," said the green, crawling on top of her matching leaf.

The yellow caterpillar joined to feast but was stopped as her green friend arched, rearing onto her back legs in a threatening manner.

"Go to the yellow leaf," she said.

"We need to prepare," said the yellow. "That one's wilted."

"Trust me," she said again.

"Why won't you share?"

"We're not here to eat," said the green. "Stay still and not another word."

"It's not fair!"

The green caterpillar reared again and twisted her body, knocking the yellow caterpillar onto the wilted leaf. Nutrients remained in the veins, green-striped like her, but the blade was not worth the struggle.

"I'm sorry," said the green. "Be quiet and still."

A bird-shaped silhouette emerged and the yellow caterpillar with the green stripes understood. Sometimes preparing for the future meant not doing anything at all, such as innocently lying in wait while a not-so-innocent world carried on.

Survival is important for becoming something new.

The fire-winged finch landed next to the fallen branch with its monstrous shadow blocking the sun. The winged giant hopped around the leaves, looking for food, pecking between pebbles and twigs in the dirt.

The green and yellow caterpillars were invisible to the bird, camouflaged against their similarly colored leaves.

A second finch landed, chirping, followed by a

third, their heads cocking from side to side, as they fed on marching ants. Each bird looked the same, wings black in areas like burn marks, although one hopped to compensate for a seemingly broken leg. With the last of the ants eaten, the birds flew away, leaving the caterpillars safe once again.

"Thank you," said the yellow.

"You would have done the same for me," said the green.

"Yeah."

The caterpillars fed until their bellies filled and the bright orb in the sky fell beneath the horizon. They had traveled nearly across the plane of grass to a white picket fence next to a rosebush. Both would burrow underground by the roots, which is where they would begin their transformations.

"Are you ready to pupate?" asked the yellow.

"I think so, but I'm scared."

During adolescence, both had discussed when and where they would build their cocoons. Neither knew how to construct the protective shell, or even how to dig, but they'd figure it out, together. How difficult could holometabolism be?

"We'll do it together," said the yellow.

"Promise?"

"Even if it hurts."

Near the fence, they came to a silk bridge.

"What is it?" asked the green.

"I don't know."

"Looks like a shortcut to me."

The silk bridge led directly across a deep, dark gorge in their path. Taking the bridge offered more time to solve the pupa dilemma.

"Let's take the long route," said the yellow.

"Looks strong enough to cross," said the green.

"I think we should continue the way we were going."

"Trust me."

The same trust had saved her from the birds.

"Come on," said the green. "I'll go first to make sure it's safe."

The mostly-green caterpillar stepped onto the silk. She struggled with footing, but managed to crawl out a ways.

"It's sticky," she said, "but strong enough to hold us both."

The mostly-yellow caterpillar watched her friend crawl halfway across, and then tested the silk. She had sixteen legs: six thoratic or true legs bunched at the front of her body, eight abdominal prolegs, and two larger legs in the back. With all sixteen fighting the tackiness of the bridge, it would take much effort to cross.

She had her true legs secured when the silk rope shook.

The green caterpillar writhed, body flagellating.

"What's wrong?" asked the yellow caterpillar, but her friend was silent, the segments of her body wriggling, mandibles chattering wordlessly.

A shiny black creature pounced from the shadows, biting into her friend, its long forelegs hitting her body, hitting her face, pushing her down as she fought, and then scurried effortlessly out of sight.

"What is it?"

As the green caterpillar squirmed, the long-legged creature hurried onto her again, pincers sinking deep. Her green friend flailed, falling onto her side, sticking against the silk. The next bite made her still. The attacker relaxed, slowly circling around and then on top of her. Long black legs held an equally black body high into the air to reveal a red splotch on its belly.

She had never seen anything like this before, but the red warned of evil.

The silk vibrated as the yellow caterpillar pulled free, as if she had plucked one of the strings. This caused the creature to step off her friend a moment and advance, but then it returned to her friend, wanting nothing to do with her.

The yellow caterpillar could only crawl away in a slow escape.

"I'm sorry," she said. "I should have gone first. I should have led. We should have taken the longer path."

She mourned her friend and would have to figure out holometabolism on her own.

"I'm so sorry."

She crawled the long way around, avoiding the shadowy gorge, to the other side of the rosebush.

Underneath the cover of the thickest branches, she burrowed under the moonlight.

The yellow caterpillar found comfort as she spotted her friend, encased in a cocoon, nearly camouflage against the white silken bridge.

Her friend was on her way to transformation, she knew.

The shiny black creature had returned to the shadows.

"We will fly together soon. When it's time."

No longer alone, the mostly-yellow caterpillar with green stripes nestled underground near a patch of dandelions, and white tuffs of what remained of older flowers. This was where she would shed the last of her skin, to reveal her own cocoon, which would offer protection while her body broke down into undifferentiated imaginal cells to reform and shape a beautiful moth.

DEATH'S-HEAD

Julie sat on the end of the bed, hair damp from the shower, body damp from sweating. The phone cord coiled from the wall to the bed. Had she called Frankie to apologize? The phone in her lap yapped at her to hang up, so she returned it to the wall. She waited for the doorbell, for Frankie to knock, but Frankie had come and gone. The fact Julie was clothed and made presentable told her it wasn't part of her imagination. She'd make it up to her later.

The shakes caused her to dry heave into the bathroom sink.

She had to dissuade her body from needing the drug. This unfortunately meant she needed more of it. Quick research on the internet about withdrawal symptoms revealed the shaking and sweating were minor, beginning symptoms. What she needed to worry about was her heart. High levels of *Drakein-5* could lead to heart palpitations and cardiac arrest, sudden death. Julie checked her pulse and found it beating at about two beats per second. One-twenty. Sometimes she could feel those palpitations, like someone jabbing her in the chest with an icepick. A thermometer she found under the guest bathroom sink displayed a temperature of 102° Fahrenheit / 39° Celsius. The back of her hands reminded her of her grandfather when he was still alive with Parkinson's.

Deep breaths. Long, deep breaths.

Calling for an ambulance would put her back in the hospital. A last resort.

Julie took the thermometer with her, as well as some of Earl's colonidine pills—one of the prescribed medications for high blood pressure she found at his bedside—and a mix of over-the-counter magnesium and fish oil pills. Earl took the same pill cocktail daily to help with his own heart condition. Safe or not, she didn't have much of a choice. She took one of each and called for a cab.

Someone using her heart as a pincushion, Julie imagined. Tiny fingers holding mini needles, and jamming them into her heart every few, random minutes.

103°.

"Where to?" the driver said.

She offered the street corner because she didn't know his exact address.

Her pulse had slowed, but not by much.

When they arrived, the shaking had turned to jitters.

She wished Frankie had taken her.

104°.

Julie couldn't remember paying the driver as she knocked on Chase's door, but she was twenty-four bucks lighter, and no longer sweating. She rang the doorbell and waited, and then rang it again and waited even longer. Most would leave at this point, but it was a code. A quick third ring meant 'customer.'

Chase answered the door and greeted her kindly. He wore a black pinstriped business suit, dark red shirt, and white tie.

"I didn't expect you back so soon. You look absolutely stunning, like a cat chewed you up and puked you out. Please, for the love of all things holy, come inside."

She staggered past him.

"Sit the fuck down already before you hurt yourself."

Chase disappeared into the kitchen, returning with a wet washcloth and an open bottle of water. He sat next to Julie on the couch and dabbed the washcloth against her forehead and across her cheeks. He pressed his lips against her forehead, held the kiss for a moment, and pulled back—something Julie's mother used to do to check for a fever.

"You're burning up. Drink this." He handed her the bottle. "Slowly."

Julie leaned back.

"Jesus, what happened to you? You're ghostly white, almost pellucid."

She thought of telling him the truth, then thought better of it.

"You don't need to tell me. I can see you OD'd and were admitted to the hospital by the catheter mark on your hand."

Chase left the room and brought back a penlight. He sat next to her, pried open her left eye with his fingers, moved the light across her vision and then checked the other.

"You're clean though, so what gives?"

"I think I took too much."

That's all she gave him.

"Definitely took too much, but how much you think is too much may be different than how much is too much. What are we talking: twenty drops, half the bottle?"

Julie's knees shook.

"How much do you have left?"

A worried expression.

"The whole fuckin' bottle?"

An eight-milliliter bottle of Visine typically yielded forty eye drops or more, although it could hold twice the amount. Since a syringe of *Drakein-5* added to the total liquid volume of the Visine bottle, this amounted to nine milliliters of combined solution, typically fifty drops of the drug per bottle. Julie had taken five doses before injecting an additional syringe of concentrated *Drakein-5* into her bloodstream. She had dropped an equivalent of thirty doses, or sixty drops.

Always dilute it, he originally told her. *Don't drink it, don't inject the shit directly, just dilute it. One drop in each eye is all it takes.*

She wanted to ask what would happen if taken undiluted.

"You didn't drink the bottle, did you?"

He was concerned about the bottle she had purchased, not the syringe she had stolen.

"No."

Chase set the penlight in his shirt pocket and rubbed his lips with his fingers.

"I've never seen anyone react this way to *Drakein*," he said.

Julie didn't believe him. "I need more," she said, digging into her pockets for the money, an ugly mess of bills. She counted out a hundred and ninety-six dollars.

"I don't sell partial bottles, Julie. You know that. I don't count the drops and sell them individually. It's five hundred per syringe. I'm nice enough to throw in the Visine."

She was dying on his couch and he wanted to talk about ethic.

"That's how I do business," he said. "And since you've sold for me before, you know there's a hundred dollar cut if you sell one for me, which makes your cost four. Let's just say what you have in your wad of sweaty cash is two. That's half. But here's what I'm going to do for you, little flower. I don't do this for anyone. Remember that."

He reached past her, uncomfortably close, for a bottle on the table on her side of the couch, staying a moment too long. He shook the bottle, toying with her.

"This is mine. A little over half full, I believe."

"Thank you," Julie said, reaching for the bottle.

He pulled it away, slightly out of reach so Julie leaned into him.

Be a good girl and give me some sugar, she heard her father saying. *One of each color for being a good girl.*

"I'm doing you a favor and you won't speak a word of this."

Chase took her money and raised an eyebrow until she nodded.

"How much was your cab fare?"

"I'll find a ride."

"How *much* was your cab fare?"

"Twenty-four."

He handed her thirty and then the bottled dragon, not quite letting go.

"You're going to do me a favor first."

Julie imagined the worst, but would do anything.

He pulled the bottle from her tight grasp and stood in front of her as she pocketed the money he had let her keep. Then he straddled her knees as she leaned back into the couch. She swallowed hard as he held her chin and tilted her head back.

"Open your eyes, Julie. It'll be a lot easier," he said, twisting off the lid to the bottle. "Seriously, Julie, what do you take me for?"

She looked to the ceiling and rolled her eyes back.

"One drop."

[drop]

"In each eye."

[drop]

She blinked in the drug, an instant rush.

The shaking ceased. Chase un-blurred and stepped away and a faint gray aura floated off his body like smoke. Julie couldn't remember the meaning for gray, though she had studied auras and their color meanings online after first experiencing the visual effects of the drug. It clung to him as he moved around the room. She felt for her pulse and found it slower.

Sexual feelings hit her next, but not for Chase. Skin melted from his face, ran along his arms, and dripped from his fingertips, dissolving before any of it hit the floor. She blinked it away. Her body fell into the seat of the couch, the fabric soft and exotic and wanting to be touched.

Chase returned with the penlight and filled her eyes—the left eye before the right—the light dancing, his skull jutting from its skin in strobes.

"That's better," said the gaping jaw. "You just needed a fix."

Julie ran her nails through a visage of his face. He had leaned back—her mind not caught up with the present—so her fingers traced the space between them.

Her body instantly reacted to the *Drakein*. Her hands offered a red fiery mirage, similar to heat rising from asphalt. Never before had she seen the auras so soon after dropping, nor the horrid images. Only after prolonged use had she wanted to fuck someone so badly, even Chase, but he didn't seem interested. Chase looked to his watch and sighed. He didn't want her there; he wanted her out of his house, "fixed" enough not to die on his couch.

When she put the thermometer in her mouth, he smiled, stood, and left her there. He disappeared for some time and returned with something hidden behind his back.

"103° is feverish, but lower," he said, kneeling in front of her. Drink the rest of your water, flower."

Julie drank the rest of it.

"I need to ask you something, Julie, now that you're good for a while."

"Anything you want."

His eyes changed. The smoke wafting from his body darkened.

"You've got some dragon in you, which means you're less likely to lie to me. Lying would not be good for you."

A gun moved to his lap.

He knew about the syringe.

The gun didn't point at her, but rested on her knee.

"When a customer doesn't fulfill payment, for example, or when one of my associates with whom I do business decides to take my product to sell it, but doesn't sell it, and then runs off with my product or the money he or she made from my product … I sometimes use a guy to get one or the other back. You should know exactly where I'm going with this, but maybe you're too high to comprehend. What color am I, Julie, what do you see?"

White with an aura of—

"Black."

"Good, then you are seeing clearly. What do you see in my eyes?"

He was looking to the gun; silver reflected in his eyes.

"Trust."

"You see trust?"

She had known Chase long enough to understand he appreciated honesty more than anything, so Julie nodded.

"Do you see my dilemma, Julie?"

She wanted to stand, but the gun became heavier.

"And now you're here to buy more product, with barely enough cash to cover half a bottle, and for some reason I'm selling it to you and buying you cab fare. There must be something wrong with me. You think? To be able to sell you more? You don't happen to have it on you, do you?"

"No, I—"

"Didn't think so. I can't discount what you took. I can't do that. It's just not right. Five hundred for the syringe. You need to come up with it by—" Chase looked at his watch. "—well, it's almost nine now, so let's say you have until noon to get either my product back, or my five hundred. You have until noon, or I put a fucking hole through your face myself, and then I go to your house, where you live, anyway, and I justifiably put down Grandpa Earl and Grandma Barb and find a way to take my compensation."

Earl and Barbara weren't really her grandparents, but Julie lived with them sometimes and thought of them that way and until now, she hadn't worried about their safety. Chase's roots reached deep and had dug into her life, tilling through the dirt like hungry worms.

The barrel pointed at Julie now, but only because Chase shifted to pull a cellphone from his pocket. He dialed a number and turned on the speakerphone. It rang twice.

"Yeah …" said a voice that sounded like her father.

"It's Chase."

"I know. Says it on my phone."

The voice from last night.

"You never called or messaged last night after we last spoke. I'm beginning to think you don't love me anymore. You seeing someone else? I'm beginning to miss you." After a short silence, Chase looked right at Julie and said into the phone, "Any luck tracking down Elliot?"

Julie's chest physically hurt from her heart pounding.

"Last night I was able to track him for a bit, but he was with someone."

"That hasn't stopped you before."

"At a bar. The place was packed and I spotted a few cops hanging around."

"And?"

"And what?"

"Did he see you there? Did he recognize you?"

"Why would he recognize me?"

What did Elliot have to do with anything?

"Listen, are we going to answer each other's questions with questions, or are you going to tell me the rest of the story? There I go. Another question. No more questions."

"There were complications."

Chase raised an eyebrow and waited.

Julie craved more of the drug to take off the edge. A skeletal hand held the revolver on her knee and she imagined it spider-crawling up her leg. She wanted nothing more than to stand and avert the anxiety. A restless leg got Chase's attention and he stood up himself and circumnavigated the chair, like a vulture awaiting a wounded creature to die.

Why was he avoiding telling Chase she was with him?

She imagined Chase was reeling to ask "What kind of complications?" but avoided yet another question to answer a question, bringing the long silence over the phone.

Why's he letting me listen in on this conversation, to make a point, to protect me? Why would he want to protect me from my father? Did Cal know he'd gone after his own daughter? Coincidence? More questions awaiting answers.

"He left with some girl at the bar after a few rounds."

Julie knew this part of the story well and didn't want to hear it. She remembered looking through the smoke, past Elliot, to the man with the dark sunken eyes and hacked up hair, as if he'd shaved it himself during a drunken bet, and the way he admired her with his burn scar face—so disgusted, so sickened—and how Julie had thought he was just some pervert gawking at her. She had made a joke about him to Elliot, to get him to laugh, to get him to talk.

"I trailed them for a while."

Julie hadn't seen her father in over three years prior to that night. She had told enough people that her father was dead over the last few years that maybe she had finally come to believe it. She hadn't even recognized him from across the bar ... from only a few feet away when he staggered into Elliot's home with a shotgun at his side, forcing the long barrel into Elliot's mouth, forcing them to strip, forcing them into having sex, something they'd both wanted before he had intervened.

Just push it down and out of your way, Julie. It won't bite.

"—and when they pulled up to his place, I parked behind them."

Hungry hands and thirsty mouths in the car.

"But something didn't settle well, you know?"

"No questions."

Her father had watched the entire time: Julie straddling Elliot on the seat, un-tucking his shirt, not caring to breathe during their tangled embrace, wrapping her legs around him, his hands crawling up her back, Julie wanting so desperately at the time to peel out of her clothes as she grinded against him.

"And then they honked at me."

Her back arching against the steering column, Julie remembered. It almost made her smile thinking of it again.

"Neighbors' lights flicked on, people peering through mini-blinds and shit. I swear to you, Chase, they turned around and saw me, and other people were looking, too."

Her father had watched from his car as some guy made out with his daughter, face sucking face, hands going around and underneath clothes, both heading to the door so they could go inside and fuck each other, Julie backpedalling barefoot through the sprinkler water with her hand down some guy's pants, both barely making it to the door and neither caring about the glossy half-eaten red splotch of mouse a black cat had left for them as a present on the porch as an eager house key desperately tried to fuck an innocent keyhole on the blood-red door, a color symbolizing *passion*, which really meant *suffering*.

And once they were inside, her father had followed. He had wanted to prove a point, to ridicule them both, but by then the drug had overwhelmed her. Maybe Julie let it happen, taking the man underneath her and guiding him inside. Her father watching. Perhaps, deep down, she had wanted to prove her own point, to let him know he had lost control over her.

Julie dropped *Drakein* again to kill the memory.

Chase shook his head.

The little apparition girl, Hannah, stood in the hallway, as transparent as steam rising from hot asphalt. The see-through girl waved to Julie before heading down the hall.

"I took care of it," her father said.

"What about the girl," Chase said. "How did you handle her?"

"Restroom?" Julie whispered to Chase the next time he circled round and faced her. She couldn't take it anymore. The voice—her father's voice—so cancerous.

Now? he mouthed.

"Girl stuff."

She thought of the vision with the blood spilling out of her.

Save her, Hannah had said.

Chase pointed with the gun to show her the way and said into the phone, "Do you know where you can find her?"

"I know where to find her."

"Really."

Chase, toying with him.

"Brenden Memorial Hospital. She OD'd last night."

"Why doesn't that surprise me?"

Their voices fading …

Julie tried not to listen but could not help but listen as she followed Hannah. Over her shoulder, Chase transformed into a horrid hallucination; his body black, as if burnt, a dark substance bleeding out of him as he spoke to her father and listened to his mix of lies and truth. Fiery demon eyes bore onto Julie. The phone moved to his ear, the speakerphone turned off.

Quietly, he said, "How would you know she OD'd?"

Hannah waited for her outside the restroom. Reese nested in her wiry hair, a pearl-translucent outline of the tarantula she had remembered from childhood. The girl took the spider in her hand and held it out to Julie. One of the creature's front legs reached for her, and an all-to-familiar memory surfacing from the night prior— the Elliot-sized skeletal spider leading her into the kitchen, tapping on the glass, wanting out of its prison.

Her fingertips touched the dead girl's fingertips and Reese crawled onto her palm. How easily she could crush it, she thought, but those were her father's words sullying her mind.

Overheard from the hall: "You didn't take care of her … No, she's in *my* house, withdrawing. This is your problem, not mine!"

She let Hannah lead her inside and shut the door and could see through the girl's translucent body to the sink, and above it, the mirror. The bathroom smelled sterile like the hospital. The reflection revealed a tired Julie with a hand held outward, a little girl of about three standing before her; the transparency overlaying the girl's facial features on Julie's pregnant stomach.

And then the baby bump was gone.

"I need to get out of here," she told the girl.

The hallucinations were driving her mad.

Julie's reflection flashed a nasty sight of her face melting away and then returning to normal. Bloodshot eyes looked upon her in their dark sunken sockets. Sweat dappled her brow. She had to wean of the drug and stop the dragon's hunger. Every time she fed the beast, it only wanted more. Julie forced the eye drop bottle into her pocket, despite the craving. She thought her hand shook, but it was only Reese moving from her palm to her wrist.

Hannah regarded the spider in the mirror with a smile and looked to Julie. "Don't be afraid," she said.

The see-through tarantula from long ago climbed Julie's arm. It took much effort not to brush it away. It moved slowly, each of its many hairy legs taking turn. She felt him even through the long-sleeved shirt.

"He wants to help," the girl said.

At her shoulder, Reese pried at the neckline, pulling up the thin material and somehow turning himself around at the same time. Cold legs tickled her neck, a sensation similar to the effects of taking a few drops of *Drakein-5* traveled down her body.

"It won't hurt," the girl said.

The spider burrowed underneath and bit into her.

Warmth entered her body, but not pain. Hannah was right. Reese bit into one of the cutting scars near her clavicle. He stayed there a while, drawing the darkness out of her, Julie knew. Soon she no longer shook. Julie put the back of her hand against her forehead. She had cooled, the fever breaking. The continuous draw from the spider pulsated synchronously with her heartbeat. In her reflection, the blood in her eyes pulled back into her body, the purple in her veins—once highlighted by the bathroom fluorescents—lightened until they were faint, her drained white skin gaining color.

Reese crawled out from under her shirt and he was no longer spectral, but charred in color. And he was no longer clammy; instead, he was brittle, delicate, and lighter, possibly hollow. Black ash footprints dotted Julie's arm as he traveled to her hand. His forearms reached for the bathroom counter. Julie leaned forward and Reese jumped onto it, creating a layer of black dust beneath the chiral body like a Rorschach ink splotch. One leg at a time, he specked the sink with his disintegrating body, climbed the splashguard and made it to the mirror. His front legs, like feelers, tested the glass, which, as Julie had supposed, had the consistency of water. Tiny circles wavered outward as he passed through. A moment later the surface returned placid.

On the other side of the mirror, Reese looked like the spider she and Frankie had caged in their little plastic aquarium.

Julie reached for the glass to find it impenetrable, unknowingly passing her hand through Hannah's body.

"He ate the bad stuff," she said to her in the mirror, "the bad stuff inside you."

"Why?" she asked, pulling down the shirt.

In line with the three parallel scars from her youth there was now a fourth.

Why had she—

"You okay in there, Julie?" Chase said from a few feet outside the door.

Julie covered herself, the way she had when caught doing something bad, and turned on her heels, expecting a hand to come banging against the door: Mom or Dad.

The girl was gone.

She sank to her knees.

Any moment her mother's voice would slice the silence.

Open the door so Daddy can—

"Julie?"

"I'm fine!" Realizing it wasn't her mother calling, Julie toned it down. "I'm fine … I just had to … I'm feeling a little sick from coming down. I'll be out soon."

She flushed the toilet and ran the sink water for influence.

"I was worried about you. I had to take that call. I'm sure you understand. He sends his regards, by the way." Chase laughed and followed it with, "Only kidding, flower. So, listen. You have me in a pickle here. My guy says he met a friend of yours last night while taking care of some business for me. He mentioned 'some girl' running around with a mutual friend of ours. Some *girl* … Go figure. Two clients. And they randomly crash into each other. I'm sure you're aware of what happens when people owe me money and don't pay me back. A horrible night, I imagine."

A long sigh.

"This is a business. Supply and demand, product vs. payment. Clients demand my supply, my product, and I demand payment … or bad things sometimes happen. Economics 101, with caveats. Make sense?" He tapped on the door with either a knuckle or his gun.

"Yes."

"Good. Anyway, really long story short, we talked, and he says you, another of my clients, are no longer in possession of my product. Now, we both know he's correct because here you are, knocking at my door. Okay, figure of speech. I'm actually knocking on my own door for some reason with you behind it, hiding. Seriously, can we stop talking through this damn door?"

"I'll be out in a minute," Julie said, looking for any kind of makeshift weapon.

Not a lot of options. There was a toothbrush on the counter in a holder, a bottle of cologne, mouthwash, a plunger and brush next to the toilet. Chase could simply open the door and put a bullet through her skull and he'd be done with it, problem solved.

"We can get some coffee going, get you off of this high, and we can talk face to face and figure out how exactly you're going to pay me back. Unless you have some kind of secret stash at home or feel like robbing your own fake set of grandparents, I'm not sure how you're going to manage all this. I think we're at a stalemate here. Isn't that what you call it when two people play chess and neither can move, neither can win? Or am I thinking tic-tac-toe?"

Nothing useful under the sink, unless she suffocated him with toilet paper. She found her weapon in the medicine cabinet.

"I don't want the half bottle anymore," she said. "I'll give it back and you keep the money I already gave you and I'll get you the other two hundred before noon."

"Three hundred, love, but you can't take a bite out of the pizza and expect Round Table to take it back while you scrounge enough cash to pay for the pizza you stole from them the day before. Life's not so easy. The world no longer plays charity."

"You sold me half a bottle."

"Product, Julie, by the slice. But don't worry, I told him I'd take care of this one. 'On the house,' I told him. He's not going to be coming after you, because I'm handling this one myself."

Julie held an old-fashioned razor: four inches of handle, four inches of blade, folded upon itself. She opened the blade. She'd cut the bastard if she had to; that's what she was good at anyway. But Chase wouldn't enjoy it. She'd cut him deep.

"We're going to be civilized about this, Julie."

A click, like the sound of a hammer pulling back on a revolver. He was going to do it now. Chase had taken her father off speaker-phone while she was in the restroom.

What did he say to Cal? What did he promise?

He was going to take care of things himself, he'd said.

She had taken money from Earl once before and could do it again, but she'd promised herself she wouldn't, not ever. She had taken a few hundred from the Heimlichs without them knowing, and had put it back without them knowing. No, she wouldn't do it again.

The doorknob turned, ever so slowly.

"Julie?" he said.

She imagined Chase pointing the gun forward, chest level, maybe head level, with one hand on the doorknob. Had she locked it? She had locked it, but couldn't remember if she had turned the lock mechanism vertical or horizontal. She no longer had until noon to figure things out; she had until right now.

"I want you to trust me, Julie. I want this to work out between us. Really, I do. This is a business in which I take great pride. I want to introduce you to someone so you trust me."

"I bet you do," she whispered.

"Will you let me do that?"

Julie edged closer to the door and positioned herself perpendicular with the hand holding the gun barging through any moment. He'd probably only need one shot, but she wouldn't give him the pleasure. She'd cut his hand right the fuck off.

The door unlocked. The doorknob turned and then stopped.

She'd have to cut deep and then go for the other hand. She'd have to cut through the tendons, or whatever let the fingers do their work so he couldn't pick up the gun.

"I want to introduce you to Colt," Chase said as the door opened.

Colt was a gun; she knew enough about firearms.

As soon as she saw his hand, she came down with the razor, hard and fast. The blade sliced through most of his wrist and stuck.

Chase let out a horrendous noise.

He wasn't holding a revolver; he had been holding a bobby pin—no longer able to hold it—that fell to the floor with a splash of blood. She had sliced through nearly everything but bone. An arc of red painted the door and Chase quickly capped the spout with his free hand. The gun tucked into his belt on the back of his pants. The click she had heard was not a hammer pulling back on a Colt, but a tumbler flipping over as he picked the lock—a simple doorknob with a single hole in its center. She had needed to unlock her own bathroom door in the past, learned the trick from her father.

Julie had nearly sliced open the boy standing next to him.

In shock, Chase introduced his son, which looked exactly like him, "Colt, this is Julie. Julie, Colt."

He couldn't have been older than four.

"I'd have you shake his hand but I'm afraid you'd slice it off now can you grab me a towel or something and help me out here! Agh! Jesus, Julie, what the *fuck* are you thinking?" Chase risked a look at the wound and shot another arc against the door.

Two bloody circles dripped red to the floor, as if a giant vampire had sunk its fangs into the door to bleed it out.

His son, Colt, stared at his father's wrist, mesmerized.

White towels soaked up the red.

"If the bleach won't take it out," said her mother, "you're paying for a new towel, out of your allowance. We won't be keeping spotted towels. Every time one of us wipes, it's your blood we're smearing around, Julie. You want your father and I dabbing your blood over our faces when we wash up, is that it?"

"No."

Julie never received allowances.

"Remember the capris you bled through at school? Classmates pointing at you and the red splotch between your legs … blood doesn't come out, Julie. It stains. And we couldn't bleach your pants, could we?"

"No."

"You'll be paying for a new set of towels if this doesn't come out. I don't know why I try with you sometimes. You better pray Jesus forgives girls who cut, Julie. Cutting is suicide practice for girls who want to go to hell. God gave you a body and every time you slice into it, you're disrespecting the body given to you. You think God appreciates you doing that?"

"No."

Her mother spread the hand towel over the washing machine and poured a capful of Clorox bleach over it, and rubbed the material together. She pulled a knob to start the water and upended the bottle over a crumpled end of the towel to let bleach soak into a clean area. She pulled Julie closer with a hard yank of her elbow before forcing the strap of Julie's tank top down over one shoulder and dabbing the wound.

"Oh, this stings, Julie." Chase clenched his jaw and hissed through his teeth. "What were you thinking?" He looked to his son, perhaps realizing how close she had come to slicing the boy open instead.

"I'm so sorry, Chase."

"You thought I was coming in here to kill you?" He reached for the bobby pin but couldn't pick it up with the injured hand; his fingers were lifeless, disconnected. "What was I going to do, pin-the-hair-away-from-your-eyes you to death?"

Julie was lost for words.

"Colt, go to your room. Play with your LEGOs or something until I come get you."

The boy ran.

"I was going to give you until noon to come up with the money, but now we'll have to reconsider. Christ, this hurts."

Blood sprayed from his wrist as if he'd placed his thumb over the nozzle of a garden hose, but it was only a hallucination. His wrist steadily dripped as soon as the visual passed. Chase was in shock and bleeding out; he'd already lost a significant amount.

"We need to call you an ambulance," Julie said.

"You *do* love me."

"Where's your phone?"

"You still don't have one?"

"No."

As if anticipating the call, Chase's pocket vibrated.

How can you not own a cellphone? Elliot had asked her in the car.

Everyone I know has a cellphone. Why would I need one?

She remembered wanting to taste him as his question came out low-pitched and slow, his face pulling away, the dragon messing with her in so many ways. She had reached one hand around his neck and her other deep into the right front pocket of his pants.

See? I'm never more than a few feet away …

Julie grabbed another towel for Chase and pulled out the cellphone, trying not to recall anything more from the previous night.

"Who is it?" Chase asked.

"Unlisted."

"Well, it's him again. He's around the corner and can wait."

She ignored the call and dialed 911.

"Yes, we need an amb—" Julie said, but that's all Chase allowed her to say before he let go of the gash and ended the call.

More blood.

"I don't need an ambulance," Chase said, placing a hand on Julie, mostly for support. "You think I've got insurance? I have a guy for this sort of thing."

He pulled away to rewrap the wound and a red hand silhouette stayed behind on her shoulder, like a bloody smear of smashed tarantula, right where the illusionary spider bit her.

Reese.

"I really *should* kill you, though. This is a lot of blood we're talking about here and this is an expensive outfit."

Chase was one of the few men she'd met who referred to a suit as an outfit.

He made a motion for the gun, but Julie lunged forward and grabbed the wrist she had sliced, her fingers sliding between what felt like guitar strings and slick heat and it was enough to bring Chase onto his knees, giving her the opportunity to take the gun he'd tucked into the small of his back. Hands shaking, Julie stepped back, pointing the Colt in his general direction but to nowhere in particular.

After making a strange mixture of grunts through clenched teeth, Chase composed himself and rose to his feet. He had turned paler and started to sweat. He slid in the mess, but quickly righted himself.

Somewhere in the struggle, Julie had dropped the cellphone, which again vibrated on the bathroom floor and worked its way through the blood, as if floating over it.

"Quite the predicament," he said. "Here I stand, or stagger really, holding myself together, quite literally. If I let go and try for my gun, the blood lets loose. Maybe you're brave enough to pull the trigger before anything goes down. Who knows? I could bleed to death just from letting go of my arm. Maybe I try anyway and you take a shot and it goes through me and I keep coming at you and take my gun from you and put a hole in your fucking head. Self-defense plea will work because this is my house and I'll claim *'I've never seen this druggy whore in my life, Officer.'* You think they'll buy that? What do you take me for?"

The buzz of the phone vibrating against the floor.

"It's probably not for you."

"I want out of this," Julie said, not entirely sure if the splatter-dripping walls and the rest of the gore around her was an illusion caused by the drug, or in fact reality.

"Look, I want to rewind the last few minutes of life and stop you from nearly cuttin off my freaking arm, but that's not going to happen either."

"I'm serious, Chase. I want out of this. I owe you money, and I'll get it to you. Somehow. Not by noon today, but I'll get it to you. But then I'm out. I never met you. You never met me. We don't know each other from this point forward."

"You're really doing this to me."

Julie's father droned from the floor.

"And you promise not to send my ... not to send him after me.

I want nothing to do with him, not ever. He's the reason I'm here. Did he tell you what he did? Did he tell you he followed us back to Elliot's house?"

"I know all that, Julie."

"Did he tell you he followed us inside?"

"Julie—"

"Did he tell you what he *really* did, that he made us take off our clothes, forced us to do things in front of him?"

"Give me the gun. Pointing it at me is getting annoying."

"He probably didn't tell you the details 'cause he's a sick fucking bastard! Did he tell you how he *really* watched us, what he made us do? He put a shotgun in Elliot's mouth while he forced us into having sex. Killed Elliot. Did he tell you that? I didn't think so. I want out of this. I'll get you the money, I swear, but I want out!"

"He takes care of things and sometimes oversteps boundaries—"

"He made me shoot the syringe up my arm," Julie said, extending her wrist to Chase.

"*That*, I didn't know."

"That's why it's gone and why I was at the hospital, why I can't get down from this high and need a fix just to level. I want out of this. The dragon, I don't want it anymore. Either you come after me and I shoot and you die, and maybe *I die*, or I keep pointing this gun at you until you bleed to death, or we come to an understanding so neither of us dies and you get your money and I walk away for good."

"The gun's not loaded, Julie."

"Fuck you," she said, stepping closer and steadying her aim.

"Julie, how long have you known me? When have you ever seen me with a gun? Never. You're tripping out on this drug worse than I've ever seen. I have a kid in the house. You think I'd ever open my son up to that? It's not even a real gun. It's his. It's a toy, Julie, not even metal. You pull the trigger and it makes sound effects like some kind of alien plasma gun. Now can you answer the damn phone?"

"What?"

"I can't answer it."

Chase's face had changed since she had cut him: his cheeks white, face splotched with beads of sweat, eyes sunken within their sockets; and it wasn't a hallucination. He slid onto the ground, his legs slipping forward, hands reverently folded.

The weight of the gun wasn't right.

Plastic.

"There's … in the contacts of the phone, there's someone by the name of Keene. Simply says Keene. Call that number and tell him I sliced open my arm … I don't care what you tell him, but get him here." He looked at the red around him and added, "All of this was in me?"

The gun had an ON and OFF switch, and a volume wheel.

The doorbell rang with nobody to answer but Julie. She expected her mother to call from the kitchen for someone to answer the damn door already after two chimes and a follow-up knocker attack. Three quick taps and she knew it was Frankie.

"Hey," she said, swinging open the door.

"Hey."

It was freshman year of high school for both Julie and her best friend. They stayed close throughout the years and sometimes hung out in the spans between school ending and dinnertime, the hours before Julie's mother returned from work at the nursing home, a job she had taken to manage the bills after Cal was sent to prison. They usually had until seven, unless Frankie had to babysit her two younger sisters.

"I need to ask you something," Julie said. "Something serious."

"Danny Parker? No, he's a douche."

"About my dad."

"What about him? He's got another eighteen months or some-thing, right?"

"Seventeen, I think. Did he ever … you know—"

Julie had tried asking her once, but they were both a little drunk after hanging with the aforesaid douche—who they'd coaxed to steal a bottle of Stolichnaya from his parents to mix with Red Bull—and Frankie would either change the subject or raise a hand.

Asking was nearly as worse as seeing Frankie's expression sink into disgust.

The doorbell rang with nobody to answer but Julie. Chase held onto his wrist like a writhing python; his son, Colt, sent to his room; and Julie, pointing the plastic toy at Chase, wanting moments ago to end his life. The doorbell rang a second time, and instead of the knocker following, the back of someone's hand pounded against it.

"Chase?" a familiar voice called from the front door.

"Your father?"

"The day you came over with Reese and the aquarium, the day we played on the swings in the backyard and you went inside and disappeared for a while, and then I found you sitting on my parent's bed not wearing anything and crying. I know you remember that, Frankie. I asked what you were crying about and Cal was there with you and said you had an accident and needed to change and then he shut the—"

"Well I can't answer it, obviously," said Chase.

Again, the pounding.

Julie wanted another drop. Just one. The bottle in her pocket pressed against her leg. The blood on the tile splashed upward like a wave and then settled, all within a second. Part of her knew it wasn't real. Chase's aura had turned lemon yellow by the time she dropped the gun. She retrieved the warm, slick phone.

"Call Keene. We'll drive to him. Someone will drop you off after, wherever you're currently staying. I don't really care at this point."

"I'll call a cab."

"You'll call my guy."

"What about your son?"

"You're not watching him; you're coming with us. Colt will be fine. Keene's daughter can watch him. Shouldn't be a problem. She's sat for me before." He pondered this and then yelled across the room, "Colt? Daddy needs to run out for a few hours. Put on a movie or something after we leave and wait for Lacie. You remember Lacie?"

"Yeah," said a faint, scared voice.

"She's going to look after you until I get back."

He motioned for the phone with his uninjured hand.

"Chase?" her father said from the front door.

"Coming!"

Julie found Keene in the contacts and dialed, put it on speakerphone. Chase didn't move until it rang the first time, and then she followed him out of the bathroom. He moved slowly.

Keene answered on the fourth ring.

"Chase, you've caught me at a bad time. Can I call you back?"

"I need a favor. Now."

A sigh, and then, "You got it. What happened?"

Chase turned his head to Julie and said, "There's been an accident. Let's just say a straight razor accidentally sliced open one of my wrists and I can't move any of my fingers on that hand."

"You got it wrapped tight?"

"Thanks, yes I'm fine, and you? Yes, I've got it wrapped!"

Julie coughed into her hand.

"Tourniquet?"

"I've got it wrapped with my other hand. If I let go for even a second I'm a walking blood sprinkler. It's fuckin' bad, man."

"Who's that with you? I heard someone cough, wasn't you."

"So what?"

"So tell that person to find something to use as a tourniquet or you're going to bleed to death. And then you need to go to the emergency room. You got some plastic tubing, or a coax cable or something? How much blood have you lost?"

"You know the small sodas at the concession stands at movie theatres that aren't so small? We're on our way to you."

"No, you're not. You're going to the hospital because I can't fix that shit, but first you're going to wrap your arm, as tightly as you can, above the elbow."

The doorbell rang a few more times.

"You said you can't move your fingers?" said the phone.

Chase concentrated on his hand, as if willing his fingers to move.

A dead tarantula on its back, legs in the air … still.

"No."

Julie started to undo Chase's belt and thought of Elliot and their awkward-backward pedaling up the walkway to his place. She carefully unlaced the belt from the loops of Chase's pants and coiled it above his elbow, which caused a final spurt of red from between his fingers. She knew about tourniquets and pulled the leather hard until she thought it might hurt, and then some—it had to be tight enough to cut off the blood circulation to the rest of his arm— and tied it off. There was a pained expression captured on Chase's face, followed by a curiosity they both shared, and then he let go of his wrist. After a small welling of blood and a release of air, Chase rewrapped the wound in the towel.

"We have it in a belt," he said, motioning Julie to follow him out of the bathroom and into the entryway. "It's not gushing."

"Good."

Chase unlocked the front door.

"We'll be there in five minutes," he told the phone.

"You'll be in the ER. I could sew your wound, but your tendons are cut and you'd eventually lose the arm. I'm serious. Go to the hospital, Chase. I can't fix this."

"I can move my pinky a little … no, I'm just shaky."

After a ghostly twist of the knob, the door opened and there stood her father, Calvin Stipes, with his buzzed hair, dark, tired-looking eyes, and the burnt rose tattoo climbing his neck. His trench coat partially covered the shotgun. A skull jutted momentarily from his face as he stood in the doorway, apparently unable to find words to express his confusion. A thick trail of red led to the bathroom behind her and Chase, Julie knew, and his eyes moved from the violence left behind them to the two people who had come from that direction: Chase holding a blood-soaked towel to his wrist, a belt strangling his arm above the elbow, weak and staggering, barely able to stand on his feet; and Julie, splashed in his blood and holding him upright.

Either Keene hung up on Chase, or Chase hung up on Keene.

"This is Julie … Julie, well, you two have already met. Now that we are well acquainted, we need to leave. The two of you can catch up in the car, but we need to go."

"What the hell happened?"

"What happened is that you drove me to the hospital a few minutes ago and we're already in the waiting room waiting to be seen, and for some strange, other-worldly reason, our minds have traveled outside of our bodies and back into this house somehow and our past-selves are conversing about leaving while our present- or perhaps future-selves are waiting for the doctor."

"Why did you bring your daughter here today?" the doctor said.

It was their first visit to Dr. Stanter. Julie's mother called him 'the shrink' but had never explained why. He was quite tall and wore square glasses midway down his nose so he could see through them if he needed to while taking notes, but more often looked over them as he spoke. Dr. Stanter had wanted to see Julie privately before their consult, but her parents wouldn't allow it. She'd heard them arguing about not caring whether or not it was part of his process to interview her first, as well as how much all this nonsense would cost if he couldn't fix Julie's problem. The door the doctor had closed—so Julie wouldn't have to hear—did little. She wouldn't have 'opened up' to him anyway, as the shrink put it. Frankie had been her best friend for years to earn such trust; Julie had never seen this guy in her life.

"Because of this," said her mother, reaching for her.

Julie retracted in her chair, but her mother's ever-extending hands were always conquering. There were never chairs big enough in which Julie could hide. Sometimes Julie dreamt of her mother chasing after her in an empty field, with arms dangling at her sides, giant hands brushing the ground, elongated fingers able wrap completely around Julie's waist if she caught up to her. She often awoke the moment a talon fingernail touched between her shoulder blades, a bead of sweat trailing her back like a faint memory of her mother's touch.

Julie shifted in her seat when her mother exposed the scars.

"Are those cuts self-inflicted?" he said, taking notes.

"Of course they're self-inflicted," her father said.

"That's why we're here," her mother said.

"I really suggest I speak with Julie in private before we go any further. Julie, do you mind if your parents leave the room?"

Julie looked to her father and then to her seat.

"We're a family and we work things out as a family," her father said. "Whatever you ask in front of Julie you can ask in front of us."

"Is that okay with you, Julie?" the doctor said.

Julie looked to her father again.

"Julie," the doctor said, gaining her attention. "Are you okay discussing this topic in front of your parents?"

"He's asking you a question, Julie," her mother said.

"Mrs. Stipes—"

"Elizabeth. My mother was Mrs. Stipes."

"Elizabeth, please don't interject or I will have you removed from this room without your discretion. Both you and Calvin. I'm asking Julie this question. Not you. Not your husband."

"You can't—"

"Believe me, I can, and I will. If I have even the remotest of suspicion you or your husband have caused injury to your daughter, I will call the authorities and have you removed until disproved. The two of you bringing Julie to see me in the first place helps your case; however, please don't force me to get Child Protective Services—"

"I wouldn't lay a hand on my daughter," her father said, standing. "Liz, let's leave Julie in the doctor's hands. We're here to help her, not hurt her. And if that means us leaving so they can talk in private for a while, then so be it. We have nothing to hide, Dr. Stanter."

"I'm not leaving my daughter alone in here with—"

"Elizabeth."

She stayed seated and leaned forward. "Why would she cut herself? Please, just answer me that and Cal and I will leave the two of you alone, for as long as you need. Why do people cut themselves? Is there anything we can do?"

"Julie's cutting will take some time to ascertain. It may not happen today, and it may not happen over the course of the next few sessions, but we'll do our best find the cause and a resolution. Julie's rather young to be doing this sort of thing, from what I've experienced, so it could be a number of things. Cutting is a means of letting emotional pain escape. Psychological pain blocked—and released—by physical pain, in other words."

"Is it a cry for attention?" her father said, grabbing at her mother's hand to try to get her out of her seat. "I've read cutting can be a cry for attention, but if that's true, why would she be doing it in private, where no one can see?"

¤ ¤ ¤

"You're cut up pretty bad, too."

"*Badly*," Julie corrected.

She watched her father's eyes through the rearview mirror as she sat behind Chase, who rode in the front passenger seat with the shotgun leaning against his leg. Every once in a while Cal snuck a peek at her in the backseat through the mirror and Julie quickly looked away. His face had been fried beyond recognition. He had sheared his head and had lost a significant amount of weight while in prison, but his eyes were the same. He had weathered over the years, his leather skin starting to wrinkle around the neck, where the red rose tattoo climbed out from his collar. Each petal edged in black, as if the flower had survived the fire with him.

"Really, I'm fine," said Chase. "Don't worry about me. Find me a drugstore where we can purchase a sewing kit and bandages and we can do this ourselves. I don't need this hand. I'm right-handed. I'll just use this useless one to wave at people from now on."

The towel wrapped around his wrist had turned completely red.

Julie wormed a finger under the bandage covering the gash on her wrist where she had sliced herself open with part of Elliot's jawbone, feeling the crisscrosses of thread. She let the tip of her fingernail enter the wound.

"Julie, do you mind if I take a closer look at the cuts?"

She shrugged. With her parents out of the room, Julie didn't see a problem letting Dr. Stanter see the marks. She pulled down the corner of her shirt.

He slowly rose from his chair and leaned down to her, pushing the glasses up the bridge of his nose as he made a squinty face.

"Three cuts, side-by-side, all the same length and equally apart. Forty-five degree angles rising left to right." After returning to his seat and jotting more notes, he said, "Some of these cuts are old. The lowest one was recently reopened, am I right?"

Sometimes instead of cutting she'd simply slide a fingernail across the wound to slice it back open, would leave it there while it stung, and would then make it sting again and again.

When the stinging subsided, blood had started to seep into the gauze covering her wrist.

"You two get in some kind of wrist cutting contest? What happened back there?"

"Well," said Chase, "she must have tried killing herself sometime at the hospital. My guess, based on her lovely patchwork, maybe it was an accident. I don't know. With that much dragon in her system, who knows? And then she decided to pay me a visit to buy more *D*, if you can believe such a thing, and right after I got off the phone with you the last time, I paid her a visit in the ladies' room to see what was taking her so long and she sliced me open. Nearly killed my kid! I think that about sums it. Did I miss anything, Julie?"

"I didn't try to kill myself. I OD'd on your shit after this asshole made me shoot an entire syringe of *Drakein-5* up my arm!"

"What syringe? You sold her an entire syringe? I thought you said it was only bottles."

Lies.

"She *stole* the syringe last time she bought from me."

"Doesn't look like she'd have that kind of money."

"Then *you* can pay me back. Be her Daddy. Fill those shoes."

"'*What syringe?*' Don't play stupid," Julie said. "You come back into my fucked up life the moment someone important enters into it, someone I connect with emotionally, someone who levels me out, who I think will understand me, and you end it. You're the reason all this happened. All of it. And you stuck that thing into his mouth and killed him."

Julie pitched forward and grabbed the shotgun, her entire body shaking as she sank into her seat. She flipped the weapon around and put it to the back of her father's head.

"You put this in his mouth and killed him."

"What are you doing, Julie?"

She pressed the barrel hard against his neck and tried to pull the trigger, not caring if they crashed or hit a passing vehicle head-on. She wanted him dead, but nervous fingers only slid around the shotgun, her eyes not wanting to move away from her father, as if magnetized to the rose on his neck where she intended to shoot him. She wanted to see his face explode and flower out and through the window.

"Julie," said Chase, "you're reacting to the *Drakein*, and you're on your way to getting us all killed. As soon as we get to the hospital, we're going to check me in and get me all patched up, and then we're going to admit you, I promise. They'll flush out your system or whatnot and bring you back to reality. Whatever happened between you two ..." His words were fast and concentrated but it may have been the drug speeding him along.

The hospital hadn't flushed away the drug.

Cal remained focused on the road, despite her threat.

The little bottle in her pocket screamed for her. A single drop in each eye after all this came to a close and her father was out of her life for good.

She pulled against the trigger and a silent blast sent a load of buckshot through the center of the flower as it blossomed from his opening face, the darkest shades of red spraying through a shattering window. And then everything pulled back in, the shot rushing reversely through the air, the various shades of liquefied life drawing back through his head and into the hole and sealing up neatly inside as he recomposed.

He turned to her, his face gone—no gaping hole, but a flat surface of smooth skin.

"You need help," his faceless face said to her.

"I'm dying here," Chase said, white and sweaty, the color drained out of him. He slid around in his seat and leaned his forehead against the dashboard, dripping onto it.

Her father's eyes returned to her in the rearview.

"Put down the cane and help Chase."

She had tried pulling the trigger on her father's walking cane, the end of which she held flush against his neck—a simple black cane with a shaft like a shotgun barrel. The stock pushing into her shoulder was nothing but a silver handle in the shape of some kind of reptilian head. She tried remembering her father at Chase's door. He had leaned weight against the weapon, using it as a crutch. His staggering walk. The shotgun and the cane: one and the same. She now pointed the stupid thing at her father, willing to kill him with it.

The cane writhed within her hands, the smooth surface turning scaly, the serpent's mouth opening with a black forked tongue tasting the air, and then instantly hard and cold in her hands and transforming again.

"I need to get out of here," Julie said, dropping the cane.

She reached for the handle and pulled, but the door was locked.

Her father watched from the mirror.

"What are you doing?"

She unlocked the door and the handle worked this time. She pushed as wind pushed back. They were probably going seventy or eighty down the freeway as the road blurred beneath her. Pressure from the cabin warbled in her ears. The door locks clicked, meaning her father had pushed the button to trap her inside, but the door was already ajar, yet too difficult to open. She let it close and tried the window; halfway down, it stopped from some kind of built-in safety mechanism.

Glancing to the cane/gun/snake at her side, she found it lifeless and still, and to the reflection of her father's eyes, she found them frantic.

Julie managed to squeeze her head and arm through the window frame and felt pressure against her armpit as the vehicle slowed—her father slamming on the brakes and veering to the shoulder. She withdrew into the car, kicking the glass.

Chase laughed in a way close to crying.

The *bam! bam! bam!* of her feet against the glass.

Gravel under the tires spattering against the undercarriage.

Her father's words indecipherable amid the chaos.

She kicked out and on the fourth attempt the glass shattered like a spider web, yet held together. She kicked repeatedly, the breakaway glass ripping like completed sections of puzzle pieces. She remembered finishing puzzles as a kid, and then peeling the image apart afterward into four or five bigger pieces to put back into the box.

Julie climbed out the window—not nearly as easy as climbing through the mirror in the hospital room. Shards of glass in the frame raked her skin through her shirt as she slipped out and fell out onto the gravel. She tumbled and rolled, but not much. The vehicle slid to a stop next to her. She was on her feet and running to the fence adjacent to the road when she heard her father call out her name, as his door slammed shut. She looked back only once: her father reaching through the broken window for his cane and then limping after her.

The barbed wire fence came up to her chest and she easily climbed over. The wheat field beyond was dry and dead like the afternoon air. Stalks rose four feet from ground to sky and brushed lightly against her skin as she passed through it, reaching for her, tickling her. The field moved with the breeze and it reminded her of blackbird flocks soaring as one, a single entity working together, moving like dark clouds through the sky with attention deficit, first in one direction, and then another. The gold surface shimmered with sunlight.

Waterlogged soil made it difficult to run through the field. The wheat, planted in rows, created divots as wide as her feet. Running parallel to the path of the rows made it easier and soon a flattened

line of wheat led her father directly to her. She had created what looked like a tunnel through the field.

Cal had made it to the fence and struggled over it. He fell, his pant leg sticking to the barbs. "Julie," his faraway voice called, barely audible over the sounds of the field.

Julie reached into her pocket for the bottle of *Drakein*, eager.

She unscrewed the cap and lost the bottle, which landed in a brown puddle, floated amongst mosquito larvae and bits of wheat. Hesitating, she grabbed the bottle and kept going, trying to feed the urge. Drug tears ran along her cheeks, the drops missing her eyes.

"Julie!"

Her ankle stuck between hardened rows of dirt and twisted as she fell. The Visine bottle launched forward and disappeared through the field, through Elliot. She had nearly fallen onto the translucent arachnid skeleton and stared ahead at his headless bony body, at arms and legs split apart to form eight appendages, at an arched back and hollow ribcage, at clavicles dangling like pedipalps around the cervical portion of his spine, which now resembled a mouth. Barely visible under the sun. Barely Elliot.

A clammy leg touched her ankle and the pain dissipated.

"I'm so sorry," she said.

She let the spider crawl on top of her, one leg at a time, the weight of Elliot's body hardly there at all. Somehow she knew he wanted to help as he slowly advanced. And she let him.

Julie reclined until her back met the wet ground. Spreading her arms and legs, she allowed Elliot to crawl completely onto her, pinning her, two legs holding each of her arms and legs. What was left of his body pressed against her own and if he still held human form, they'd be close enough for sex, but instead the sacral part of his spine pressed between her legs. If he still had a head, they would be close enough to kiss, but instead the palps of his spider form caressed her neck and exposed the three parallel scars near her shoulder.

Warmth coursed through her entire body as the creature bit into her, drawing heat from her arms and legs, through her groin, through her chest, up into her neck, out of her body and directly into the spider. Electricity. A Jacobs ladder through her spine. Her eyes clenched shut as Julie imagined the two of them back in Elliot's home: shedding clothes, exploring hands, eager mouths, bodies entangled and grinding. Julie on her back, allowing him inside. She came as the spider held her down, her body convulsing, body shuddering. She wanted to wrap her arms around him and pull him close, but she was immobile like a winged bug on a pinning block and she liked that even more—the inability of control, the vulnerability of allowing her body to react how it may. Arms and legs immobile, she arched beneath him, head tilting back.

Elliot drank the *Drakein* out of her and crawled away.

As hurriedly as the sensations filled her body, they departed.

Julie opened her eyes to find the arachnid skeleton no longer transparent, but solidified and ashy gray, the color of Reese years ago. A familiar flaky leg brushed her own. The leg paused there, prompting her to follow, before carrying on.

Cal called her name, much closer.

Collecting herself, Julie followed the spider through the field. A headrush dizzied her the moment she stood, legs shaky, but her mind cleared with each step. A breeze cooled the sweat on her skin. She didn't need a thermometer to tell her she had broken the fever.

The last of the drug dribbled out of her neck like warm milk against her skin.

Elliot and his eight appendages moved quickly through the wheat, the body turning every so often to check if she still followed.

Walking turned to jogging turned to running to keep up with the spider legs disappearing into the field. She followed him through waves of grain until his path ended at a small clearing surrounding a stagnant pool of obsidian water. The spider took a drink and then simply stood there, peering into the surface.

Julie joined him, touching the water with her foot. It reminded her of the polished black stones she and Frankie once stole from a gem show, which appeared solid but were semi-transparent when held up to sunlight. Something as red as the dead mouse on Elliot's doorstep shimmered beneath the surface. Elliot saw it as well.

The rose.

She knelt next to Elliot and splashed away the top layer of muck. The flower waited an arm's length below. Julie watched an involuntary hand disappear into the black, and then her entire arm, up to her elbow. The side of her face lapped the tepid water. Petals brushed fingertips before a hand on the other side wrapped around her wrist and pulled her inside.

Julie wasn't supposed to go by the pool alone but that didn't stop her parents from not watching her while they drank from the silver cans—*you can't have any of these sodas, silly*—in the neighbor's front yard. She skipped around the water's edge, humming a made-up tune, waiting for Frankie to come over so they could play.

A fuzzy black caterpillar with white hairs and a red spot on its back crawled along her index finger. The little guy reached her nail, so she turned her finger upside-down so he could crawl to the other side. She put the thumb in his way so he'd crawl over it next, but nudged him loose, onto his back, and a wrongly-timed wind rolled him off her hand and into the water. He was light enough to float, but his legs struggled and he squirmed to stay alive.

Kneeling next to the pool, she could almost reach him, but the waves from her fingertips pushed him away. She leaned out farther, one hand on the edge and the other reaching for her friend, and the hand holding her upright slipped.

She somersaulted and went completely under and swallowed water, breathed burning water through her nose, swallowed more. Her arms flapped like the caterpillar, legs kicking. Julie's toes touched the bottom, but only with her head completely underwater. Every time she found the ground, she pushed, able to gasp a mouthful of air with her head tilted straight back before taking in more chlorine down her throat. The fire behind her nose burned as she coughed into the water. A blurry wet world surrounded her. She found the edge of the pool but her fingers slipped on the slimy surface as her toes slid on the curved wall below. The next time she found the ground and pushed, her lip smashed between her teeth and the rock edge, the water around her clouding red, and then she couldn't feel the wall at all, only more water and more water and more water and—

Julie stared at a wavy sun from under the surface.

Someone leaned over the edge, a dark-skinned hand reaching down, an adult hand, Frankie's mom. A smaller Frankie silhouette knelt next to her.

Hannah knelt next to Julie in the trial room. White surrounded them both. She had somehow fallen through the pool of rancid water and wound up in the familiar, featureless room, lying flat on an unseen floor. Like the spider moments before, Hannah was no longer see-through and resembled an ordinary young girl in a flower-pattern dress.

"I don't know what's real anymore."

"You're real," Hannah said.

The girl held out her hand for Julie to take, her touch real.

"Where's the man who took you?"

Hannah pointed above—if there even existed such a thing as 'above.' Forward, backward, left, right, up, down … none of it mattered in this world. She wasn't even sure how Hannah had escaped. Perhaps he only chased her with Julie around, only existing in her mind.

"He'll be here soon, but that's not him."

Like a rip in fabric, the white above them opened. One of Elliot's giant gray legs tore through the invisible ceiling, which rippled around the appendage to reveal an outline of blue sky—the open field from which she came.

"Did you pull me here?" she said to the girl.

A nod and a smile like her own.

"You were reaching for me," the girl said.

Another of Elliot's legs pierced the hole, prying through, reminding Julie of the smaller spider she had imagined crawling out of her uterus. Halfway exposed, the arachnid skeleton teardrop fell silently next to them. The blue gash in the white remained open.

"He'll be here soon," Hannah said.

Elliot expanded from his lumped form and stood on all eights. Although clean, his body shook like that of a wet dog.

"He's still chasing us," the girl said.

"He's always going to chase us, isn't he, as long as I let him?"

Together they walked through the white, Julie leading the way this time. Elliot stayed a distance behind, protecting them.

"I'm not sure where we're going."

"We're going to the rose," Hannah said.

"We are?"

A red dot bled the whiteness ahead.

"You're not sick anymore," the girl said.

She had forgotten about the bottle—lost somewhere in the field. She no longer wanted it, no longer craved the dragon.

"I guess not."

Julie rubbed her shoulder.

The scars were light in color, flat, old.

"Did your friend help?"

"A few friends helped."

They came upon a withered rosebush, with thick dry branches covered in large thorns, dead if not for the single glowing flower rising directly from its roots. Power emanated from the flower. Julie felt it as strongly as the *Drakein* that had called for her. The rose bloomed brightly alive from roots and branches once dead. She touched the petals.

"I'm not going to run anymore."

"Julie," Cal said from afar.

He had joined them in the whiteness, the spider holding him at bay, side-stepping to cut him off, nearly as high as the man's waist.

Elliot reared, four legs reaching as the others balanced the creature in place.

Cal kicked the spider to the ground and continued advancing.

Elliot rose from his crumpled mass, attacked him again with a raised femur, the tibia and fibula bones hitting him hard in the back.

"He can't hurt me here," Julie said under her breath.

Cal whirled and wrapped his arms around one of the femurs. The smaller bones dangled over his back. One of his muddy boots pushed the spider's body the opposite direction. A few snaps and one of Elliot's legs disconnected from the hip. He connected again with his foot and the spider backed away, if only for a moment, before stalking Cal from a distance.

Julie put herself between her father and the girl, protecting her, protecting the rose.

Cal limped forward. Something about not right.

Emotionless, he raised the femur, similar to how he had raised the shotgun to her chest at Elliot's—denting her left breast with the barrel, squeezing the trigger, knowing he had already fired both rounds—and the man in the trench coat, the man without a name who she later determined was her father, with the self-buzzed haircut and the week-old stubble on his cheeks and the burnt skin running along his neck and over part of his face, he smiled again, like he had before. He lowered the bone and limped closer.

"You're not my father," Julie said.

"Give your daddy some sugar," he said, but those weren't really his words; they were the words of a man long dead.

"You're not him, I see it now."

Her father had died in prison, like her mother said.

"What did your mother ever know?"

"She knew enough to have him put away."

Her father hanged himself in his cell after setting fire to the sheets on his bed, some of which he'd tied around his neck before jumping off the metal frame to end his life, like her mother said.

His eyes moved to Hannah at her side.

"Your mother played along. Let things happen …"

"Why did you do it?" Julie said.

"Your mother's the one who did this to me," he said, ignoring her question. He pointed at his neck. "She smashed a bottle of Bacardi 151 against my face while I was lighting a cigarette. Did she tell you that? Caught nearly my whole damn face on fire. She called the fuckin cops from the hospital the day she turned me in for what I did to you, the day she did this to me. The shrink … he tried to tell her, but she was too damn stubborn to listen. Couldn't believe I'd do such a thing to my own daughter, let alone your little negro friend. Did she tell you all that?"

"She must have, or you wouldn't be able to tell me," Julie said. "I control you here. You do what I say. Say what I want you to say."

"What can you do," he said, intimidation more than question.

"I could paralyze you while my pet spider slowly devours you. Would you like that? I could do that. I can. But I won't, because none of this is real."

"I'm fuckin real."

"Everything you say, I must already know." Tapping her forehead, she added, "It's all buried in here."

An ugly smile.

"Why did you do it?" Julie said again.

Crimson from the glowing rose reflected in the black of his eyes, demon-like. Hannah held the flower in both hands, plucked from the lifeless rosebush.

Julie pointed to Elliot, who was about to strike.

She almost let him.

"Why did you put us through … what you did to us?"

The man resembling Calvin Stipes couldn't answer. Julie didn't know, meaning he didn't know. She'd have to ask the man on the other side of this reflection because they were not the same, no, although they could pass as twins. Doppelgängers.

He stepped closer.

"You can't hurt us here," Julie said.

"I'm sorry, Julie—"

"You're only saying that because—"

"No, Julie. I'm sorry, but I was trying to tell you that you're wrong. I can hurt you here, more than you know. You've been capable of hurting yourself for years. Imagine what I could do with that mind of yours. I can make you take out your knife …"

Julie pulled the pocketknife from her jeans.

"I can make you expose the blade …"

She flipped it open.

"And put it against your skin …"

The blade sliced into her shoulder, only as deep as the previous cuts, only as far as Julie had ever allowed.

"Stop it!" Hannah said, stepping around Julie.

"I could do this over and over and over again," he said.

Hannah offered the rose and he stopped. He dropped Elliot's leg at his side and held out his hands eagerly. She allowed him to take it by the stem, and he held it to his neck, the red transferring from the flower to his skin, the petals curling, burning, crumbling like ashes from his fingertips, transforming once again to a rose tattoo.

Julie buried the knife into its petals.

Life sprouted as she pulled out the blade, red spattering the encompassing white.

Falling to his knees, the man she once thought her father gargled out of the hole in his throat, trying to say words Julie wouldn't allow him to say, trying to wrap hands Julie wouldn't allow him to wrap around his neck to stop the bleeding.

Elliot pounced on top of him, biting into the wound, not feeding from him, but injecting his venom—the *Drakein* pulled from Julie. Shooting him up with the drug.

The dragon burned through him, bubbling his skin.

Elliot's spider form lost color, becoming translucent.

Hannah faded as well.

The whiteness brightened, absorbing everything, as if capturing the scene in a slowly-taken overexposing photograph. The film blazed, charred, turned black. Liquefied around her.

Julie collapsed and fell forward, immersed. She swallowed it in, breathless and gasping as the darkness flowed down her throat.

The hand reaching through the water wrapped around her child wrist. Frankie's mother yanked her out of the neighbor's pool, slapped her back to help her cough out the chlorinated water she had swallowed. A soft hand on her wrist: Frankie, asking if she was okay. Blurry turned less blurry as the black caterpillar with the red spot tickled her arm. And then a strong hand at her neck—her father's—as he shoved Frankie and her mother aside.

A powerful force pushed at the back of her neck to keep her head below the murky black. A heavy hand. Tepid water flooded her face.

Still holding the knife, Julie flailed, swinging blindly behind her, connecting.

The hand moved up and grabbed her hair, pulling her head back.

"Why won't you die?" a scratchy voice whispered in her ear.

The black world around her exploded with color as he lifted Julie out of the water and shoved her aside. She was back in the wheat field, at the stagnant pool. The man resembling her father had caught up to her. The knife buried into the side of his neck, to the hilt, directly centered within the tattoo rose petals.

He staggered and felt the handle.

"What do you want?" Julie asked.

"I want you dead," he said, limping forward, perhaps realizing the knife would be safer to leave in his neck. He looked around for the cane or the shotgun or whatever he had carried with him, but it was gone, lost in the water during the struggle.

"Why did you kill Elliot? Why did you make us do those things?" Julie stood and faced him. "What did we ever do to you?"

"You got in the way," he said, his voice hoarse, gurgling. *"Damn it!"* he said, once again toying with the handle. He revealed a sliver of metal and winced.

"I was in your *way?* All of this, because I was in your *way?*"

"Hey," he said, his voice hoarse, his next words bloody, "don't shoot the messenger."

He thought this was funny.

"Fuck you."

"I was there for Elliot, not you. You got caught up in the middle of it. I could have taken your life as well, but I was considerate. Hell, I thought I was doing you a favor making you inject that shit. Thought it would kill you softly. Like putting down a sick animal."

Elliot's story about helping the injured cat die came to mind.

"Thought you'd simply fall asleep and never wake up. But it did something to you. Turned you on like a sex-starved teenager. I watched a while. What's wrong with that?"

"Everything."

"I thought you'd OD and die. But somehow you survived, so now I gotta put you down for good. And this time I won't be so nice 'cause *this* fuckin stings."

He charged and tackled Julie to the ground.

She landed with her shoulders against the water, his body smothering her, knocking the air from her lungs. Julie had thrown her hands up in defense at the last moment, putting them by his face. She gripped the handle of the knife like a lever and pried. As his body contorted, she managed to roll him aside.

Grabbing his ankle and part of his leg, she attempted flipping him onto his stomach in the mud, but the leg came loose, rotating completely around in its socket. She stood over him, still unable to breathe, confused, still holding onto his ankle. She twisted and pulled and the leg slipped, exposing aluminum, kept pulling until the metal prosthetic pulled free from the pant leg. A shoe wrapped around a fake ankle, which connected to a metal shin and kneecap, and a cupped section of prosthetic previously wrapped around the man's partial thigh.

Julie stomped the knife jutting from his neck.

It took a moment to process what had happened with the leg.

The man tried to speak, but pain ate his words. He pulled the blade free and life spurted out of him.

She swung the artificial leg over him, pelting his head with an audible ping. Julie brought it down over his chest repeatedly, the air slowly returning to her lungs. He cowered, one hand to his neck, but the metal snapped his wrist. She flipped him over to fill his screaming mouth with mud, straddled his back, her knees digging into his armpits as he thrashed, pressed the prosthetic leg against the back of his neck to keep his head below the surface.

Long, opaque appendages ascended from the water, wrapping around his head; three more embraced his body and arms as Julie sprang off him; two more wrapped around his remaining leg. What was left of Elliot's arachnid form hugged the man's body from below, pulling him into the mud.

She imagined the spider biting into him again, this time to feed.

Ever so slowly, the man in the water stilled.

Julie knelt onto his back and reached around the body, around the skeletal legs, through the black water to her elbow. Her knee ground against a revolver hidden in the back of his pants. She thought about taking it, but left it there. The keys were in his right front pocket. She rinsed them in cleaner water and let the surface turn placid.

Her reflection revealed a woman covered in filth. Wet clothes clung to her skin, her shirt pulled down over one shoulder, torn.

The man next to her had sunk lower, barely visible, his head submerged. He appeared headless. She had never learned his name. Not Cal, but so much like her father.

And like her father, he'd meant to kill her, in a different way.

His own death: callous and liberating.

The *Drakein*-laced Visine bottle stood out in the clearing. A few drops would clear her mind and relax her nerves. She picked up the bottle and unscrewed the cap, then screwed it back on, tucked the psychotropic drugs in her pocket to return to Chase—probably dead in the car.

She found the cane at the edge of the clearing and kicked it into the water before following the trail they had made in the field and returning to the car. Avoiding the barbed wire, she climbed over the fence and onto the gravel at the roadside.

Chase clung to life in the passenger seat, smiling with purple lips, his skin pale and grayish-white. Blood pooled on the floorboard, but his hand clutched the sopping towel wrapped around his wrist. He looked scared, confused, and full of pain. It would probably take him a long time to die. Even through the pain, he showed a will to survive.

She could leave him there and walk home, because he was an asshole, but he deserved something other than bleeding a slow death alone in an abandoned car.

"You look terrible," he said, excited to see her but loopy, waving a bloody phone on his lap. "Hey, Keene called. Told him we were— we were running late. He said 'tha-that that's okay, Chase.' I don't think he loves me anymore, but you still love me, Julie?"

"I still love you, Chase."

"You take a dive in the dirt or something?"

Julie opened the driver door and joined him inside. She pulled the bottle from her jeans and placed it in his shirt pocket.

"Hey, thanks," he said. His head slumped to face her. "No more dragon?"

"No more dragon."

"Cool."

Just like that, they had an understanding.

"Shit will mess with your head. Where's …" he said, pointing toward the field, "the—where's the other guy, the, the limper?"

"Dead."

He smiled again. "I always liked you, Julie," he said. "Never liked that other guy much—what was his name? Doesn't matter. You ever meet someone and hate him from day one? You're an old soul, you know? I'm asking so many questions. I fucking *hate* questions. Why am I—why do I hate questions?"

She hadn't noticed before, but the glove compartment was open in front of him and held a few Chapstick-sized containers. Inside each were syringes of *Drakein-5*.

"Let's get you some help," she said, starting the car.

He stayed silent for the rest of the ride, perhaps fading in and out of consciousness. Julie checked for his pulse a few times to make sure he was still alive. Slow and unsteady heartbeats reminded her of something by Poe she'd read once that had always stuck with her:

> *Sometimes I'm terrified of my heart; of its constant hunger*
> *for whatever it is it wants. The way it stops and starts.*

Julie called ahead so they'd be ready. Chase didn't stir until they came to a stop in front of Brenden Memorial.

"We're here," Julie said.

"That was a trip. Ever wake from a good dream and want to go back?"

"All the time."

The emergency room doors opened to medics pushing a gurney.

"No Keene?"

"No."

"That's okay," he said, his eyes closing.

Julie reached in front of him for one of the containers in the glove box and removed a syringe of clear liquid. She pushed the plunger to free any air trapped inside, and slid the needle into his leg, injecting the entire syringe of *Drakein-5*.

"This should help you go back to that dream, Chase."

"You don't have to owe me anything, not anymore. Deal?"

She considered.

"Deal."

"Think you could babysit Colt sometime? I can't *stop* with these questions. Maybe I don't like questions 'cause—that's some, that's some *strong* stuff, wow, you weren't kidding—'cause I like answers too damn much. You'll babysit Colt sometime?"

"Let's get you some help first, and then we'll see."

"Thank you, love … hey, what's her name?"

"Who?"

"There's a deep red aura surrounding you, a smaller version of you, younger. Like a girl. What's her name?"

Medics took Chase inside, but she didn't stay to admit him properly. Instead, Julie parked the car in the hospital garage and left it there. Left everything there. She walked until her legs tired and then she called Frankie.

"You okay, Julie?"

How much should she tell her, how much *could* she tell her?

"I need help."

She decided to tell her everything, and promised herself she wouldn't flinch.

"I'll be right there."

◻ ◻ ◻

The wound is the place where the Light enters you, she explained so delicately, quoting Rumi, and that scars were physical memories, reminders that your past was real.

Frankie took care of Julie, as she always had. She dressed the physical wounds and addressed the emotional, and redressed and readdressed whenever needed. Julie would have new scars to go along with her old ones, but they were now a part of Julie Stipes, what *made* her.

They talked most of the night, outside on Frankie's front porch, until stars broke through the black of sky like spatters of white paint. Julie talked until her throat felt full of cotton and razorblades, until she had nothing left to say. She told her about Elliot, about the man with the rose tattoo—who she thought was her father—and about Chase, about the spider, about Hannah, although never calling her that for Hannah wasn't her only name.

Most important, Frankie listened, whether or not she believed her story.

"How much of this was real," Julie asked, "and how much in my head?"

Neither tried to answer for quite some time.

"The *D* was laced with something," Frankie told her, because Julie had become so easily addicted to the drug, and because psychotropic drugs were simply not addictive on their own.

"Can you take me somewhere?" Julie asked.

"Not there. Never again."

"No, somewhere different. I need to know."

"Need to know what?"

"Out of all this," Julie said, "I need to know if *he* was real. Elliot. I connected with him and we *had* something, if even for a short while. Can you take me to his home? I need to see."

"Did you love him?"

"I'm not even sure I know what love is, or if I ever will, but I need to know if he was *real*, because out of everything terrible that happened, out of *everything*, I can't get him out of my head. I guess a part of me loved him. Is that love? I need to know if he was real. Please. Will you do that for me?"

"Now?"

Julie did not know the address, but remembered enough to get them there, even so late at night—the only way she remembered it. They pulled up to a gray single story home with dark trim, a single bulb illuminating the caution-taped front door with its yellow triangle of light.

"This must be the place," Frankie said, rolling down the windows.

"This is the place," Julie said.

Where I grew up, Elliot had said what seemed so long ago.

Sprinklers hissed on and sprayed the front lawn as they had that night, and a light rain pattered the windshield, not enough to need the wipers.

He had said something about the door, she remembered clearly, that it used to give him nightmares; and she had mentioned the cat, that the *cat* was creepy. Small talk, mostly.

Red doors mean passion, which also means suffering.

The same black cat from before waited on the doorstep. The feline stared at them with proud eyes, and then yawned, revealing fangs. There was nothing grotesque this time, no hallucinations masking the truth, no gore other than the mouse or mole or whatever dead creature it brought to show Elliot this time.

"Her name is Spooks," Julie said. "She comes around whenever it rains because Elliot's neighbors don't have a covered porch."

She brought you a present, she'd said.

With a red lump at its feet, the cat cried out, a sad sound. Waiting for Elliot, she knew, and would probably wait forever, even though it wasn't *his* cat; perhaps the cat thought Elliot had belonged to *him*. Spooks walked in a circle around the red lump and cried out again.

"Looks like the neighbors left him behind," Frankie said, pointing to the realty sign in their front yard, something Julie hadn't noticed before.

A bright light turned Julie around in her seat, and she remembered the headlights that had flashed them momentarily as she'd straddled Elliot in the front seat of his car, and for a moment her heart hiccupped into her throat, but these were the headlights of a truck down the street pulling into another driveway.

Elliot's car was gone, she realized.

"You okay?" Frankie asked.

"I think so," Julie said, although she didn't feel so.

"We can go if you want."

She shook her head and returned her attention to the cat.

A part of Julie knew Spooks would be there, which is why she had Frankie stop at a convenience store so she could buy a small bag of cat food at a not-so convenient price.

"I'm okay," she told herself. "This is something I need to do."

"Want me to do it with you?"

Julie wiped tears that were starting to form and nodded, squeezed her hand.

They walked together toward the house, toward a red door that meant suffering, and to a cat and the red mass of something that had also suffered and was now dead—a present for Elliot, now a present for Julie, like some sort of sick sacrifice.

The color of blood; perhaps it was a warning.

"Hey Spooks," Julie said.

Spooks rubbed against her leg, instantly purring, nose prodding at the bag of food held at her side. There was a small stainless steel bowl by the doormat that she filled. Spooks simultaneously purred and attacked the food, even as she poured, purring while eating.

"That's disgusting," Frankie said, meaning the dead thing.

"The world's disgusting," Julie said, and for the briefest of moments something inside her mind flashed, like the effects of the

Drakein, only in reverse, the mouse folding in on itself, the blood and the gore inverting and pulling back into the creature until the red mess was once more an adorable field mouse with a twitchy nose and glass-button eyes.

"And the world is beautiful," she said, picking up the cat.

"You're taking the cat, aren't you?"

"I am. She needs a home, and the Heimlichs need a cat."

When Julie first thought of returning to Elliot's, she had wanted to break inside, to cut through the caution tape, to see for herself the crimson flower left behind on the floor—proof that Elliot had been *real*; to know what had happened between them had been something factual. Like the cut on her wrist—a future scar that would later help define her—she'd made using a piece of his jawbone; she'd cut herself in order to feel *something* rather than nothing, to know that she was still alive and capable of feeling anything at all.

But she no longer needed that assurance; she'd seen it all before, had survived. Elliot Cartwright had been real, she knew, and they had known love, if only for a short while.

Moths fluttered aimlessly around the lightbulb on the front porch, some fallen dead beneath. She'd read once that male moths and other flying insects were attracted to artificial light—false belief that such things were females emitting sex signals. *Was that right? Was life and death as simple as moths flying into flames and burning against unfuckable lightbulbs?* Phototactic attraction, or phototaxis, something like that. Confusion while navigating, the artificial light radiating in *all* directions instead of linearly, and their inability to keep the light—of what they believe to be the sun or moon—at a constant angle.

She could smell their deaths.

"Must be frustrating fluttering round and round and getting nowhere," Julie said, meaning the moths, meaning herself.

A death's-head hawkmoth landed hard against the wall, skull-face prominent on its back. *Acherontia Atropos.* She'd written a story about them back in high school.

Another ghost from her past.

Life is not so linear.

There were ghosts in this house now, she knew, ghosts of Elliot in his arachnid form, in whatever forms he cared to choose, and this gave her a strange sense of comfort knowing that a part of him still lived on, even after death. And there were ghosts elsewhere, and they would also live on, like those of her mother, and those of her father, and like Hannah, which made her stomach uneasy because she was not yet ready to understand.

"What if I'm pregnant?"

SCARLET HOURGLASS

[a fable by Julie Stipes]

Everyone knew what the color signified and every-one knew the shape. Red warned of danger, of evil. The shape warned that time would soon be up if crossing her path. The mark blazoned brightly on her stomach, which meant the spider most often kept her back to the world so she wouldn't scare anyone away.

Sometimes she exposed the hourglass proudly, dangling upside-down from her eight black legs.

STAY AWAY, she projected.

The spider didn't have many friends, if any. And she was okay knowing that. Soon she'd offer new life into the world, and no longer would she be alone.

Rain had washed away most of the web she had created. Beads of water glistened on what remained. Not much, but at least it was something …

She had captured a horsefly and some sort of

beetle the day before, planning to eat this morning to appease her future young, but the little silk blankets were gone—designed to protect, to preserve—and now were washed away, wasted.

An ache in her belly reminded her she was hungry.

Always, she was hungry.

She couldn't go out looking for food, though. Food had to come to *her*. That's how life worked for the spider.

And she had to rebuild, she knew, to survive.

In order for her children to survive.

Always, she had to rebuild.

Sometimes she had to start from nothing, like flowers re-growing after plucked or mown or eaten or burned, but this was not one of those kinds of mornings.

If only she could eat the flowers …

The roses always seemed so appetizing.

But STAY AWAY, they warned, like her.

Survival was much more difficult for widows. Although her silk was stronger than all other arachnids, this meant her webs were thicker, whiter, and more visible to prey. This meant she ate less often, sometimes foregoing nourishment for days, which is why she often saved meals for later, in those little white cocoons.

At least she didn't have to start completely from scratch as often, though. Not as often as most …

Daddy-long-legs, wolf spiders, and other eight-legged or unfortunate seven-legged neighbors had to continually rebuild from absolute nothing, even after the slightest of rains. She guessed that's why

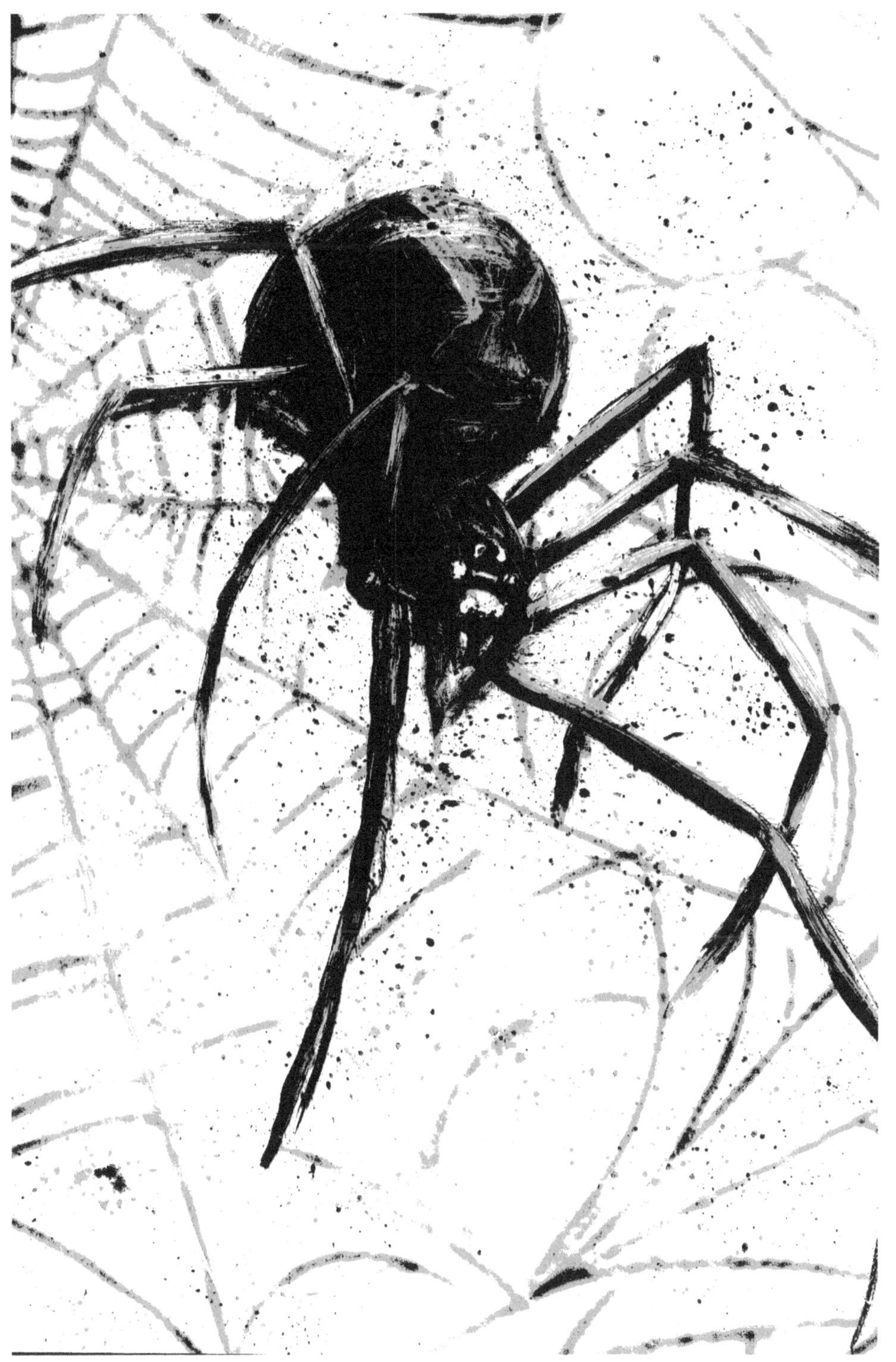

most built nests underneath the eaves, although *that* too came with risk.

Although seemingly four-legged, the strange bipeds that lived in these homes often wreaked havoc on both spider webs and their makers.

How could something as insignificant as arachnids—at least in terms of size—bring so much fear to something so large?

The world was such a strange, magical place.

Perhaps fear was ignorant to size.

Rain had damaged most of her current web, but she could easily add to the strands still anchored to the white picket fence and the rosebush below.

And so she began her rebuilding ...

What time is it?

Time to eat, the hourglass on her belly told her. Time to hide the scarlet mark and hide her body in shadows.

A hummingbird hovered near the web, possibly checking out her handiwork, but the spider's vibrant color warned to STAY AWAY for as long as the buzz of her wings held her there.

Pincher bugs skirted the web, as well as a line of black ants and an ugly bug of some sort, but none were tempted to cross the bridge she'd made between the rosebush and the fence.

They could *all* see her silk.

They could sense the danger.

The spider waited, patiently.

Always, tested by patience.

She rested one of her legs against the thick silk,

waiting for the slightest of vibrations of a not-so-lucky creature happening upon her trap, but the sun rose and fell and she stayed hungry.

The next day was equally still. Not silent, because there was a lot going on in her environment, but *still*. Not once did her web thrum with good fortune.

A field mouse scurried up the white picket fence. A creature so large would feed her for an un-guessable amount of time, and would feed her children, too, once they found their way into this world. She could take him. That much was certain. One bite and the field mouse would go down.

It would go *still*, like the warm afternoon, in a matter of moments.

The web could definitely hold the weight of a field mouse.

If not for her future offspring and ever-growing body, she could have outrun the mouse over a short distance, and ended him quickly. Life was never fair, however.

"I saw your hourglass from below," said the field mouse, "and your web. In the light, it nearly glows."

The spider ignored him. She didn't need his mockery or his insults. She needed food and the field mouse—

"And I see you *now*," he said.

She stepped out from the shadows, if only to let him know she wasn't hiding from anything.

"This is what my friends call 'the safe distance'," said the field mouse. "Our kind have seen what your kind can do. Some of our kind have even fallen to your venom."

The widow took a slow step forward. Not moving her body, but bringing one of her eight legs closer. Then she relaxed, letting the field mouse think she didn't pose a threat.

"I've seen you before," he said. "You are *alone*, aren't you?" The field mouse looked around cautiously. "I guess if you had friends, I'd be dead already."

If only he would leave her in peace. His presence alone could scare away her next meal. If only she were faster, more agile. Yet, she knew how to get rid of him. Mice weren't brave creatures, she knew. They were cowards, like the four-legged giants who walked on two legs.

All mouth and no bite.

The widow skittered across her web as fast as she could manage. The field mouse wasn't expecting her to do such a thing and nearly tumbled backward off the fence. She almost got him, her front-most legs brushing his tail.

The field mouse scurried away, hopping down and out of sight. Her empty stomach growled in anger, but the mouse was never prey in her mind, simply a nuisance that needed to go.

And in that regard, she had succeeded.

The rest of the night was still.

The children were starting to grow restless. They wanted out, hundreds of them, and when they broke free they would spill out like the seeds of a dropped fig. Hundreds of hungry children looking for food. Most would be born into this world, she knew, starve, and perhaps die, never having the chance to know what it was like to live. But not if she could help it …

Always, she would try.

The widow worked both frantically and ceaselessly to expand her web. She fully bridged the gap between the white picket fence and the rosebush. She worked all day and into the night, hungry and starving, determined to save them.

She would make sure they fed.

She would make sure they lived.

And then, if she had any fight left in her, she'd

focus on herself, because *always* she would fight. *Always*, she would try, until her dying day.

The black widow spider was nearly asleep, perhaps about to sleep the long sleep, when something plucked one of her many silk strings and sent a thrumming up her leg. A note of hope.

"What is it?" asked something greenish-yellow and wriggly.

"I don't know," said something yellowish-green and wriggly. "Looks like a shortcut to me."

They contemplated crossing.

"Let's take the longer route," said the yellow.

"It looks strong enough," said the green.

"We should continue the way we were going."

"Trust me."

"Come on," said the green. "I'll go first, to make sure it's safe." The green caterpillar stepped onto the silk. She struggled with her footing, but managed to crawl out a ways.

Her back legs stuck to the webbing.

Time was running out, so the spider danced across the silk with the last of her strength and lunged, fangs burying deep and fast. She retraced as quickly as she had attacked.

It wouldn't take long, she knew, but she always hated this part: the waiting, the dying.

The green caterpillar with the yellow stripes contorted, body arching and legs kicking, while her companion, the yellow caterpillar with the green stripes, inched away in the opposite direction.

She attacked again, not sure if it would make

the process go any quicker, but it seemed to help.

The mostly-yellow caterpillar turned back once more for her friend, the mostly-green one, so the widow stood upright on her back pairs of legs as a warning.

STAY AWAY, the red hourglass proclaimed.

And soon the other caterpillar was gone.

Working with haste, the widow spun her silk, turning the meal for her children round and round within her black needle legs.

She counted them, one by one, as they emerged into this world. A hundred ninety-six tiny spiders just like her.

Only one didn't make it, a male, born still.

The field mouse stopped by a final time.

"Congratulations, miss," he said.

He looked sincere, but looked something else as well: a shade lighter. Perhaps it was the sight of all her offspring moving in a seemingly never-ending fluid motion that set him off, or the young spider not moving at all. The field mouse disappeared into the shadows without saying another word.

She spun a small white blanket around the one that didn't make it, and carried him down to the rosebush. She walked over thorns and placed his body in the center of a rose with a color resembling the mark on her body. She tucked him in deep, where he'd be safe, at least until the flower opened under sunlight.

"To the light we shall return," she said, although not knowing why.

And then she began to rebuild as the rain turned to sleet turned to hail turned to snow …

She did what she had to do in order to survive.

No longer alone, she counted her children once more while dangling upside-down on her web. She turned over the hourglass, the rose beneath her much like a reflection.

A ROSE / AROSE

The earth is round, and so is Julie's belly, full with child; like the moon, Julie's hand rotates around the hemisphere, energy shining down and filtering through her body so the child inside knows her mother is there, on the outside.

"I feel you," the mother says.

Hannah. I'm going to call you Hannah.

"Do you feel me?"

Hannah kicks, and it hurts, but it's a good kind of hurt.

There were plenty of bad hurts in Julie's past, but none of that matters anymore. All that matters is Hannah. *Little palindrome Hannah.* All that matters is that she's born into this world healthy, has a chance to become someone special, to make a woman of herself, to be someone better than the ones who made her. Of course there will be complications, struggles, setbacks, but that's all part of life, what makes it all so interesting. She'll grow up fatherless, sure, a daughter to a young mother, sure, but so what?

Julie was raised in such a manner. Her father had been dead to her as a child, and her mother had raised her on her own, from what little she can remember. Some of her own childhood complications—an only child—included alcoholism, drugs, as well as abuses of the verbal, physical, and sexual kinds, and she'd even lived with "grandparents" for a short period of time, who weren't really her grandparents at all but a nice old couple who let her crash at their place during some bad times.

And I turned out fine.

"Can you feel the love I'm sending you?"

She presses her hand above her navel and holds it there, closes her eyes, and imagines Hannah inside the womb, feeling that hand, pressing her own against it. The energy shoots through her like a chill, and as if in response, the child turns.

"Yeah, you can feel me."

Moonlight fills her studio apartment, enough that she doesn't need to use the lights at this early hour in order to make her way from bed to fridge to couch, merely a few dozen waddles, and she'd rather leave the lights off anyway for a better view out the window, which is where she finds herself some nights, simply staring out into the great black nothing when she can't sleep.

It's a cozy apartment in Mosfellsbær, not far from Reykjavík in Iceland, where she worked in marketing until a few weeks ago for a small firm. She'd helped with editing digital and hardcopy ads printed in English, mostly, while attending an online U.S. college. Maternity leave had kicked in because of the pregnancy and she was told she couldn't come back for a while, although she still *wanted* to work. Maternity leave's not a lot of money compared to working, but she has enough to get by, enough to pay utilities, insurance, groceries, future stuff for the little one, some dining out now and then.

Iceland had treated her well, the healthcare especially. She had better insurance in Iceland on a visa for a one-year student/work contract than she'd ever had back home in the U.S. working full-time. Back home, Julie would have been denied coverage for her pregnancy, for having a "pre-existing condition."

Mosfellsbær was something new. Something very much needed. In Mosfellsbær, Hannah, not yet born into this world, was accepted as a life, not thought of as a liability.

"You like *hangikjöt?* Let's see if you like *hangikjöt.* You did yesterday."

It took a few attempts to learn the word, which translated to 'smoked lamb' and rolled off the tongue just as easily.

She'd lived in Iceland these last six months and had tried as many new foods as she could, given her budget, and had learned many new words and phrases in *íslenska.* Such a beautiful language for such a beautiful place. If she had known she was pregnant, she wouldn't have moved somewhere so exotic, but the island, and the people on it, had treated her better than she could have ever imagined, so it was a blessing more than challenge. It had been her girlfriend Frankie's idea to get away—to *run* away—from a past that had constantly chased her. Frankie hadn't meant Iceland, but half a world away from their hometown in Brenden, Washington was perhaps the best place she could have landed. Brenden wasn't far from Seattle, and considered a cow town to those in the city; perhaps she'd simply moved from cow town to sheep town.

"*Hangikjöt,*" Julie says again, mostly for practice. She can't help but wonder how long the word will last with her, how long she and her daughter might last in such a place.

Is this another string in a great line-up of strings that make up my life?

"*Mig langar til að prófa hangikjöt,*" she'd told the waiter named Kristjan, who sometimes flirted with her and she'd sometimes flirt back. *I'd like to try the smoked lamb.* She'd practiced.

"*Það er gott!*" he'd said.

She'd gone the night before, by herself, sat by the window, and when he'd taken her order and excitedly answered, she could only nod and smile because his words were foreign.

Tonight she's alone again, by a window, contemplating the baby sheep.

Straight from the container, Julie tweezes a small piece of smoked lamb, shoves it into her mouth—which has craved strange foods these last few weeks, or anything spicy, really—and tries to savor the bite, which she has to convince herself doesn't taste like smoked baby sheep.

Julie's the type of pregnant girl, she realizes, actively despised by women who are or have ever been pregnant: rail-thin with a baby bump, in other words. A trait she'd gotten from her mother.

"Are we good?" she says, placing a hand onto Hannah. "Okay. Cold lamb at—" she says, looking at the clock on the stove, "—3:18 A.M. Whatever you want, kid. You wake me up this early in the morning to pee, then you're hungry for leftovers. What next? Give me everything you've got. I can take it."

She's on the couch by the main window, overlooking not a great part of town, but not a bad part of town either because there doesn't seem to be any bad parts of town in Mosfellsbær, nestles a pillow behind her head, sets her feet up on the back cushions, and balances the leftovers on her chest. Such a different life than in Brenden: 1) It's quiet; 2) It's less expensive; and 3) You can see the stars, even when the moon's out. None of those three existed back home.

"That one's the North Star," she tells her unborn daughter, taking another bite. "Polaris. Why do I know this? I don't know. I guess I read too much, or *watch* too much. But don't get your hopes up, kid. I only know that one specifically. All those others? Well, there are a lot of stars out tonight, but all those others—"

As simple as someone flipping a switch and turning off its light, Polaris sinks into the dark blue ocean of the sky, and a needle-like pain stabs at Julie from within. Enough to crumple her on the couch and into a fetal position. The takeout spills to the floor. She hugs her stomach, instinctively protecting her child, the one who most likely caused the pain.

"Okay, so you don't like the *Hangik*—" she says, and the pain stabs her again, deeper this time, what feels like icepicks simultaneously jabbed into both ovaries.

Damn, Hannah! I feel you just fine.

"Okay-okay-okay, *ahh*, that's enough, that's *enough*, you're hurting me!" and Julie cries, much like a child.

And for a moment it's enough.

The pain lessens, and lessens, and as she straightens out her legs to relax it hits her again, even harder, and she swears a series of words in English that could work as either nouns or verbs. A contraction? This can't be a contraction. It's too early …

"*Ríða!*"

This is one of the bad hurts.

With over three months remaining of her pregnancy, Julie wonders about the pain, what it could mean, and suddenly there's a warmth between her legs, completely out of her control, like menstruation, or like she's urinated. She doesn't want to reach down, but does, to check.

Her fingers come back wet and tacky.

This isn't good, this isn't good …

Under the light of the moon, Julie's apartment and everything in it casts in black and white, like an old film, and so her fingertips appear black with the blood.

Like a crimson rose blooming, the warmth spreads between her legs, the pain taking Julie to the floor. She instinctively reaches for her cell phone to call Frankie, dials. The phone kicks back angry dial tone. It's an international call, she realizes. *I'm in Iceland*, she realizes.

911 kicks back the same.

What the hell is the 911 equivalent?

She's only six months, she keeps telling herself, only six months along and why is this happening? The cell phone, blurry and spinning, or is *she* spinning? She's pulled to the earth and spinning *with* the earth, something erupting inside—pulling and pushing and twisting inside—and it feels as if Hannah is clawing her way out, clawing her way *through* her mother to escape, and suddenly the past forces its way through the present, overlaying her memories, her thoughts.

Obsidian spider legs, each as long as her hand and each as sharp as shards of volcanic glass, one-by-one poking out from her womanhood, feeling for a way out, protruding from between her legs and finding the light and pulling the body to which they are attached outward, Julie birthing an arachnid spider the size of a small child, her *child, its spinnerets now free and pinching/breathing the open air, its body crowning, first a small black disc, like an eye opening, widening, the pupil blood-red and hourglass-shaped in this timeless moment/flash of something buried in her past—*

"Hannah!" Julie yells.

And the child wants out, takes itself out, one leg at a time until there are eight as sharp as knives and they all pull at once, twice, thrice, until a shiny black head-sized body squeezes out, and the legs pull again, and again, and again, as if Julie's body is breathing/pumping the thing out of her, the rest of its body crumpled and sliding outward and finally it's free and on the ground, awkward new legs dancing around in her fluids to find purchase, and not until they do does the body rise on its appendages, like the small bones of a child arching her back—

But the *Drakein-5*, the dragon, is long out of her.

She reaches for her monster child at her feet and says her name again, mother-like.

The spider draws back, one appendage pointing forward—

The child is not there to take her hand.

Julie blinks through the tears, through the illusion, through the confusing memory hallucination from long ago, and again finds her phone, which is no longer spinning. A quick search online gets her the emergency line for Iceland: 112. In three rings, she's talking to someone:

"*112 neyðartilvikum, hvernig get ég aðstoðað?*"

"English. I speak English. *Enska. Enska.*"

"Yes, *Enska.* What is your *neyðar* … sorry, your emergency?"

"I'm pregnant. Something's wrong."

"*Þú ert ólétt.* Are you in labor?"

"No. I mean, I don't know. I'm not due for another thirteen

weeks, maybe fourteen. Something's wrong and I'm bleeding and worried she's—"

"End of second *þriðjungi*," she says, not really to Julie. "Trimester," she says, finding the correct translation. You are at the end of your second trimester?"

"Yes, roughly. *Gróft.*"

"*Gróft,*" the woman repeats. "An ambulance from Icelandic Red Cross can be dispatched to your location. Do you request an ambulance?"

"Yes, thank you."

The spider bites into her again, which makes her cry out. She needs an ambulance. Without a car, she needs something faster than a taxi or public transportation.

"I'm showing you are at Álafossvegur 20, 270 Mosfellsbær. Is this correct?"

It sounds correct, although Julie had never pronounced Álafossvegur so elegantly.

"Yes. Álafoss Apartments."

"Please stay on the line with me."

I'm not going anywhere.

The last thing she needs in her life is losing Hannah. After six months having her in the womb, the two of them have become something special, each helping the other in their symbiotic relationship. Hannah helped Julie *through* life, while Julie *gave* Hannah hers.

She hadn't wanted her at first, when she'd learned of her pregnancy. Thought of an abortion, but only for a moment. She'd have to go through all of it alone. No parents. No husband, let alone boyfriend. And, of course, Iceland.

And her friend Frankie … half a world away.

Three weeks after landing in Reykjavík, Julie had stopped doing something she'd done since she was eleven, and a week after that found herself in a corner-side gas station market. She didn't know what they were called, the thing she was looking for—in *islenska* anyway—and for some reason she was afraid to ask, as if to buy such a thing in public was to be self-demeaning; to check for something you did or didn't want. ÓLÉTTUPRÓF, the box read, which when read by someone who can pronounce it properly sounds fancier than something to pee on: a pregnancy test. Did she want to know? Did she really want to know? Could she *be* pregnant? She couldn't be, which is why she found herself purchasing an *óléttupróf* from some guy who had probably lived on the island all his life, and why she found herself purchasing a package of cotton swabs, and a new toothbrush, and paste, and deodorant, and red nail polish, a package of gum, vitamins, and a few other things she didn't need because somehow, to Julie, this made the thing you peed on not exist so much at the checkout counter. When the man at the counter put the box into the bag with the nonessentials, the customer next in line, an older woman wearing some kind of fluffy hat and scarf, squeemed and said, "*Svo mörg börn ...*"

"Still with me?" the woman on the phone asks.

"Still here."

You're not going anywhere, she tells Hannah. She holds a hand between her legs, as if to keep the fetus inside. *You're staying right here.*

The woman on the other end stays on the line, walking her through a quick self-evaluation: asking about the blood, asking about the fall, asking about allergies to medications, her blood type—which Julie knows is AB- because it is not only the rarest of types but because she'd needed a transfusion once before—and Julie guesses the constant stream of dialogue is to keep her from losing her mind, which she's been on the brink of doing since the hallucination, her mind wandering from past to present.

Why are you doing this to me, Hannah?

Julie had tested herself twice more the week she discovered her pregnancy, each test telling her something similar: pregnancy plausible, a + sign, a silhouette of a baby. She kept all three tests lined up on her glass coffee table in the living room area, as if seeing them each day made it more permanent. She'd never gotten morning sickness—another reason for mothers everywhere to hate her—but she never got her period again, either, which is why she eventually made an appointment with a doctor. Not *her* doctor, but *a* doctor. Another reason she loved Iceland: healthcare was as it should be: universal. As a working student, Julie qualified for International Student Insurance—

"*Hvað heitir þú?*"

"Can you tell me your name?"

The words came from nowhere, and then again from a paramedic standing over her, as if he'd materialized out of a void. She had blacked-out, the world around her inverting from black to white, colors filling in shapes of an attractive man, albeit out of focus.

"Julie Stipes," she says. "*Ég heiti* Julie Stipes."

"American?"

"*Já.*"

She couldn't remember ever giving the woman on the phone her apartment number, but the paramedics had apparently found her.

They lift her toward them, Julie's body horizontal. Metal contraptions click into place and it's then Julie realizes she's been lifted onto a stretcher, and they carry her buoyantly to the back of a van with overhead lights twirling. Amid the maelstrom of color, Julie looks for the North Star, but it's gone, replaced by the bright overhead light in the back of the ambulance that's turned everything around her a fuzzy white.

"How far along are you?" a woman says.

The cold diaphragm of a stethoscope presses against her belly.

She never has the chance to answer.

"You have to make a choice," the girl in her dream says. She's maybe three years old, pushing four, strawberry-blonde hair like her mother and freckled skin that's nearly transparent, and a diffused glow about her that everything in dreams

sometimes have. There are two of her, one behind the other, but the other off to the side, as one would see the same person in blurred focus. They are the same but different, one moving independently of the other, out of sync, two separate entities trying to share the same time-space. But that's impossible; nothing can share the same time-space. Julie knows the girl is Hannah, little palindrome Hannah, because she looks like Julie as daughters look like mothers. I don't understand, *she tries to tell the girl, and then the girl, the wispy one less out of focus, pulls a flower out from behind her back, holds it out to Julie with both hands as an offering; the other shifts, her feet in a wider stance, her arms in front of her as if to embrace a hug; and so the two girls appear as one, with eight appendages. In the white-washed world, the rose glows vibrant red, which pulses like a heartbeat, Hannah's heartbeat. As if beating two-for-one, the heart of her child emits a flurry of fast pulsations. Da-bum da-bum da-bum da-bum.*

Julie wakes to hospital sounds and her first instinct is to hug her belly. She's alone in the room, on a hospital bed, covered by a thin blanket. She looks underneath, expecting blood. Her stomach still has a baby bump, but at only six months along it's nothing spectacular and Julie can't help but imagine she's lost her. Everything else seems fine. No blood.

Stainless steel hands hold fluids bags that drip into a tube connected to a catheter in her arm. An electrocardiogram monitors her heart. These various devices take care of her while hospital staff mingle in the halls. They seem to be gathered around a flat screen television mounted to the wall, these orderlies, as if gossiping about the news, or as if some kind of terrorist act as bad as September 11th, 2001 or worse just happened. The small television in her own patient room is powered off, the patient in the adjoined room sleeping noiselessly behind a drawn partition curtain with the silhouette of a woman leaning over him. And there's a third bed in the room, as if they had squeezed another patient into the already small space. On that bed is a boy of maybe seven or eight, a bag of blood dripping through a red tube connected to a catheter in his left arm while an IV bag drips clear liquid into yet another tube. His parents are huddled in chairs next to him, the mother holding a water cup with a bendy straw to the boy's lips so he can sip. A burly man enters the room, excuses himself, and joins the woman behind the curtain. More parents. One hospital room, three patients, four parents, Julie, and now a nurse writing long Icelandic words on the whiteboard next to Julie's bed.

"Hi. Who can I talk to about my child?" Julie says, holding her stomach. "I need to know she's okay." And then she adds "*Læknir?*" which she knows is *doctor.*

"*Fyrirgefðu. Ég skil ekki. Ég næ einhvern sem getur hjálpað,*" the nurse says. She holds three fingers in the air, like sign language, finishes writing something down, and leaves.

"You're in Landspítali Fossvogi, a hospital in Reykjavík." It's the boy's father, turned in his chair to face her. "She says she's going to find someone who can help."

"Thank you." She's about to ask about the hospital, why it's so crowded, but he turns back to his son, who is pale.

"Julie," says a new voice beside her.

"Yes?"

"Hi, I am Doctor Einstök—yes, like the beer—and will be looking after you today. This is Eva," he says, gesturing without looking, "and she will be taking your blood for analysis."

"Hello," she says. In front of her is a wheelchair.

"Don't worry, this is only for precaution," he says. "Will you please come with us? The hospital is, shall we say, a little busy today. We can take you somewhere private to discuss."

The doctor and the nurse each take a side and help Julie into the wheelchair, being careful with the tubes and especially the catheter. The nurse flips something up on the chair, another loud click, and transfers the IV bag to it from the bedside arm. In the chair, in a hospital gown as thin as paper, Julie feels so delicate, so fragile. She can't help but wonder about her clothes and who had dressed her and who had first undressed her. Under the gown, she's wearing nothing, her old underwear most likely cut away and thrown out.

"There we go," he says. "Now, if you'll follow us …"

Follow is probably not the right word.

They wheel Julie out into the main foyer, which is likewise crowded. She's slalomed around doctors and nurses in hallways, taken to an elevator, up one level, wheeled out to a reception area with phones ringing and not enough people to answer them, and finally to a small white room with a computer attached to a rolling cart, and a sink and counter cluttered with labeled containers; other than that the room is empty, perhaps a storage closet turned into a makeshift consultation room.

"A minute and I'll be right back. In the meantime, Eva will take your blood."

"*Blóð*," the woman says, which means *blood*, and that's all she says, first tying a cloth above what little bicep Julie has, then curling Julie's fingers for her and making her own fist with a stern look on her face so that Julie understands what she needs to do. She swabs Julie's arm and has the needle in and drawing blood in what seems a single fluid motion. A tube fills with deep red and together they wait, looking at the walls.

"AB negative," Julie says.

Eva smiles and nods, and when she has enough, this Icelandic vampire of a nurse, in another fluid motion, pulls the needle free and tapes a swab of cotton to where the needle had entered, then leaves the room.

Julie's alone for only as long as it takes for the door to close before it quickly opens.

"You've had a very long night," Dr. Einstök says, looking at her chart. "You're probably wondering about this, huh?" he says, putting his hand over her stomach, over Hannah.

She nods and feels a single tear trying to work its way out of her eye, like a single drop of *Drakein-5*.

"The room we had you in was crowded. A matter like this requires an amount of privacy to discuss. Apologies for the over-crowdedness."

He's stalling, she knows, avoiding the matter at hand, her pregnancy. The pain she'd felt in her apartment in Mosfellsbær, the blood, so much blood … *Blóð*.

She's suddenly cold inside, this special part of her now dead.

I've lost her.

"Here," he says, understanding.

Dr. Einstök widens the stethoscope around his neck. Through her gown, he puts the diaphragm against her belly, moves it around, listens, doesn't quite frown, moves it around some more, and then holds it steady.

"Listen," he says, removing the ear buds. Expressionless and apparently not a germaphobe, he hands them out for her to take. "You need to listen to understand."

Julie hesitates, knowing what she'll hear—what she *won't* hear: the bad news this doctor is trying to tell her without actually telling her: that sometimes hearing *nothing* can be more terrifying than hearing *something*. She'd first heard Hannah's heartbeat from an ultrasound a friend of a friend had given her after-hours at a vet clinic, like an animal. Now the thought of *not* hearing Hannah scares her more than anything.

She takes a breath and lets it out, puts the ear buds to her ears.

Hannah's heartbeat patters rapidly, like an echo of her dream.

Julie smiles, and the doctor offers half a smile in return.

Something is missing from that smile.

"We may need to schedule an operation," he says.

Complications.

"She's there," Julie says. "She's there. Is she going to be okay?"

The doctor looks quizzical, and adjusting in his seat says, "While you were unconscious, we ran an ultrasound, because of the bleed-

ing, and more specifically because of the amount of blood you lost."
He stops a moment and it's a big moment. "You said *she*."

"Hannah. Why, is it not a girl?"

"There were two."

"Two …"

"I'm sorry, but you miscarried the other."

"The surviving fetus is still very small. We will need to run some tests."

The first time Julie knew about Hannah, she was the size of a cashew, or so the internet told her. She'd called her a cashew until she'd grown to the size of a gherkin, and had called her a gherkin until she'd grown to the size of kumquat, and then she was a kumquat, and then a lemon, an avocado, always some kind of fruit or vegetable. At twenty-eight weeks she'd read Hannah would be able to sense light filtering in from Julie's world, that her eyesight had begun developing, and suddenly Hannah had become real. A child. A daughter. Twenty-nine weeks and her lungs and muscles were further developing. And now, somewhere between thirty and thirty-one weeks, based on when Julie could last remember having sex, she'd discovered Hannah was not alone all this time, until now.

A child is dead inside me, floating around, next to his or her sister.

"Definitely a girl," Frankie had said. She'd stayed with Julie for five days during spring break. She'd gone off to college to study microbiology while Julie had simply gone off to a geothermic wonder halfway across the globe. "I can tell the way you're carrying."

I'm carrying a dead child inside me.

Frankie was the second oldest sister of seven siblings, had watched her mother through four pregnancies and a miscarriage.

"You sure?"

"Have I ever lied to you?"

She hadn't. She'd always been there for Julie.

And now Julie would miscarry, one of them, anyway.

"There's a way you can check," Frankie had said.

"I know. I just can't afford it."

"No, not hospitals. Wait up a sec." Frankie had gone to the junk drawer in the kitchen, rummaged through until she found a pencil and a threaded needle with black string wrapped around a small rectangle of cardboard.

"What kind of mad voodoo shit is this?" Julie had said.

"You think 'cause I'm black all I know's *voodoo* magic?"

"I'm claiming voodoo 'cause you think you're gonna tell the sex of my child with stuff found in a drawer."

"Damn straight I am."

She'd watched as Frankie unwound the thread, tied a knot through the eye of the needle, and pushed the pointy end into the pencil eraser. *Ticonderoga #2.* She'd sharpened the tip—shavings falling right into the open drawer—and satisfied with her work, her voodoo, Frankie held the contraption by the thread so that the pencil dangled like a pendulum.

They'd both sat at the small round table in her nook.

"Hold out your wrist. No, your other one."

Floating inside me.

Julie had done what she was told and Frankie took Julie's hand in hers and helped it to rest on the table. She'd dangled the makeshift pendulum over Julie's open palm and told her to relax, to breathe normally. They'd both sat in silence, Frankie watching the pencil go still, Julie watching her own heartbeat on the veins of her wrist, to which Frankie gradually lowered the tip of the pencil so that it hung about a quarter-inch above Juile's somewhat transparent skin.

Slowly, the pendulum had begun to rock.

"You're making it move," Julie had sad.

"Look at my fingers. Does it *look* like I'm moving it?"

"You're moving it."

One child moving; the other child not.

"No. I'm not, *you* are. Your providence is moving it."

The tip of the pencil had rocked back and forth, back and forth, a sixteenth of an inch at a time, an eighth of an inch, gradually changing from a single line of motion to more oblong in shape, a manifestation of tiny counter-clockwise irregular rotations slowly morphing until they were nearly perfect circles, a full quarter-inch in diameter. A clock reversing time.

"Circles means it's a girl," Frankie had said, sure of herself.

Hannah, if it's a girl.

"What signifies a boy?"

"Back and forth: lines."

Asche, if it's a boy, which could also work for a girl.

"You're totally making it move."

"Could I *totally* be making it move, in perfect circles? You think I'm *that* good?"

The circumference of the circles had then narrowed until the pencil came to a stop above Julie's wrist. They'd both waited a while, each holding a breath.

"I guess you're only ever gonna have one," Frankie had said. "More than one and it stops between kids, then starts up again, either circles or lines. I've been right every time with my mom. Last time I tested her, it went circle-line-circle-circle-line-circle-circle."

"What if you tested her now?"

"Circle-line-circle-circle-line-circle-circle. Every. Time." She'd rambled it off like she'd rambled off her siblings as simple shapes a hundred times before. "I'm my mom's fourth circle."

"Have you ever tried it on yourself?"

"Yeah. No kids."

"Let me do it."

Frankie had handed the pendulum to Julie and traded places with her. Julie had let the string and pencil go still, slowly moved it over Frankie's wrist. Nothing. She'd tried it again, still nothing. She'd even tried making the pencil move, but it danced awkwardly.

"Try it on yourself," Frankie had said, and so she had.

A circle had developed, then nothing.

Hannah.

"The other child is too far along to birth properly," Dr. Einstök says, the bluntness of his words bringing her back into the now. "This is much different than—how would you say—the *hverfa tvíbura*, the syndrome where one twin is *frásogast*. When one twin is absorbed into the uterus," he says, putting up two fingers and bringing the second down so that he's pointing at the ceiling, either signifying the loss of a child, or a lost child going to heaven. He then points with both index fingers and brings them together, in parallel. "Your twins appear MoMo, or Monoamniotic-Monochorionic, which means they share the same placenta sac, but have two separate *naflastrengur*. They are both girls, identical. You understand *naflastrengur*?"

He opens the door and sticks out his head, shouting to someone in the hall.

"*Hjúkrunarfræðingur, naflastrengur?*"

A woman answers: *umbilical cord*, and he rejoins her.

"Same placenta, different umbilical cords. We are concerned about the cords, sometimes they become entangled." His fingers curl around one another. "We could try *Sulindac* to reduce amniotic fluid, to limit your child's movements, but that is high risk this early in the pregnancy. And there are other complications."

The doctor's expression hints horrific, perhaps something noticed during the ultrasound. His eyes move to the floor so as not to look at her.

Complications, a nice way of saying *Oh, the atrocious things I've seen.*

"I just want Hannah to be okay."

Julie never imagined everything happening all at once, not like this, with the last third of her pregnancy suddenly stripped away. The discovery of Asche, and her loss, is a plague in her heart not yet fully developed because everything is so right-the-fuck-now.

I wish Frankie were here. She'd help me through this.

"We will do everything we can to make sure Hannah survives. Cord *þjöppun* is too common in the third trimester. I know. It's sad I know Monoamniotic-Monochorionic because there is no translation, but *þjöppun* … eh, *compression*, or kinked like a garden hose."

She imagines Hannah with an umbilical noose around her neck.

The doctor himself looks choked, his eyes rising to meet hers.

"Cesarean is preferred between weeks thirty-two and thirty-four for MoMo twins, and you are close to that based on my observations from the ultrasound. We will administer steroids, which will help stimulate Hannah's lung development, reduce risk of infant respiratory distress. This is what I believe we should do in your situation."

Julie had seen premature babies before, on television, in the movies, always looking so small and so delicate, tiny arms and legs curled up like dead tarantulas on their backs—*like Reese*—and fighting for every breath so as not to be their last, those clear-plastic bins they were kept in, the machines and tubes and wires and *oh god now it's my child!*

And what of the other, the unborn, the one with the noose around her neck?

The girl she'd never name Asche.

"What … what will happen to—" she says, unable to get the words out.

She can't breathe, as if the noose is around her own neck, the room spinning counter-clockwise like Frankie's pendulum, impossible starlight filling her peripheral vision with blinding light, and then going black, a dark room spinning out of control. Circles.

A girl, the room tells her, singular, *and then nothing.*

"You're doing great, Julie," someone in the darkness says, a gentle voice. "Deep breaths, counting backward from ten." She's turned onto her side, a bee sting in her spine. She doesn't want to count backward; she wants to count forward … *Ten*, she says.

❑   ❑   ❑

The spider wants out of her, the arachnid child. Like sharpened metal legs, each appendage stabs at her belly from inside, the creature/child clawing its way out of her, not through her womb this time, but through her stomach. Black needles jut outward from her belly button, like sharpened-whittled-blackened bone, first one, then two, then four, piercing through, and then the bones split so that eight legs are out and reaching for leverage against her swollen abdomen, like the naked wires of an umbrella against her skin, and they pull, and pry. Numbed from pain, her stomach opens from the middle, like a flower under the sun, the red hourglass pushing its way through, the glass, breaking and tearing the skin, the red oil/sand within spreading as the slimly obsidian body of the creature/child protrudes, back-end first, spinnerets pinching the air, until the bulk of its mass is finally freed, followed by the head. The child/creature falls to Julie's side like a charred octopus or squid, its black body struggling outside the amniotic fluid. And then four hands reach down from above: two taking the dead twin at her side, two reaching inside the wound for the other, for Hannah—

"Nine," Julie says, sounding like the German word for *no*, and she realizes she is still counting backward from ten, the woman who had apparently started the anesthetizing standing tall over her, ghostlike. The faint silhouette of an apparition. She holds what looks like a face and spinal cord of a semi-transparent android, all a blur. *No, not an anesthesia mask at all,* Julie realizes—*that's not how a C-section works*—nor is it attached to air tubes of any kind. Another doctor with a facemask transmogrifies in its place within the overly bright room. He holds a long needle with a fat white handle shaped like the hilt of some miniature ancient sword, and pulls away from her, rewinding, as if he were in the middle of stabbing her with it had thought better. Clear liquid still waits in its reservoir, unused, the needle merely used to poke her. He sticks her with a smaller needle, injecting something warm into her arm.

"Where's Hannah?" Julie says, still on her side. Her back is cold and exposed, the papery gown no longer tied together but open wide. Her stomach still bulges with child.

More than one child: one alive, one dead.

"You're doing great, Julie," the doctor says, helping her roll onto her back. "I had to stop the spinal epidural because your water … *braut. Gott?* Everything is happening quickly now."

"Broke," the woman next to him translates, meaning her water.

Julie knows the word, along with the *'Good?'* that followed. But nothing is *gott*. She's fading in and out of consciousness, barely there, barely *here?* And they are trying to wake her, or to at least *keep* her awake, holding shit under her nose lest she fall into dreamland, injecting her with drugs, and she can't help but think of the vile of *D-5* she'd once been forced to shoot up her arm lest she and/or Elliot take a shotgun blast to the face, not that it mattered.

When did my water break?

The small hospital room darkens to black, brightens blindingly, her world a strobe of flickering reality. Time ticks and stalls. Seconds. Minutes. Hours. Indistinguishable.

"I'm—" Julie says, interrupted by a pain in her abdomen. A needle pokes her from within this time, either Hannah or Asche wanting out.

No, nothing is gott!

"We will not be able to deliver cesarean, but I have faith in your strength."

The doctor sets the epidural needle on a tray and with the help of the other woman in the suddenly crowded room, rolls Julie onto her back and lifts her into an upright position, knees spread lazily but pointing to the ceiling. They are prepping her for delivery, she knows, getting the stirrups or whatever they're called, laying out metal instruments, gloving hands, sterilizing, machines making all kinds of ruckus, scrubs running around like green/blue ghost streaks.

How can I be already having a child?

This wasn't supposed to happen for another few more months, but suddenly the moment is here; something she hadn't considered fully until this very moment … how much it might hurt and what it would do to her body to bring new life into this world. And now, learning there are *two*; one alive, the other …

They lift her gown or cut it away—a blur through wet and tired eyes—and squeeze a tube of cold gel onto her semi-bulbous stomach. A cart with a monitor is unexpectedly in front of her. Dr. Einstök presses a dildo-like thing against her skin, moving it around while a single heartbeat *warble-warble, warble-warbles,* or perhaps that is the machine itself, simply sonic vibrations, like someone underwater screaming *wow-wow, wow-wow.* The screen reveals black-and-white glimpses inside her body: speckled nothing, then part of a torso, a head, an arm or foot, a fanned display of two tiny bodies sharing a womb, revealed one puzzle piece at a time.

Face-to-face, the fetuses appear to be drawing away from one another after a kiss. The doctor slides his magic wand to reveal their feet, which are tangled together, and Julie has to wipe her eyes, but no, the images are clear, even through the tears and the strain are two feet, not four; and then two hands, not four. The doctor is looking for something more. The doctor is looking for Asche, and suddenly her forever-sleeping face is on the screen, expressionless, choked by her own umbilical cord or perhaps Hannah's because there are two.

Monoamniotic-Monochorionic. Momo. Naflastrengur.

The ultrasound gives Asche life, gives her movement, although Julie knows otherwise. And then Hannah's face fills the screen— *wow-wow, wow-wow*—with her smile bringing a smile to Julie's own lips before the pain once again forces her into a clenching grimace. She can't help but scream out because it hurts.

Six months, only six months …

Hannah's hands seem so delicate, forming and un-forming tiny fists as the image on the monitor moves between the twins. Hannah's fingers open ever so slightly, pawing, as if reaching out to her dead sister. Two dainty hands meeting—

(*nubs*)

no hands at all; the petite fingers brush against handless append-ages—*too many appendages*—as though Asche's hands were severed at some point, or had never developed at all, or perhaps absorbed into the shared amniotic fluid.

What am I seeing?

"*Meðfæddur,*" Dr. Einstök says, not to Julie, but to the other woman in the room, who jots the strange word onto the papers on her clipboard.

"*Aðeins viðhengi,*" she says.

Julie tries to say those same words with inflection, to let them know she's also present in the room and in-the-know, but instead the contractions turn her words into miserable cries.

She pries open her eyes to see the monitor, which moves to—

(*nubs*)

feetless appendages—*too many appendages*—dangling by Hannah's perfect toes. A trick of the light, Julie tells herself, or one of the umbilical cords folded and folded and folded into what had falsely appeared as too many legs.

"Breathe, Julie," the doctor says, and he's right.

She's not breathing at all, but holding her breath.

It all comes out at once: the breath, the fear, the insane war cry. Her sounds are unworldly yet primal. She pushes, hard. Pushes again with what little strength she has remaining.

"Breathe, Julie," someone says, now, or perhaps hours ago, "but try not to push."

Time is a broken, lying clock.

"Push," someone says, a familiar voice that sounds like Chase.

A single drop in each eye.

Julie welcomes the rush, but the drug is not there for the taking. The dragon is long out of her system. Had she thrown the last vial away, stashed it somewhere, given it back to Chase? She can't remem-

ber, doesn't want to remember, not now. No, one bottle remained. The dragon. All she wants is to push it out of her.

"Try not to push."

Already Julie is in another room.

"Get it out of me!" she screams, meaning Hannah, meaning Asche, meaning whatever creature she'd seen during the ultrasound.

"*Legháls er að stækka fljótt,*" someone says.

"You are dilating quickly," the doctor says, translating not only the islandic but the angry look on her face. "Are you ready?" he asks.

No-no-no-no!

The contractions hit her again, buckling her.

"Let's see where we're at," the other woman says, Ava, looking between Julie's legs, which at some point had found their way into stirrups. "Yes, very quickly. *Very* quickly."

She trades places with the doctor and takes a different syringe from the metal tray and plunges its needle into a catheter attached to Julie's arm, injects the entire thing into her bloodstream. The rush is instant, and welcoming, filling Julie's entire being with warmth, a white spark of electricity shooting up her spine, blinding her with something akin to orgasmic ecstasy.

The drug transports her to another where and another when.

Julie's been here before, a place the little apparition girl had called the trial room, albeit the last time she'd fallen through glass in order to find herself wandering within the white. The little apparition girl had been Hannah—or who would eventually become Hannah—there to lead her to a flower ... No, not to show her a flower blossoming, but something terrible.

"Bad things happen here," she had said.

"What kind of things?"

The girl had looked to her feet, then—Julie remembers it clearly—and had shrugged, as if too afraid to say anything, as though revealing truths from this possible future might erase her potential for ever existing.

"What kind of things, Hannah?" Julie had asked.

The girl had simply pointed at Julie in the mirror—but where is the mirror now?—as blood welled beneath the paper gown in her reflection, a dark crimson stain against the white. She had watched it flower through the fabric, running down her leg, a sharp cramp bending her in half. Julie had grabbed at phantom pain, then, and grabs at it now. She had pried her fingers away, expecting menstrual blood, but her fingers had come away clean. In the past—or precognitive future—in the trial room, wherever and whenever that may be—Julie had looked down, the blood gone, despite the intense but otherwise familiar pains of a period.

Ghost pain troubles her again as Julie faces not a mirror this time but herself in the empty white. Looking down, the lower half of her hospital gown wells with blood, which flows down her inner thighs. Sticky red covers her fingers.

Hannah is not here this time, to help her, to guide her through whatever this is, but if she were, she'd be rocking on the balls of bare feet, Julie knows without a doubt, rolling the fabric of her dress between her little fingers.

As quickly as the blood in the mirror had appeared, then, it had disappeared. Julie clearly remembers the intense pain of what had happened—as it happens now—like a hot coal migrating past her stomach and beneath her intestines. She feels something moving inside beneath the baby bump, something hard, something pushing back.

What is the opposite of déjà vu?

"Can you feel it kicking?" Hannah had said.

Her unborn self? What would become of Asche?

"Can you feel me kicking?" the little apparition girl had perhaps wanted to say. "Can you feel her kicking? Can you feel us kicking?"

"I feel you," Julie tells the white. "I feel both of you now."

Pain drops Julie to the floor, as it had then. The pressure inside her round belly moves lower and severe cramping makes her cry out in the empty room. Her scream reverberates off the walls—if there are any walls—and the sound is inhuman, demonic, the frustrated way Death must sound when touching a shoulder and the person attached to it doesn't die. She looks underneath the hospital gown again and lifts her fingers from her crotch. They came back tacky and red, as they once had in her reflection.

Uv àjéd.

And then she remembers what had happened next, and what would thus happen now, but she is no longer afraid. She is willing. She, as the doctor had asked, is finally ready.

Julie's body contracts as blood spills freely from between her legs. The tips of two black, skeletal appendages tear out of her. She feels the urge to push, and when she pushes, more of the creature comes out. Slimy, jointed black legs claw at the air, each nearly eight inches long, stretching her body wider, multiple elongated legs grazing her skin, cutting into her like knives—like hesitation marks, like the cuts she had sliced into her shoulder when she was a child—as they struggled in the wet for leverage to escape.

With every push comes a jolt of lightning through her body—

[flash]

"I need you to push," the doctor says, and then *"Ýttu erfiðara"* either to Julie or the others in the room. There are three: Dr. Einstök, the woman from before, and the hazy image of a man standing behind them. Through the strain, and because of the lighting, this third person appears to have smoky wings trailing from his back, or her back—for a lack of features—nearly touching the fluorescents above; his/her face is a blur, or not there at all, his/her hands held at the sides, as smooth as batons.

"I *am* pushing!" Julie screams, but she's not. The pain is too much, even with anesthetics or whatever the woman had injected her with failing to numb her below the waist.

Julie's fists could be crushing walnuts.

Elliot's jawbone, she imagines, digging her nails into her palms. She holds onto that visual, now holding two pieces of bone, one in each hand. She squeezes until she conjures his imaginary teeth cutting into her skin, digging into her life lines. Cutting herself to feel *something, anything.* And then she once again clenches her teeth—

soon they will shatter—and pushes, pushes, pushes, willing the thing out of her. She pushes what feels like daggers. Breech. *"Fætur fyrst?"* she manages to ask, knowing the words.

"No, *höfuð fyrst. Gott,"* the doctor says. *"Mjög gott!"*

The woman next to him says, *"Króna,"* a single word, like the constantly changing aura around the sun, and without translation, Julie visualizes what they are seeing: Asche's crown, Julie's body opening wider to allow her passage into this world. Somehow she knows it's her and not Hannah. Her head reflects in each side of the doctor's glasses as twin gray irises.

I am the vessel, Julie thinks, a lyric of some song long ago or maybe the title.

She pushes as the doctor's eyes widen, his expression mostly hidden by the facemask, but fear of the unknown is there, hiding. The woman next to him steps back with a hand to her mouth. The featureless man/woman behind her steps forward, still out of focus, his/her angel-like wings spreading to blot out the light of the room.

"Push," the doctor says, his voice less confident.

She pushes. Pushes. Not breathing, but pushing. The sun between her legs burning. The son between her legs both pushed by Julie and pulled by her doctor. She pushes. Not breathing, but pushing. Until she feels her first daughter's lifeless body sliding out of her, infinitely long, until she's finally out, along with something else, a knot of unknown. Julie finds air, takes in a deep breath. She expects the child to do the same, but the child is incapable. The child doesn't cry. The child cannot breathe. The child's not held by her feet and slapped on the back to clear her lungs, for they had never fully developed to breathe on their own. The stillborn child is simply cradled, the noose tight around her neck. The twin reflections in her doctor's glasses ... the first of the twins ...

The color of ash.

An umbilical cord is clipped with precision, and then a second time, a third. A mess of cord. The doctor playing Cat's Cradle with the spider web her spinnerets have woven over the last six months. Untangling the first-born.

Hannah is still inside her, needing out. *Now.*

She imagines the second body churning within her body, the head turning toward the welcoming light of the room, which is no longer unobstructed by the dark aura of imaginary wings—the faceless and out-of-focus stranger merely a trick of shadows.

"You're doing well, Julie," the doctor says, turning toward the other woman in the room—the *only* other person ever *in* the room. Ava. No, not Ava, someone else.

She's a—

(ljósmóður)

midwife. Julie remembers the word in both languages at once, and she is also seeing the lifeless child through a blur of tears, for she is also crying as she accepts the lifeless body and takes it away. For the briefest of moments, Julie sees Asche before the midwife turns and leaves for another part of the room, out of sight.

Asche, a name for either a boy or a girl.

[flash]

The child is out of her and taken away, but not by the doctor. He's taken by the aura-winged, out-of-focus 'other' with seemingly no hands of his/her own, with no face, with no special features at all; this is why Julie thinks of him/her as a genderless 'other,' as though from a different time and place, perhaps another realm of existence altogether. Another where. Another when. A guardian, she muses. A guide.

Without hands, he/she somehow holds Asche, as small as a bundle of socks, cradles her, leaving a bloody trail in the floorless white that disperse like wet footprints on hot sand.

It's her own blood, Julie realizes, looking—

(is there such a thing as down?)

at her hospital gown.

He's/She's whispering to the child: "Lives of great men all remind us / We can make our lives sublime / And, departing, leave behind us / Footprints on the sands of time."

Julie's heard it before, some sort of religious poem. Frankie used to have a poster on her wall with those same words, or ones slightly altered. There were so many versions and snippets of similar poems about god or whatnot. But the prints left behind by this ghostly visage are far from those normally left behind by foot, for he/she is also seemingly without feet. If they can be called legs, they disappear into not sand but absolute nothing as he/she continues whispering: "My precious child, I love you and will never leave you / Never, ever, during your trials and testings / When you saw only one set of footprints / It was then that I carried you."

As the 'other' and the unbreathing girl grow distant, the two become one and dissolve into a small ball of red light, too bright to even—

"Hannah is on her way," the doctor says with an intense but sad countenance. He changes his focus to the next child—*she will always be my daughter*—to the burning sun between her legs, to the *króna*, to a new crown forming. Julie reaches out with motherly desperation, wants to hold her, more than anything else in the world. Moments ago she hadn't known of her existence, but wants to hold Asche nevertheless. Like a supernova, light explodes around her.

She's alone, at first. The endless white is completely silent; it is here she finds peace, if only for a moment. Temporarily blinded, she walks through the nothing, following a now-vanished path of red dots. The white seems to go on forever, although there's no necessity for direction or valuation for distance or space. No north or south or east or west. No footprints or blood spots to guide her. Only past and future. Progression and retrogression. There is only white, until Julie happens upon the rose.

Blood no longer seeps through her hospital gown as she leans down to the glowing red flower. Julie is clean—how she had first found herself in the Land-spítali Fossvogi hospital in Reykjavík—and for now feels no pain.

The rose is there for her, she knows, for Asche. Perhaps left there to find. Perhaps a part of her. It rests upon the tiny body and pulses steadily on behalf of a heart. Touching its petals, Julie is met with warmth and a never-before-felt energy that surges through her every fiber.

Hannah is there, too, still in Julie's swollen belly; the unborn child kicks, wanting out—but Julie is numb to any discomfort.

Still with child, and with a still child.

Half-pregnant; half-mother to not-so-identical twins.

The child at her feet, Asche, is perfect in every way. She wants to be held and so Julie holds her, rocks her gently, sings a lullaby with made-up words because she doesn't know any. She nestles her in the crook of her arm and places a free hand over Hannah, sings to her as well.

"I know it's difficult," says a voice, "but I need you to push, just one more—"

[flash]

Sudden pain inverts the room, and Julie realizes she's back in the delivery room. An electrocardiogram or some other device hollers warnings, along with the metallic clanking of instruments. Islandic words flutter between the others in the room, but they mean nothing. She's blind, and at first imagines a hand held over her eyes—the faceless and out-of-focus 'other,' perhaps—to keep her from seeing what no one should ever see; but then those fingers widen, like mini-blinds twisted open. Julie pushes, as instructed, and when she can no longer take the pain, she stops, her world slowly solidifying back into place in a series of steamy lines: the doctor's head, bloodily-gloved hands between her legs, her hospital gown soaked red.

A second labor.

He cuts at something—or had already cut, she understands—making room for Hannah, lest Julie vaginally tear. An *episiotomy*, she'd once read, *a surgical incision into the perineum*.

The child is small, but so is Julie, and the pressure lessens.

"We are nearly there," the doctor says.

And no, he's not holding—

(her father's pocketknife, her *own* pocketknife)

a scalpel … for Julie can see the top of Hannah's head peeking out now, reflected in the doctor's glasses as she looks over the gown. Not a pair of gray eyes this time, but *pink*, her own white skin around each pupil-less iris and the mirrored fluorescents giving the doctor fiery, bunny-like eyes—*tapetum lucidum, their light-reflecting surfaces nearly glowing. Like the rose.* The thought of a rabbit or bunny or any other animal staring at her exposed body is enough to make her laugh, to stop her from pushing.

"Can't stop now. I know it's difficult," the doctor says, "but I need you to push one more time. One … long, *hard* push."

One more push. One more push. One more push. How many more times is he going to fucking say it? Just one more push—

(of the needle, of the drug)

Never had she so desperately desired a dose. A single drop, just this once. She'd brought a bottle with her to the island, she suddenly remembers. *Is it back at the apartment?* An eight-milliliter bottle of Visine laced with *D*, a final gift from Chase before she'd said her goodbyes—for saving his life after first almost ending it with the unfortunate slash to his wrist; that was Chase's sardonic humor. Not that Julie planned to ever use again; her fight against the addiction is simply knowing she *won't* use. "I own you," she'd said to the bottle more than once in the past. *In my purse? In my purse, here at the hospital.* She'd had it with her in her carry-on luggage, the bottle under three ounces and TSA-approved. Sure, she had to ditch her Diet Coke at security to help save lives, but the drug had made it through easily enough. A single drop in each eye to help ease the pain.

Julie screams, a deafening sound—

[flash]

◻ ◻ ◻

As the flower's light begins to dim, so does the child. "No-no-no-no," she says, trying to grab her, to hold her, but Asche is not really there and her fingers easily pass through. The perfect little body fades, synchronous with slowing pulsations of the rose-light, until their shared heartbeat is still.

(you can't stop now)

The flower blackens and curls, petals turning to ash.

(I know it's difficult)

He disappears and so Julie grabs for the rose instead, which crumbles within her fingertips and turns them gray. She finds herself alone in the white, once again, until a stab deep inside her gut bends her into a fetal position.

(but I need you to push one more time)

Hannah is on her way. You have to think about Hannah now.

(One ... long, hard push)

Save her.

(You can do it)

Save her, the little apparition girl had said.

On her back, Julie spreads her legs and props up her knees, finds the strength to push to push to push—oh god—to push and she reaches down to feel what's happening because she cannot see—a crown, the top of Hannah's head—her body open so impossibly wide why the fuck would anyone ever want to fuck?— and pulls her hand back only to find it covered in gore and shit—is that shit?!—like trying to piss out a mango—and suddenly she's both laughing and crying through the pain and the hurt and biting her lip to stop herself, tasting the blood and feeling the child passing through—blóð, blóð, blóð—yes, I can taste the blood, motherfucker—and reaches down once again with both hands and feels the head—Hannah's entire fucking wonderful head—gently touching an ear, a nose, a brow, like a baby doll, and once the shoulders are free Julie grabs the slippery child and begins to pull and slide and push and—eeuughh!—has to remember to breath, just breathe—please be alive, please be alive, please be alive, Hannah—if only to give her the strength for one ... long, hard push—

The whiteness brightens, absorbing everything, as if capturing the scene in a slowly-taken overexposing photograph. The film blazes, chars, turns black. Liquefies around her—

[flash]

As a child cries in the delivery room, Julie cries, or it's all in her head. She's lost an entire trimester of pregnancy, and an unexpected second daughter, but Hannah is finally here … her daughter, little palindrome Hannah, still tethered.

"Can I hold her?" Julie asks, reaching out.

"*Brothætt,*" he says, looking to the midwife. "*Brothætt?*"

Inaudible pulses on the monitor: Julie's heartbeat.

"Fragile," she says, translating.

The doctor clamps the second umbilical cord, cuts it free, and returns attention to Julie. "We would normally wait a while before"— looking to the ceiling for the word—"disconnecting you from her, but time is important. *Það er mikilvægt.* Hannah is very small. Nearly full-term, for twins, but still considered premature because of her size. She will go to pediatrics from here where they will—"

"I want to hold her."

"They will take care of Hannah, run tests, clean her up, and keep her warm; what we would normally do here after birth, letting you hold her for your warmth. She will require assistance for some time."

Inaudible pulses on the monitor, slowing.

"Will she be okay?"

"She will be okay."

Julie watches as the midwife gently takes the child from Dr. Einstök. With a soft cloth, she wipes away some of the mess covering her pink body. Hannah is tiny enough to fit within two barely parted hands. Mostly hairless and wrinkly and alien. Another man in scrubs is already in the room to take her and, once again, her child is handed off like an overfilled vase in a relay race, on her way to another part of the hospital.

"You will need to pass the placenta now," the doctor says matter-of-factly. "This is normally considered the third stage of delivery, but in your case it will be the fourth, no?" He says it like a joke, and Julie knows he's smirking behind the mask, although nothing seems remotely humorous. "And you are *blæðingar … blæðing …*"

"Hemorrhaging," the midwife translates. "We can make you comfortable for this part, which is much easier. You're through the hard stuff. It's easier if you're sitting more upright."

"You will need to push, only a little," the doctor adds.

Inaudible pulses on the monitor, slowing.

Together, they help Julie clamber the birthing bed and—

"There we go," the doctor says.

Julie avoids looking down, avoids looking into the reflection of bloodletting offered by his glasses. The placenta slides out of her, like a partially filled water balloon, one half a raw chicken breast the other an ashen and cancerous lung—how she imagines the sac appearing between her legs, split symmetrically—and is not painful in the slightest, not like the labor, as it makes an awful sound coming out of her.

Inaudible pulses on the monitor, slowing.

The electrocardiogram or whatever it's called holds her attention; rather draws it away from everything else happening in the room. Her pulse displays in jagged jolts every so often, the number to the right of it dropping, dropping, dropping. The blood pressure displayed, double-digits over double-digits, is lower than before, but she's unsure if that's good or bad, the numbers meaningless. The pulse becomes a long flat line as she slides down the bed.

Like a Polaroid photograph developing in reverse, the delivery room slowly turns from white to black, inverting, and then outlines of color breaking through and forming into shapes. Dr. Einstök is there, if only by voice. He's suturing her back together—*a cut, a tear,* the last line coming into focus is the thread. Julie's body: numb.

"You gave us quite the scare, but you did fine. *Frábært. Flutt.*" He laughs behind his mask and taps the plastic device clipped to her finger with the hand holding the suture needle. "The pulse oximeter fell off when you shifted down the bed."

It takes a moment to process.

"Where's Hannah?"

"Hannah's in another room," he says, eyes squinting. The suture needle and string shoots skyward before diving back down. "There are further tests we need to perform, but she is doing well."

"When can I see her?"

"Soon. You need rest, and your child needs rest. You have both gone through something quite incredible, much stress. She is a beautiful girl, 1.445 kilograms."

"What is that in pounds, ounces?"

"She's a little over three pounds." He cups his hands together, either to show her the size of her daughter or to reposition the needle. His glasses reflect two miniature vaginas and the two halves of cut skin below, which he's so delicately sewing back together.

The blood is gone, she realizes, and her gown now clean. Everything is clean.

"There," he says, and snips the line, satisfied with his work. As if reading her thoughts, he backs away and says, with the familiar muffled voice of all doctors behind masks, "You fainted, blood pressure too low. Thirty minutes ago. You were—" he says, swiveling, his interpreter nowhere to be found, "*blæðingar ...*"

"*Blæðing,*" Julie says. "I was bleeding."

"Yes," he says, closing her knees back together. He then taps metal arm holding the half-empty bag of blood labeled with HEILBLÓÐ in bold type, connected by catheter to her wrist. AB stands out on the bag in even bigger capital letters within the thick outline of a square. "You required a transfusion. Much better. *Miklu betra.* We cleaned you and changed your clothes. And a different bed as your reward," he says motioning with his hands.

"When will I be able to hold her?" she says, meaning Hannah, meaning Asche.

"She is much too, eh, *brothætt.*" Under his breath, he tries coming up with the word on his own, "Broken? No, not *broken* …"

"Fragile," Julie says, remembering from before. "But I can see her?"

"Yes, Hannah is much too fragile to be held. And yes, as soon as we have her stable, and you stable, you can see her. She's in *gjörgæsludeild* and doing well. Most of her tests are precautionary, so when you see her, don't be alarmed. We will monitor her all day and all night to keep her healthy, alive. You do not understand *gjörgæsludeild.*"

Julie shakes her head 'no.'

The ceiling once again holds his answer: "NICU."

"Neonatal Intensive Care Unit," Julie says.

To keep her healthy, alive.

She imagines Hannah's petite form sprawled out in a clear-plastic box, wires attached to all parts of her body, machines monitoring her every breath or perhaps breathing *for* her, vitals displayed as numbers and shapes on screens for as long as they must. Julie's seen intensive care babies before, on television and in movies, knows how ugly it can be, the NICU, with parents holding hands over their mouths to cover emotions, as if their hands are miming the breathing masks, their fingers miming the tubes—

Where do hospitals keep the dead?

"That's ointment on your bottom lip. You bit yourself during labor, not too badly. The catheter," he says, tapping a clear tube of liquid connected to another port in that same multi-access catheter, "is an IV to help with, eh … *purrka?* No. *Hydration. Saltvatn, bíkar-bónat, sykur, kalíum.* I'm sorry. I do not know these words in English. Salts and sugars. Like clear Gatorade for your entire body to drink. Your body was very thirsty, why you fainted."

"When can I see Asche?"

"Ash?" her doctor asks, not comprehending. "*Aska, aska, aska.*"

"When will I be able to hold her?"

The simple use of the pronoun is enough to deflate something inside him.

"You want ... you want to hold her, the other child?"

I need to feel.

Julie nods 'yes.' "Is that okay?"

Until now, she hadn't realized she'd wanted to. Could she? Would they let her? What do hospitals do with stillbirths? She imagined she'd be required to fill out a death certificate for Asche, along with a birth certificate for Hannah, a yin and yang of life and death, but that's as far as she's considered, having only known about the existence of both children—*I'm the mother of two children*—for a short while. Until today, she'd only known of Hannah, and thought she'd had another three months before bringing her into the world.

And now ... now there are two, yet there is only one.

"I need to see her," Julie says, "and hold her."

"You want to hold her," Dr. Einstök repeats, mostly to himself. "*Fjandinn,*" he says, like a curse word; perhaps it is. He stands, paces the room. "Are you sure?"

Another nod 'yes;' she is certain.

"Your other daughter," he says, "she was stillborn long before you delivered."

"I understand," Julie says, a lie.

"Her cause of death was most certainly from cord entanglement, which we discussed. But I am uncertain how long this was happening. There were ... *fylgikvillar*, eh, complications much earlier in her development. Quite uncommon. I have read about similar complications in birth, but never before with stillbirth. Do you really want to know this?"

I need to know.

"Yes," she says, shaking.

He hesitates, perhaps sees her determination as a new mother, maternal instincts and intuitions already surfacing.

"I can bring up this information on a tablet, in English, if you would rather read about her condition in privacy before making your decision." His lips turn into flat bracket. "Or, if you have a smartphone, the hospital has decent customer Wi-Fi and you can research on your own after we move you to your recovery room in a few hours. Your belongings will be there."

He's looking for a way out, Julie knows, for some things are just too difficult for one person to tell another. Some things unable to be unseen.

"Yes," she says, "I would like that."

"We can also swaddle her, if and when the time comes, so you see less."

I need to see.

"Yes, I would like that, too," Julie says, another lie.

He stands there a moment, in case she changes her mind, she knows.

"Thank you, but this is something I need to do."

"*Verði þér að góðu*," he says, a phrase she recognizes: 'You're welcome.' "You should rest," the doctor says, and nods, as if understanding there's no way in hell Julie will ever find sleep until *knowing* and *seeing* and eventually *feeling*.

"It's called congenital amputation," he says, and leaves the room.

The door closes behind him, an audible click.

For the next few hours, the two words haunt her mind: congenital amputation. She's alone in the delivery room, for the most part, her thoughts sometimes interrupted by one of the nurses checking in on her, to see if she needed anything, to remove the blood transfusion after the bag had emptied. Julie watches the IV drips fall into the little reservoir before trickling down the tube and to her arm. Pain is minimal, more of a constant discomfort, but she knows there are drugs involved that are keeping both pain and comfort at bay. Wonderful drugs. Her various medicines and dosages, written in black Dry-Erase marker on the whiteboard by the door, despite their foreign spellings, are unintelligible. Scribbles, mostly.

Like the seconds of time, the IV drops tick by agonizingly slow. Yet this does not alter her decision about Asche. She needs to be with her, and then with Hannah.

A nurse pushes a wheelchair through the door at either 7:27 A.M. or 7:27 P.M. Although hospital walls are adorned with clocks, with the lights left on, hospitals are much like casinos in that mornings and nights are sometimes mistaken for one another. According to the whiteboard, the nurse's name is Rós, and she offers a nice morning smile, as though she'd only recently started her shift and still had the energy to smile.

Julie quickly learns Rós doesn't speak English, barely a word of the confusing language, except for 'ready' and Julie's name because it's printed on the whiteboard and on her wristband and charts, but she doesn't hold that against this woman because likewise Julie doesn't speak much *islenska*, and is she not the intruding party?

The kind woman points to her own chest and says, "Rós."

Rose, of course your name is Rose.

She's a nice flower and helps Julie into the wheelchair, which is ultra-modern, made of either fiberglass or carbon fiber-something, but, like all wheelchairs, still clunky, noisy, cold, and uncomfortable.

I'd kill for underwear, for real clothes.

With the meds wearing thin, it hurts to sit, as if feeling every stitch—in an area Frankie liked referring to in their youth as 'the taint.' She'd always hated that term.

Taint my problem.

"Ju-lie?" the nurse says, the second syllable inflected.

Ready to see Hannah, and to hold Asche.

"Yes."

Not ready for any of this.

The rest of her body violated and stretched. The baby bump is still there, but not so much. She pulls her hospital gown against her skin, arms wrapped around her chest. Breasts sore. She fights the sense of everyone staring at her as nurse Rós wheels her around the labyrinthine hospital.

"Why is my left nipple leaking?" she asks, but she knows its colostrum, her body not yet ready to produce milk. This is the *pre*-milk. She had read about the leaking months before, and about nursing pads she could wear within in her bras like maxi pads for her nipples. She had also read that they could bleed after nursing, which had terrified her. Julie isn't wearing a bra now, just the gown, and so the liquid seeps through the thin material. She covers herself, feeling exposed, feeling like she had once before: forced to undress in front of Elliot.

Cramps eat her from within with their sharp cannibalistic teeth.

Frankie Jones had warned her of something called postpartum abdominal pains. Frankie had experienced her own mother—*of seven kids*—go through such a thing after giving birth to Frankie's youngest siblings. "Afterpains," she'd called them.

"After you deliver Hannah," Frankie had said, "your uterus will contract, shrinking back down to its original size. Lower abdominal cramps. With my mom, it seemed worst the first few days, but gradually got better, maybe over the course of four or five weeks, maybe longer, I don't know. She'd try to hide it. She'd hide a lot of things. You'll pee a lot, too, so you should practice Kegels. She said it wasn't too bad the first time, but got worse with every child. My mom would sometimes pee a little after sneezing …"

"Ju-lie?" the nurse says again, wheeling her into the recovery room.

"As ready as I'll ever be."

Rós and a male nurse, already there and waiting, could be fraternal twins: tall, light blond/blonde hair, not heavily built but thick-limbed and big-shouldered, as if wearing American football gear under their scrubs. She imagines the two competing in caber toss on the weekends, or maybe playing rugby. They lift Julie's seemingly weightless body, one on each side of her, and place her on a new bed. After some rapid indecipherable dialogue between the two, the woman offers Julie another of her smiles and they leave her alone in the cold room.

Julie's purse waits on the tray next to her, and it takes her a while to gather the courage to look for both the vice and the *de*vice calling for her.

She rifles through disarray, mostly to see if everything is there, mostly to see if her "eyedrops" are there. She finds her cell phone first, 58% battery life, enough, and brings it to life. After opening the internet browser, she Google-searches "congenital amputation," the two words that had haunted her since her doctor had spoken them with his *I'm sorry* voice. The free hospital Wi-Fi is indeed decent. Wikipedia is the top link, and upon tapping the words with her finger, a framed box appears at the top of the page that reads:

> This article includes a list of references, but its sources remain unclear because it has insufficient inline citations. Please help to improve this article by introducing more precise citations. (August 2014) *(Learn how and when to remove this template message)*

Great, Julie tells herself, *I'm one of those people who gets all her information from Wikipedia, "the free encyclopedia,"* as it clearly states, *or WebMD.* She's stalling, she knows, reading the unnecessary text, the menu on the left, the tabs on the top-right, the small print, trying not to move her eyes down to the middle of the screen, to the bold and scary phrase she's there to define, which stands out as repulsively as an hourglass on a black—

> *"**Congenital amputation** is birth without a limb or limbs, or without a part of a limb or limbs."*

She sets down the phone, screen first. "*Without a limb or limbs, or without a part of a limb or limbs.*" She thinks of her dream, or whatever that had been, the blackened spider child prying out of her. She'd seen the limbs, those handless limbs … And there was more to be read, and so she grabs the phone again, not wanting to but needing to, and reads further:

> "It is known to be caused by blood clots forming in the fetus while *in utero* (vascular insult) and from amniotic band syndrome: fibrous bands of the amnion that constrict foetal limbs to such an extent that they fail to form or actually fall off due to missing blood supply. Congenital amputation can also occur due to maternal exposure to teratogens during pregnancy."

Julie fights the urge to click the hyperlinks attached to the foreign words and phrases—amniotic band syndrome, teratogens—and scrolls to the next section labeled "Causes."

> "The exact cause of congenital amputation is unknown and can result from a number of causes. However, most cases show that the first three months in a pregnancy are when most birth defects occur because that is when the organs of the fetus are beginning to form. One common cause is amniotic band syndrome, which occurs when the inner fetal membrane (amnion) ruptures without injury to the outer membrane (chorion). Fibrous bands from the ruptured amnion float in the amniotic fluid and can get entangled with the fetus, thus reducing blood supply to the developing limbs to such an extent that the limbs can become stran-

gulated; the tissues die and are absorbed into the amniotic fluid. A baby with congenital amputation can be missing a portion of a limb or the entire limb, which results in the complete absence of a limb beyond a certain point where only a stump is left is known as transverse deficiency or amelia. When a specific part is missing, it is referred to as longitudinal deficiency. Finally, phocomelia occurs when only a mid-portion of a limb …"

The phone vibrates and Julie nearly drops it, her heart thudding. An incoming call notification covers the article. FRANKIE JONES, the phone reads, along with her number.

She knows something's wrong.

Julie wants to tap the red circle on the display to send her to voicemail, or to at least silence the phone and let it ring out, but she can't. Not this time. She'd pushed Frankie away in the past and had promised herself she'd never do it again, no matter what. Not even with something like this. Even after slapping her across the face, Frankie had been there for her through terrible things, had stayed at her side, always. Julie taps the green circle instead.

"*Hæ.*"

"Hey?" Frankie says. "That's all I get, just 'hey'."

"Yes, but I said it in islandic, it only sounds the same."

Seconds pass on the little timer on the display, three seconds, four; although it's an expensive call, Julie doesn't care, and she knows Frankie doesn't care.

"You know something, don't you?" Julie says to break the silence. "You always do."

"Hannah's here, isn't she. I can feel her," she says, followed by a soft hiss of static. "But how can she … you're only …"

"She is. And yeah, a little early. I'm in the recovery room, waiting to see her."

Asche is early, too, but neither of us ever knew there were two. She can't tell her that, though, not yet. She *would*, just not now.

"A *little?*" Frankie says, and is silent for a while. "You sound hoarse. Not just from, you know, labor, but from something else. What's wrong? Something else is wrong. Wait, why are you *waiting* to see her? Shouldn't you be holding her?"

"By 'little' I mean 'nearly three months.' She's small, so—"

"She's healthy?"

"I— I think so. Look, Frankie, I had to pick up, to talk to you and hear your voice, but can I call you back? I was going to call you anyway, but they just wheeled me in here."

"Wait, you seriously, like, *just* finished giving birth? Yes, girl. Call me back. Oh, Julie, I'm so excited for you, and for Hannah. I should fly there. I can totally fly there and see you. We can talk about it later, though. I'll hang up and look at flights. You get some rest, and when you see her, give her a kiss for me. Okay. I'm hanging up now. I love you, Julie."

"I love you, Frankie."

Three words is all it takes to keep a friendship alive, especially from a distance. Simply answering a call, a text, an email, an instant message. Communication is the language of love. And to not love is to not live.

Julie had taught herself that—through experience, through trial and error.

"Frankie?" she asks, but Frankie is gone.

She stares at the phone, still stuck on the ended call, afraid that pressing the Back button will return her to the page for *congenital amputation*. But she hits the back button anyway, reads the rest of the article, clicks the links and learns new words and phrases. She learns everything there is to know from merely reading about the subject, until her hands shake and are no longer able to hold the phone.

She was stillborn long before you delivered.

"I need to hold her, to see her, to feel her," Julie tells the room.

The smart phones finds its way back into the pocket of her

purse, in which she rummages for what had also called her. Next to her apartment keys, Julie finds the *Drakein … the dragon.* Simply holding the bottle is enough to calm her nerves, the drug not necessarily there to use, but to not use. Yet the bottle is light.

Like a foul-mouthed angel perched on her shoulder, Frankie whispers in her ear: *This shit got you here. What good will it do you now?*

"You're right, Frankie," Julie tells the empty room.

The outside of the bottle is wet, the label starting to peel away. Somewhere in its travels, the lid had come loose, spilling the last of the *Drakein-5* into the bottom of her purse—most of it gone, evaporated, wasted.

And good riddance, Frankie whispers in her ear.

Julie rubs her fingers together, the mostly-evaporated substance now semi-oily, like essential oils. She wonders what would happen if drops of pure *D-5* were added to a diffuser and vaporized to breathe.

Shaking the bottle, Julie realizes the entire bottle is empty, every last drop. She looks at her hands, as if they hold the answer, and they do.

Don't even think about it, Julie.

Her index finger and thumb are wet, barely, but the drug is there, the smallest of doses.

As she rubs the last of the dragon into her eyes, the rush is not quite as instant this time, and the effects different than before, as though thinned. She hadn't used in six months—the entire term of her shortened pregnancy, not knowing what it might do to Hannah— so perhaps the effects diminish with the drug's exposure to air.

I guess this one last time is all right, Frankie whispers in her ear.

Julie looks to her hands, both of them, expecting the many bones to come gushing out to grab her, but instead her skin—luminous and nearly translucent—holds them back. The shaking in her hands visibly lessens. She is ready for her daughter, ready to test those senses, ready to say those three little words for the first and last time. Julie tosses the Visine bottle across the room, making a basket in the garbage can.

When the recovery room door opens, the sudden sight of Dr. Einstök does not frighten her, nor does the woman from before, Ava, who embraces a swaddled bundle close to her chest like a child holding her dolly. The three of them stay inside their bodies, never exploding into gore, merely emanating a strange kind of visible energy around them.

Diffusing watercolors.

"Julie," Eva says, "this is—"

"Asche," Julie says. "Asche Stipes."

"Is that the name you've decided?" Dr. Einstök asks.

Julie nods, holding out her hands.

Will I need that for the death certificate? She imagines she will, and notices the doctor writing the name on his clipboard.

Asche Stipes on the death certificate, and Hannah Stipes on the birth certificate. No middle names, for their mother was also born without one. She'd thought of incorporating Elliot Cartwright somehow, to make him a part of their lives in the subtlest of ways, but both his given and family names were masculine, and how would she ever explain them? *Elli* or *Wright* might work, but she liked the names better without.

"We thought you might want time alone with her," Eva says, but I'll be outside the door. You can press the call button next to you when you are ready for me to take her away."

Take her away, Julie thinks as she is handed the child. *Yes, they will have to take her away at some point.*

Through a haze, and because she is bundled tightly, Asche could be a sleeping child. She's no larger than a baby kitten and fits easily within Julie's cupped hands, barely there. Clean, smiling, with only the slightest of color imperfections around her neck—a hangman's birthmark; otherwise, perfect in every way besides the ashy skin.

"Thank you," Julie says. "I would like some alone time with her. Not long."

To say hello and goodbye. Aloha, as they say in Hawai'i, meaning both.

"We have a grievance counselor on staff," Eva says in nearly perfect English. Short, petite and brunette, she could very well be from the States. "And a Christian priest if you are religious and wish for a blessing. We also have a—"

Religion is having erroneous faith in that your faith is neither faith nor erroneous. Is that a proverb? she wonders, her mind wandering. *A terrible fortune?*

"—and can put you in contact with someone from Útfararst-rofa Kirkjugardanna, a funeral home in Reykjavík, and they can walk you through the process of what will need to happen next—"

Cremation ...

Burial ...

"All of that can be discussed later," Eva says, glowing, bringing Julie back into the real world. "An autopsy is not necessary, unless you request one—"

"But again," Dr. Einstök interrupts, "a discussion for later." He motions to Eva with his hands in a manner that implies they should go and leave her be.

"Yes," Eva says, looking down. "Take your time and I will be right outside."

Julie nudges the blanket, inspecting the mostly hidden child.

"Hannah is doing well," the doctor says as she leaves the room, as if to balance bad with good. "And she will be ready to see you within the hour. Unfortunately, you will not be able to hold her for a few days. *Brothætt*," he says, drawing her attention from the child. He smiles, seeing the understanding of the word on Julie's face. *Fragile.* "Her blood pressure, and heart rate, is still stabilizing. I would say three days, maybe four at the most, but you can hold Asche for now, for a while. If you need anything, please let us know. I will be monitoring Hannah until then. She looks very much like you, I can tell, even this early. Many *líkindi* ... eh, similarities? Likeness, much like Asche, here," he says, pointing, "but ..."

Try not to get attached to this one, his body language reads.

"The call button is at your side when you are ready."

You will need to let her go.

"Thank you," Julie says. "For everything. For this. I know it's probably not common for a mother to want to hold her stillborn child, but I— I need to hold her, for just a minute."

"Of course," he says, and without another word leaves the two of them alone in the small room, the door clicking behind him.

She holds the forever-sleeping child, not knowing what to say, not knowing *if* she has anything to say. Her body, cocooned in the white swaddling blanket, seems supernaturally small. Smaller than any of the dolls she'd ever held as a child. She rocks her, as she had practiced rocking unmoving toys in her youth, tempted to tilt her head back so that her eyes might flutter.

Her eyes are blue like yours, the doctor had said, meaning Hannah.

Identical, Asche would also have those same eyes.

"Hello Asche," she finally manages. "Hello sweet and sleeping child. I didn't even know about you until today, or yesterday, or whatever day this is, and for that I am sorry. I should have known about you. I should have taken better care of myself. I should have gone in for check-ups more often. I should have been more responsible. I hope you understand that I never meant to hurt you. And I hope you understand Hannah never meant to hurt you."

A rainbow of auras wavers around her tiny body, every color imaginable.

The *Drakein*, Julie knows, or perhaps something more.

She blinks through heavy lids.

I need to see.

There is more to the child, Julie knows, or perhaps something less because of her condition. Congenital amputation. She'd read all about the subject, but had avoided pictures.

Complications, the doctor had said.

There were complications, Chase had said.

The two memories clash as one.

The dragon, had it done this to her? *No,* Julie tells herself. A dragon is a symbol for protection, not the opposite. If anything, the drug had protected Julie through all this, and had later protected Hannah, and yet Asche … *No, I cannot believe such a thing.*

Asche stirs, wriggles, but only in her mind, and so Julie holds her closer, the body so delicate, so fragile, and much like a chrysalis—the hardened body of a butterfly pupa. That's how Julie imagines the still child, as a life not *mal*formed, but not quite *trans*formed. The body full of imaginal cells ready to do their magic, yet unable to continue because of an interruption. Asche, between stages. Between life and death. Stuck in the middle of a metamorphosis. She had written stories in her youth, one a fable involving a butterfly and a moth, for they had fascinated her with their odd transformations from one stage of life to the next.

I need to feel.

Julie touches the child, and pulls away. The body is rigor—such a terrible word—as she expected, the skin smooth and cold.

You would have become something beautiful.

"A child … my child, so very beautiful. If any part of you can hear me, know that I will always think of you. I will always love you as I will love Hannah. I will love you the same."

Asche lay partially within the blanket, her abnormalities hidden. Had she developed fully, had the first of two cords not tangled around her body, she would have become Hannah's identical twin, but no, she is as light as a wad of feathers, not quite half the weight of a normal newborn, not the same as—

"Lanie," Frankie had said. "You should name her Lanie."

"Why," Julie had said, not so long ago.

They had been looking through a book of baby names Frankie had found for her at a thrift store. They'd flipped through the pages and called names out at random—and sometimes not-so-random— along with their meanings if either raised an eyebrow.

"I don't know," Frankie had said. "I've always liked that name. It means *path* or *roadway*, like a *lane*, I guess. I kind of like that. You've gone through a fuck-ton, Julie, your path bumpy. The road less traveled. Remember that stupid Frost poem we had to memorize?"

> *Two roads diverged in a yellow wood,*
> *And sorry I could not travel both*
> *And be one traveler, long I stood*
> *And looked down one as far as I could*

"What about Hannah?" Julie had said, "H-A-N-N-A-H."

"Where'd you come up with that name?"

"I don't know. It just came to me, has a certain symmetry."

"Hannah," Frankie had said. "Isn't it called something, when a word can be spelled the same way forward as backward?"

"Yeah. What's it mean?"

"I just said what it means: when a word can be spelled—"

"No. *Hannah*."

"Oh, right," Frankie had said, flipping through the names. She'd stopped somewhere in the first third of the book, then turned a page at a time. "Hannah," she'd said, "spelled with either an 'h' at the end, or without, or with only one 'n' and no 'h,' or even spelled *Chana*, with a 'c,' is a Hebrew name derived from … I don't know what all this shit is, but basically it means *favour*, spelled F-A-V-O-U-R, or *grace*, as in: 'He [God] has favoured me [with a child].' *God* and *with* a child are in brackets. I guess it means God fucked you and got you pregnant."

"He sure did."

"In the book of Samuel, Hannah—spelled the way you want to spell it—was incapable of having a child. I'm paraphrasing here, but basically she prayed for a child, or something, and God gave her a child. Jesus. How many times does this happen in the bible? Immaculate conception …"

Then took the other, as just as fair,
And having perhaps the better claim,
Because it was grassy and wanted wear;
Though as for that the passing there

Seventh grade seems so long ago. Life had been so graceful then, her childhood so innocent and unmolested, the poetry confusing then, but so meaningful now.

I need to know.

Julie unwraps the blanket, slowly. Needs to know what she and Elliot had created, what her own life choices had created. She peels away the layers, blinking through the tears, through the last of the drug. The child hatches, too many arms and too many legs unfurling like the fronds of a fern. Handless, footless. Gray. Asche's wrists and ankles had not developed enough within the womb to hold the bones of her arms and legs together, the limbs split at the elbows and knees. Four smooth arms and four smooth legs. The child's body, beneath the head …

Arachnid, like her father during the worst of the hallucinations.

Julie blinks again, the drug doing what it does best: altering reality; yet the *Drakein-5*, perhaps because of dissolution, rubbed into her eyes in its thinned and oily state instead of dropped into each eye as designed, does its opposite. The abnormalities draw together, not in a rapid splash of gore, but as a slow relocation of how things ought to appear. The split arms merge, as well as the legs. Tiny hands and tiny feet emerge where they should be. The body, no longer cold but warm, and no longer hard but soft. Lungs inflate, a mouth opening to take a first breath. A heart beats. The still becomes unstill. The child squirms. The ash skin bleeds, but only with color. The dead child comes to life, stretching within Julie's hands, fingers clawing.

This is what Hannah looks like, and feels like.

The first moments after delivery are the most important, she knows. She'd read about mother and infant bonding months back,

preparing her for this exact moment, not with Asche, but with Hannah; she'd expected to give birth to one child, not two, and to hold onto that child close those first few hours, skin against skin. But they had taken Hannah away. What would become of their bond now that they were separated? How would they bond through an incubator, or plastic tray, or wherever they kept her in this hospital? How would they bond without touch? This is why Julie holds Asche now, she knows, *for* Hannah. As twins, they shared a magical connection, as they had shared a single placenta, as they had shared her womb, and although they cannot share the same world going forward, they share it now, in this moment, through this embrace, throughout whatever hallucination this may be.

She rocks the child gently, places a finger within a miniature hand, sings her a lullaby—made up words—and begins to wrap the swaddling blanket tightly around her body once again.

When her daughter's eyes open, they are blue and beautiful.

Hello, Hannah.

Julie presses the call button. She has said her hellos to one child and said her goodbyes to the other. She wraps Asche back in the swaddling blanket and watches the sleeping child. The pink skin drains of color. The limbs contract and curl. The soft body hardens.

Alone once again in the recovery room, Julie watches her phone vibrate on the tray holding her purse. UNKNOWN NUMBER, the screen reads. She lets it go to voicemail.

No one has this number, other than Frankie.

NEW VOICEMAIL, the screen reads. .01 seconds.

The phone rings a second time: UNKNOWN NUMBER, and a third a few minutes later: UNKNOWN NUMBER. Neither goes to voicemail, but the time between reeks of desperation. She's tempted to answer if there's a fourth, but for the next hour the phone is silent and offers only the date and time and battery life. She'll need to find a charger.

She can't think of a single other person who'd call. No one has the number, other than Frankie, and her landlord, and maybe her bank. Probably a sales call.

Chase?

"For, you know, saving me, I guess," he had said, handing her a full bottle of *Drakein-5*, the one which now sat empty at the bottom of the garbage can across the room. "Take it, love," he had said. "You put me here"—*a hospital room much like this one*—"I know, but, well, you *took* me here, is what I'm trying to say. Slicing me open was an accident, if you can call it that, or a misunderstanding. 'There is no such thing as an accident; it is fate misnamed.' Someone said that. That bastard Napoleon Bonaparte, I think. Anyway, it doesn't matter; that's all in the past. The past has passed. I'm still tripping a bit. Okay, a lot. What matters is that we are both alive, and that's all we can ask for, am I right? Of course I'm right." He was right. "Listen, Julie—"

The past is a tree without roots.

She'd had to see him, to make sure he was okay, and had snuck into Brenden Memorial the same way she'd snuck out after her own intravenous trip, albeit not wearing stolen clothes, but her own. Chase had given her money—*hush money*—and she took it without hesitation, and he had given her the bottle, the only thing he'd had on him at the time besides the toy plastic gun, which had sat beside him. He was still so high from her injecting him with the syringe that he probably would have given her anything.

"If you don't want it," he'd said, pushing the little white bottle into her hands, "Sell it. I don't care. Do whatever you want with it. You came back to see me. Besides a few visitors—in some of the strangest dreams I've *ever* had these last few days—you're the only one who's come to see me. Well, except Colt. Speaking of which—I love valium, by the way, is that what they're pumping me with? Where am I? Where was I?"

"Speaking of which—"

"Right," he'd said. "Call Lacie for me, will you, love? She can bring Colt here so I can see him. Every child needs a father, right? Even one like me."

"I want out of this," Julie had said after calling, and he understood, even high.

Goodbye, Chase.

She hadn't heard from Chase after that last visit to the hospital, but she hadn't owned a cell phone then, either, so it couldn't be him trying to call because he didn't have the number. Could it? Could he have tracked her down? No. They'd had an understanding. He was part of the past now—a misnamed fate, a root.

"Every child needs a mother," Julie tells the room.

A text from Frankie chimes not long after.

How you holding up? How's Hannah?

Haven't held her yet, Julie texts back.

What?

Within the hour, or so I'm told.

Which hospital?

Julie reads her wristband for the spelling, which autocorrect doesn't like. The wristband is something she will keep forever, she knows, along with Hannah's. Asche hadn't worn one, because she'd never lived, or because she hadn't had hands to hold one in place.

Landspítali Fossvogi. In Reykjavík. Why?

Cuz I'm headed to Iceland!

What?

Booked, roundtrip. I fly out tomorrow!

No way!

Yes way!

An emoticon of a heart, three times.

An emoticon of a middle finger.

This is stupid, Julie texts. *I need to hear you. I'm calling you.*

The call doesn't go through at first, until she realizes she can't simply tap Frankie's name in the contact list. She adds the international prefixes, eager to hear her voice, manually dials her number.

"You're coming here to see me," Julie says before Frankie has the chance to answer. "You're kidding, right?"

"I fly out of Seattle at 4:00 P.M., Icelandair, and board at 3:25. Apparently, they fly nonstop out of Sea-Tac now, so I'm taking a red-eye. A little less than seven and a half hours in the air. I land at 6:15 A.M. your time. I fly kinda over the Arctic or something. So, basically, I'll see you tomorrow morning, or the next day. I think. What's the time difference there?"

Julie can tell Frankie's reading her itinerary from a computer screen. She's known her long enough to distinguish her serious voice from her joking voice.

She's actually coming here.

"Frankie, it's so expensive."

"Shut your face. I've been saving up for a trip anyway. I wasn't planning on *Iceland,* but why the hell not? And I'll crash at your place, so I'll be saving on a hotel anyway."

"I have to stay at the hospital a few days. I'm not sure how long."

"You're *not* going to talk me out of it, if that's what you're trying to do. I've already booked my flight, *non*refundable. I'll be there a solid week and can watch over your place when I'm not with you. Don't you have a cat or something to take care of?"

"Iceland, Frankie. I don't have a cat."

"What I'm saying is that I'm coming, no matter what."

"Look, Frankie—"

"You're *not* talking me out of it."

"No, I mean there's other stuff you need to know."

The silence is much too long, like a mere few seconds of dead air on the radio, a forgotten song or commercial.

Julie doesn't know what to say, or how to say it, but Frankie needs to know why she delivered three months early.

She needs Frankie to know that she was coming to Iceland to celebrate a birth, but would also be there for a funeral.

"I've been reading about preemies," Frankie says.

More of her voodoo.

"You're in the category of either 'very preterm' or 'moderately preterm,' based on the six-month thing, so I know Hannah's going to be small, like half-size.

Another beat of silence.

"She's in the NICU, right?" Frankie says.

"She is," Julie says. At some point, she had started crying again.

"And I know there can be complications that early."

"I held her," Julie says.

"Wait, what? I thought you couldn't for a few days."

"Not Hannah. She was *so* small, Frankie."

"What are you talking about?"

"Asche. I held her. She looked like Hannah, only … only smaller, and … but she looked just like her in all other ways. Identical. I went into labor early because Hannah was a twin. *Was.* Past tense. I was pregnant with twins, and miscarried the first. I had to deliver Asche, before Hannah, but she was already gone … a long time gone. But I held her. She was so delicate, and beautiful. I need you here, Frankie, more than anything. I need you to help me figure out what to do. Why did I ever come here? Why didn't I stay?"

"Twins," Franke says, as if she understands everything.

Circles means it's a girl …

Hannah, if it's a girl …

"What signifies a boy?" …

"Back and forth: lines." …

Asche, if it's a boy, which could also work for a girl …

I guess you're only ever gonna have one, Frankie had said then.

"You were only meant to have one," Frankie says now, breaking the silence.

◻   ◻   ◻

She cries for the next few hours, both sad and happy tears, but eventually runs dry. Frankie will be there with her, soon, and knowing that is comforting. The clock on the wall reads 3:45 and Julie knows it's early morning because of the lights and the skeleton crew of hospital staff. She's supposed to 'get some rest,' but how? Somewhere, someone is watching over Hannah, but who?

The covered platter of hospital food at her side remains untouched, the paper cup of water next to it empty. She's also supposed to eat, but doesn't have the appetite.

8% battery life, the phone displays.

Rummaging through her purse, Julie finds a charging cord, and remembers last seeing the adapter portion plugged into the kitchen nook back at her apartment. Álafoss Apartments, #2, Mosfellsbær. *Shit.* She texts Frankie the address, having forgotten to after their call, and plugs the useless cord into the phone. 7%.

"I'm going to need you," she says, looking around the room.

A machine against the wall has a handheld USB device of some kind plugged into it, but would it charge her phone? Couldn't hurt. She gives the cord a gentle tug and pulls it free, the machine letting out a constant, high-pitched whine.

Nope.

Julie presses the call button, and by 3:51, a man in scrubs checks in on her. Like the others before him, he smiles, first looking at the whiteboard on the wall—which on the bottom left reads ENSKA HÁTALARI, meaning that she is English-speaking, according to the last nurse. Julie isn't due for medication for another three hours, and so he looks confused.

"You pressed the call button?"

"Not really an emergency," she says, nodding. She holds the phone by its cord, like a dead mouse. "But kind of. Is there a way I can get a charger for this? It's my only way of reaching anyone."

"*Já*," he says, and by 4:00 and 6% he returns with one, perhaps his own, as well as another cup of water with a bendy straw.

"*Þakka þér fyir*," she says, meaning 'thank you.' "That's the only other phrase I know in Icelandic, the first phrase I ever learned, but seriously, though, thank you."

He nods politely, probably thinking he'll never see the square adapter again—because phone chargers tend to disappear after loaning them to friends, let alone complete strangers—and plugs her phone into the wall for her, within reaching distance. He takes the platter of food, feels the weight and lifts the lid, and then sets it back down. "The Jello is good, to at least have something in your stomach. Everything else is … okay, but you should eat."

"Is everyone here this nice?"

Considering this a moment, he says, "It doesn't take effort to be nice, only to be the opposite. My sister used to say, 'Every muscle in the face is needed to frown, not many to smile,' but I'm sure all sisters used to say that."

And this makes her smile because Frankie had once said something similar, and she'd always thought of her as a sister.

"Is there anything else I can do for you while I'm here?"

"Maybe another blanket?"

There's one already in the room, she discovers, as he opens a cabinet. It's not much, but he unfolds the blanket and lays it over her bare feet.

Sometime during the early morning hours, Julie had fallen into a deep sleep, for the next time she opens her eyes the clock is a few hours ahead, the hospital more alive with activity. Her cell phone displays 7:07 A.M., although she'd slept like the dead, as if she'd slept the entire day away and not a few measly hours. 74% battery.

Frankie won't be here until tomorrow morning, Julie realizes, but that's okay.

Finally hungry, she starts with the Jello, then moves on to the sandwich, which is cucumber and a soft white cheese. A few bites settle her stomach. At some point, the water at her side had been replaced with orange juice, with two pills in a smaller plastic cup next to it. She drinks greedily, and swallows the pills one at a time, even though the cramps have subsided.

She will need to arrange a few things for Asche, she realizes, walking to the closet-sized restroom to pee. She leaves the door open because who fucking cares. While sitting on her white thrown, she Google-searches terrible things: 'what do hospitals do with still-born babies,' and 'disposition of the body after stillbirth,' and 'death certificates' and 'Icelandic funeral practices.' She learns more than she wants to know, but everything proves useful.

Apparently, traditional Viking funerals involved cremating the deceased in pyres, although the common practice followed traditions of the country's predominant denomination, the National Church of Iceland, such as the *kistulagninar*, a wake attended only by family and close friends. Frankie and Julie, in other words …

If I handle everything here.

Embalming is not commonly practiced in the country, either, she learns—against church practice or something—so her best option is cremation, her preference anyway, although she'd be required by law to purchase a casket for the cremation. Old laws. Old traditions. This prompts another unusual search on her phone: 'baby caskets.'

What kind of a casket would be required for Asche's small form?

The caskets, like miniatures.

What kind of urn for her *cremains?*

She'd never heard such a cruel word until today, and imagines a Viking funeral pyre, a raft, aflame, floating into Kollafjörður.

I'll need to go back to the States. I'm a mother now … No longer a student learning calculus and biology and dissecting the English language, but a girl learning to become a woman learning to become a mother. What was I ever thinking coming here?

The last thing she reads is an article titled "Disposition of the Body after Stillbirth."

"Is everything all right?"

Asche becoming Ash.

"In the restroom," Julie says to the new voice, although nothing is 'all right.' She flushes the toilet and says, "I'll be out in a second." It hurts to wipe, but that's the least of her problems, and it takes her more than a second as she thinks of pyres.

Ash joining the sand in the ocean.

The grievance counselor shakes Julie's hand, as if handling a business transaction. The handshake is liver-spotted age and tired bones. She's here for emotional support, to help Julie through making tough decisions, and from the tender handshake and her idiosyncrasies, she's apparently done this before. Julie understands about half of what the woman says, but she is presented with three options:

1) *Burial.*

Julie can work with a funeral home to make arrangements, a place called Útfararstrofa Kirkjugardanna is highly recommended, or she can contact the cemetery sexton directly. 'Sexton' is the toughest word to decipher, but her phone proves useful once again. It would also possible for Julie to do the burial herself, on her own land, if she were to own land. Working with a funeral home would not be required, although advantageous, for the staff would have better knowledge of burial laws and could offer further grief counseling if she so needed.

"I'm on a temporary visa," Julie tells her, "a student visa."

The woman smiles, lets her know there are other options available, although her child's body would not be able to be embalmed prior to shipping overseas because embalming is indeed uncommon in this country, considered unnecessary. In order to have Asche buried at home, in Brenden, Washington, this would require—

2) *Cremation.*

"Not all funeral homes have a crematory, but they can all make the necessary arrangements." The woman sounds nothing like this, but this is what she implies with her wise words, and how Julie would later play out their mostly-single-sided conversation.

"Cremation will give you time," she says, to a certain extent, "to determine how to give tribute to the life you've lost."

She's not 'lost;' she's right here at the hospital.

With a cremation, it would be easier to return Asche to Brenden. She could get one of those little metal urns made for children, like those she'd seen in her research on the throne.

"You can then choose to either take the cremains, or to have the crematory discard them. Most choose to take the cremains, either to keep or to bury. And you also have the option of—"

3) *Förgun.*

Such a horrid word. At first Julie thinks the counselor is trying to say foreign, but after having her repeat the word, the woman translates it as, "Disposal," as if tossing away garbage.

"They can place your dead child in a plastic baggy and throw her in the trash."

The woman does not say this, of course, but Julie takes it as such, as biohazard. "My recommendation is for one of the first two options," she says instead, or something similar. "From my experience, young mothers—nearly *all* mothers—prefer either burial or cremation, but it is not my position to give advice, only to give you your options, since this is a lot to take on all at once. This latter option, however, since you are not from here, gives you more time to say goodbye. You would be able to have her with you for as long as you like before making a permanent decision. Where you are, emotionally, how much you are connected to her …"

I've said my goodbyes.

"An obituary can be published in *Morgunbladid*, the nationwide newspaper; its title means 'The Morning Paper.'"

Julie wonders if she means 'morning' or 'mourning.'

The grievance counselor says many other things; she's nice, after all, has probably gone through hundreds upon hundreds of patients—and much patience—like Julie. This means nothing to the counselor, most likely desensitized into an emotionless automaton, although it means everything to Julie. This woman has helped other miscarry-mothers, but how many had gone through this exact scenario? She's there to help, but too much is lost in translation.

She leaves behind pamphlets on loss, and on postpartum depression for Julie to read/translate later, *Þunglyndi eftir fæðingu*, leaves behind a copy of *Morgunbladid* so she can consider the wordage of past obituaries, one of the child obituaries circled in red pen …

What's her name?

Julie doesn't even know the woman's name, or was told and had already forgotten. Her mind is lost as she shakes a hand—that skeletal hand—and says goodbye. Her mind is already on the second child: Hannah Stipes; she can see her within the hour.

The pamphlet on postpartum depression is a tri-fold. Foreign words surround illustrations of a cartoonish-looking new mother holding an infant, but Julie is anything but sad and so she tosses the paper aside. Her fingers shake from either lack of sleep or anxiety.

New-mother fear pumps through her like adrenaline.

What if I don't bond with Hannah? What if she doesn't accept me? What if we've been separated for too long? What if something's wrong? What if Hannah doesn't stop crying when I hold her? What if I don't know how to hold her? What if I drop her because I don't know what the hell I'm even doing?

This isn't postpartum depression, Julie discovers, but postpartum anxiety. She reads about the subject on her cell phone to pass the time.

A porcelain doll, she imagines, *shattering at my feet.*

"Motherhood is like magic," Frankie had said, back when some of these same questions had run through Julie's mind early on in the pregnancy. "That's what my mom said, at least. She got pregnant at sixteen with my oldest sister and had to drop out of high school. Had no clue what she was doing, and you've got a few years on her. Motherly instincts come naturally."

What if I leave her alone, for only an instant, and someone snatches her?

That was her biggest fear—not losing Hannah during the pregnancy, as she had lost Asche, or losing her during labor, but someone simply *taking* her away.

Many nights, while pregnant, she would startle awake from dream, shaking—as she shakes now—arms outstretched like the cover of some 90s pulp horror paperback; Julie reaching for a child no longer there. Not a newborn, but a girl old enough to walk on her own. Strawberry-blonde. Sometimes three or four years old, sometimes as old as seven. A flower-pattern dress, every damn time, like the one Julie had worn as a child. Calvin Stipes is sometimes there, her father, leading his granddaughter away by hand, sometimes holding her in his arms and running—*from what, his own daughter?*—and sometimes it's the man with the burn scars on his neck doing the same, only limping, or the man with the tattoo of a rose. *Were they not the same?* Always, Julie reaching out, in pursuit but never gaining. And then the nightmares would fade as easily as they'd come, the girl and whoever was taking her would evaporate with her own realization of dreaming, the remnants of the man holding her daughter's hand dematerializing.

The doctor had in fact taken Hannah away, and Julie had reached out for her, like in her past dreams. And someone had taken Asche away—not the doctor, not the midwife or a nurse, but some ethereal being neither live nor dead, neither male nor female, with wings unfolding behind him/her as easily as heat lifting from a desert road.

"With life there must come death, and with death, life.
That is the balance in this world. The pure shall not leave

> *in death, but be guided to other worlds. If one must be*
> *guided, another must be protected to live, and if one must*
> *live, there must surely be balance with death."*

Where had she read that before? The passage comes to her all at once, like a photographic memory, but the words give her hope.

Asche, was she guided?

Julie's hands shake. She can no longer hold the phone, which has since blackened and offers a digital display of time and nothing more. Nearly an hour had passed, but how? Time had slipped away while deep in thought. She'd see Hannah very soon, and this was both comforting and terrifying. Any moment now. Any second. The door would open and she'd be guided to the NICU to not hold her, not drop her, but to finally see her. And when she'd reach out her hands this time, they would find glass and not pass through.

Hannah, protected to live …

She had read that meditation helped with postpartum anxiety, and so she takes a deep breath and slowly releases it through slightly parted lips, lets her hands go lax. Closing her eyes, Julie focuses on the clock on the wall, not watching the time, but listening to each tick of the second hand, willing them to slow. She lets her mind go dark, tries to think of nothing at all.

What time is it? she wonders after a while, for the room is silent.

"It's time to see Hannah," Dr. Einstök says.

Julie opens her eyes and finds herself sitting upright on the recovery room bed, legs crossed, hands held to either side. When she splays her fingers, they no longer shake. She calmly admires the old scar running parallel to her life line—Elliot's path, carved next to her own.

She had expected a nurse or her midwife to take her to see Hannah, not her doctor, but she's glad to see him. He holds the handlebars of a wheelchair and smiles.

"Are you ready?"

Julie nods, unfolding her legs.

He helps her off the bed and into the chair.

"I thought I'd take you myself," he says, wheeling her around.

He pushes her through a more secluded, quieter part of the building, somewhere close to the NICU: the library of endangered children. Soon they round a corner and the narrow hallway opens to a room marked GJÖRGÆSLUDEILD. Julie had expected a large room with rows upon rows of newborns, yet he brings her to a smallish sterile white room, with partitions separating waist-high rolling carts. There are only three carts in the room, each holding infant incubators—what Julie thinks of as miniature plastic greenhouses—but only the middle one is occupied.

Hannah.

The newborn lies on her back, eyes closed, one arm at her side, the other held across her chest and covered entirely by gauze and tape to hold a catheter in place, one leg stretched downward, the other held at a ninety-degree angle, toes bare. Most of her lower half hides in diaper. A bandage covers her stomach, although her chest is exposed and adorned with a heart monitor and its single black cord. A white cap conceals all but her face, a few wisps of dark hair peeking beneath. Held in place by an elastic strap and blue pads pressed tightly against her cheeks is a proportionally large breathing mask with a clear ribbed tube, which splits her face symmetrically and arches over her tiny head. Her mouth is sealed shut by another strap of tape casing a thin tube. Her limbs are thin, stretching every so often. Ten fingers. Ten toes.

She is beautiful.

"She is doing well," the doctor says.

So peaceful, so innocent.

On either side of Hannah's greenhouse are large holes, four total, so that hands might have direct access; enough for two parents to reach inside, Julie realizes. Two.

I'm a single mother. Alone.

Hannah, although covered by a clear-plastic rooftop, is otherwise exposed, and easily small enough to fit through the holes. Someone could reach inside and take her if they wanted to, but Julie tries her best to push that thought away. Through teary eyes, Julie watches her child breathe, watches her sigh, watches her *live*. Then it dawns on her: she can touch her child.

As if sensing her thoughts, the doctor says, "While you may not be able to hold Hannah against your chest, at least for a few more days, you can at least touch her, which we feel is important at this early stage. Skin to skin. Mother to daughter. *Móðir til dóttur.* You will need to wash your hands, of course," he says, motioning to the sink.

Julie stands from the chair, places a hand on top of the plastic.

"Hello again, Hannah."

She washes her hands for perhaps longer than she needs to; they shake under the water, but only because she is tired, having only slept for a couple hours at most.

What if my touch breaks her? What if she is made of glass and I am made of stone? What if all this is not even happening? What if I'm still back in Brenden, tripping on Drakein-5?

"Ignore your what-ifs," Frankie had once said to her, "or you'll die trying to answer them. Life is too short to worry about what might never happen."

"Julie?" the doctor says, and she turns to him.

"Sorry."

This is happening, she knows. She is here. This is now. Asche is gone, but Hannah needs a mother as much as any mother needs a child. Even if she has to go through it alone from this point forward. No, not alone. She will never be alone.

"Hannah, you are my life now," Julie says, drying her hands. "I have you."

And I will always have Frankie Jones.

This is enough to make her smile.

Julie hesitates, takes in the room. Hannah is there, waiting for her, machines not keeping her alive but making life a little easier for her, for now, or so she is told. The doctor demonstrates how to hold the child within the plastic box without hurting her—miming the actions without actually holding her, instructing Julie on what she could and couldn't do, what to touch and what not to touch, reminding her to warm her hands before reaching through—and then he gives them space. He'd be around the corner if she needed anything at all.

"You can do this," she tells herself. "You can do this."

And if I go back home, I will have a place to stay.

Earl and Helen Heimlich had opened up their home to her—the closest thing she'd ever had to one, anyway, and she was always welcome back. Earl had told her as much the day he drove her to the airport as she was leaving for Reykjavík. "The door is always open, Julie," he'd said. "Whatever and whenever you need, our home is your home."

"You can do this."

As soon as Hannah's healthy enough to leave the NICU, and able to go 'home,' she'll take her back to her cozy apartment in Mosfellsbær, and as soon as she's able to fly, she'll head back to Brenden ... to the Heimlich's ... close to Frankie.

I don't have to go through this completely alone.

"Hi," Julie says, approaching the incubator. Again, she touches the plastic, keeps her hand there a while. "Believe it or not, I'm your mother. I know. Hard to believe, right?"

I need to feel.

And I can.

I can!

"Don't be scared," she says to the child, or maybe to herself.

Julie drops both hands, holds them just outside the holes, and for a moment wonders if some unexplainable force pushes back, for they are unwilling to go any farther, as if it is not air separating her hands from her daughter but invisible glass.

"You can do this."

She expects a solid surface, like the many mirrors she'd mentally gone through in the past, but her hands find their way through this time because there is nothing there at all.

With an unrelenting heart hammering within her chest, Julie wills herself to go on, to touch Hannah, and there's an incredible energy suddenly between them, something powerful, as if eliciting a touch might spark an electric shock. *Nothing is so painful to the human mind as a great and sudden change*, Julie remembers. She once quoted that line from Mary Shelley's *Frankenstein* for a school project. Touching her, will it bring her to life?

Her skin is warm, thin …

I will give her all my life, and all my love.

ACHERONTIA ATROPOS

[a fable by Julie Stipes]

A moth once emerged from her cocoon after drowned by a morning rain. Water seeped into the soil around her home, softening the outer shell. The scab-red case split as tiny legs poked through, introducing her dark world to light. She chirped through the struggle, but eventually freed all six of her legs from the pupal exoskeleton and rose out of her dirt grave.

"You have a face on your back," a voice in the oak tree said, "a gray face."

The moth, exhausted from her transformation, simply listened.

"I saw a dead cat once in a field and the face on your back looks like the dead cat's face. A skull, they call it. You have a skull on your back."

"What colors am I?" the moth said.

"Besides the face, you're darker than the mud around you, like a starless night."

"No colors at all?"

"None that I can see, but your wings aren't

ready yet. You need to let them stretch a while. Maybe you should perch up here, let them breathe."

The moth with the skull on her back shook the dirt and crawled toward the trunk of the giant oak. She traveled the exposed roots, hazy from the long sleep, skittering in zigzag paths.

"You're a strange looking bird," said the voice above.

Do birds eat moths? she wondered, remembering the finches when she and her friend were still in caterpillar form, how they eagerly pecked at the ground searching for food, for things that wriggled. She wanted to ask if the voice in the tree was that of a bird, but if a moth asked a bird such a thing, it would draw suspicion.

"I'm unique," the moth said.

"What were you doing in the mud?"

"Sleeping."

"You're not a bird, then. Can you fly?"

"Not yet. My wings are wet."

"Don't worry, I won't eat you. Moths are too powdery. No, I prefer worms and caterpillars."

The moth didn't want to tell this potential bird she had not yet learned to fly, that before her long sleep, she was wriggly food to the creature. Instead, she kept her wings back to cover her caterpillar-like body. At the trunk, she climbed, claws hooking into the bark, and her wings slowly opened.

"I knew you were a moth."

The moth chirped quietly, wings stretching.

"Birds can't climb, not like that, and you're smaller than most birds I've seen. Big for a moth, though."

"I used to be a caterpillar."

"But you've transformed. You have wings."

"Does that change who I am?"

"It changes everything. We're nearly the same. Why did you chirp?"

"I was scared, thought maybe you'd consider me a bird."

While climbing, the moth's eyesight improved, her dizzying walk steadying as she adjusted to her new body. Walking was much easier when she had more legs. Six didn't seem enough, the new ones so much longer.

"Besides, how can a bird eat something with wings?"

She recognized the fuzzy outline of not a bird, but an orange butterfly.

"You're a monarch."

"I led you to believe I was a bird because I thought you might be a bird."

"Have you seen my friend?" she said to the butterfly.

"What does she look like?"

The moth looked for the white cocoon of her friend on the silk bridge, but the cocoon and the bridge were both gone, perhaps washed away by the rain. A new, different bridge filled its place. Maybe she had already hatched and flown away, unable to find where her friend had burrowed.

"I'm not sure. Similar to me, perhaps."

"Then no, I haven't seen her. You have some color under your wings."

"I do?"

"Yellow. And stripes on your back, too, like a

bee. Your forewings are mostly black and brown like bark, but I think your second set of wings may have some yellow. Stretch them out."

The black and yellow moth extended her reach, exposing her hindwings. With her new eyesight, her peripheral vision extended beyond what she was used to. The hindwings were almost completely yellow, but she could not extend them far.

She was nearly to the monarch and climbed the same branch.

"I've seen moths before, but none like you."

"My wings are small," said the moth.

"Give them time," said the butterfly, her body still, but her beautiful, delicate wings paddling the air. "Most hang upside-down after the *eclose*, to let the wings expand and dry. I bet yours are three times that size when they're ready."

The moth dug into the branch and dangled over the edge, her wings pointing to the ground far below. She let the wind blow against them. Gradually, they emerged.

"Think you can fly now?" said the butterfly.

"I'm not sure," said the moth. "I've never done it before."

"It's easy," said the butterfly. "Flap."

The moth crawled upright to join her new friend on the branch, extended her wings fully, and then batted the air. An erratic flight, but she flew.

"Like that?"

"Like that."

She tried again, landing against the trunk.

"Your wings are loud," said the butterfly, "and you look like a queen bee. I wonder if they'd let you

take some. Maybe they wouldn't notice."

"Take what? Notice what?"

"There's honeycomb in a tree in the woods and it's full of honey, which is so much better than nectar, I've heard. I can show you. Maybe you can distract the bees."

"Have you tried honey?"

"Not many butterflies have, if any."

"Wouldn't the bees be mad if we took some, even a little?"

"Just a taste," said the butterfly. "They make too much anyway."

"Just a taste?"

"Follow me, I'll take you there."

The moth fluttered behind the butterfly until

they happened upon a honeycomb in a woods buzzing with bees.

On one of the highest branches of a black oak, the honeycomb draped like a blanket.

Hundreds of worker bees covered the surface while others patrolled the air.

The butterfly landed on the branch of a neighboring tree, so the moth joined her.

"It looks dangerous," said the moth.

A few butterfly corpses surrounded the base of the tree.

"Not for you," said the butterfly. "Some of my past friends have tried to get the honey, some stole a taste, but none returned. You're different, though. Unique, like you said. You look like them. You even smell like them, and your chirping sounds similar to their queen, so you'll fit right in. You have nothing to lose."

"Better than nectar?"

"Better than nectar. One taste and you're hooked."

Hesitating, the moth flew to the honeycomb, landing as far as she could from the bees. They crawled over the nest in waves, around and over each other.

As a caterpillar, she had always relied on her friend for courage. Things were different now that she had transformed. Along with acquiring a new form during the long sleep of caterpillars, she had somehow developed courage, and independence.

The moth with the skull on her back snuck closer, chirping, displaying yellow for all to see.

A single bee crawled toward her, touched her

wings, and let her be. Another crawled over her back, but otherwise ignored her, so she crept closer to the masses.

When curious bees approached in droves, she made her noises and they hurried away.

The reluctant moth extended her proboscis into the honey.

From the other tree, the orange monarch butterfly urged her onward. Below: broken butter-fly wings and death.

Hundreds of bees watched, some investigating; none seemed threatened by her presence.

They *accepted* her.

She took a drink—a taste, is all—and the honey filled her with warmth. One drop.

An instant rush.

The butterfly was right.

She thought again of her caterpillar friend, wishing she were around. Perhaps she hadn't survived the attack from the eight-legged creature.

Her new friend landed beneath her on the honeycomb.

"Think it's safe?" said the butterfly.

"I don't think so," said the moth. "You should go back."

A few bees flew toward them.

"With you here, it's safe."

"I'll bring you some honey," she said to the butterfly.

But it was too late.

The moth scurried to her friend and covered her fragile body with her large black wings as the bees descended. One landed next to them, trying to

get to the butterfly. Another landed on the moth's back, but her skin was too thick for the stinger to pierce. She screamed, beating her wings against the assault. One sting and either would be dead like those below.

"A taste," the moth said to her friend, protecting her.

The butterfly extended her proboscis to taste the honey.

"Thank you," she said, sliding out from under the cover and fluttering away.

The moth trembled and shook her wings and batted the bees until they were no longer a threat, until the butterfly was out of harm's way. As they retreated, she smoothed out her wings, embracing her beauty, the black and brown and the yellow. She had truly transformed during holometabolism, and in many ways. Once again, she sampled the honey and let the energy surge through her while a white sun warmed her body.

"I have a skull on my back," she told the world.

The bees continued in their labors as pollen fell around the death's-head hawkmoth in a morning glow of brilliant color, coating her wings with life-magic.

"Someday I will fly to you," she told the sun.

LIFE-MAGIC

Was life and death as simple as moths flying into flames, Julie wondered, a resurfaced memory from not so long ago, *and burning against unfuckable lightbulbs?* This last part made her laugh. Had she seen a comic strip of something similar? Was that what brought up the strange visual? For the transmogrified, it was phototactic attraction and nothing more, she knew. Phototaxis. It all seemed so binary for the simple yet complicated creatures: the difference between light and the absence of light; white and black; morning and evening; dusk and dawn. At night, would moths attempt fly to the moon as they did the sun during the day? The light switch by the door: off or on, life or death.

The burnt powdery wings of moths; she could smell their bad choices as easily as she could still smell the old ink on these pages.

What more could moths do other than to follow their instincts, their attractions?

Julie held the manuscript for "Acherontia Atropos," a few measly time-aged pages stapled together, which Frankie had told her once was a *faux pas*—a tactless act in the world of publishing. She was still in high school when she'd written the thing, so who cares. Was it any good? Who the fuck knows. They were never questions in her mind, but for some reason she'd kept her favorite stories she'd written all these years, stashed away in what her mother had called a 'hope chest.' *Hope to what, someday remember in case I forget?* 'Memory chest' would be a better term for such places to hold things through time.

Across the top of the title page, her English teacher had crossed out the all-capped ACHERONTIA ATROPOS with a red pen and had written in cursive: *No one knows this term. Why not call it something like "The Death Moth" or "The Death's-head Moth" instead? Why the Latin? Fables are meant for children, no?* This was followed by a quote Julie had later learned was plagiarized from someone named Michel de Montaigne: *"How many things we held yesterday as articles of faith which today we tell as fables."*

She was wrong, yet was right.

The story was a fable, like the others she'd written in her youth, typed out on an antique Royal typewriter because antique typewriters were "in" at the time, something cooler than using a personal computer, laptop, or tablet, and her teacher gave her more credit that she was probably due. Another A-. Always a positive followed by negative with Mrs. Ruptier's grading of her work, like a cut into something smooth.

There was more room for mistakes punching those old finger-worn keys, Julie knew, which also meant more care. She'd spent a hundred bucks on the Royal, had cleaned its typebars with lighter fluid and a brass-bristled brush, thanks to YouTube, and cranked out stories with titles like "Scarlet Hourglass" and "The Fox and the Field Mouse"—which she'd originally titled "Apodemus" because that was Latin for 'field mouse' and because the story was always more about the mouse than the fox anyway.

"If everyone stopped using Latin, wouldn't the language die?" she'd once asked.

She eventually retyped some of her earlier stories to stash away in the chest, such as "Eclose," which had originally been titled "The Long Sleep of Caterpillars" for fear of others not understanding the term for change. Julie had written that particular story when both she and Frankie had been going through the transition from childhood to womanhood. She and Frankie were the caterpillars, of course.

Modifying the titles meant re-typing the title pages entirely, but Julie never minded. She often found typing therapeutic, something to do other than cutting into herself … although both temptations tugged at her fingertips now and again. *Bleeding onto the pages*, perhaps.

The typewriter was in the chest as well, underneath the stack of stories and other memorabilia, still functional after all these years, never in need of a power source or recharge. The machine would work *ad infinitum*, again and again in the same way; forever. Would outlast *her*, even, waiting for other people's tales long after her own was done and over with.

A sheet of white paper lay against the platen, a single sentence typed onto the almost middle of the page, in all-caps, like a title of some new story of Julie's life left untold:

THE MAN N THE MIRROR.

"The man in the mirror?" she said aloud, but that wasn't quite right. The spacing was off around the letter 'N' and a few of the letters sometimes gave her trouble, she remembered.

Julie removed the old Royal from the chest and set it on the floor, sat in front of it, cross-legged, perplexed. She hit the hard return a few times to bring the page down, loving the old *clunk-clunk* sound, then pressed the smaller Lock key above the left Shift key. She carefully typed the entire alphabet in capitals, with spaces in between, each letter stabbing the paper with separate cold metal arms. And then she made harder attempts at the two troublesome keys. The 'A' and 'D' took more effort, so that the paper read:

B C E F G H I J K L M N O P Q R S T U V W X Y Z A A A D D D

"The man *and* the mirror," Julie said. "The man and the mirror."

She had apparently left herself a message from the past in this 'memory chest.'

But this particular story, albeit simply a title and nothing more, wasn't for or from a fable like the others. The 'man' in the title killed such thought, and so she rummaged through the rest of her saved treasures. She found yearbooks from Brenden High School, a few faded pictures of her mother taken in black-and-white, some sort of medal with a ribbon, Polaroid photos of her and Frankie through various years and awkwardness, one of Julie with her first crush, one with her first kiss. What was his name? School notes passed back and forth through class, folded various ways and scribbled haphazardly, a newspaper of 9/11 showing the second plane crashed halfway through the building not yet smoking, another proclaiming BIN LADEN IS DEAD, handmade friendship bracelets, her first bra, a mood ring gone black, her cutting knife, a two-dollar bill, some foreign coins she'd collected over the years, pen-pal letters, a dried red rose.

And then she found it: a receipt from her time working at Home Depot. Although the wrinkled paper was thin and nearly torn in half and the carbon printing faded, the receipt was for a single item. A wall mirror, with tax, for $87.78.

Eighty-seven seventy-eight, a palindrome number.

The man and the mirror, had she ever known his name? Why had she kept the receipt? *No, not a receipt*, she remembered, *a copy of a receipt*. After this 'man and the mirror' had made his purchase, she had handed him the original, and then had made her own copy, which she had done for all palindromic totals because it was something fun to do while working at the HD.

But why had she kept this particular receipt, after all these years? Why not any of the others? Because the man who had purchased the mirror in her checkout line could have been a doppelgänger for Elliot Cartwright. He could have been his twin, or at least a close cousin. Same cropped hair, same half-smile. And he had looked at her the way Elliot had looked at her all those years ago—not like prey, but in a way that implied he wanted to be preyed *upon* by her, as if drawn to her magnetically, emotionally, spiritually, not merely sexually … perhaps even connected to her very soul. She could still picture him now, better than any photograph.

"I broke our last one," he had said, and for some reason that had intrigued her at the time in all that it implied. 'Last,' she understood, not meaning 'previous' but 'final.' And he was broken, much like the mirror, and she had wanted to help.

The memories now flooded in like spilled water: his penetrating eyes, as if they led to other wheres and other whens; the way he carried himself—dignified, vulnerable, adaptive; the way he turned back to look at her just as he was leaving the store, catching her with a broken smile of her own, catching her trying not to notice him leaving. So much like Elliot. "I'll see you again," those eyes read, and she had believed them, although they had looked so alone.

This was three years after Iceland, three years after Hannah was born. She had forgotten about him until now, upon seeing the title of his unfinished story. She had left herself this clue, to perhaps find him one day.

The last fable she'd ever written was "The Fox and the Field Mouse," and so she began reading that story first, hoping for clues. *Perhaps he was the fox, perhaps the field mouse*, Julie thought, and then remembered the dead mouse on Elliot's doorstep, the red blotch. *Perhaps the fox.* She took a felt marker and crossed out the title, wrote APODEMUS instead, the original title.

APODEMUS

[a fable by Julie Stipes]

"You are alone, aren't you?"

The field mouse looked around cautiously. He wasn't much afraid of spiders in general, but this one, this kind, with the shiny black body and bright red stain on its belly, sent shivers down his back. They *were* loners, for the most part, but many loners in a concentrated area could be trouble.

"I guess if you had friends, I'd be dead already."

It wasn't such a nice thing to say, even to a spider. He felt bad for saying it. He thought of apologizing, but the damage was done and the spider charged across her web, those eight legs surprisingly fast.

She had caught him off-guard. The field mouse nearly tumbled backward off the fencepost. Agile, the field mouse somehow managed to escape, quickly darting across the white painted wood, hopping to the trunk of a nearby oak tree, and back to safety.

Was that a spiny leg that had brushed my tail?

He thought so. He had nearly brushed death.

Never again would he take that shortcut. Likewise, he would never take the shortest path to the gardens, which ran parallel to the woodpile, where such vile creatures like this shiny black spider lurked. He saw them sometimes, hiding in the many shadows.

"Stay away from the pile," his friends had warned.

He'd gone there once, after a hard rain, like the one the night before. The wild mushrooms were plentiful around the base of the pile, often growing directly on the wood. He hadn't seen the spiders, then, but knew they were there, the same way he knew stars still filled the sky when the sun rose and turned the world above light blue. The same stars, every night. Rain had washed away the spiders' webs and they'd rebuild, he knew. And sometimes they hid, like the stars, waiting for the sun to go down. Without the sun, shadows were no longer shadows and their hiding places opened up to the rest of the world.

That thought scared the field mouse more than anything at all.

The garden was abundant with life.

Various lettuces filled one box, carrots in another, along with the usual tomatoes, beans, squash and a few fruits. The garden was filled with moving life as well. Bees pollenated the flowers, a hummingbird stuck its proboscis into a hanging feeder filled with red sugar water, beetles and ants roamed the box tops, and the air buzzed with insects and chirped with birds. Freshly watered by the rain, a few of the planter boxes had soil tunneled by worms.

The orange and white pup drew the field mouse's attention, however. Never before had he seen such a strange-looking creature.

He thought of it as a pup because he or she seemed young and dog-like, yet had cat-like features, such as the pointed ears that stood straight up, and the bottlebrush tail. It dug its nose into the corner of a planter box on the opposite side of the garden.

A cat surely wouldn't do such a thing.

Quietly, the field mouse edged along the base of the nearest box. Curiosity called for a closer look.

A brown nose rose from the soil and turned his direction. Marble eyes saw him.

The field mouse froze.

A cat would properly pursue, head low to the ground, eyes never leaving its target. A cat would stalk him, ears back and tail flat, one paw slowly moving in front of the other.

A cat would glide across the ground in this slowest of motions until close enough to pounce. He had watched a few of his friends go this way to the great beyond.

The orange and white pup, however, surely an adolescent, by the look of him, paid no further attention. The nose buried once again into the soil, prodding, and returned with a small potato wedged in its mouth.

The field mouse unfroze.

A cat would never eat a potato.

The foreign voice of a human called out across the yard and the orange and white pup fled.

When he returned home to the nest in the field, the mouse forgot to mention the sighting of the pup in the garden. His mind was preoccupied with baby arachnids.

"I think we should move to another field," said the field mouse, "or at least farther into the field. I don't want to risk the lives of our children."

The mother of three mice snarled, her whiskers furrowing beneath the pink dot of her nose. "But we've moved three times already," she said. "We seem to be distancing ourselves from food."

"We'll find more food," he said.

"Running away from our problems is not always the best solution," she said. "Sometimes we need to face them."

The field mouse thought of the path to the garden. The shortest route ran along the woodpile of shadows and through the white picket fence by the oak.

"I'll help protect the family, Daddy," said his youngest. She showed a defensive stance.

"Me too," said her brother, doing the same.

"You will do no such thing," said their mother, pushing a piece of carrot to their third child.

"I just want for all of you to be safe," said the field mouse, "and well-fed. If we decide to stay here—"

"We're staying here," said the mother.

"Like I was saying, if we decide to stay here, we need to abide by a few rules. And this goes for all of you, even me. No exceptions."

The family of field mice quickly ate, intrigued.

"No woodpile."

"But the mushrooms—" his youngest said.

"Soon the woodpile will be overrun. It will no longer be safe. It's not safe now. We will have to find mushrooms elsewhere. I can begin my search tomorrow. I know how you all love mushrooms. But, no woodpile means no shortcut to the garden."

"Please tell me we haven't lost the garden," said the mother.

"We still have the garden," he said.

This caused a great sigh of relief.

"It's a long path around the house, I know, but it's a safe path. Who knows? Maybe I'll find us a nice patch of mushrooms along the way."

All three of the children brightened.

"No playing by the oak tree."

"There's a lot of oak trees, Daddy," said his daughter.

"No playing by the oak tree by the white picket fence. Nearest the house. The one with the cracked trunk where the squirrels are always stashing their finds."

"There's lots of other oak trees, Daddy."

The field mouse didn't mean to exclude the pup sighting in his family's morning discussion. He had merely forgotten, distracted perhaps by his fear of the spiders. He had forgotten all about him until later that afternoon when he explored the long way around the house to the garden.

Part of an orange and white tail poked out of a tangle of wild blackberry bushes running along a small creek.

Potatoes and berries: such a strange diet for such a strange-looking creature.

Silently, the field mouse followed the creek until he skirted his 'safe distance' with the pup. The tail was motionless. He watched long enough to determine that the pup had most likely fallen asleep while eating the wild blackberries.

"Pup?" said the field mouse, and he waited.

The bottlebrush was still.

Cats wouldn't eat potatoes. Cats wouldn't eat berries. But cats *would* stay motionless, for what seemed lifetimes, before they pounced. This creature surely wasn't feline, and if he or she were readying to pounce, it would pounce in the opposite direction of the tail, which now pointed straight at the field mouse, for he had slowly crept closer to investigate.

"Pup?" he repeated.

He was no longer a 'safe distance' away and was certain he could be heard.

The tail lay motionless.

Upon closer inspection, this wasn't even the same pup. The tail was larger, darker, aged.

Creatures that ate potatoes and berries surely didn't eat mice. This thought ran through his mind over and over again as he approached.

"Hello?"

Even if it were sleeping, the field mouse was sure his voice would be heard and the creature would startle awake.

Yet the tail remained still.

Something was wrong.

The smell told him this, as well as the inedible fungi that had sprouted around the fallen creature. Mushrooms only ever grew on things that were no longer living. And the white larvae, like ever-bending grains of rice, only fed on things no longer living.

He continued his exploratory journey around the house. The long path to the garden took three times longer than the shortcut past the woodpile, yet it was much safer. Instead of the typical shadow cover, the sun warmed his travels, and it was comforting. The sun seemed to rid the world of vile creatures.

"Hey, you're new," chirped a finch.

"Not new, really," said the field mouse.

"Haven't seen you before. Seed!" The finch, with its yellow beak, pecked the ground. "Nope. Rock."

The bird hopped along the ground next to him, pecking, shaking her head, pecking.

"Seed! Nope. Piece of wood. Where you headed?"

"I'm on my way to the garden."

"Where you from?"

"My family and I live near the rosebushes on the other side of the house."

"Roses by the oak?"

The finch hopped, pecked.

Nearly everything she picked up in her beak, she shook back out. She followed alongside him.

If they were ambushed by a cat, at least the cat would go after the much distracted bird first, though the field mouse wouldn't wish such a fate on any creature. It was a horrible thought and he felt bad for even thinking it.

With exception to the wings, they were about the same size.

The finch was so distracted, in fact, that she didn't even notice he hadn't answered her question about where he lived. He lived by the red roses, but didn't tell her this.

"Seed! Yep, seed."

"Have you ever seen an orange and white cat that isn't really a cat? Big, bushy tail, with ears as tall as you and me?"

"Cat here's gray- and black-striped," said the finch." She pecked the ground a half dozen more times before saying, "Only cat I've seen. Does it yip?"

"I'm not sure. The one I saw dug for potatoes in the garden." He decided not to mention the one he'd found by the wild blackberry bushes.

"Potatoes?" The bird snatched a twig, shook it free, and kept hunting. "Not a cat. Fox. You saw a fox."

"What's a fox?"

"Not a cat."

"Thanks," said the field mouse. The bird wasn't much to talk to, but he felt safer having her there.

"Caterpillars!"

The finch flew off and landed next to a few birds that looked just like her.

When the field mouse finally made it to the garden, the fox pup wasn't there as he'd expected. He wondered if the pup knew about the dead fox in the wild blackberry bushes.

Perhaps they were related. How could the pup react to seeing such a thing? Perhaps the pup was lost, alone, scared …

The distance between the nest by the rosebush and the garden was going to be a problem.

Three times the distance meant three times the amount of time it took to get from one place to the other, and three times the effort to move food from the other to the one place.

It took most of the day to move a carrot, a bundle of strawberries and a stack of peapods.

"I don't see how this is going to work," he said to his family. "We need to move to the other side of the house."

"I like it here," said their oldest child.

"Me too," said the next.

"Me too," said the next.

"And our family is only getting bigger," said the mother. "A few more are on the way. We're in no condition to just pack up and move. Any luck finding mushrooms?"

The field mouse thought of the dead fox.

"None that are edible."

The children seemed disappointed.

"I can help look tomorrow," said his oldest, although she was far too young still to scavenge.

The field mouse thought of the fox pup digging for potatoes on its own, perhaps too young to scavenge.

"Maybe she can go with you tomorrow," said the mother.

He thought it over.

Together they could move twice the food. If only the boys were older, they could all go out and bring in four times the amount of food in the same amount of time. Toward the end of summer they'd be old enough to scavenge as a pack.

"Tomorrow you can come with me," he said to his daughter.

"I don't want to go," she said, "but I agree with

Daddy. We should move. Not to the other side of the house, though. We're field mice. We should be in the field."

"Absolutely not," said the mother.

"We *have* relied on the garden more than we should," he said. "The garden won't always be here. It's gone every autumn, and stays gone through winter, and not until late spring each year do we get to live in this paradise."

The family sat idle, pondering the idea.

"After the babies come," said the mother, "and only after they're old enough to move safely. We can all work hard over the next few months, pack as much food as we can and store it here. We'll move only when we're absolutely ready to move."

The youngest two didn't seem to care.

The oldest seemed excited.

The mother looked concerned.

Later that night, when the children were fast asleep, he asked her if she had ever heard of a fox.

"Orange and white, you say?"

"With ears like ours."

"The size of a cat?"

"But not a cat."

"Do they eat mice?"

"This one didn't want to eat me."

He told her about the potato.

"I think he may be an orphan."

The pup was there late the next morning. The garden was once again alive with life. Instead of digging for potatoes, the orange and white fox bit into an unripe green tomato and pulled it free from the branch. With his head low, he ate.

"I like your taste in food," said the field mouse.

The young fox rose from the ground, startled, and took another bite. "What if I liked eating field mice," he said.

"Do you?"

"Nah, I'm messing with you. Others might, but I stick to vegetables. If it talks, I won't eat it."

The fox ate the rest of the unripe tomato.

"You should try those when they're red and ripe," said the field mouse.

"I've only ever had them like this."

"First season here?"

"I don't know what a season is, but we've only ever seen green ones. Only been here a few days. I don't think we're supposed to be here, though," he said, his nose pointed to the house, "because the thing that lives in there scares us away."

"You keep saying we and us," said the field mouse. "Where's the rest of your pack?"

"The last time the thing with the scary voice came outside, he had a dog. My mom and brother were on one side of this place and I was on the other. The dog chased them away."

"Where are they now?"

If foxes could shrug, this one shrugged.

"I don't know. My mom always said that if we ever get split up, or lost from one another, that we should meet here, by these boxes. We got split up three days ago. Maybe they got so lost they forgot their way back."

The field mouse somehow knew the aged

tail he had seen poking from the wild blackberry bushes belonged to this poor creature's mother.

His brother, if the dog didn't catch him, too, was most likely lost and alone like this pup.

"I'll help you find your family," said the field mouse. "I'm good at following tracks."

"Mom always said to meet here if we got lost."

"I have an idea. If you help me bring a bunch of food back to my place for my family, I will help you find *your* family. We can make trips from here to there all day, so if they return to the garden, you'll see them. If by the end of the day you don't, meet me back here in the morning and together we can try to find them."

"You promise you'll help me find them?" the fox asked.

"I promise."

Seven trips back and forth between the garden and the nest by the red rosebush yielded enough food for weeks.

The fox taught the mouse about reburying the root plants—the potatoes, carrots, and beets—to make them last.

This was something he had never thought of before. Basically, transplanting the vegetables.

"That's why I dig roots so much," said the fox, a clever pun.

He was a fast digger and did most of the work.

"Just watch for moles," he said. "They'll steal your food without you even knowing it.

The mother was hesitant at first to let the fox

into their home, but after seeing how willing he was to help and how gentle he was around the children, she quickly grew fond of him.

"What does your mother look like?" she asked. "How will the two of you find her?"

The fox did the shrug thing again and said, "She looks like me, I guess, but her tail has a black spot on the very tip."

At those words, the field mouse's heart sank. The tail poking out from the blackberry bushes had a black mark on the tip. He must not have hidden the apathy well, because the fox's expression saddened.

"You've seen her," he said.

The field mouse nodded.

"And my brother … did you see him as well?"

The field mouse shook his head.

"We'll look for him in the morning. You can stay here tonight."

That was the last they spoke of the long sleep.

The fox led him to the edge of the garden to the place where he had lost track of his family.

They took the shortest route, which meant passing the woodpile and then the white picket fence by the oak tree, an area of the farm now flourishing with spiders. With the fox at his side, the field mouse felt safe and the spiders hid in the shadows.

"Here," said the fox. "The three of us were here when the door opened and the dog started the chase. I ran that direction," he said, pointing to the east with his snout, "and my mom and brother ran that way."

His snout turned to the west, toward the open field where the field mice had earlier discussed moving their home.

Even after several days, the tracks were still visible. Heavy paw marks chased smaller, faint paw marks from the past, which they followed into a present field of tall grass and shrubs. A few matchstick trees spiked the sky.

They happened upon a hollowed out stump.

"This is where the chase split."

A single, smaller set of tracks led toward a gathering of manzanita. A larger set of tracks, trampled upon by a heavier set of dog tracks, most assuredly, led to what the field mouse could only believe were the wild blackberry bushes along the creek bed.

"Your brother went this way."

The fox sniffed the ground, turned his head, and looked the direction of his mother. At this level, the fox and the field mouse were the same height, and for the first time they were eye to eye.

"Do you really think he's still alive?" said the fox. "It's been three days and—"

"You and your brother are the same age?"

"Yes."

"Well, it's been three days and *you're* still alive. Alone, you've found a way. And there are no tracks that follow his into the field. Alone, he has also probably found a way."

With this new hope, the fox sat upright, towering over the field mouse. The warm sun shimmered yellow off his orange coat of fur. His ears perked at the distant sound of a dog barking from the opposite direction, but he seemed unafraid.

Along the way, the manzanita slowly overtook the field. The farther they ventured, the less the sun's heat tired them. The creek had somehow wound back around to join them. It was much cooler, the ground damp and soft.

"Mushrooms!" exclaimed the field mouse.

They sprouted everywhere around the flaky, brown and red branches of the manzanita.

He grabbed a mushroom cap.

"Are they good?" the fox said.

"*Are* they good," the field mouse replied, not as a question.

The fox sniffed suspiciously then took a bite.

"Well?"

"Delicious."

"I can see why your brother chose this direction. Me and my family could *live* out here. We seriously could and just might. This is paradise."

"Brother?" said the fox, looking around.

"This way," said the field mouse.

The tracks ended at the creek, but he could see that they started up again on the other side.

Rocks large enough to hold his weight worked as a dry bridge to cross the water. Seven hops and he was across. The fox leapt over the entire thing in a single bound, his back feet splashing in the water at the edge.

Together, they followed the tracks as they appeared and disappeared in the dirt, until they ended completely at a hole dug into a mound. The field mouse was about to ask what it was, thinking of snakes and other nuisances in the wild, when the fox told him.

"It's a fox hole."

The black mouth in the ground looked ready to swallow.

"Brother?"

Scurrying from within the mouth caused soil to rain from its dirty lips.

The field mouse hunkered behind the hind legs of the fox, ready for the worst of things imaginable: the head of a large snake to emerge, or the legs of a hairy tarantula, or perhaps some kind of ground-dwelling owl.

Instead, a black nose poked out, followed by a white and orange snout speckled brown from burrowing in the foxhole for who knows how long. The fox's brother sprung from the hole. Without the dirt, the two would look nearly identical.

They brushed noses and danced playfully around each other, the field mouse backing away carefully to avoid getting trampled.

"He got Mom," said the dirty fox.

The brother must have found her on its own, such a horrible thought. Images of the aged fox tail filled the mouse's mind, along with thoughts of the dog …

"I know," said the clean fox. "My new friend told me." He motioned to the field mouse. "He helped me find you."

"Thank you," said the dirty fox. He turned to his brother. "I got lost and couldn't find my way back to the place Mom told us to go if we got lost."

"We can live here now," said the clean fox. "You can, too," he said to his new friend.

"The place is full of love!" the field mouse said to his family later that evening. "And life, and places to hide, and fewer things to hide *from* … So full of love!"

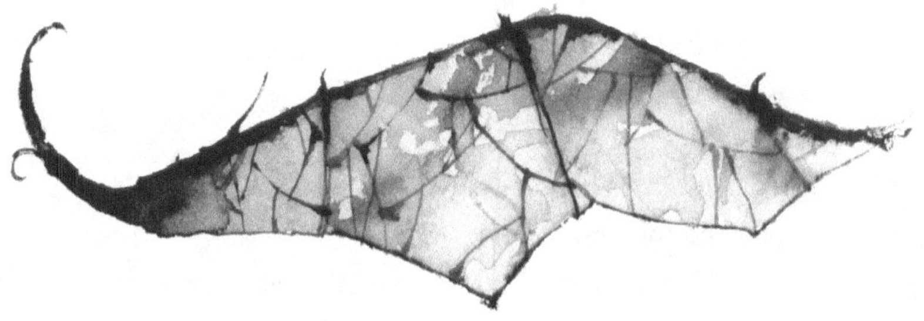

ENSO

Julie gave each of the four fables their appropriate titles, whether in Latin or not. She read each in turn, then swapped their order and read them again, repeating until she'd read each and every possible sequence. What she found was that the order did not matter. The short tales worked together as one, creating a larger, nonlinear, almost circular story not merely representing moments in *her* life, but *all* life.

And she was not one animal, but perhaps many, perhaps *all.*

She was the caterpillar.

She was the moth.

She was the spider.

She was perhaps none of these things.

Ensō, she thought, remembering a mediation class she'd taken on Japanese ink painting, the symbol often used to express a moment the mind is free to let the body create.

She bound the four fables in no particular order with a paperclip, and from her desk pulled a sheet of paper and covered the stack of pages. She then freehanded counterclockwise a giant black circle using a single stroke of the felt marker. Her *ensō* symbolized a moment of pure enlightenment, representing both the universe and *mu*—the void—with both elegance and strength. Inside this void, Julie wrote those four letters, giving her collection a title.

Julie thought of Elliot and his place in this history—*her*story—of fables, and couldn't help but think of 'The Man in the Mirror,' whoever *he* might be, for that story was yet to be told, not a part of her past, like the others, but her future, perhaps stuck somewhere in the *mu*, still *waiting* to be told.

She pulled the single sheet of paper from the old Royal typewriter, read over THE MAN N THE MIRROR title once again with its missing letters, smiled, then crumpled the page into a ball and held it tightly within her palm, for palms held stories of their own, with every wrinkle meaningful. "The Man in the Mirror" was not her story to tell, and so she'd never force herself to write it like the others; instead, she'd play her part, if that's what the story required, as one of its many characters.

"What's his name?" she asked the room. "What's *his* story?"

SOMNAMBULISM
/ I SUMMON LAMBS

[an anagram]

Without love, life is not worth the effort.

Put the barrel of a gun in your mouth, pull the trigger, and show the world you're made of flesh and bone and gray matter and nothing else, because without love, true love, the type of which palpitates your heart every time your eyes make contact with a significant other, well, without soul-to-soul connection, then what are you but organic substance? What are you but another loveless, pointless man waking up each morning to rinse and repeat recursive tasks to get you through the day?

Why suffer through it?

Others depend on me, and for whatever reason I cannot allow myself to let them down. Either pride or dysfunction is the reasoning. I have a son. I had a wife. The tense of the verb tells the story. Matty is fifteen now. I still call him by his nickname, which is probably why he doesn't talk to me. He calls me Aeron. Not a father, or his dad, or any sort of acknowledgment to our relationship. His mother, Karen Stevenson, kept the surname following the divorce and still clings onto it, mostly for Matty's sake. She says it's so his friends at school won't ask questions, so he won't have to explain why his parents got divorced. I'm sure they know. Everyone knows.

I could skirt around the truth, but it's better to let it out, to let the horrid matter splatter onto the walls because I still taste oil and metal.

Karen wanted a few days without me around while I stayed behind to sort out inner demons. She kissed me on the cheek and told me to call if I needed her.

The solitude brought a gun to my head. I loved her. Matty, too, and I couldn't let the darkness inside my head spread to them.

I called my reflection Norea, a mirrored version of my name. I thought of the various means of ending my life to pull this off, but a revolver seemed easiest.

The man looking at me through the other side of the mirror needed to see what I wanted him to see, so I moved the barrel out of my mouth and to my right temple. Norea moved the barrel to his left. Perhaps he controlled the marionette strings at this point and wanted me to see. I can't remember pulling the trigger that first time.

A single bullet hiding amongst six chambers decided our fate. I spun the cylinder and pressed the barrel against our head a second time and pulled the trigger without hesitation.

With a shaky hand, I raised the gun a third time.

Pull the fucking trigger, he said.

He smiled, and then pulled it for me.

Voicemail, meaning he saw my name and chose to ignore the call.

"Hey, Matty, it's me. I haven't heard your voice in a while and wanted to say hi. Your birthday's next week and, well, I'm sure you know that, but I was hoping to maybe take you out for pizza or something, play some arcades, or maybe see a movie. Call me back when you can."

No return calls or texts.

I try his mother with a text because I know she won't pick up with my name on her display. Surprisingly, she calls *me*.

"Aeron, you've gotta stop this. If he doesn't want to talk to you, he doesn't want to talk to you. You can't come to me every time he doesn't answer his phone."

"His birthday's tomorrow."

"And you think texting me will make him want to spend time with you?"

"I'm his father."

"Right now he doesn't want you to be. He's a teenager now. He would rather spend time with his friends. And he should. We all go through that stage."

"The stage where you don't acknowledge your father's existence? He hasn't returned my calls in nearly two months, Karen. His last text to me was *k*, a single letter."

There is silence from her end, revealing she cares, and a sigh. Even after all these years, silence is a language we both understand.

I imagine a finger in her hair, twirling, her eyes to the floor, one foot rubbing the other.

"What do you want me to do, Aeron?"

"I don't know. Tell him I called."

"I will."

"Tell him I have his present."

"Do you?"

"Yes."

Another moment of silence means she's shaking her head, looking to the ceiling or to the clock perhaps.

"What is it?"

"A new helmet."

"Jesus, Aeron …"

"I want him to be safe. It's black with flames on the side. He'll like it. And gloves—"

"We sold the bike."

"What?"

"Have you been taking your meds? The bike's been gone for months. He hasn't wanted to ride since he broke his collarbone."

"Again?"

"A year ago. He broke his collarbone last spring. Remember?"

Karen never wanted Matty to have a motorcycle, so I got him a BMX. A tire slip on a dirt ramp had sent Matty over the handlebars and landing onto his side. It was a clean break.

"You haven't been sleeping much, have you?"

"Some."

Why suffer through it?

When I sleep regularly, it's four or five hours per night. Some doctors think a week of sleeping like this will put a person in a state similar to constant drunkenness, with longer exposure requiring psychological evaluation.

"Have you been sleepwalking again?"

"Maybe. Hard to tell living alone. Sometimes I wake up in strange places, so maybe."

Somnambulism.

That's what my psychiatrist calls it. Differentiating between dream state and reality is often difficult, which is probably part of the reason for the sleep deprivation. A fear of falling asleep. What if I don't wake up? What if I can't wake up? What if the reality I think I know is the dream, or vice versa?

"Aeron, you still there?" It's not Karen, but my doctor.

My watch tells me three hours are gone. Reality is a blur.

"What do you see?"

I see two black dragons holding hands and kissing with their tails braided together, the image split symmetrically down the center, but not entirely. It's the first Rorschach inkblot test Rae shows me. It could be a butterfly or some kind of facemask, but my first thought is a pair of dragons, so that's what I tell her.

My shrink's name is Angel Rae, which I think is a rather beautiful name, but I always call her Rae. Calling her Angel or Dr. Rae never sounds right. I expect something like 'interesting,' but she simply switches cards.

"And this one?"

"Some kind of demon face. A butterfly-shaped demon face."

"And this one?"

The next card shows an oily squashed butterfly with elongated antenna horns.

"A butterfly."

"The second image that comes to mind, then."

"A face."

"Good. Point out what you see."

"It's *my* face. Here, the eyes," I say, pointing to the round inkless areas on either side.

The sockets around the empty stare resemble my own features, as if looking into a mirror in a dark room with my face covered in black mud. I see a half smirk on the right side of what resembles my mouth, which would be my left. Karen used to point out that sometimes when I smile, only one side of my face reacted. Bell's palsy. She always called it the Stevenson smirk because everyone in my family shares a similar smile.

I point to the lips, which are curled, a darker section of cheekbone, a fleshless nose, an evil brow, sharp ears that furl like the dragon wings on the earlier picture.

Rae stays on this one the longest, the others merely flashed in front of me.

"Do you remember this card from before, Aeron?"

I shake my head.

"You think this one looks like you?"

"Sort of."

"Last week you called this one Norea."

◻ ◻ ◻

My heart skips a beat for the first time in ten years. She is that beautiful. And I recognize her. Soul mates, living together, laughing together, in love. There's a pull between us. The world is forcing us together, or perhaps to remember an alternate past.

We're both shopping for food, and I spy her spying me, looking over her shoulder, not in a 'Why the hell are you following/stalking me' manner, but an intentional 'I want you to notice me noticing you' manner.

She smiles, as I do, with only one side of her mouth. Her piercings are many but accentuate her remarkable features: two small hoops in the lobes of each ear, a few a little higher up, and one on her bicuspid. She's somewhat of a Gothic type; this usually doesn't interest me in the slightest, but my heart tells me otherwise. Strands of hair dyed purple. A doll.

I know her.

I know I know her.

The cart is still empty and I aimlessly push it around the produce aisles. I can't remember why I'm here, but I must be out of food.

This girl is petite. As she reaches for the roll of produce bags, her midriff reveals part of a tattoo in solid black to skip my heart another beat. I have a thing for tattoos. She's not my type, but types must change over time.

Like a schoolboy with a crush, I look away, push my empty cart past her, to more food that doesn't seem to want my attention, and as I pass, I feel her eyes at my back. She's watching me. I somehow know her well, and know it's what she would do in such a moment.

What I don't expect is the giant brown bag of potatoes she drops in my cart before disappearing around the corner. And I feel her smirking.

◻ ◻ ◻

"Why are you telling me this, Aeron?"

Somehow I made it home and had Karen on the cellular. I don't remember finishing my shopping, nor driving home, yet I'm in the middle of putting away groceries.

"I mean, it's great you're finally showing interest in another human being other than me and Matty, but this should be something you tell your friends about, or Doctor Rae."

"We *are* friends."

"I know, and I love you, Aeron, but ..."

Karen is home, pressing two fingers against her temple.

This, I know.

There are no signs of potatoes and I wonder whether or not my mind had made up the encounter entirely. Was I perhaps in some kind of lucid dream?

"Did you talk to her at least?"

"I can't remember."

"Well, if you see her again, talk to her. That's the only advice I can give you. If there really is some kind of cosmic or karmic connection between you, something will happen. If it doesn't, it doesn't, but at least you tried. Remember how long it took you to gather up enough nerve to ask me out?"

"It took two weeks to ask your name."

"And we had a class together. People, this woman at the store ... you may never see her again. Time's not always on your side."

As I admit to questioning her existence, I see the bag of potatoes next to the stove.

Time is constant, at least in this existence. Without time on my side, I have no chance.

"You're right. The next time I see her, if I ever see her again, I'll talk to her."

"Good. It will be good for you. Look, I need to go, but did Matty ever get back to you about his birthday tomorrow?"

"Hold on."

If he had, I can't remember.

I check the call history and text messages, but his only text is the *k* and he hadn't returned a call in a solid month.

"Nothing."

"Stop by tomorrow around seven. He and his friends are going go-cart racing, but he'll be back at that time. Join us for pizza."

"I don't know what to do anymore. He's disowned me."

"You can be here at seven. Don't stop trying to be a father. Eventually he will see through the past and realize you still need to be in his life. But return the damn helmet. Get him an Apple gift card and tell him it's to put toward a new iPhone. I can't afford to get him one."

"Karen, do you remember why I called?"

Rorschach was obsessed with these damn butterflies. Rae holds up another and I'm tempted to call it a moth to test her reaction.

"I see a bat, spiraling downward."

"Interesting."

Her first use of 'interesting.'

"You see motion in this one, or movement?"

There's a spiral-like pattern in the center of the card, as if ink poured in such a pattern before the paper folded in half to create the symmetry.

The next image looks similar to hands forming the gesture for 'bird' in sign language, thumbs linked together and fingers mimicking wings.

"This next image is a bit different from the rest," Rae says, holding the card.

All the cards up to this point were black ink splotches on stark white paper. This one has a few drops of red amongst the black.

"What do you see?"

"A black face with red eyes."

"And this one?"

"The same face with blue eyes."

"And this one?"

Rae expects the reaction. It's the same card from our last session, the one I told her was me, my face, my smirk, the same card I unknowingly told her was Norea sometime before, only in this depiction he has red eyes and flame hair. Thoughts return of the girl at the store.

"How do you feel seeing this, Aeron?"

"May I see the card?"

She hands it over and I hold it to my face like a mask.

"How would *you* feel seeing something like this?"

"I don't think it looks like you, Aeron."

"Imagine looking into the mirror each morning with this guy staring back."

"Norea."

"Why is the hair on fire?"

"Why do you think Norea's hair is on fire? Significance?"

"Someone set him on fire. It's the first thing I thought of … the eyes burning." I remove the card from my face and return it to her. "In front of the mirror, all those years back, I saw this face, my face, but with those same eyes looking into me, through me, through the glass."

"The glass you shot."

I remember the incident clearly: the gun moving from my mouth to the side of my head, a few more clicks of the hammer against empty spun cylinders, my mind cloudy, my hands and eyes heavy like the Colt .38, and finally the hammer finding a round, the gun pointing wayward, the bullet drawn to the man in the mirror—his face, not mine.

"Maybe Rorschach saw something similar when looking into the mirror."

"These are not Rorschach inkblot tests. These are your drawings from your time with Dr. Milton. Do you remember making these?"

She shows them to me again: black symmetric faces with red eyes, blue eyes, fiery hair, some with deep scarlet expelling from the mouth or from empty sockets.

"These are copies of the drawings you created, under his care, hung on your walls."

All the damn butterflies, the bat, the masks … they can't all be mine: thick black ink, ballpoint, charcoal, paints.

"These aren't inkblot tests?"

Rae shakes her head and writes something down.

"Maybe *he* made them," I say, considering the implications.

It means he's still around—this man on the other side.

"Aeron, when was the last time you looked into a mirror?"

¤   ¤   ¤

Three pills set me right. I wash them down with Kraken rum. Not a good thing to do, I know, but for the moment it's what calls me.

"Matty. Matt, it's me again." I sound like an idiot, but sometimes fathers are idiots. "Hey, I'll be at your mother's at seven."

Answer your phone, I want to say, but I suppress a sigh that hopefully won't cross over into the message like some ghastly spirit.

"Anyway, I'll see you then."

I toss the phone onto the bed and fight the urge to stare into the bathroom mirror, afraid Norea will be there. Either he's there or he's not there. I want to see, but I don't. The last image burned into my head is my reflection in the mirror: my head bursting open and flowering red onto the walls—his head, not mine—and glass snowflakes falling around me.

The phone rings. Karen.

"Where are you?"

"At my place. Why?"

"You were supposed to be here at seven."

The alarm clock on the nightstand reads 7:27.

"Hold on," I tell her, checking the call logs.

I left Matty the voicemail at 5:25.

Somewhere, two hours had slipped, another poke through the fabric, reminding me of String Theory, of multiverses layered one on top of the other. Where am I in this string knot? Which string holds me in place, or do any of them? I imagine a quantum elevator door opening in some unknown when and where to let me out.

There must be another me to fill these gaps of memory, these jaunts through time.

"I'm on my way."

"Matty's still with his friends, but he knows you're coming over, so don't look bad by not being here when he gets home."

Home is a sad word when you're on your own.

For Matty, home is his mother's. Twenty years from now, he'll visit for Thanksgiving or Christmas or other gatherings to see his mother and he'll see it as *coming home*, while my place will forever be referred to as 'Dad's place' or 'Dad's apartment,' or simply 'Dad's.'

"Aeron."

"Yes?"

"Take your meds."

Karen lets me stay until nine. She'd let me stay longer, but I feel out of place without Matty there. The untouched wine in her glass and her incessant tidying tells me she's uncomfortable with me waiting on her couch with an unopened birthday card on the coffee table.

My face is a mask of sad adjectives.

Why can't these be the moments that slip away?

I taste metal, but it's only a memory.

Sorry excuses of pencil sketches cover the table. Some resemble those Rae showed me, yet none seem drawn by the same hand. I use a red ballpoint to fill in recognizable eyes, which is funny considering eyes are the only parts of you that truly connect in mirrors.

When was the last time you looked into a mirror?

Years.

There's one mirror in the apartment—the bathroom—and it's lonely. A fear of the unseen/unknown keeps it on the wall. The things you don't see scare you most: the figure out of focus, the monster off-camera, what may or may not be hiding or watching from the shadows.

And so the mirror stays, in hopes that whatever lives on the other side of the glass will not be there—a form of control; without the mirror, I wouldn't have the choice of looking or not looking.

The light is always on in the bathroom. Soft white outlines the door, competing with moonlight earnestly permeating through the bedroom window. I have a suspicion Norea is afraid of the light, as I am afraid of the dark. Perhaps *he* turns his light off for *me*.

The world is quiet, but for the braying of my neighbor's sheep.

On the morning that follows, I discover a lamb generated the awful noise. It's a marvel such sounds can come from something so small.

The body walks awkwardly, as if learning to stand for the first time. There is no sign of the mother. My guess is the mother gave birth the night before, which would explain the death pleas keeping me awake. Besides finches pecking the soil, the lamb is the only creature within the small fenced yard. Why would someone raise sheep near an apartment complex?

The weedy, overgrown yard could provide sustenance for a fully-grown sheep, but this baby, this lamb, needs its mother's milk.

This makes me think of Matty, once a lamb, now nearly fully grown into a sheep, or a Matt or Matthew, and how he still clings to his mother. He wants nothing to do with me.

I don't even call Karen this time because I'm tired of hearing the same disappointing words. I'd rather listen to the sad braying of the lamb than be told my son's a teenager and needs space from his undeserving father.

"He's been through a lot," Karen would say, meaning what *I* had put him through.

Sketches wait for me on the table, those I created after my last session with Rae: some in Sharpie, ballpoint, paints. I even tried both hands. My black butterfly faces are pathetic, as if drawn by a shaky child. They're not symmetric in the slightest. Sorting through them, I can't help but wonder if she lied.

Perhaps the creator still hides behind the glass.

The bathroom light flickers to reveal a silhouette face outlined in white on the mirror. I don't remember turning it off. A piece of paper with a familiar image. I peer through the doorframe, not yet ready to confront any part of my reflection in the dark.

I keep the paper on the outskirts of my peripheral until it's directly in front of me, head level. And then I'm looking at a mask: black outstretched wings donned in thick acrylic. Scotch tape holds the painting in place, my face perfectly covered.

After avoiding reflections in rearview mirrors and restaurant restrooms and windows and whatnot for the last however many years, I see his eyes through holes ripped in the wingspan.

Four hands with black-stained cuticles reach to the face and two find the surface wet.

Closing my eyes, I turn off the light.

◻ ◻ ◻

Ten-year-old memories fill the darkness.

The girl from the grocery store, she's behind the counter at a Home Depot ringing me up for a mirror. She's a few years younger. Her name badge reads JULIE.

[the letters are red and the last three characters are larger than the rest]

Is this a gift?

She's curious, but I don't know why.

A replacement. I broke our last one.

I had shot it, in fact.

The amount flashes on the monitor as she scans the barcode on the box. The price is a number palindrome, or perhaps an anagram.

That will be eighty-seven seventy-eight, she says.

I sign the check and hand it to her.

Is there anything else I can help you with?

She brushes the blonde hair out of her eyes and rests a hand on her waist. She's wearing a pair of tight, low-cut jeans, and a loosely worn orange smock. As she bends sideways to move the mirror, the beginning of a black tattoo dragon peeks out near her pierced navel. It looks too good to be fake, at least the part I can see.

Sure, Julie. As a matter of fact, there is something you can help me with … you can [the memory faded] … something about the most terrible episode of—

[puzzle pieces, hammered in place]

Me, staring.

No, this will be all.

There's something about her.

I hand her the check and she hands me the receipt, avoids eye contact, and rings up another customer. She's short, cute, and fit, but also somewhat rebellious, which isn't a bad thing. And I'm married, at the time, so there ends the fantasy.

In the reflection of the glass doors, I notice her smile.

And then I remember the letter and the rose—

"How were the potatoes?"

Suddenly Julie is in front of me, years later: the present. Neither of us pushes a shopping cart. I remember standing in front of the bathroom mirror with a black wing mask covering the face of my reflection, and I remember closing my eyes and turning off the light, but everything after is gone. A dream long lost after awakening.

The dragon connects these multiverse strings. I know this, but I'm not even sure of the day or time, but I'm back at the grocery store, meaning I'm foodless and two weeks of my life have fallen into the void. My mind rambles as she waits for an answer.

"Exquisite," I say. "And thank you, by the way."

The potatoes are most likely still in the bag at the apartment.

"You looked like you could use some potatoes," she says. "You didn't *have* to buy them, you know. Did you know 'potato' comes from the Spanish *patata?* I wrote an essay about the history of potatoes for school once. 'Potato' used to refer to what we now call sweet potatoes, but the English mixed up the plants a long time ago so now the name's fucked up forever. Little things change the bigger things sometimes."

She realizes I'm not good at breaking the ice and keeps the conversation going.

"You recognize me. Not from a few weeks ago, but from before that. I can see it in your eyes. Do you know me? Do I know *you?*"

"Your name's Julie."

[puzzle pieces]

"It is, which means you're a stalker because I don't recognize you at all; although you have a familiar face."

"In another life you sold me a mirror at Home Depot. I remember your nametag."

"*Right*, the mirror!"

"You remember."

"No," she says and laughs, but it's a sweet laugh. "I haven't worked at HD since my girl was three, a long time ago, but *wow*, amazing memory. What's with the flower?"

In my grasp is a blood-red rose.

"I'm not entirely sure."

"You don't know where you got it?"

"Nope."

I must have stolen it from one of the vase bouquets in the floral department during my outage, but the stem is warm, meaning I've held onto it for a while. Meaning I've walked the store aimlessly and without a shopping cart for quite some time.

"You're odd. I like odd."

Out of my element, I hand it to her, and she gives a half-curtsey and blushes. She brings it to her lips, closes her eyes and inhales.

"It doesn't smell like anything," she says, "but it's beautiful."

"Likewise."

"I don't smell like anything? I guess that's a good thing."

She's playing with me, yet drawn to the flower.

"The beautiful part."

She pouts and I'm instantly in love with her.

"Since you don't remember where you got it, you must be a kleptomaniac/romantic, so I thank you for stealing this flower in my honor, kind sir. And no thorns. I love it."

The rose remarkably resembles the one I left for Karen the day I put a gun to my head. I had tried to kill my reflection, the reason for purchasing a replacement mirror and meeting this girl all those years ago. I had written my goodbyes on notepaper, placed with a rose on top of Karen's pillow:

> *… I took the effortless way out by pulling the trig-*
> *ger and ending it all, but know that it was not me*
> *I was aiming at. I had to kill the demon inside,*
> *and through my body was the only way.*

The words of the letter still haunt me, every single one. I try to forget them, but they are always there, waiting. Writing the suicide note to Karen required tapping into a dark place; years later, that place is still a part of me, a black splotch of cancer.

I never give flowers as a token of love. I explained it to Karen once, which is why I chose the rose as my last gift to her. Gifts given with love should last only as long as the love of the expressed affection. A flower is a gift of temporary love, which should last only as long as the flower. With the falling of petals, so falls the affection. A gift to express eternal love—such a gift should last forever.

And now this girl, this beautiful stranger, she's turned things upside-down. I don't want this to be the last time I ever see her and I've given her a rose.

"I want to see you again," I say. "Before this flower dies."

She peels a petal and lets it flutter like a fallen butterfly. Peeling another, the half-smile becomes whole and her eyes rise from the gift. She keeps peeling and I understand.

I want to tell her everything …

Without life, love is not worth the effort.

Rae wants to talk about it again: the incident. I tell her about the mirror, about the phantasmagoric blood rivulets clinging like melted wax over my reflection. She's heard it all before. Not illusion, she tells me, but 'the representativeness heuristic of a man escaping his mirror world.' She has long words for everything to describe this precognitive detachment from reality: depersonalization disorder, disassociation fugue. Call it what you will, I saw the insides of my head blown open and splashed on the glass. I saw the man on the other side of the mirror trying to escape—through my face.

This wasn't the day he/I put the gun to my head, but a few days prior. While washing my face at the sink, I looked up to see this premonition.

"Dissociation is often a coping mechanism," she says, "a psychological defense to help in tolerating stress. At the nonpathological end of the continuum, daydreaming and sleepwalking are common examples of dissociation. As you continue down the continuum, there are nonpathological altered states of consciousness—"

"I have no fucking clue what you're talking about."

Her eyes flicker like the shutter on a camera and capture me in a moment of confusion. A table separates us. We each have coffee in ceramic mugs. The coffee shop smells of roasted beans and a mix of vanilla and caramel. Somehow, she sits in front of me, holding her mug with both hands, perhaps to keep them warm, and I'm afraid to ask Julie what we're talking about, or how long we've been here.

"I lost you there for a while, didn't I?" she says.

Is this a date?

"This doesn't have to be a date," she says, as if reading my mind. "We can be future friends chatting over cups of coffee."

I could apologize, but the Karen voice in my head would probably tell me that sorrys are leaking insecurities.

"Someone once told me to never apologize for the things I can't control," I say, "so I need to come up with an excuse other than 'sorry'."

"Saying you're sorry can also be an expression of empathy. It doesn't have to be an apology. But you have nothing to be sorry about."

She is Karen's opposite.

A safe question: "What made you decide you wanted to come here with me?" Perhaps I could figure out what brought us here.

A not-so-safe answer: "I asked you, and you said yes."

I smile, or at least try to smile, but my face is broken. The coffee is hot, which means we sat down not long ago. Jagged water percolates down the window overlooking Briar Street, but it's always raining in Brenden, which means it could be any gray morning of the week.

"You only smile with half your face."

"I have a few things wrong with me."

"Not *wrong*," she says, "*unique*. That's why I asked you out. You seem interesting, and there's not a lot of interesting left in the world. Tell me something dark about you. Something you've never talked about before."

"Do shrinks count?"

"You have a shrink? Me too!"

"Don't get too excited about it."

"No, shrinks don't count. In fact, tell me something you've only told your shrink. That'll make it more interesting."

When she moves her arm to brush the hair out of her face, I see the rose. She had broken off most of the stem, the flower over her right ear. In some cultures, this means she's looking for a mate, so I half-smile again; the left ear would mean she's taken. It's not the rose I gave her at the store because she'd torn that one to shreds in order to see me. Had I given her another?

Time is no longer a stranger.

"Someday, I'm going to fix that other side of your smile."

"Your mouth does the same thing."

"*Finally*, someone has the balls to tell me. Believe it or not, you're the first. Kind of fucked up, huh? Going around your whole life with a Picasso face."

My laugh causes her to laugh.

"There it is!" she says. "It was only hiding."

"What?"

"When you laugh, your face isn't broken and the other side of your mouth works. You need to laugh more. That's the only thing wrong with you. That, and you don't have a name."

"I haven't told you my name?"

"Nope."

"And you still asked me out?"

"Well, I *assumed* you had one."

"And, I gave you a flower."

"That's part of the reason."

"I'm Aeron, with an *e*. Aeron Stevenson."

She takes my hand and formally shakes it.

"It's a pleasure to make your acquaintance, Mr. Stevenson, but I hope someone's told you sometime in your life that spelling it with an e makes it feminine."

"An *a* and an *e*. A-E-R-O-N."

"And now you're even more interesting."

She doesn't let go of my hand and instead brings it down to the table and puts her other hand over it, warm from the coffee. Her hands, so delicate. She's wearing those black gloves with the fingers cut out to expose nails painted black.

"Anyway, what were we talking about?"

"Everything. But specifically, you were about to tell me something dark about you. Something from therapy."

I realize she's warming my hands.

Why not?

"Past or present?"

"I like this game. Which is more difficult to talk about?"

"The past."

"Then we'll work up to that. Present, then. We'll take turns, but no lies, no padding the truth. This will be our thing. Deal?"

"No judging."

"Fuck no."

"Deal, but no laughing."

"We see who we really are through laughter."

She's right.

"I may or may not be seeing sheep in my nonexistent neighbor's yard. They keep me up at night sometimes."

I love the half-smile that forms.

"My turn," she says. "Sometimes I buy cigarettes and pretend to smoke them in public. Most guys see it as a turnoff."

"The baby lamb's the loudest."

"Secretly, I like second-hand smoke."

"My therapist thinks the sheep are representations formed by imagination to force me to pursue the loss of my parents; the baby lamb is me, calling for my mother."

"My therapist thinks I smoke them."

"You lie to your therapist?"

"Sometimes."

"That's awesome. I should try that."

There's an awkward silence because I'm ready to open up to her about my past.

"We really don't have to talk about anything if you don't want, but this is nice. We could just sit here and enjoy each other."

She spreads out my fingers, massaging each one individually, and then the meaty area connecting palm to thumb.

"You're less tense," she says, admiring and tracing the lines. I'll read your palm next week if you let me."

"You can do that?"

"A little. Me and my friend Frankie used to do it. You can learn a lot from a person that way. And I like your hands. That means you're stuck seeing me next week. You okay with that?"

The hand she's holding … I roll up the sleeve with my free hand to show her the crisscross scars covering my wrist and forearm. There are dozens.

I expect her to let go; instead, she follows the trails with her fingernails, as if reliving the glass from my past.

"Something dark," I say.

Julie lets go, but only to pull the neckline of her blouse down and to the side.

¤ ¤ ¤

"You're manifestations of my clouded psyche," I yell out the window. It's 3:30 in the morning and the sheep won't stop with their braying. I count six. Seven. They're multiplying. Counting sheep should put a person to sleep, not keep them from it. They roam, ignorant of time. The sun is three hours from rising. The baby lamb is gone. Perhaps they are calling for him.

An unknown number rings twice on my cellphone.

"Hello, this is Aeron."

"Hey, it's me."

I look at the number again because it's Matty's voice. He never calls. Before answering, the little Karen voice in my head reminds me to call him Matt.

"Matt ... haven't heard from you in a while."

"Mom says you should have my new number, and I wanted to thank you for the birthday card and money for the phone. She said you waited around for me. Sorry I missed you."

Who was this guy? Not Matty.

"Still there?"

The question makes me wonder if it's been seconds or minutes or hours.

"Still here. Just surprised you called, but glad you did. I never got a chance to wish you a happy birthday. Liking the new phone?"

"So far."

"Why the new number?"

"Can I ask you a question?"

"Anything."

"I know we don't talk much, but I was wondering if I could get your advice. It sort of has to do with the new number."

"I'll do my best," I say, hoping my mind doesn't go on vacation.

"There's this girl, Erica Lock, and we've been seeing each other for a long time, six months. But now there's this other girl."

"Dangerous territory, Matty."

I regret calling him that, but for once he doesn't seem to mind. He also doesn't seem to mind that we haven't talked in over a month. And now he's calling for advice on a girl, or girls. I look at the phone for the time and date, but it's only the day after yesterday.

"I know, but it's not like that. I mean, it is, but for her, not me."

"What do you mean?"

"She's been seeing this other girl, I think. They hang out a lot after school and she's always finding excuses for being around her instead of me, like I'm a third wheel. We've been arguing for weeks about her, and a few days ago she said she spent the night at her house and she said something happened, but only once. But that's still cheating, even if it's with a girl, right?"

"Yes, it is. If something *happened* between them, whatever that may be—and you don't have to tell me about it, please don't—but if they … well, if they shared something together, even a kiss, or some kind of *moment*, for a lack of better words, then it's cheating."

"And that's what I told her."

"Did the two of you break up? If not, you should."

"We did, but then she started calling again. We got in this big fight over the phone and I told her I never wanted to see her again, but she keeps calling and texting. That's why I changed my number with the new phone. Luckily, she's never been to the house."

"That's intense, Matt. What kind of advice are you looking for, though? It sounds like you made the right decision. I'm not sure if I could add anything."

"I guess I was looking for assurance, you know? I can't talk to Mom about this, and there's no one else I can talk to. Most of my friends are *her* friends."

"You did the right thing, Matt."

"Thanks."

Silence, but for once not an awkward silence.

"I wasn't late on my birthday because I was out with friends.

That's what Mom thinks and what she probably told you. I met Erica for coffee. We talked for a couple hours, her crying mostly, but I ended the relationship. But now I don't know what to do. She thinks I'm going to tell everyone at school she's a lesbian, but I'd never do that to her. I hate her now, can't even stand hearing her name, but I'd still never do that, out of respect. I'd never call her out. We have all the same friends, so hanging with them—"

"Look, Matty. My advice to you is only going to be more assurance, because you're handling everything right, in my opinion. I know it's tough, and trust me on this, but you need to get your own friends. Friends outside her circle of friends. If you want to remain friends with some, that's fine, but you need your own friends. That's the best advice I can give you. Do you have any feelings for her, anything at all?"

"I'm not sure, I just feel so alone now."

"You need to forget about her as quickly as you can and move on. You're a good-looking kid with an old soul. Girls will be flocking over you. But ignore them. That's my advice. You will never find love by looking for it; love will find you when you're not looking at all."

"What do you see?"

I see two black dragons holding hands and kissing with their tails braided together, the image split symmetrically down the center, but not entirely. It's the Rorschach inkblot test Angel Rae first showed me. It could be a butterfly or some kind of facemask, but again, my first thought is a pair of dragons, so that's what I tell her.

"And this one?"

This is a new card.

"A Death's-head Hawkmoth."

"That's very specific. You have typically referred to these types of images as butterflies. Why a moth this time? Why such a specific species of moth?"

"It has a wide striped body, larger than the others. And the human-like skull on the ... the area between the wings."

"The thorax."

"Sure."

"The back of this card is labeled *Acherontia Atropos*, which is the less common name of the Death's-head Hawkmoth. There are three similar species: *lachesis*, *styx*, and the *atropos*, named after the apportioners of death in Greek mythology. Atropos, in this case, was thought to cut the threads of life from all living—"

"Styx ... as in the river Styx?"

"The river of the dead."

"And the third, what's it called?"

"Lachesis, who was thought to allot the correct amount of life to a being."

"Like the little bald doctors in *Insomnia*."

"I am not familiar with that story."

"Stephen King's novel. There's a character who can't sleep who starts seeing auras, like colored marionette strings connecting every-one to the heavens. The little bald doctors walk around with shears and cut the strings when someone's time is up and they die. Two good doctors named Lachesis and ... not Styx. I think it was Clotho, or something similar; but there was a bad doctor named Atropos. Three total."

"Sounds like Stephen King knew a little something about Greek mythology and these three fates. I may have to give that one a read."

"He knew something about insomnia, I can tell you that much."

"What else about this image comes to mind, Aeron."

"The skull, or the face on the moth's back ... it's eyes are hollow. If enlarged, the face looks like the picture I told you about, the one Norea left for me on the bathroom mirror."

"Did you bring it with you?"

I pull the drawing from my pocket, unfold the paper, and hold it to my face like a mask, looking at Rae through torn holes.

◻ ◻ ◻

Small hands wrap around my head, cold fingers covering my eyes. This would typically freak me out because I don't like people touching my face, but the hands are comforting. I know they're Julie's by the touch and smell.

"Guess what color shoes I'm wearing."

"You're not wearing shoes; you're wearing sandals."

"No fair, you saw me coming."

"I've only seen you twice, and both times you wore black sandals. The first time at the store you had black flip-flops. The last time they were dark brown leather and had a clasp behind the ankle with silver flower rhinestones."

"You're good at this game," she says. One of her hands falls to my neck and stays there as long as it can before she circles around and sits across from me at the table.

"What's your dominate hand?"

"Right."

"Your left hand will show me what you were born with and what you can expect in the future. Your right will show me what you've gone through in life."

Julie takes my hand, and she can have it as long as she wants.

She holds my thumb in one hand, wrist in the other.

She stretches my thumb until the skin is smooth, massages my fingers from base to tip, one at a time, and then gently rotates my thumb toward the palm.

"Relax. See the lines, how they bunch?"

"Is that bad?"

"No, it's stress, which never goes away, but accumulates."

"You've been through shit. This line," she says, tracing a path from my index to my wrist. "This is your life line. Well, you have two, but this really long one tells me you have a lot of vitality. You're also cautious with relationships, which is good for me, I guess."

"What's the smaller one next to it."

"Extra vitality, or perhaps you're living multiple lives at once, multiple planes of existence, maybe. And you're going to live for a long time. See how far down it goes? And the circle in the line … something terrible happened to you, or you were hospitalized for a long time, or maybe both."

"Hence these lines," I say, flipping over both my wrists.

She flips them back.

"This broken line," she says, relaxing my fingers. Her pinky slides across my palm below the base of each finger. "This is the heart line, but that doesn't mean you have a broken heart. See how it begins in the middle? This means you easily fall in love, again, good for me, but it also shows you don't have a good handle on emotions. The circle here means depression, but we'll work on that."

"Does the break in the line mean anything?"

"Emotional trauma."

"Makes sense."

"How am I doing so far? Keep going?"

"So far, you know me as well as my shrink, so yes. Please."

"This one's the head line," she says, tracing another broken line below the heart line. "But it's not what you think. It has nothing to do with head. Your thoughts are inconsistent and you might have a short attention span."

"Hey, look, a table!"

"Strange, it doesn't say you have a sense of humor. Anyway, it also tells me you've had to make some big decisions in your life. Keep going?"

"Please."

She caresses a jagged line to the right of my life line.

"Are you sure? Not everyone has a fate line."

"Yes."

"You can't say I didn't warn you. Okay, this one's the fate line, also known as the line of destiny. You can see it better if you cup your hand a bit. See how it's deeper than all the others? This tells me your life is mostly controlled by fate."

"What do the breaks in this line mean?"

"It means you're prone to change, because of people like me."

The sheep bray at midnight. Sounds like some sort of spy code, but it's the first thing I think of when looking to the glowing 12:00 of the clock on my nightstand. The numbers blink, meaning power's lost, and that the nine-volt battery in the clock is dead as well.

I expect sheep in the neighbor's yard, but the lot is vacant.

And then I hear them again, behind me, on the nightstand.

My cellphone brays.

A message from my little lamb: *dad, can you text?*

Me: *Yes*

The cellphone tells me it's a barely after ten o' clock. The last time I fell asleep before ten was in high school with Karen. I wait for his message, wondering if my ears had played tricks on me with the phone. Perhaps—

Another bray.

Matty: *she wants to meet for coffee what should I do?*

Me: *Girlfriend with girlfriend?*

Matty: *dad …*

Me: *sorry*

Matty: *but yes*

Matty: *she says we need to talk*

Matty: *she says shes stupid and sorry*

Matty: *still thinks about me*

Every text message from Matty sounds like a sheep strangled. I imagine his fingers dancing over the cellphone, putting a poor creature to death each time he hits Send, while my fingers hunt and peck for the right letters and constantly go back for corrections. I imagine Matty—Matt—patiently waiting for his father's slow response.

Me: *Matt, she IS stupid and should be sorry. Still think about her?*

He takes a while to respond, which means I either said something wrong, or he's deeply considering his answer. It gives me time to check my phone settings. Under text notifications, 'bray.mp3' is selected for Matt's number. I check some of the other contacts, but only Matt's number is setup to kill sheep. Before I can change it, another sheep dies.

Matt: *no*

Me: *Good. Someone give her your new number?*

Matt: *note on my locker*

Matt: *notes*

Me: *Tell her to pound sand*

Matt: *lol k*

Me: *You deserve better*

Matt: *thanks dad*

Me: *Anytime*

No more sheep die, but I leave the ringtone in place, having my suspicions where it came from. I send Julie a text: *sheep?*

Julie: *The only sheep you need to worry about*

"Matt says you're seeing someone," Karen says.

"We've been out a few times."

"I knew something was up; you seem happier. I can always tell when you're happy because you stop talking, and when you listen, you really listen."

"And I've been sleeping, believe it or not."

"Must be *some* girl. Speaking of which, Matt's been quiet lately, too. Is everything okay with his girlfriend? That's bad, I don't even know her name. I know the two of you have been talking because he won't talk to me. He says it's 'guy stuff' and finds some excuse for ending the conversation. Tell me he's okay and I'll leave it alone."

"He's working through some stuff, but he'll be okay."

"Promise?"

"He's fine."

"Good, and I'm glad he's talking to you again. This new girl of yours seems to be a good influence on you. I can tell in your voice you're doing better. Speaking of which, Matt's been hanging out with a new crowd. Should I be worried?"

"Let me see your other hand," Julie says, taking my left. She's nervous, something she's never shown before, hand trembling. "I want to read about your future this time. I'm not as good at this part, but it will be fun."

"What does it say?"

My heart skips a beat.

She pulls me forward, leans over the table and kisses me.

"I think it said that would happen."

▫ ▫ ▫

Rae leans back in her chair and writes in her notepad. In front of us are scattered images of butterflies and moths and dragons and faces.

"I want to talk about Norea," she says, reaching for the drawing my other self had left for me on the bathroom mirror. "Are you no longer afraid of him?"

"I saw him the day I pulled that picture off the mirror."

"What did you see?"

"Eyes, connecting through the mask. I saw that I had nothing to fear. I saw myself, through *his* eyes, *my* eyes, the *same* eyes. And knew he saw me. At first, I hid behind the mask because I knew he was doing the same. Why else would he put the painting there, and why else would he have cut out the eyeholes? He wanted us to meet.

"The painting was taped on the glass, eye level. Maybe he created the paper mask, or maybe some part of my subconscious created the paper mask without me knowing, but either way it was there, waiting to be worn. We met through the holes in the paper.

"I turned off the light because I thought he might be afraid of it, like I'm afraid of the dark, so I turned off the light to let him know I was no longer scared, and that he should no longer be scared.

"The eyes glowed: one red, one blue, but I wasn't scared and I knew he wasn't, either. We leaned closer to the glass that separated us and I somehow knew the blue eye on the left was mine—his right; the red eye on the right was his—my left."

I hold out my left palm to Rae: "Future."

And then hold out my right: "Past."

"The last time we tried this, there was no mask, and we both weren't ready to meet, so things turned out poorly, hence all these scars over my arms. But this time … this time we were ready, so I pulled off the mask and we faced each other."

"What did you see?"

"Nothing but black for a while. No glowing eyes, nothing. But then my eyes adjusted to the dark and I could make out shapes in the reflection. Minimal light came in the room from under the door, and slowly I could see a shimmer in my eyes if I looked closely enough. You ever stare at yourself in the mirror for a good length of time with the lights turned off? I used to be afraid of doing that before. Now I know there's nothing to fear. My reflection, Norea, he's just a part of me, always has been and always will be, and I'm a part of him. And then I turned on the lights to find us both smiling."

I flip over the picture in front of us.

Written on the back of the mask in black ink:

Aeron | noɿɘA

"My name and his name, with all the letters reversed except for the middle letter … this is all I found after turning on the lights."

She shows me her tattoo, all of it, and now I can't stop thinking about dragons.

◻   ◻   ◻

"How long have you been off the medication?" Karen says.

"I'm on a new kind of drug, but three days."

"What's her name?"

"Do you believe in coincidences?"

Julie takes my hand and doesn't answer right away.

"The first time we ever saw each other," she says, "what was that, over ten years ago? I felt some kind of connection with you. Something happened, and something else happened, and then countless other things happened that made that exact moment happen. One hiccup and the world changes for everyone."

"Like the butterfly effect. Moths, too, I guess."

"Exactly. I lied earlier about not remembering you. I do remember you. I remember you buying the mirror and I remember watching you leave the store. I even remember the exact amount on the register because I was really into palindromes and anagrams at the time."

"How much was the mirror?"

"Eighty-seven, seventy-eight."

"Just imagine all the happenings that have led up to this point."

"You never ate the potatoes I gave you, did you?"

"No, but that was a good hiccup."

The way she holds my hand within both of hers as we walk is comforting.

"I also remember you saying 'I broke our last one' when I asked you about it, and I have wondered ever since how you broke it. Something dark?"

"Something dark. I shot it with a handgun because I missed my head. The last thing I did before seeing you that first time. I couldn't find a broom and dustpan, so I used one of the towels to clean up the glass around the sink and floor. I threw everything away in the dumpster behind Home Depot, and then I went inside to purchase a new mirror, one with a better reflection."

I don't expect her to pull away, but to pull me in close, and that's what she does.

"There are no coincidences," she says, "just appropriately timed incidences."

THE END OF THE BEGINNING

"What do you need?"

Julie needed something hallucinogenic, an escape to the fantastic, something that would bring her to a new plane of existence and blur reality. *I need all that,* she told him, although she didn't know why, and didn't know what she was looking for, what might provide everything she craved. Something stirred inside, something primal, and it wanted out.

"How much are you willing to pay?" he said, holding a white pill.

She had saved over the last few weeks from odd jobs, babysitting and whatnot, not sure if that would be enough to get her anything good. His tone implied he'd take something more than money, but she wouldn't give him that. She was a sexual being, sure, but that didn't make her a whore. Julie pushed his hand off her leg.

"I can get whatever I need," she said, "but I'm not interested in *E*, or you."

"I'm going to point you to a friend of mine who knows a guy makin' something that will blow your mind, something to difuse."

He held out a blank business card with a phone number scrawled on one side, and next to it he wrote a name.

"Have you heard of *Drakein-6?*"

ORIGINAL CONCEPT ART

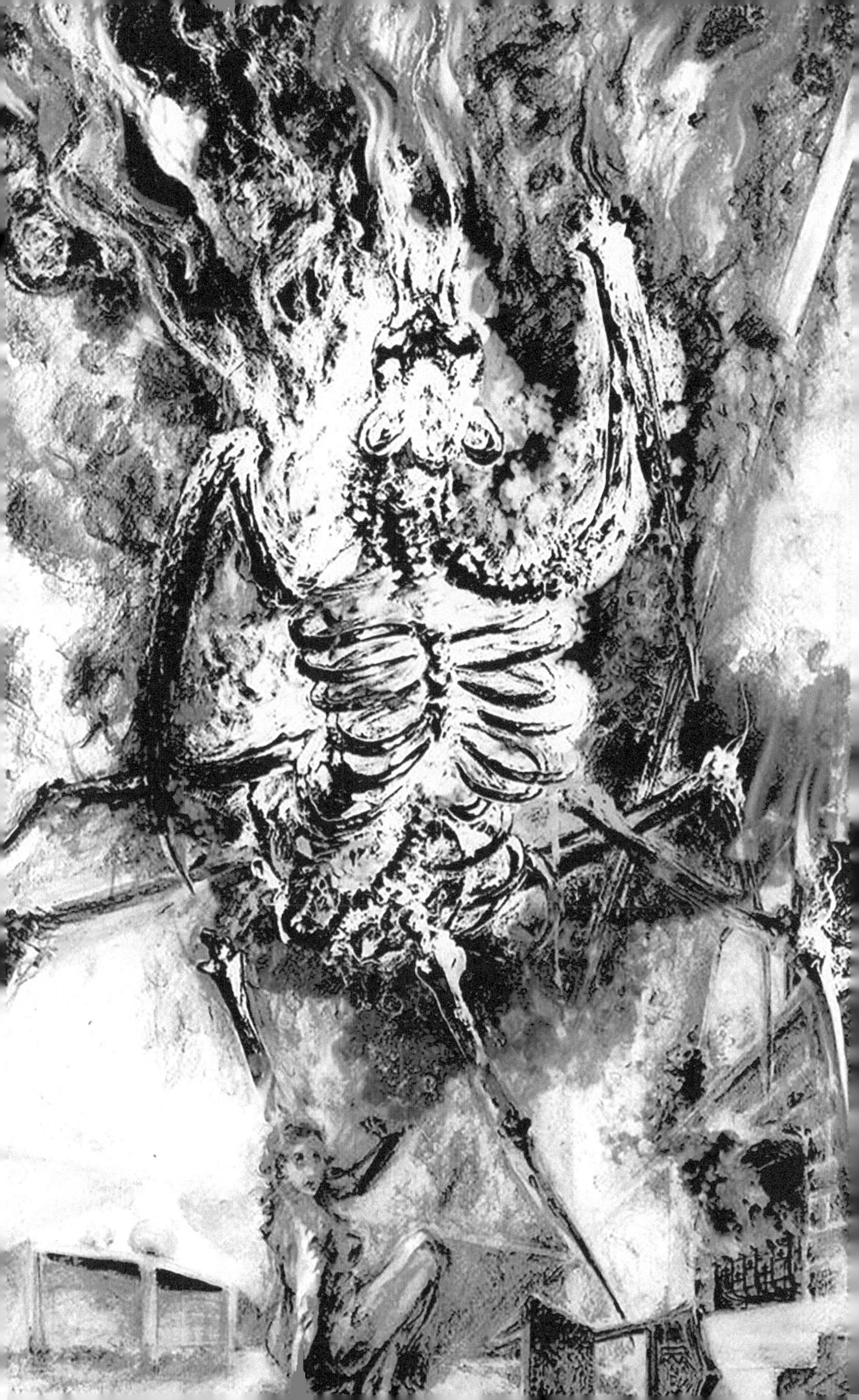

ABOUT THE AUTHOR

Michael Bailey is a recipient of the Bram Stoker Award (and eight-time nominee), Benjamin Franklin Award, and a three-time Shirley Jackson Award nominee. His novels include *Palindrome Hannah* and *Phoenix Rose*, and he has published the fiction and poetry collections *Scales and Petals*, *Inkblots and Blood Spots*, *Oversight*, and *The Impossible Weight of Life*, the novelette *Our Children, Our Teachers*, and *Agatha's Barn*, a tie-in novella to Josh Malerman's serial novel *Carpenter's Farm*.

He is the founder of the small press Written Backwards, where he has created speculative and psychological horror anthologies such as *Pellucid Lunacy*, *The Library of the Dead*, five volumes of *Chiral Mad* (the fourth co-edited by Lucy A. Snyder), and dark science fiction anthologies such as *Qualia Nous* and *You, Human*. He served as the co-editor for the anthologies *Adam's Ladder* and *Prisms* (with Darren Speegle), and *Miscreations: Gods, Monstrosities & Other Horrors* (with Doug Murano). Many of his books raise money for charities.